THE MOUNTAIN
OF SOULS

MARCUS LEE

THE MOUNTAIN OF SOULS

THE CHOSEN BOOK I

Paperback ISBN: 9798369874448
Hardback ISBN: 9798374588323

For more information visit: www.marcusleebooks.com

First paperback edition Feb 2023
First eBook edition Feb 2023

CHAPTER I

'Hold on, and don't let go.'

I look around, wondering if there will be more instructions, but the door to the room has already closed. I'm gagged securely and have been told by a masked captor not to remove it. Whilst my hands and feet are free, I don't dare untie the gag, not yet.

Others are crammed into the room with me, all in soiled clothing, filthy from their journey here, wherever here is. Everyone is wide-eyed and scared as they look upon each other for the first time. It seems we're all roughly the same age, although of varying size.

I want to scream and cry for help, but that will be a waste of energy.

A moon globe hangs from the ceiling, adorning, and lighting the room we've been herded into. The floors, walls, and ceiling are covered by panelled wood. As my fingers absently trace the grain, I discover the wall surface is marred by hundreds of scratches, whereas the floor and ceiling shine with a deep, polished lustre.

Despite still being held captive, at least I can now walk around. It's the first time in two weeks that I've been allowed out of a small crate that confined me like a caged animal. Two weeks in a box stinking of panic, fear, and claustrophobia, my only company the desperate voices and tears of unseen others.

Hold on, and don't let go.

What does that mean, Malina? I ask myself.

I study my surroundings while most of the youths sit on the floor, exhausted. Some try to untie the gags, which are so tight that it's hard to breathe.

Thirteen leather loops hang from near the moon globe above me. Another is placed in each corner of the room - seventeen in total. I wonder what they might be for. Seventeen loops, but over twenty people. Hmmm.

Even on tiptoes, they're just beyond my fingertips. As I lower my arm, I catch the gaze of a filthy, blond lad taking note of what I'm doing. His hair and cleft chin suggests an Astorian bloodline, and he has the strangest eyes.

There's a distant jangling of chains, followed by a grinding noise, and then the floor begins to shudder.

Those sitting, scramble to their feet, as with a lurch, the floor splits down the centre. Everyone moves quickly away from the gap as the floor shakes and begins to slide back beneath the walls.

It isn't long before the distance between the two sides of the floor is about two paces wide. Cold fetid air rises from the depths and I retreat away from the edge with growing unease.

Hold on, and don't let go.

The bigger boys begin shoving anyone and everyone smaller out of the way, so they can get closer to the corners' transient safety, and being one of the smallest, I can't even get near.

Two boys are trying to open the door, banging on it, pushing their shoulders hard against the unforgiving wood but to no avail. Relentlessly, the floor continues to move, and the gap between the two halves becomes ever wider.

Moans of fear fill the small room, and several boys and girls are crying. A puddle of urine gathers at the feet of a boy, and everyone edges away.

Don't just stand here! I admonish myself. I'd always been quick of mind in the orphanage, but here I am, freezing from fear. I quickly move to the open edge of the floor and gaze down into the black abyss. The moon globe that easily illuminates the whole room doesn't shed enough light to penetrate to the bottom. The air that comes from below is foul. It reminds me of the back of the butcher's shop situated behind the orphanage. It assaults my senses, smelling like rotting meat.

If the floor continues to open at the same rate, people will soon start to fall in, and being small, I'll be one of the first.

Do something!

I look at the loops in the middle of the ceiling. It's still an easy jump to grab them, but I'll be left hanging over a horrifying drop, and for how long, I don't know. I'm skinny, malnourished, and it's unlikely I can hold on for long. I'd have preferred the straps in the corner, but I can't get through the press of bigger youths.

Another lurch, and those banging on the door move away as the floor retracts further.

Everyone here has the same filthy, disowned look I have. No one wears fine clothes, has good shoes, or even a semblance of styled hair. They're all outcasts, perhaps orphans like me. No one will miss us if we die here.

Hold on, and don't let go.

My heart has never beat this fast. I make a decision and my hands shake. It's hard to catch my breath past the thick gag, but it's now or never.

I take two steps back, then propelled by trembling legs, leap and catch hold of the dangling leather. My sweaty palm slips, and I expect to fall, but as my weight bears down, the leather loop tightens around my hand, lending me its support.

Tears course down my cheeks. I've been frightened many times in my life; fear is nothing new, but this! Sobs wrack my body. Below my feet is nothing but blackness, and those words resound in my head.

Hold on, and don't let go.

Swinging my legs, I bring up my other hand to grab the leather and only then note the wide-eyed gazes of everyone huddling against the walls directed at me.

Suddenly, the blond boy runs from the group and leaps, catching hold of the loop next to mine. He sways wildly back and forth, but his grip is sure and strong. Once again, our eyes meet. One of his eyes is blue, the other green. To have different coloured eyes is to be considered cursed in Astoria, and those born with this defect are usually killed at birth. I'd never seen anyone with them before. Then again, most people have never seen yellow eyes like mine either. We stare at each other for a while, and I can sense his terror, but he manages a brisk nod.

Others quickly follow our lead with a pounding of feet and squeals of fear.

The grinding gears screech louder, and the floor retracts faster. The largest boys have claimed the loops in each corner of the room, securing their safety. They bully everyone else away, fists pummel those who are too slow to move. Only the strong will survive, the law of the streets.

The distance between the floor and the central straps widens, and a small girl gathers her courage and leaps. She doesn't make it. With a gag tied firmly around her mouth, she can't even scream as she disappears, arms and legs flailing, to be swallowed whole by the darkness.

My tears follow, falling into the depths along with others from those now hanging around me.

There are only two straps left vacant in the middle of the ceiling, and a further two girls run and jump. Thankfully, they make the distance and hang on, knuckles white, swinging backwards and forwards like ripe fruit.

The smell of fresh faeces fills the air, nauseating, overtaking the smell of rotting flesh.

I want to vomit in fear and disgust at the smell, but know that if I do, the gag will cause me to choke, so I swallow the reflex down.

All the loops are now taken, yet two boys and three girls are still pressed tight against the walls, the edge of the floor mere inches from their toes. They try to dig their fingers into the wood, desperate to find a purchase.

Now I realise where the hundreds of scratches have come from.

The two boys look around desperately. Having failed to secure the corner loops, they now eye those of us dangling from the middle of the ceiling.

I guess what's going through their minds.

Please, no!

The two boys, arriving at the same decision, leap as one. There are no free straps left, and they're too far to have made it anyway, but they leap nonetheless and grab onto the ankles of the girls who'd last made the jump.

Seconds later, all four disappear into the pit, arms and legs kicking.

Not long after, the three girls trying desperately to hold on to the wood panelling follow, their deaths strangely quiet.

As I look around, fifteen of us hang on, arms trembling, sweat, tears and urine dripping.

By the time the floor is cranked back into place, only twelve remain.

Everyone falls to the floor. The smell of fear is rank, and I know my own stench adds to the thickness of the air. How long we wallow in misery and our own filth is hard to say.

My hope that this ordeal is over is shattered when the gears start rumbling, chains jangle, and the horror begins all over again.

This time around, I struggle to hold on from the very beginning. My hands are tired, and the loop I've chosen is damp with sweat. Quickly the pain in my hands, arms, and shoulders becomes excruciating. Maybe I should just let go, fall into the dark embrace of the pit, and end the torment?

My moans are pitiful through the gag as death approaches and whispers to me like a friend. Just as I'm about to give in to that seductive voice, the Astorian boy comes to my rescue, his hand closing over mine. It hurts, his grip is powerful, but now I can't let go even if I want to.

The floor grinds shut again, and as I land, collapsing in exhaustion, I'm shocked that just eight of us are left.

The door to the room opens, and a robed and masked woman enters. The eyes give away her sex, as does her movement; graceful, purposeful, feet placed with certainty. Yet every step somehow exudes the potential for violence, like a predator stalking prey.

'You will say nothing. You will do as you're told without hesitation. There are to be no questions. If you fail at anything, you will die. If you question anything or disobey my command, you will die.'

The voice is slightly muffled by the cloth mask, yet the message is simple and chilling. Like a cat, the woman stalks amongst us, a glistening, tiny dagger in her hand. With swift movements, she severs our gags.

I draw in a deep breath, almost choking at the stench but so grateful at being able to breathe freely.

The woman walks toward the door, pauses, and looks over her shoulder, beckoning for us to follow.

'My name is Lystra,' she says. 'Follow me if you want a chance to live.'

***

We scurry along corridors illuminated by torches. Their flickering red light creates a hellish ambience, and I wonder if I should have let go of the loop after all, and embraced sudden death.

The air here is tinged with dampness, and I fear some disgusting spores will take root and fester in my lungs if I survive. Our soiled clothes only add to the foulness of the air.

Sobs and whimpering accompany the scuff of stumbling footsteps as my rag-tag group of filthy survivors follow Lystra, too scared to disobey or be left behind.

She halts at a closed iron-reinforced door, and we hang back, not daring to approach too close. After a quick search within her robes, she produces a key and turns it in the lock. It swings silently open under her touch. Fresh air wafts in, and following a flick of Lystra's hand, we file past, heads bowed.

As I step into the open, the horror I'd just survived briefly fades. I gawk in wonder, for although I stand in something akin to hell, it's a hell overlooked by the heavens.

I'd witnessed a training ring before, outside the soldiers' barracks in my hometown, and there's no doubt I'm standing in one. Yet, despite its familiarity, it's as unlike that training circle I knew as fire is to water.

My rag-tag group and I stand in the heart of a mountain or maybe a dead volcano.

Way above us, blue sky and clouds offer a tantalising glimpse of heaven, and indeed, the interior slopes of the mountain are covered in trees and vines, lush and colourful. I can see birds flying amongst the foliage and animals leaping around.

Yet, as my gaze travels downward, the vista begins to change. First, the mountainside from halfway down is blackened, stripped of natural growth, and looks to have been burnt down to the bare rock. Then, below that, it's been fashioned into a coarse, circular wall.

Above the wall on the far side of the circle is a balcony upon which five dark-robed figures stand, observing us as if we were nothing but insects scurrying around their feet.

Set intermittently within the wall are doors, and from them, groups of filthy, frightened youths spew forth. Shortly there are about sixty of us staring around, a mixture of wonder, hopelessness and fear plastered on our faces.

Stop gawking, Malina. Take stock!

I'm standing at the perimeter of the training ring ... but what a ring. It measures about two hundred paces across, with a raised circular dais in the centre. Robed guards hold crossbows at the ready wherever I look.

I don't know how long I've been standing here, but Lystra's sharp voice cuts through my thoughts.

'If you want to live, you won't be the last to the dais and back again.'

Silence greets her words, not that anyone would dare question anything. Then I see movement from the corner of my eye, and as I look around, I can see the other distant groups of children streaming toward the central dais.

Almost as one, we turn and throw ourselves into this race for life. The bare rock of the training circle floor is uneven, and my bare feet hurt with every step. Six of my group are already pulling ahead, and I strive to run faster. Running was never my strong suit, and I haven't eaten sufficiently in weeks. I feel weak, and my gasps for breath quickly turn to sobs.

A tubby boy runs next to me as we lag behind the others. We're still fifteen paces from the dais as those ahead turn and race back toward us. I can see his wide eyes snatching glances at me as sweat pours down his face.

Come on, Malina, I urge myself. *Faster!*

Then as everyone runs past, skinny arms and legs pumping, I find myself alone as I reach the dais. I touch it with my hand, then turn back.

I'm too slow, and worse, I can barely see. Tears and snot stream down my face, running into my mouth as those ahead finish the race. Finally, I catch up to the group, lungs heaving.

No one looks up except for him with the strange eyes. On his face, as if clearly written, I can see relief for himself but also sorrow as he looks at me.

Lystra draws a long dagger from within her sleeve and stalks toward me.

RUN!

Despite my survival instinct telling my legs to move, I don't have the strength. I wish I could, although to where I don't know, but anywhere to be able to draw breath a few more times would suffice. Maybe I'd have used the time to look at the sky and see the clouds a final time.

Yes, the clouds.

I tilt my head back.

Look at the clouds closely, Malina. You won't see Lystra, her blade, or even feel it!

Death will end this nightmare.

Lystra's footsteps approach and stop.

I'd heard it said that when death is upon you, all your memories flash in front of your eyes. I just wish I'd had happier ones.

***

I'd been happy for a short time, once. Such memories are wispy and intangible, but sometimes I can remember what it felt like.

My father had owned a fishing boat. It was small and needed only five men to crew it, but it put food on our rough wooden table and enough coins in his pocket to pay for the rent of the rickety house I spent my first years in.

I can barely remember how he *really* looked; he was so rarely around. He had to be up early, before dawn and returned well after sundown. But I recall a rugged face hidden behind a full beard, wild unruly hair, and twinkling eyes.

I knew when he smiled, for those eyes would crease, and he'd lift me up and swing me around until I cried with laughter. He smelled of the sea, salty and fishy, but sometimes of grain spirit too.

If he came in smelling of that, I remember my mother and I had to be very quiet.

My mother. Full of warmth and smiles, who endured many jibes because of the yellow eyes, ashen skin and pitch-black hair we shared. My father had been the only man willing to marry her, for people muttered that she had evil blood in her and looked like some dark creature of the night. But, even if she'd looked that way to them ... to me, and to father, she was beautiful and her heart pure.

Many were the fantastical stories she'd regale us with late into the evening, the flickering candle adding frightening shadows to already scary tales of old.

They'd been good times with just the three of us, and then my brother had arrived. Karson.

I was five when he was born, but whilst my mother and I were happy, my father wasn't.

Why? I'm not sure. Karson was a lovely baby, full of smiles and funny noises. But I think it meant my father had to work more, taking fewer days off to feed an extra mouth. Karson also looked like my mother and me. The hair, skin and eyes were unmistakable.

A year later, in the middle of autumn, there'd been four weeks of unseasonable, constant storms. No one was foolish enough to go out on those white-capped waves, higher than a house, and no money had come in. It was the worst weather anyone could remember.

My father wasn't around much then, even if he had the time. Instead, he spent what little money he'd saved on grain spirit, not the rent, and the money collectors' visits had grown more frequent. Finally, one night, they'd beaten my father and threatened to have us evicted.

The last time I remember seeing my father had been the following morning as a shadow in the moonlight when he'd donned his oiled skins. The wind was raging outside, howling like the spirits of the dead. He'd leant over to give me, my mother and my sleeping brother a kiss. He never did this. Yet as the memory flashes through my mind, I realise that somehow he feared he wouldn't be coming back. He was right.

How quickly life can change.

Within days we'd had to move to a tiny, filthy room above a tavern, with just a curtain separating our straw mattress from mother's.

To keep a roof over our heads, she'd had to do *things* that made her cry inconsolably every night. I had to take care of my brother, leading him around the town when my mother *entertained* guests. Then one day, about three years after my father's death, she'd brought the wrong man back, and her cold, white body had kept us company for days. Upon finding out, the tavern owner had reported us to the orphanage, and we'd never even had the time to see our mother buried before we were carried kicking and screaming to a filthy cage on the back of a wagon.

The only redeeming thing about being taken to the orphanage had been going there with Karson. His little arms had given the best hugs, keeping me warm and the heartache at bay, giving me a reason to survive, to fight.

It was dangerous inside. The warders were brutal, and the older children merciless, picking on us for our looks. But we'd made it through the initial months, establishing our place. I was small, but I'd fought tooth and nail to protect my little brother, and every night his little arms and heart magically gave me the strength to carry on.

We were inseparable and often knew the other's thoughts without the need to talk when in a dangerous situation. It wasn't quite magic, but it *was* something extraordinary. We kept this ability to ourselves, a secret advantage for perilous times of which there were many in the orphanage.

A year into our incarceration, Karson died. It took only four days from when he first coughed for the lung rot to kill him. I wasn't allowed to go near him in case I'd caught and spread it, and he'd died alone, and I'd died inside.

There was nothing good to remember in the following years, just an endless fight for survival.

Then, two weeks ago, I turned fourteen. Even though I hated the orphanage, I'd been dreading the day, for my coming of age meant my time there was over.

There are worse places than an orphanage.

The orphanage had put me up for auction, along with a dozen other filthy specimens. I understood why. The orphanage only managed to provide food and shelter to those left at its door by raising money ... by selling children as they came of age at fourteen.

As I'd stood on the auction block, looking at the screaming faces, both men and women raising coloured wooden batons to indicate a bid, my heart had sunk. Who knew where I might end up? Rolantria, Suria, Tars, or maybe I'd stay in Hastia.

The best I could hope for was to be taken into some wealthy local merchant or noble household, work the kitchens, clean the rooms, whatever was required. Being bought to work in the fields wouldn't be too bad either, despite the long days. Most slaves in those positions could expect to live into their late twenties.

The worst would be if I was bought by a brothel keeper or the army. With the brutal war for independence ongoing, conscription was now commonplace. Either outcome would be horrendous and lead to an early and probably gruesome death.

One by one, those around me were sold, and as they recognised their fate when the winning bids were cast, I studied their expressions. Many tears were shed, and I witnessed the crowd's laughter rise to match the misery of those whose fates were sealed.

For whatever reason, conscious or otherwise, I'd been the last to be presented to the crowd, and the noise had buffeted me like an angry wave, leaving me dazed and reeling to be the focus of so much energy.

As my eyes flickered from face to screaming face, sickened by bulging eyes, stained teeth, and painted cheeks, my gaze had locked with the one face in the crowd that showed little to no emotion whatsoever. I couldn't place where he was from. Neither his clothes nor features gave that away.

His gaze was blank, chilling even, like looking into the eyes of a dead fish. The urge to look away was nigh on overwhelming, but the alternative was the mayhem surrounding me. For some reason, that cold stare of death brought some kind of comfort, and so I held on to it.

Dead eyes raised his hand and kept it there, the baton he held aloft indicating he would continue to increase on any offer.

Instinctively I knew that while I held his gaze, his arm would stay up, and slowly the screaming crowd quietened as those who competed for my ownership conceded the fight. Then, as fast as it had started, the madness of the auction was over, and relief washed over me, mixed with a sense of foreboding.

I was pulled roughly from the platform, and a metal collar was secured around my neck. The auctioneer marked a stained ledger with hands so filthy, he could have used his finger to write with, let alone the quill and ink he used.

'Er name's Malina,' he'd advised *dead eyes*, but received no words in response, just a couple of coins; the value of my life. Without saying a word, he took the chain attached to my collar and led me through the filthy streets of Santarian, the city where I'd spent my entire life.

It was a coastal town, and many was the day I'd spent working on the docks under the watchful eye of the orphanage guards. I'd both loved and hated those times. It was the closest to freedom I'd come with the salty breeze upon my face. I loved looking out in wonder at the white-capped waves beyond the bay despite the fact they'd claimed my father. Yet our guards were far too liberal with their whips, and the screams of the gulls matched my own all too frequently.

Yet what lay beyond the horizon might soon be at my feet, for my new owner had led me directly to the docks.

One of the rules beaten into us children whilst at the orphanage was never to ask questions. Even lessons such as learning to read and to write were mostly done in silence. The interaction between the strict teachers and us, the pupils, was limited to beatings if the answers written on the chalkboard were incorrect.

So, as I'd walked, my eyes had darted around, taking in everything. I'd known to keep silent, not saying a word until such time as he, my master, might ask a question.

Of course, I was worried, intrigued and curious about what line of work he was in. He didn't have the opulent clothing of a merchant or noble or a farmer's well-worn and patched apparel. His hands were not stained by clay or dye. His clothing was bland, functional, not so dirty as to be filthy, not so clean as to be new. The only things that stood out were his gaze and how he moved. Among the bustling streets, he'd seemed to manoeuvre between the jostling bodies without making contact, whereas I was bumped around, with many curses following me.

We'd reached the docks, and there amongst the war galleys was a cog, a small merchant ship.

The first thing I noticed was that in contrast to the decks of nearby vessels, which were busy with activity, the cog's deck seemed strangely silent. No fish or crates were being loaded or unloaded, and no bandaged soldiers rested, crying in pain. This was the calm amidst the storm.

The second was its flag, flapping gently in the breeze, bearing the insignia of the weeping eye. It was from the Isles of Sin, one of only three neutral nations in a world at war.

Nonetheless, I'd paused briefly in dismay, earning a sharp yank on the chain that had sent me tumbling forward. The Isles of Sin were where the dregs of humanity had historically been sent if they escaped the death sentence.

I'd been led up the gangplank onto the ship, where a woman met us with nothing but a nod before I was taken down below into the cramped hold.

It was then that I realised things were going to go from bad to worse.

The sound of despair and misery filled the hold. Sobbing, crying, begging voices echoed in the enclosed space where over a dozen crates were stacked side by side. The smell of faeces and urine made me gag, and I was shown to an open crate near the end.

As I looked inside, I noted a small hole in the bottom. I'd turned with wide eyes to look at the man who led me there, but his cold gaze brooked no disagreement as he indicated for me to get in.

Inside there had been nothing but a small seat. As the crate door closed, there was a grate I could look out of that let air in, however foul it might have been. There was also a small hatch latched from the outside.

Then, as the man moved away, the lantern he'd carried went with him, and I'd been left in the pitch black, with the crying, the stench, and misery.

The vessel had set sail almost immediately. Thereafter, retching had replaced the other sounds as the small vessel was thrown around like a toy on the ocean waves.

Two weeks later, the ship had docked. The thump and cessation of movement indicated to us that a destination had been reached. The crate I was within hadn't been opened; instead just unloaded, put on a cart, and then rocked and bumped to an unknown destination. It had been night-time when we'd docked, so although I'd peered out the grate, I could see very little.

The next thing of note was being dumped from the crate and herded into the room with the moving floor.

Fast forward to the race, Lystra approaching, her footsteps stopping and the clouds. I catch my breath, noting how one is shaped like a face ... the face of my brother.

A dagger flashes ...

***

Lystra's weapon finds its mark. It makes a strange sound, almost like a wet slap, and my stomach spasms.

But the scream that follows isn't mine and drags my eyes downward.

Instead, Lystra's dagger is buried deep in the stomach of the tubby boy who'd run alongside me and turned back early before reaching the dais. As his legs begin to give way, she eviscerates him.

I watch through disbelieving eyes as he collapses to his knees, insides slipping through his clasping fingers to coil on the floor. He topples over, trying feebly to scoop them back in, but as the blood gushes from the horrendous wound, his movements slow until, with a final sigh into the silence, he lies still.

Sadly, his death doesn't bring an end to the horror. Far from it; it's too early.

The day passes in a blur, and the different groups around the circle merge. The tests, games, challenges, name them what you will, are only brought to a close as the light fades. The prize for not coming last in these? The chance to face death over and over again.

I'm incredibly fortunate. After the race I thought I'd lost, the challenges are based on dexterity and agility rather than size and strength. I've always been nimble, and that ability saves me.

Now, as I look at the roughly forty faces around me, it's hard to fathom we're all that's left.

My feet are bleeding, my hands raw, the skin gone from both elbows and a knee. Everyone else is in a similar state. We're in a rough cell, sat on the cold, stone ground, with a guard standing tall at the door, forestalling any escape attempt.

Escape.

Never has a word seemed so important. I want to be anywhere but here.

Buckets are lined up against a wall. After death and fear, I suffer humiliation by relieving myself in front of everyone else. Every breath is a cocktail of foulness; an accumulation of blood, faeces, and urine hangs heavy in the air invading every pore of my body. Not that I'd been clean before, but this is a new level of wretchedness.

I feel a measure of satisfaction that the guard is also breathing in and tasting the same rotten air.

Two more guards enter, wheeling a wooden hand cart between them. On it is a metal cauldron, wisps of vapour coming from the top.

The smell of food wafts momentarily into my nostrils, briefly driving away everything else, and my stomach growls. I start to get to my feet, as do the others around me.

'Sit down!' shouts a guard, his voice booming in the small enclosed space, and no one dares disobey. Not now, not when we understand that our life is worth less than nothing.

One of the cart guards takes a bowl from beside the cauldron and beckons us over one at a time.

Why have I never been called up first in my life? I'm worried there will be none left.

I collect mine third to last.

My wooden bowl is greasy but full to the brim with steaming hot, watery broth. It has things floating inside that might be meat or vegetables, but possibly something else entirely. Nonetheless, I slurp it as fast as possible, burning my throat; the law of the orphanage.

Except for cries, moans, and desperate pleas for mercy that went unheeded, no one had dared to say anything, so a voice raised in complaint causes our heads to whip around.

We're all roughly the same age. However, the boys are mostly bigger than the girls, and one such boy is prying away a bowl from a girl's fingers. She quickly stifles her complaint, but the high-pitched outburst, however short, draws a guard over to her side in a heartbeat.

As with Lystra, there's no hesitation, and suddenly we have two new corpses keeping us company.

I allow the remains of my broth to cool before finishing it. No one will be stealing anyone's food if that's the punishment.

My stomach grumbles, and I hear others too, yet no one dares ask for more.

I lick my bowl clean before it's collected, then sit like a pig awaiting the butcher's knife.

The guards withdraw, and the door closes with a bang that hurts my ears. I don't hear it lock, but why bother. Fear keeps us prisoners very efficiently.

A small, barred window in the cell overlooks the training circle. Its meagre opening allows light to illuminate the room, but that begins to fade rapidly.

I push myself back against a wall and cautiously look around from under my bedraggled hair. My clothes stick to me, almost every part of me hurts, and my mind fills with images of the countless deaths I witnessed.

My body shakes uncontrollably. Never have I been so frightened in my life.

There's no way I'll be able to fall asleep. I'll probably ...

***

Daylight encroaching into the room like a ghostly hand, dim, barely seen, rouses me despite my exhaustion.

I take stock of myself as I come to my senses. If possible, I feel worse than last night. My joints are stiff, especially my fingers. The wounds on my elbows, knees, and knuckles have scabbed as I slept. To add to my discomfort, my clothes are rigid, having dried out from whatever I'd dampened them with in my horror.

I gauge those around me, and my attention is caught by the dead boy and girl lying alone on the floor. Everyone has shied away from them, and they lie side by side, almost as if embracing. Their ghostly skin looks white against the grime and blood that enshroud them.

How can they look so peaceful?

Now is not the time for such thoughts. My eyes are damp, and whilst everyone in the room has cried at some point since arriving, I determine to present a strong image. If I'm to survive, no one must know how weak I feel.

As so few are awake, I creep to the latrine buckets and close my eyes, hoping I'll make no sound. Unfortunately, my bowels are not well, and the heat of shame flushes my face at the awful noises and fresh smell I create. Even worse, there's nothing to wipe myself with.

I don't want to sit down now I've finished and have my clothes stick to my filth, so I remain standing.

How long will it be before the guards, Lystra, or any of the other sadists come to get us? I don't know. But I sense that if yesterday was bad, then today will be worse.

I need to be ready.

Reaching out with my skinny arms, I circle them to loosen my shoulders. Despite my disgusting trousers, I do squats and then stretch the back of my legs. I'd been shown these exercises at the orphanage infirmary when I recovered from a brief bout of joint fever, and they help loosen me up.

A few of my cellmates are awake, including the boy with the strange eyes, and they watch with interest. Several get up to emulate me, and the cell comes to life.

My scabs break open, but strangely it's a relief, for I now have better flexibility despite the pain and blood I can feel seeping from the newly opened wounds.

The door opens, slamming against the wall, and the few asleep, awake in an instant.

A robed figure stands in the doorway, dark eyes glaring, muscled forearms crossed.

'Outside, now!'

He holds no weapon, but nor does he need to.

I scramble not to be last, and I'm safe and outside the door amongst the first half dozen. My stretching stands me in good stead because so many others who hadn't, shamble after as if they're seventy years old.

The training floor is still in shadow, and I expect the only time it's ever fully illuminated will be at noon if the sun passes directly overhead. Otherwise, only the top half of the steep slopes may see the sun's rays for long.

My feet stick slightly to the rough ground, a tackiness caused by blisters opening, yet I'm not alone in my suffering. A trail of blood is behind us, and the day's torment has yet to commence.

Turning my attention to the central dais, I'm concerned by the thick poles erected overnight now circling it. Starting with a short pole, barely knee-high, the circle goes round and round, the poles progressively standing higher. The tallest one is at least six times the height of a man.

After yesterday, I know what they'll be asking for even before Lystra comes striding toward us, eyes as piercing and sharp as a sin-hawk's talons.

~ 16 ~

'You will, one by one, attain the top of the highest pole, then make your way directly down without retracing your steps,' Lystra explains.

I'm right. I knew what was coming, but I think all of us did by now. There's no need for threats or promises of what will happen if we don't finish the course or do as asked. We've seen enough to never forget the price of failure or cheating after just one day.

'Line up,' a guard barks, holding his arm out.

He wears a black hooded robe, but he's young, maybe only several years older than us, and his eyes look as distant and removed as the moons. We scramble to put ourselves in line as quickly as possible, not knowing if even being last in this will find us staring death in the face. Fortunately, we move fast enough to not warrant such an outcome.

Suddenly the boy at the front of the line doesn't appear so relieved as he recognises he'll be first.

Lystra turns her gaze upon him.

'Go.'

The boy jogs to the first pole and steps up, catching his balance. He quickly glances back at us, his eyes full of fear.

I know my eyes look the same, and already I feel myself shaking. Someone cries further down the line, and even in my state, I can't help but want to go comfort them, but I daren't move.

Instead, I watch intently as the selected boy progresses up the spiral, leaping lightly from pole to pole. At first, he's tentative, but then, as his confidence grows, he starts to gather pace, eyes focussing on the poles in front of him.

In everything we'd done so far, it had been a competition. Come last, and that was the end. But in this challenge, it seems completing it will be enough to survive. Therefore, despite not knowing the boy, I root for him.

'Come on,' I whisper under my breath, and as I glance about, others have looks of encouragement and hope in their eyes.

If he can do it, it will boost everyone's confidence, and he's starting to make it look easy; until he makes a mistake.

He looks down and suddenly realises how high he is. He freezes, fear taking hold, thin grimy legs shaking.

Silence reigns. Lystra and the guards watch intently, waiting for further progress, but the boy is unmoving, terror having stolen his ability to act, perhaps twenty poles from the end.

I don't want to watch his terror; I'm afraid I'll be infected. Instead, I gaze beyond him, and there, high in the sky, are beautiful white clouds. If only I could be up there, and that one, yes … I can see an image forming, a face …

Lystra reaches out a hand, catching my attention, and a loaded crossbow is placed into it.

Please move! I scream silently.

A deep thrum, and the boy moves, falling limply to hit the ground with a thud.

'Next!' Lystra's voice sounds flat and emotionless.

I want to take that crossbow and beat her and all the guards to death with it. I've never thought of killing someone else before, and the idea shakes me. My eyes rove around to see if there's a chance to escape, but every door to the circle is closed, and even if I try, I can't outrun a crossbow bolt.

Two more fail. I'm about ninth in line, grateful to be so far back when Lystra walks down.

'You!' she commands, snatching away my brief feeling of security before picking a boy to go after me. As I numbly walk to the challenge, it's as if the world holds its breath.

Without a doubt, everyone's eyes are fixed on me as I step onto the first pole. Strange how they appeared so thick and sturdy from a distance, but they barely seem wide enough now that I'm standing on top.

My heart hammers frantically, breath coming in short gasps.

I'd counted the poles, as we all probably had.

Fifty poles.

Forty-nine, forty-eight.

I determine not to look down, just count backwards in my head.

Twenty-five, twenty-four.

I've completely shut out the training circle, the wall, the mountainside, and anything that might make me appreciate how high I am.

Twelve, eleven.

My feet are in a terrible state, and as I step to the next pole and push with my back foot, it slips. I twist even as I fall, grabbing the top of the pole, a fingernail tearing off.

'Nooo!' The cry escapes my lips, and I hold on, legs shaking, arms trembling.

I'm so tired. If I just let go, my aching body cajoles me, I could fall, then rest on the ground. Yet my mind knows the truth. I'd be broken, in agony, and death would follow.

My survival instinct, which had served me so well in the orphanage, kicks in, and I wrap my legs around the pole, anticipating the impact of a crossbow bolt, knowing I have but a moment to get moving, to do something.

Pushing with my legs, I pull simultaneously with my arms and manage to gain the top of the pole, and still no crossbow bolt.

I stand, legs shaking. They barely hold me up. Fear has robbed me of strength and the confidence to move.

Step!

But my legs won't obey.

Step!

It had been easy till now, and yet I can't move. I'm dizzy, swaying, and close to overbalancing.

Wouldn't it be better if this were all to end?

I look at the sky. It must have been a still day, for the clouds hadn't moved. Where was the cloud? Yes, there! The cloud with the face of ... my little brother.

'Move, Alina. You can do it, Alina. Move!'

I hear Karson's voice chirruping in my head. It can only be him, using the nickname he'd given me because he'd always struggled to pronounce the M in Malina. For him, not only can I conquer fear, I can move mountains.

As the crossbow thrums, I step forward, and the bolt whistles past my ear.

I keep moving.

Ten, nine, eight ... and before I know it, I'm on one, and no more crossbow bolts have come to claim me.

I'm so high up, but it doesn't bother me now. Instead, the tears that run down my face are of sweet joy at my little brother's voice saving me at the time of my greatest need after all these years.

Was his voice a figment of my imagination or really him?

My exhausted arms and legs wrap around the pole, barely holding on as I lower myself down.

The wood is rough, yet my feet, which almost caused my death, now help save my life.

My bloody soles lubricate the pole, and I feel myself slide a little. I turn my feet inward, harshly rubbing first one then the other against the wood. The skin inside my arms also tears, helping further.

The ground rushes up to meet me, and I collapse at the base of the pole.

A guard comes over and kicks me toward the line. I crawl, leaving a bloodied trail behind.

I'm lucky. I get to rest and catch my breath. This will hopefully give me an advantage in whatever comes next.

***

I barely register who succeeds or fails after me. It's hard to focus through the pain, but at least my numerous injuries now simply hurt as one.

A guard drops a piece of stale bread into my lap, and I barely have the strength to chew and swallow the gritty fare, but I force myself. A short while later, he comes back with a bucket and a ladle, pouring water directly into my parched mouth. I cough and splutter. It's too much, yet at the same time, not enough.

The poles are removed and the dead bodies of the fallen piled upon one another. I watch with morbid fascination. It's an unnecessary reminder of what awaits. Arms and legs poke out like sticks from a bonfire. Then, as if in response to my comparison, a fire begins to grow inside me.

This is not where I'll die, at least not today!

'Form a circle around me NOW!' yells Lystra, her voice as cold as a winter's day.

Before I can even react, I'm being kicked and dragged into position. Other children are more fortunate and scramble into place themselves.

'Survive this, and for now, your ordeal will be over. Fail, and your life will be over!' Lystra barks, and nods to a guard who steps into the circle to drop two cudgels. Two others walk outside the ring of children, then simultaneously push a boy forward to the centre.

'Kill or be killed!' Lystra shouts.

If my heart beats any faster, I fear I might faint. The blood rush I experience fills my veins with nervous energy brought on by fear and the primordial desire to live at all costs.

One of the selected, hulking and dark-haired with a cruel face, doesn't hesitate. While the other boy looks around, eyes full of tears, *cruel-face* stoops down, scoops up a cudgel and without hesitation delivers a crushing blow to the back of the other's skull.

There's a sickening crunch followed by complete silence as the struck lad crumples to the floor without a sound. Blood flows, creating a gooey puddle.

The pile of bodies has some new sticks added to it.

Minutes later, the next fight starts, and it's equally gruesome. Two girls attack each other ferociously, desperate to stay alive. They end up so badly injured that a guard slits both their throats.

This is an essential lesson to everyone yet to be called. Not only must we win, but remain standing at the end, not on our knees.

When a hand pushes me forward, I'm strangely calm, for death's grip is no longer as fearsome or unfamiliar. I scoop the sticky cudgel from the ground and absently note it's covered in matted hair and torn skin. It's not unwieldy and feels strangely comforting in my grasp.

I study my opponent.

Despite the ashen face, his gaze is confident, and why wouldn't it be. He's tall, while I'm barely half his size with much shorter arms. We circle each other, both wary of the previous fight's outcome. He swings several times without commitment, and I gauge his reach as I duck away.

I daren't block his weapon with my own, he'll simply bash it from my hand, nor can I get in close to land a blow of my own. There's no dodging these weapons, and being shorter, my head is very vulnerable if I close the distance. But I know what I'm going to do. The question is, can I do it?

He swings, and I step back, giving ground, offering no threat, but when he swings again, so do I, but not to meet his weapon. Instead, I duck and swipe at his hand as his cudgel whooshes over my head.

'Aargh!'

The crack as my weapon connects fills me with hope. A moment later, his cudgel bounces across the ground.

Tears stream in dirty rivers down his face as he runs at me, arms outstretched. If he can bear me to the ground, he'll have a chance. Yet my nimbleness stands me in good stead, and as I twist away, my cudgel is already swinging and connects with his knee.

His scream of agony makes me falter for a moment, and I look around the circle as he writhes on the floor. Lystra's gaze locks with mine, and there's death written across her face.

Kill or be killed.

I retrieve the boy's fallen cudgel and return to where he's lying on the floor.

'Please. Please, no!'

He raises his hands as I bring the cudgels down in a flurry. Now death is upon him; the boy finds the desperate strength to block blow after blow with his arms despite them breaking under the multiple blows. However, soon he can lift them no more, and I barely have the strength to raise mine.

As I look into his brown eyes, there's resignation mixed with terrible pain. Perhaps even a hint of relief.

I drop one cudgel and raise the other in both hands over my head.

I'm so grateful that he closes his eyes before I deliver the killing blow.

***

It's approaching evening.

As I look around at the other eight survivors in my group, most sit and stare blankly ahead, no doubt trying to process in their minds how their lives have suddenly changed. I've never considered my life held much value, but till now, I've never considered it utterly worthless.

My hair is damp beneath my fingers, and I'm shocked at how short it is now. Everyone else has just received the same treatment.

First, a no-nonsense haircut in a room with a waterfall cascading down the side, the water draining through a metal grating set into a flagstone floor. After the scissor treatment, we'd been ordered to strip and stand under the freezing water. No one had dared disobey, and we'd all shivered uncontrollably under the pummelling, but after we finished, it was the cleanest any of us had probably been for most of our lives.

Yet nothing could wash away the trauma we'd just experienced so quickly.

Only eighteen survived of the forty-odd who started the day. Where the other nine are sleeping, I don't know, nor do I care.

We're wearing clean linen tunics and trousers, dyed brown. Our old clothes had been so fouled, burning them had probably been the only recourse. Our numerous wounds were covered in sticky salves that had taken away some of the pain and are now bound with the whitest linen bandages I've ever seen.

I'm washed, in clean clothes, on a bunk with fresh sheets. The cell we're in isn't exactly spacious, but neither is it cramped. A moon globe hangs from the ceiling glowing softly, indicating there's immense wealth behind this operation, for magical items are rare. The floor is bare rock, swept clean, with no sign of rodent droppings.

In the far-right corner of the room, a wooden table and chairs take up space, whilst opposite them, a small doorway leads to a toilet area.

None of us could do much more than fall to our beds when we were shown in by Lystra and two other robed escorts. She'd told us not to leave the room unless summoned, as it would be viewed as an escape attempt. *'I'll see you in the morning,'* her last words as she swept from the room without a backward glance.

With the threat of imminent death receding, a little strength and perhaps hope returns.

On the table is a large cloth draped over something.

I groan as I lever myself upright, hesitantly crossing the room, but if we're allowed to go to the toilet, it must be alright to walk around. I approach the table, limping heavily, cautious of my damaged feet, and pull the corner of the cloth up and peek underneath.

My stomach rumbles in wonder, and I pull the cloth away to reveal nine bowls of food: meat, vegetables, and bread, with some goblets of water.

For as many years as I can remember, all I've been fed was stale crusts, cold gruel or some watery broth and yet here before me is a veritable feast.

I'm tempted to start eating as quickly as possible. That had been the law of the orphanage. Eat fast to protect your food, then try to grab more from those who were too slow. But, instead, I turn back to the others, who sit like propped-up corpses, eyes staring into nothingness, consumed by their thoughts.

'Look,' I say, my voice hushed. Yet when no one pays me any attention, I repeat myself louder. 'Everyone, look at this!'

Heads turn slowly toward me, drawn by the sound of something other than fear in my voice. The next moment, we're sitting around the table, the trauma forgotten, as we eat the most divine meal.

It's strange to be eating and crying at the same time, but all of us are.

Nobody speaks beyond my first words, perhaps scared of the consequences. We tear into the food, lick the juices from our fingers, rub them around each bowl and lick them again. The water is clear and the freshest I've ever drunk. It's only when the moon globe begins to dim that exhaustion hits us all like a blow, and we stumble to our beds.

Yet as I lie down, the horror returns. Faces flash through my mind, screaming, pleading, followed by images of broken corpses. How can I possibly survive what the morrow will bring? Despite being bandaged and fed, I'm broken.

I must find a way to escape! Maybe with the others helping, we can do this together.

For a while, my mind remains positive, but as reality crushes my dreams, my last thought is wondering how I'll die.

***

CHAPTER II

I awake from the deepest sleep I've ever had in my life.

Initially, it had been plagued by the worst kind of nightmares, the ones it's impossible to wake from. Unsurprisingly, everything from the last two days had initially repeated itself over and over, but then they'd gradually faded.

Now, as I lie on my back, the moon globe on the ceiling brightens, and I remember the *nightmares* had turned to dreams, full of a sense of well-being.

How is that possible?

As consciousness takes firm hold of me, my heart beats faster as fear of what might lay ahead in the next minute, hour, or day sends a kaleidoscope of horrific images through my head.

However, confusion strangely dispels my growing sense of panic.

I lift my hands in front of my eyes, turning them around.

Yesterday, my hands had been bandaged to cover the torn skin, the blisters, and the weeping wounds. Likewise, my arms, legs, and feet had been a mess of ripped flesh.

Yet, as I inspect myself, there's pink, healing skin: no scabs, tears, or bindings. My arms are the same, and when I move my legs and wriggle my toes under the warm blanket, I feel the absence of injuries there too.

The others are beginning to stir, with not a bandage in sight.

I feel rested, stronger than I have in years.

What kind of magic is this?

My complaining bladder forces me up, the rock floor cool beneath my feet.

I feel stiff as I pad into the toilet area. Even this room is larger than anything I've ever lived in.

There's a low, sturdy wooden bench over a fissure in the rock. The bench has holes carved in so I can sit and relieve myself. I don't know how deep the fissure is, but there's the distant sound of flowing water. What a luxury not to have to use buckets!

Back in the main room, the others are standing. Not only does everyone have those looks of well-rested amazement on their faces, but I notice they look healthier and fuller. My arms also seem less skin and bone.

The food we eat is bread, cold meats, and water.

'How the hell are we going to get out of this place?' a girl with the most beautiful dark skin asks.

'We don't even know which way is out and what's outside if we do find a way,' mutters a black-haired lad, keeping his voice low. 'We arrived here on a ship, remember. So, we've no idea where we are.'

'Why are they feeding us such good food if they're going to kill us?' another girl asks softly.

'The best thing to do is eat this food and get our strength up,' growls a big lad.

'Agreed!' another boy nods, and that's enough to stymy any more conversation.

No further words are said as we tuck in, yet we continue to exchange glances, gauging each other, and there's confusion behind everyone's eyes.

We must all be thinking the same thing.

Where's the horror? Where are our wounds? Why are we being fed like royalty and have beds to sleep in?

We hear a cough and turn to see a guard standing at the entrance to our cell.

My feeling of well-being threatens to vanish, but the guard simply beckons, and we hurry over.

He points to our beds.

'Boots!'

As we turn, to my amazement, beneath the end of my bed is a pair of short leather boots. I've never owned proper boots before. I want to inspect them, such is my wonder, but we know the cost of coming last, and we're all back at the door in moments.

As with the other guards, his presence is foreboding. He's tall, muscled, with scars crisscrossing his forearms.

I look at myself. I'm dressed in the same cut of clothes as the guard, and a strange feeling of unity briefly washes over me.

As a group, we follow him silently through narrow, rough-hewn passages, our way lit intermittently by moon globes. He leads us to a door, and my insides clench, for it's grated, and beyond I can see daylight and the dais that marks the centre of the training circle.

Fear returns, and a low moan escapes my lips, echoed by those around me. I'd left the horror behind for a moment, but now it seems we're going to meet it face-on again.

With a grunt, the guard swings the door open, and we hesitantly step through.

The other nine survivors are on the far side with a guard of their own.

'Follow me and keep up,' our guard orders, breaking into a slow jog.

The pace is leisurely as we follow, and my heart, which had started hammering when I saw the dais, begins to settle down as we move easily around the training circle. My boots fit perfectly, and I can't believe I'm wearing some for the first time in my life that weren't my father's.

I furtively study the others and catch those strange blue-green eyes of the blond lad snatching glances at me in return. I nod, and his lips hesitantly form a smile. It's almost as if showing anything other than fear or trepidation is unsuitable.

This makes me think about what happened on this very ground. But even as I change the focus of my attention, I shake my head in confusion. There's no sign of the blood, vomit, and faeces that was here only yesterday, let alone the bodies.

The guard increases the pace a little.

I feel refreshed, strong, and I'm amazed at how my body has the energy to respond.

As we do circuit after circuit, I note the dark balcony jutting from the mountainside I'd caught sight of yesterday. As I peer upwards, I can see dark-robed figures standing silently, observing. Were they the same ones from yesterday? Is it for their pleasure this is happening? Yet my thoughts don't dwell on them; instead, I fantasise about how I can get out of this place.

The whole day passes in the presence of our guard, the other group distantly shadowing whatever we do. We run, we rest, we do different exercises, we rest. Our guard is stern and demanding, yet not cruel, and perhaps because we do everything he asks, he offers no threat of violence.

Food is *actually* brought out to us, nothing special, but more food. Food that leaves me full, something I can't remember ever experiencing before last night.

Nothing we do is too strenuous, and to be in the fresh air with the green slopes of the mountain high above us, the birds circling in the air, and new boots on my feet is as close to contentment as I can remember.

It's strange. How can my thoughts in one moment be full of yesterday's horrors and the intent to escape, and then the next, I feel a sense of serenity where so much blood has been spilt?

Eventually, darkness begins to fall.

The guard leads us to the waterfall room, and we cleanse together, the other group joining us briefly. The water is so cold, but beyond the initial shock, it leaves your skin burning as if on fire, and the shivering stops. Afterwards, we dry ourselves on rough linen towels and find fresh brown garments awaiting us.

I'd have never thought it possible to wear new, clean clothes, least of all two days in a row.

We return to our cell.

Since breaking fast, no one has uttered a word.

The guard warns us to not leave and then walks away, his footsteps fading. I'm tempted to sneak out after him to see where he goes or if a way out of this place is obvious, yet the idea fades almost as quickly as it forms.

Why? Because there's food laid out on the table again and a goblet of water for each of us.

After such a long day of exercise, I tear into my food alongside the others, devouring it and washing it down with water.

'We should make our escape,' I venture in a hushed whisper. 'We must get out before it's too late; we should try and escape tonight!'

Emphatic nods meet my suggestion.

'There isn't even a door on our cell; more fool them,' observes a brown-haired boy with a serious look to his features. 'We can be gone before they know it.'

'Should we go now or wait till the middle of the night?' asks a girl.

The boy with the strange eyes raises his hand in caution. 'We should wait a few days instead,' he says, backed by a smile, his words a little slurred.

'Why? Haven't you got the stones for it?' growls a big lad, leaning forward threateningly. 'Need to pluck up your courage?'

I expect the argument to end there, but *strange-eyes* firmly shakes his head, undeterred.

'No. I'm just thinking with my brain, not my muscles! Don't you think they'll be expecting us to try and escape? Wait a few more days, and they might let their guard down. With the good food they're feeding us and a couple of nights' sleep, we'll be much stronger and can make better speed when we do get out of here!'

Strange-eye's words make sense, but a few more days could see us all dead.

A staring contest begins between the two boys, but when the bigger one yawns, his jaw cracking, he nods in grudging acceptance.

'He's right,' he says, jerking his thumb at *strange-eyes*, and that's the end of tonight's escape attempt.

Overwhelming exhaustion seems to come upon us simultaneously, and everyone stumbles to their beds. I place my boots under the end, noting with interest that the others do the same, and we crawl beneath the blankets.

As I lie there, in my thoughts, I see my little brother's face; he's trying to say something to me. I strain to hear because he seems worried ... but then sleep claims me.

***

Lystra looks down at us from the small platform upon which she stands, her eyes expressionless. I think she'd be considered very beautiful if it weren't for the menace surrounding her.

'The vomiting and nausea you experienced in the early hours of this morning was due to the tincture of silk spice added to your food before you slept,' she says. 'You'll be relieved to know that it has no long-term ill effects. As you experienced, they're incapacitating and will take effect around four hours after consumption. You cannot overdose on this, so the amount administered is not an issue.'

I can't believe it. We'd been purposely poisoned. The memory of what we'd all suffered makes my stomach cramp briefly, and I taste bile in the back of my throat.

What's wrong with this place, these people?

I take a breath, finding strength at the injustice of everything to ask a question, but before I can voice it, Lystra pierces me with her gaze. It's a look full of such pent-up violence that I promptly close my mouth again, fear gripping my insides worse than any cramps.

'You will not talk in my presence unless you're asked a question or are given leave to. You may all nod to show you understand!' Lystra says forcefully.

I want to shout at her to go to hell, to let us go. I want to scream so many obscenities, but instead, I just nod and see others do the same.

I'll be gone soon, I console myself. A couple more days, and we'll escape.

Yet, unsynchronised movement catches my eye. One lad, big-boned and tall for his age, shakes his head, slowly at first, then with growing vehemence.

'What the hell is going on? I don't want to be here! Let me go!' Tears stream down his face in both confusion and newly resurrected fear.

Be quiet! I scream inside my head.

Lystra smiles. It even extends to her eyes as she walks toward him, and I begin to relax.

There's no anger on her face, no hint of disappointment. Not even as she ruffles his hair, takes his head gently between her hands, and then snaps his neck. It cracks loudly, like a dry twig being broken.

The girl closest to me bites her knuckles so hard to stop herself screaming that blood runs down her chin. My fists are clenched tightly, and my knuckles shine white.

Lystra slowly lowers the boy's head to the desk behind which he sits, smoothes his hair down, and then returns to her platform.

'Listen to me and hear every single word I say. I stand before you, and I see the fear and hatred in your eyes, and yet a decade ago, I sat where you are. I'd been starved like you, taken from an auction block like you, and had just watched everyone die around me, just like you. I was frightened, disorientated, and yet here I stand, alive and unbowed, with the power of life and death in my hands.

'You think your position unjust, unfair. Well, had you been bought by someone else, most of those who failed would have still died in time, beaten to death for some infraction or simply for their owner's amusement.

'The rest of you would also have perished, frozen in a barn during winter, or died from illness as your body was too weak to fight it off. Maybe your end would've been a dagger to the belly from a cutpurse after your mouldy bread or from a client left unsatisfied by your body. Death awaited you anyway, and it would have been a blessing, for your lives would have been so miserable that perhaps the most likely cause of your death would have been by your own hand.

'There are only two ways out of this place.' Lystra points to the dead boy. 'He just chose one. There will be many times when death seems the easier option, and it's a route hundreds before you have taken and one that many others will take in the future. The other way is to overcome the challenges you face, accept this as your life, and realise that before you in the distance is an opportunity beyond your wildest dreams. You simply need to find the strength of body and will to get you there to seize it.'

Lystra pauses, allowing her words to sink in.

I look around the room, and my gaze locks with the boy with the strange eyes. I think he's the only other survivor from my original group.

The moment is interrupted as Lystra draws a deep breath.

'Today's lesson will continue.'

***

We study for hours as black-robed men and women intermittently bring different herbs, plants, and roots to lay on a table at the front of the room. We begin to learn about the different textures and scents before and after infusing in water and food. All these, Lystra tells us, will have unique effects, from simple sleep to instant death.

It should be hard to concentrate, but Lystra's commanding tone and the corpse of the dead boy in his chair remind me of the consequences that await if I displease her. Why we're learning this is beyond me, but anything that distracts my thoughts is welcome, and I'm strangely fascinated to study something known by apothecaries who hold high station in any society.

In the corner of the room is a sunglass. I'd heard about them but never thought to see one. It's about four hands tall, marked with the twelve hours of the day and night. Inside is a ball of flame that burns brighter throughout the day as it rises to the top of the glass to indicate noon and thereafter begins its descent, gradually dimming as the day wears on.

It's one in the afternoon when Lystra calls a halt.

'Follow me,' she commands.

The eight of us dare do nothing but obediently fall in behind her as she leaves through a different doorway into a corridor beyond.

After the classroom's smooth lines, this passageway affronts my eyes. Deep cracks cover the walls like crazed spider webs, whereas the floor has been neatly finished, with barely a flaw visible.

Lystra pauses.

'At the end of this corridor, within a room, food awaits. But to eat it, you must earn it. That's the underlying principle of our methods here. So, reach the end of the corridor without touching the ground.'

She pads away down the corridor.

My empty stomach growls in anticipation of the food. I turn to the others, and for whatever reason, the stopper is suddenly removed from my bottled-up emotions. The next moment I'm on my knees, sobbing quietly. Yet, I'm not embarrassed, as my emotional outpouring triggers everyone else's.

To have the violence come back so suddenly after a day of respite and tranquillity has broken me. I must compose myself quickly, or I won't last the day.

'I'm Lotane Mul,' a voice whispers.

Kneeling before me, *strange eyes* smiles cautiously.

'Thank you, Lotane,' I whisper back.

Why we hadn't exchanged names till now, I don't know. Maybe it was because we were scared to get to know one another. Dealing with someone's death is easier if you don't know them.

I wrap my arms around him briefly, grateful for this show of human warmth, not forgetting he'd also saved my life at the beginning.

'I'm Malina.'

We know we don't have the luxury of time, so we stand, and everyone makes quick, hushed introductions.

'What now?' asks a lad with brown hair who'd spoken at the table last night. He's just introduced himself as Delon.

I study the walls and reach up, pushing my fingers into a deep crack. I then do the same with my feet just above the floor and begin to edge along the passageway.

Am I being foolish?

Unlike Delon, who obviously thinks I am, Lotane and everyone else follows my lead.

Even as I edge along, I can see him looking down the corridor; it's empty. With a brief, wary smile, he jogs quietly past to near the end and climbs up.

I tense, waiting for Lystra to appear and something awful to happen, but when it doesn't, a girl called Tirana drops down from the wall and creeps ahead. The rest of us continue our slow, painful progress, straining to hold on with our fingertips and toes.

My arms and wrists ache horribly, but I'm too wary of letting go. Curses from a boy called Nestor carry to me ever so softly as the others behind Lotane grumble at my slow progress, encouraging me to go faster. I bite back a caustic response. Why hadn't some idiots gone along the other side?

It seems to take forever to reach the end of the passageway, where the walls smooth just before the doorway. I jump down, hands shaking. Moments later, Lotane joins me, followed by the others. Delon and Tirana have already gone ahead to undoubtedly claim the wolf's share of the food.

With a brief smile and a jaunty tilt of his head, Lotane steps through the doorway, then stops almost immediately, but with everyone pushing from behind, he stumbles forward, and we follow him into the room.

Inside, there are four tables with two chairs each. Platters of food await on top.

At one table sits Delon, opposite Tirana, dead eyes staring at the feast in front of them.

Despite her having taken two lives moments before, Lystra smiles widely as if greeting her own children.

'Perhaps I wasn't clear enough with my warning. Perhaps this,' and she points at the bodies, 'is my fault. What do you think?' she demands, looking at me.

I shake so hard I can hardly get the words past my lips. 'It isn't your f-f-fault,' I stammer.

Lystra nods, eyes as cold as ice. 'We don't want to kill you, nor do we want you to die. You cost hard-earned money to buy, to bring here, to feed. I can assure you that I take no pleasure in today's deaths, for they were unnecessary, but they neither listened nor learned.'

Who is the *we* she's talking about?

'Have you learned?' she asks, fixing Lotane with her stare.

Lotane nods sharply, biting his lip.

Lystra laughs, but it's flat, without humour. 'In which case, you may all sit and eat. No talking.'

I sit opposite Lotane on a rough wooden chair while the other four pair off. Dyowne sits with Nestor, and a girl, Alyssa, sits with Garlin, the large boy who'd wanted to leave last night and challenged Lotane.

Between us are two bowls of rice, two of meat, and a further two of vegetables.

Lotane takes a bowl of each and lifts some meat to his lips with a glimmer of a smile.

Swiftly I grab his wrist.

There'd been something in Lystra's laugh which gave me pause. Don't ask me exactly what. She showed so little emotion, but maybe it was how she posed her question. Then, of course, was our previous encounter with food poisoning and the morning lesson.

I pry the greasy food from his fingers and bring it to my nostrils. Sure enough, there's the subtlest smell like wet ashes ... the scent of demon grass. I shake my head subtly as I pass it back.

Lotane smells it, his brow creasing. His eyes convey his thanks as he discards it, then checks the rest of the meat in his bowl while I do the same to mine. His entire bowl is corrupted. Next, we check the rice and vegetable bowls. Once again, one bowl of each had been poisoned.

Is everything here a game, where to lose is to die?

I'm so engrossed in my angry thoughts that the sound of choking barely registers until Lotane's shocked eyes, staring over my shoulder, make me turn around.

Garlin holds his throat with both hands, sweat running down his pallid face as he tries to draw breath.

I stand, reacting quickly to see if I can help, but only make it one pace before Lystra is in front of me, the sting of her blow spinning me from my feet.

'Sit down,' she hisses as I gaze up through tearful eyes. 'Watch and learn, all of you. Watch and learn,' and her tone grabs everyone's attention.

'This is how someone will die if they ingest food laced with demon grass. It's a painful, drawn-out death, brought on by the throat swelling so that insufficient air is drawn into the body. Look at his eyes as they bulge from their sockets; note the hands clasping at his throat. Death occurs within three minutes of ingesting. The only way to save someone who has eaten demon grass is to allow them to breathe until such time as the body's reaction wears off.'

Lystra draws a thin-bladed dagger from within a sleeve, and I watch horror-struck as she holds Garlin's head back, pushing it into his windpipe. Withdrawing it quickly, Lystra pinches the wound, opening it up, and air whooshes in, inflating Garlin's lungs even as blood flows over her fingertips.

'Hold the wound open for long enough,' she says conversationally, while blood splatters her with every hiss of air Garlin exhales, 'and breathing will, in time, resume normally. Of course, you then have to worry about infection from the incision you've made and sealing the wound.'

She looks at her hand, holding the wound open, then releases it, whilst with the other, she drives the dagger into Garlin's eye, leaving it in, the hilt flush against his socket as she lowers his head to the tabletop.

'HE didn't learn his lesson!' Lystra shouts angrily, staring at Lotane, no doubt aware that he remains alive because of my intervention.

'Now, you'll finish the meal in front of you. To stay alive, you need to be strong. To be strong, you need to eat. But more importantly, you need to learn. Everything I teach you could mean the difference between your life and death, either here and now or later in your lives ... *if* you live that long. I can see in your faces that you think your death is but a matter of time, and you're right. But it need not happen here, today, tomorrow, or the day after.

'You may hate me. You might even want to kill me but know this. I can keep you alive if you but LISTEN, so heed my words if you want to live.'

***

I sit opposite Lotane. He's pale and clasps his hands together in a vain attempt to stop trembling. The fast-beating pulse in his neck is almost hypnotic. I wish I could return the hug he'd given me earlier in the corridor, but I don't dare.

I quickly apportion our untainted food and start eating, not only because I'm hungry but because of Lystra's instructions.

Growing up in an orphanage had conditioned me to take orders and carry out tasks without delay or complaint. Failure to do so always led to punishments, ranging from being beaten with a stick to solitary confinement.

Was this really so different?

Well, yes. In the space of three days, I'd witnessed dozens of people die violently right in front of me. Before now, I'd only ever known death to approach quietly, except perhaps for my mother's passing, and I hadn't witnessed that.

Yet, if I put that to one side, the differences were strangely positive ... good food, clean clothes and a bed that hadn't been shared with a thousand insects for whom I was a midnight feast.

Even the rules are the same. Obey without question, without hesitation.

Somehow, putting it this simply in my head removes my fear; the phrase I'd chosen seemed familiar, like I'd heard it recently. I look around further, purposely avoiding Lystra's gaze in case it forbids me from doing so. I keep eating while observing the others.

No matter what Lystra says, we'll all wind up dead before long. Escape is the only option. The realisation fills me with hope, but my head begins to pound.

'You'll follow me when I leave this room,' Lystra commands, distracting me from my train of thought. The pain recedes, and I redouble my efforts to eat and finish quickly.

Shortly, Lystra strides out through the doorway. We all hurry after her, an avalanche of noise and fear. To the contrary, she moves ahead; cold, calm, full of poise and silence. We keep a respectful distance behind. She hasn't asked for it, but a cold aura suggests getting too close will lead to violence.

Suddenly she stops and turns around, exuding disapproval. We retreat before her advance until we're back at the doorway again.

Nothing is said. Who will she choose to kill?

The silence grows, and I can sense the cold hand of death approaching like an unstoppable wave.

The walls! Yes. She wants us to follow using the same method that got us here.

I edge past the others, icy fingers crawling down my spine as I move within Lystra's reach. Fortunately, as I slide my fingers into the cracks between the blocks and pull myself up, the danger passes, and she stalks away. I catch Lotane encouraging Dyowne to follow. Her flame-red hair would give her a fearsome look if it weren't for the tears running down her cheeks.

The return journey up the corridor takes longer as everyone's arms are tired. Fortunately, the footholds are deep, and I press flat against the wall, my legs taking most of my weight.

Lystra nods to me when I jump down. A sign of recognition for doing something well, perhaps? She swings away, back to the room full of herbs and plants.

Everyone's attention is undivided as Lystra introduces us to further species of plants, herbs, seeds, and leaves. They range from those that take away infection to others that induce euphoria if smoked. Each is presented to us in natural, powdered, and dissolved forms.

'What seed is this?' Lystra demands suddenly, pointing at Alyssa.

'A Dandron seed.'

'And what happens if you drink an infusion with one seed?' Lystra barks at Lotane.

'It brings on diarrhoea within the hour that lasts a day.' Lotane's voice is hesitant, nervous.

The silence that follows is deadly. How can emptiness hold such menace? I'm sure Lotane's given the correct answer, but I can see tears form in the corner of his eyes, however hard he tries to stop them.

'Well done,' Lystra acknowledges, then begins asking us all questions.

It's a fretful afternoon. Wrong answers aren't met with death this time, but by the time the lesson is over, we all have the mark of Lystra's hand upon our cheeks. Her blows are so swift that even had we dared try to avoid them, it would have been impossible.

The sunglass shows it's early evening when Lystra stops and leads us from the room back toward, then past our sleeping area. There are no handholds on the walls, so we scurry after her.

Then we come to an open doorway we remember only too well.

Lystra stands to one side, and we file through.

Three boys and a girl wait within the room, all dressed in brown like us, faces reddened from being struck.

As the door closes, we hear those terrible words again.

'Hold on, and don't let go.'

***

Fortunately, when we'd had to endure the room with the sliding floor a second time, it had lost some of its fear factor, perhaps because we'd already overcome it and knew what to expect. Thankfully, through unspoken assent, the boys had let four of us girls, me included, take the corner straps. That way, we hadn't needed to hang on for as long. Being in the corner meant we were the last to stand on the floor and the first to drop back down.

We'd all survived.

Now, I'm in damp, clean clothes again, following a guard back to our cell.

When I'd been in the orphanage, the filthy clothes I wore stayed on for a whole month. They were only removed when I took a monthly bath in water so grey, scummy, and cold that I hated getting in. I took my clothes into the water with a block of soap and had to the count of one hundred to clean away the accumulated grime and stench before giving way to the next in line.

I often wondered if that water was ever clean and what it was like to be first in line when the water was clear, sparkling, and perhaps even hot.

We walk in silence. The four newcomers stay together at the back, and I begrudge them joining us. Two loom ominously, a real threat if any more physical contests await. Yet more imminently, this could affect our escape plans.

The guard ushers us inside our cell when we arrive, and I note an extra bed as there are now ten of us. Every bed is freshly made. The smell of newly washed linen hangs in the air.

'Don't leave the room unless summoned,' the guard warns.

The newcomers squirm uncomfortably under his lingering gaze before he turns away, the gentle scuff of his footsteps slowly diminishing.

By silent assent, we all move to the table now the room is to ourselves.

The newcomers take one end, while what remains of my group takes the other. Two are obviously brothers, hulking brutes with slate grey eyes indicating Icelandian blood.

'What happened to the rest of your group?' I ask. 'There were another five of you training in the circle yesterday.'

Lotane quietly passes out plates of food. No one eats, not yet. Everyone smells the food, tasting the tiniest amounts in case it's been tainted.

I fear the answer, even as the question leaves my lips.

The slightly smaller of the two brothers looks at me with disdain. He has a crooked nose and has perfected a sneer which he uses to good effect.

'They were sent home yesterday!' he says, picking away at something in his ear.

'Really?' The words burst from my lips before my brain kicks into gear.

'Are you really that dumb?' he laughs, happy at making me look stupid. 'Ugly, pasty, with piss yellow eyes, n dumb on top. You shoulda been killed at birth!'

I can feel my face burn red and bite back an angry retort. He is way too big to antagonise, and it had been a dumb question.

'Did they die during the tests today?' Nestor prompts.

I wonder if his question will be deemed too obvious and earn him a stinging insult, but with a final sneer at me, the boy shakes his head.

'No. No one died today, although this slow fool,' he says, jerking his head at his brother, 'almost ate some poisoned food before I saved his sorry ass.'

Several plates of food are moved to the end of the table. They don't smell right, and Lotane starts handing out the rest as the boy continues.

'It was last night. The other five wanted to escape. I told 'em we should wait a day or two, but they didn't listen. Fools never do! So, we all had to go. I knew if they made it without us, there'd never be another chance, as the guards would be on alert for another attempt.

'We were going to go in two groups, less likely to be seen. Us lot,' and he nods to the other three, 'decided to go second. We were about to follow when we heard the shouts n screams. The guards dragged their corpses back to bed as a warning. It was horrible waking up to those blank eyes!'

'We were planning to escape in a couple of nights,' Alyssa croaks, her voice thick with shock at how close we'd been to suffering the same fate.

Lotane had saved our lives with his words of caution.

'Good that you didn't,' the older brother mumbles quietly.

Quiet introductions are made as we eat our fill.

Through luck or design, five boys and five girls, including me, now share a room.

I take a moment to study my fellow survivors.

Bardel, with the crooked nose and sneer, superior and spiteful ... he makes it clear he doesn't like me or girls in general. Kralgen, his bigger brother, dark and brooding, is somewhat slow, less talkative, and therefore marginally less odious.

Larn. I'd initially considered him a girl with those delicate eyebrows, slight nose and full lips. Yet he has a deep resounding voice and seems pleasant enough.

Nestor. Short with thick, curly dark hair. He always seems to be listening and rarely says anything.

Then, there's Lotane.

Tousled blond hair, often smiling, dimples, with those strange eyes. He'd saved my life, and then I'd saved his. I feel a bond because of that and the occasional looks we share. Now he's saved my life again by voicing caution about our escape.

The other girls are Alyssa, Dyowne, Orphea and Fianna.

None of us girls are large. We share the same skinny arms, and I wonder if someone like Lotane helped them to hang on the first time around.

Alyssa keeps her head down, unwilling to make eye contact with anyone.

Dyowne stares at Larn, intrigued by his looks.

Orphea is studying everyone, a little like me.

Fianna. She's sitting next to me at the table, head resting on my shoulder. I don't know quite what to make of it, but after the terror of the last days, I'm happy for some human comfort, and if I'm the sister she wants to lean on, so be it.

I'm not willing to let the subject of escape go. Every day someone dies; it won't be long before we're all dead.

'So, if they're keeping an eye out for an escape attempt, how do we get out of here?' I ask, eyes looking around the table, gauging the willingness to pursue the idea despite hearing what happened to the other group.

My head throbs a little from the stress.

'Dead, seems the quickest way,' Bardel barks with a wicked grin. 'Why don't you try that?'

Nestor shakes his head, whether at Bardel's comment or something else, I don't know.

'These passages are a maze. We need to know them before we can even consider escape,' Nestor says, his face thoughtful, rubbing his temples. 'We need to know exactly where we're going, or we'll all be taking Bardel's way out.'

The truth is painful to hear. We can't risk an escape until we discover the route.

'But we'll be stronger by then,' adds Fianna with a fleeting smile as she pops a piece of meat into her mouth.

Lotane studies me, and I flush a little under his scrutiny.

'Have you other thoughts?' he asks, those eyes of his strangely unnerving.

My mind is drawn to the room with the moving floor.

'It must be near where that terrible room is. We were taken there straight off the boat,' I muse.

'Good thinking,' Lotane acknowledges.

'Any fool could work that out,' Bardel smirks, tearing a chunk out of some bread as if by being vicious with his food, he can emphasise his insult.

My face burns again.

'Then what does that say about the boy who didn't work it out,' asks Lotane, laughing softly to take the sting from his words as he looks at Bardel.

'Hah.' Bardel raises his remaining piece of bread in a mock salute.

I smile my thanks at Lotane, and those strange eyes crease in amusement.

'I'd hate not to taste food like this again if I escape,' mutters Orphea, and that comment strangely mutes the conversation as we dwell on her words.

I consider my companions around the table as I chew. Everyone savours every morsel, and no one tries to take another's food. It's a luxury to eat slowly, enjoying the taste before swallowing. The food is a little salty making us thirsty, and we all drain our water.

'We need to keep looking for a way out of this place. But until an opportunity presents itself, we do whatever it takes to survive,' Larn says, his voice ancient and deep. 'I don't know about you lot, but I'm planning on coming first in anything I can, and I suggest you do the same.'

'He's right,' Fianna trills, her voice high and light, contrasting with Larn's. It's almost painfully sharp when heard directly after. 'It's the only course of action we currently have. Bide our time, be clever, do everything we can to see another day, week, or month.'

The conversation dies down, and we finish every crumb, every drop of water.

After dinner, I use the toilet and chuckle. I could get used to not using a pot, a tree, or squatting over the edge of a quay or a windowsill when relieving myself.

On my return, I want to carry on talking; get to know those who surround me. Understanding who you can trust and who has your back is as crucial to survival as recognising when to run or fight. So far, it seems Lotane and Fianna might be two such allies.

The moon globe is dimming, and tiredness overwhelms me. Looking around, I see yawns from everyone. There'll be no more talk tonight.

As I move to lie beneath my blanket, looking up at the ceiling, I try to order my thoughts.

Larn's advice to follow the path of least resistance and comply with everything was sage counsel. That path leads to food and safety, assuming I can undertake whatever is demanded of me.

Yes. Whatever it takes, I'll do it. There's nothing wrong with self-preservation.

However, deep down, I know something is fundamentally wrong with this line of reasoning and feel uncomfortable. So many have died; it's obscene. By complying, I'm complicit in what's going on here. If I'm to live, my goal must be to find a way to escape this place. There's a darkness here, and it's so seductive, showing you the sweetness of life next to the horrors of death.

I know I'm right, but as I think further about how I might escape, pain builds inside my head, and the more I concentrate, the more nauseous I feel. Even over dinner, initiating this train of discussion had made my head throb.

Stay, a voice inside my head suggests.

Is it my voice?

Stay.

The pain eases the more I consider this one word and its implications.

What about all those who have died and those who'll no doubt die in the coming days?

Yet the answer appears in my mind as if placed there.

Those who had died would have died in early course anyway. Lystra had said that. It was cold, unpalatable, but also the truth.

I'm in a clean bed, fed and satiated, wearing fresh clothes of a quality I'd only ever seen on merchants. No rodents, no lice, no fleas, no rushing my food, no leaking roof, no draughty windows. A toilet, a bed, and other youths my own age around me.

What if I put aside all thoughts of escape and threw myself into surviving this place?

The pain disappears, replaced with a sense of well-being.

Yes. If I can forget the pleading faces, the terrified eyes, the passing of so many lives prematurely, then I might find something here that's been absent from my life for so, so long.

But what might that thing be?

Just before sleep takes me, the answer shines in my mind like a star.

A place to call home.

***

CHAPTER III

The moon globe brightens, flooding the room with light, rousing everyone before it settles down to a pleasant luminescence.

Sleep had come swiftly and deeply. This time no nightmares, only dreams full of strangely comforting whispers.

Deep sleep is unusual for me. The orphanage was a dangerous place, and you learned to sleep whilst still maintaining a measure of wakefulness. I could be awake in an instant to the softest scrape of a bare sole or the whisper of disturbed air if someone passed close by, yet I'd not been aware of a thing for two nights in a row.

I sit up and gaze around. Everyone is there, blinking as if it's the first time they've seen light in a week.

What is it about this bed, this place, that makes me sleep so well?

I look down, realising that the blanket and sheet are sharply creased as if recently unfolded.

When I'd last awoken, my wounds had been newly healed. Now even the pink skin is gone, and there's no trace of any injuries. As I consider this, the answer appears in my mind as if placed there by some unseen hand.

My first observation was accurate. None of us has seen the light of day in at least a week.

Perhaps I should worry about this, but it seems stupid to further question the sense of well-being that fills me, and if I've been asleep for a week or however long, there's no harm in that if I awaken refreshed and healed.

There's food on the table, laid out neatly, and my stomach rumbles in anticipation as I rise to find myself feeling stronger than ever, albeit somewhat stiff.

Cautious smiles mirror mine as we sit at the table, and we take our time sniffing the bowls before tucking in, relieved. Nothing has been corrupted.

It's strange to see people examining themselves as they eat, almost as if not recognising their bodies. We've all noticed it.

'Is it just me, or was that the best and longest sleep ever?' Dyowne asks, her long eyelashes setting off her dark eyes.

Murmurs of assent and nods are the only response.

My appetite is raging, I just want to eat, not talk, and everyone is of the same mind.

Lotane looks at me, and I wonder if he's going to say something when his eyes lift to gaze over my shoulder, and whatever he was going to voice remains unspoken.

'Finish your food quickly and meet me in the classroom.'

Lystra's cold voice spurs us into wolfing everything down before scrambling to the hallway.

We edge our way swiftly along the walls ... walking doesn't even cross our minds.

Lystra sits on a table at the head of the room we'd previously studied in, surveying us as we enter.

'You may sit.'

A wave of her hand, and the lesson begins.

We cover old and new, and to my amazement, when questioned intermittently, no one gets anything wrong. It's strange, everything seems so familiar, and answers come to my mind even as I'm about to shake my head in defeat when asked a question.

We finish the morning session without a face being struck or the promise of death falling upon our ears.

Lunch is held in a vast, unfamiliar cavern with a smooth floor. It would have been an enormous undertaking of labour for this to be created, even if the ceiling remains jagged; unfinished. On the far wall is an intricate carving of a majestic man on a plinth with arms outstretched.

Sheltered behind his godlike presence are men, women and children gazing up in awe.

But it isn't the carving, however incredible, or the food that catches our interest the most.

We're not alone.

Of course, there are guards, Lystra and other instructors, but also groups of three or four young men and women dressed in black. They're several years older than us, and as I watch, they leave, carrying themselves with the same surety that Lystra exhibits.

Lystra sits at the head of our table, and food is placed before us.

It feels surreal.

Only lords, ladies, or people of wealth have people wait upon them and serve them food. Yet here I am, having a bowl of hot meat and vegetables brought to me along with a goblet of water.

Automatically we check our food, and Kralgen pushes his bowl to one side.

Lystra nods, and a new bowl is placed in front of him. He checks again, and we start to eat.

From the corner of my eye, I study Lystra and eat at her pace, ensuring we finish simultaneously, and the others do the same.

I'm used to rules and happy to follow guidelines. I'm even happier to eat and be alive, sitting down with the threat of violence now strangely absent.

Does everyone else think about this place as much as I do? Have they already accepted their place in this strange new world? Had I been chosen to serve a merchant; I'd have accepted my place already. I doubt escape would have even crossed my mind.

'Come,' orders Lystra.

Even the simple act of standing, she turns into a flowing, graceful movement. One moment static, seated; the next, with no indication of adjusting her weight, she's upright. It's almost as if I blinked for too long.

We follow, trying to emulate her silence as she glides across the chamber through a doorway, and shortly we find ourselves standing in the training circle once again.

'This time, the young men and women we'd seen earlier occupy the far side. Their bodies are gleaming as they limber up, oiled skin accentuating their defined musculature. There's a sureness of movement, a confidence in everything they do.

'You've just survived your first purge, whereas those Chosen,' and Lystra sweeps a hand toward the distant figures, 'have survived their last. Those you see are now godlike in their abilities compared to those in the world you and they once knew. Now, all that remains before them is the Revelation.'

I exchange glances with the others. We survived our first purge, which means there'll be more. Yet, I'm also intrigued by what the Revelation might be. I focus on Lystra as she takes a deep breath.

'Yet, be warned. Surviving your first purge will not guarantee your survival. Do not make the mistake of thinking yourself special because you've made it this far. That error will prove deadly. From every ten who make it to where you now sit, only four or five usually survive to the end of the journey ahead!'

I look around in dismay for being one of the weakest in the group; the odds aren't in my favour.

'You've no doubt wondered where you are and what your place is here. Now I'll share some answers to those questions and more,' Lystra continues.

'Firstly, this, your home, is called the Mountain of Souls. It's located on a large volcanic island called Furness, one of several that make up the Lizard's Reach, far to the south of the Isle of Sin. There are several reasons why we're here, one of which is to ensure no one escapes,' Lystra explains seriously.

'There are many ways you can die but doing so while trying to escape is the most foolhardy and wasteful of them all. Large ships only come here intermittently, and the fishing boats you might find cannot survive the storms or hundreds of leagues of rough seas that separate us from land.'

Lystra's cold eyes dwell on us all one by one, and I feel stripped bare by her gaze. She knew we were planning to escape! If her words are true, we're stuck here with death our constant companion. My shoulders slump along with my spirits.

'However, what I'll now share with you might bring light to the darkness,' Lystra says into the silence. 'It's time to understand your destiny!

'In a world where we all serve, it's who we serve that matters,' she begins earnestly, 'for they have the power to either give our life meaning and a sense of fulfilment or strip everything away from us entirely.'

Lystra pauses, letting the anticipation rise.

'You're training to serve the only one who is worthy. One who will bring purpose to your life and peace to the world. Under the guidance of the Serpent Order, you're training to serve The Once and Future King!'

Excited murmurs meet her announcement.

We're training to serve a king!

Even though I've never heard of him, my head spins as I try to grasp the enormity of what Lystra has said. To serve a king, even if just part of his household, is a privilege beyond compare.

Lystra raises her hands, eyes bright, shining with fervour.

'You'll be told more in time and even meet the king if you progress far enough and earn the privilege. But now, you'll understand why so much is demanded from you. To serve the perfect king, you must be perfect yourselves!'

Lystra allows us a moment to assimilate her words, then leads us back inside, and I cast a final glance at those distant figures. To attain such physical perfection … to serve a king, perhaps it's a worthy goal, way above what I would otherwise have achieved.

The mood of our group has changed; I can sense it. Backs are held straighter, heads higher. Despite what we've endured, this revelation has indelibly altered us.

Even though it's only early afternoon, we return to our sleeping chamber. Whereas before our silence when we followed was fearful, now it's contemplative.

The passageways already seem less ominous, the closeness comforting, not claustrophobic. We file into our room and turn to face Lystra as she stands in the entranceway.

'The rest of this day is yours to consider my words. You may explore the mountain as you wish. However, it will be obvious where you're not allowed to enter or exit, and you must not interfere with anything you see. Return as soon as the moon globes dim. This is the red zone, so any red arrows on the walls will direct you back here if you get lost.

'From here on, you'll have limited privileges, which will grow in time if you continue to embrace what's before you. However, absolute discipline must be maintained at all times and will be rigorously enforced.

'Failure to complete any training to the highest standards will result in your termination. Talking disrespectfully or foolishly during instruction by myself or another master may result in your termination. It should also go without saying,' and her steely gaze holds each of ours in turn,' that any escape attempt at any time will result in your termination.'

I stand there, listening as Lystra continues. The other rules and expectations she lists are strangely familiar, and I can hear the words in my mind before her lips form them.

'The final, important rule is that you finish your water every night.'

Lystra's tone is heavy, like a rock, leaving no room for doubt as to the importance of all these rules, including the last.

'You may have realised already that this helps you sleep and heal. Without these periods of recuperation, you'll have no chance to survive the journey ahead and reach the ultimate goal. As with all rules, failure to comply will end in your termination.

'Do you understand?' Lystra demands, having concluded her speech.

'We live to serve,' we answer in perfect unison.

How strange …

***

Lystra leaves, yet despite her departure, we're scared to do anything.

Kralgen and Bardel hunker down on the edge of a bed and start an animated discussion. I'm a little jealous that they have each other.

'Shall we explore?' asks Fianna, standing next to me, her hand upon my arm.

She's hesitant, as am I, but I nod. Despite Lystra's warning, here's a chance to see if it's the truth about there being no way out. The strangest thing is, I'm not sure if I want that anymore.

I look up, catch Lotane's eye, and incline my head toward the passageway, an unspoken invitation to join us.

'I like him enough, but he might be cursed!' Fianna warns, leaning in, turning her head so Lotane can't hear as he approaches. 'You shouldn't have invited him.'

She's referring to an old song about Ardenthal the Betrayer, slayer of Asyliana, a Queen of Astoria. Ardenthal had been Asyliana's lover, with eyes of green and blue. Since then, this rare defect is viewed with distrust, and Astorians born with such eyes don't see their second dawn.

'It seems to me that we're equally cursed. After all, we're here too,' I laugh softly, feeling the need to stand up for Lotane.

'Thanks,' Lotane says, nodding to us both. A warm smile makes his cheeks dimple.

I'm unsure if he's saying thanks for the invite or overheard me standing up for him, but it doesn't matter.

It's a genuine smile, and I can't help but return it.

'Who goes first?' he laughs, with a hint of nervousness.

It's a feeling I share. Our chamber gives a sense of transient safety, but outside its confines, horrors previously awaited.

As we stand deliberating, Kralgen, Bardel, and Orphea pass by us, and after a brief pause at the door, Bardel pushes Kralgen through.

I tense, half expecting a tortuous scream, but my courage returns as Bardel and Orphea follow without incident.

'I'll lead,' I offer, and step through the archway, but whereas the others went left, I turn right. I don't like Bardel, and it's not just his comments. It's hard to put a finger on, but you learned to read people quickly in the orphanage and only survived if your instincts were correct. I want to keep my distance from him wherever possible.

The direction I chose leads to the hanging room with the retracting floor. For some reason, a morbid sense of fascination draws me to pause outside, looking in briefly before moving on.

'Why did you bring us this way,' Fianna asks softly, her hand clutching mine. I'm sure she'd felt a chill just like I had when we'd looked at where so many had perished over the years.

'I have a feeling it's because near here is where we first entered the mountain,' Lotane offers quietly with a raised eyebrow.

I chuckle quietly. Loud noise seems inappropriate in this place, and voices also carry easily along the corridors. It's true. I want to see where we came in. Will a giant skull be carved into the mountainside, with its open maw marking the entrance?

I laugh at this childish thought and explain it to the others who smile mirthlessly.

'Somehow, I think it unlikely,' Fianna says. 'Yet it'd be entirely appropriate. Now, let's be quiet. I feel like the walls listen to everything we say!'

At the end of every passageway, coloured arrows are painted on the walls. It's reassuring to know we can find our way back to our sleeping chamber. Infrequently we pass by guards, who stand blocking steps, and we fall silent as we near them. Whilst their looks aren't filled with anything other than boredom, it's apparent they won't be forthcoming with any answers should we ask questions.

At every intersection, I follow the widest corridor. My footsteps aren't chosen by random, far from it. There's an occasional parallel scuff along the ground, and we were brought to the hanging room in crates on carts. I'm therefore positive this is the way we entered. It's also noticeable that no arrows point in the direction we travel, only the opposite way.

Shortly we turn into a large cave, on the far side of which is the entrance into this mountain. It's a large opening, and in the distance, far away, can be seen the sea. It's empty, devoid of ships.

My heart aches to see the waves up close, to taste the salty sea breeze. Why does the sea call to me so much? Maybe because my father's spirit resides within, or it represents freedom away from this place. My head pounds as I contemplate the last thought.

Hundreds of crates like the ones we were brought in are stacked along one side, wagons and carts on the other. Dozens of guards, as well as robed figures, are present.

'We definitely shouldn't be here,' hisses Lotane, and takes my hand and gently pulls me back along the tunnel, Fianna hurrying after us.

'Let's see where the blue arrows lead,' Fianna suggests, and sets off.

I'm strangely reluctant to let go of Lotane's hand. It has a reassuring strength, but he initiates the release, and I follow them both.

Several times we stop to look through open doors. The chambers beyond must have been naturally formed, for no human hand could have carved such huge spaces from within a mountain. Only the floors have been levelled. Every chamber has a purpose; in one, there are targets; another has ropes hanging from the roof, while others are used for storage.

Throughout, moon globes provide light.

We pass by other sleeping quarters but don't trespass. Fresh blankets are on the beds, and some have dirty plates left on tables, demonstrating that this place is home for many more than just us or those we saw stretching in the training circle.

I'm about to suggest we turn back when Fianna leads us to a door. The training circle can be seen through the metal grille.

'Come on,' Lotane suggests when we pause. 'Let's get some fresh air.'

He brushes past Fianna and me, and we step out tentatively behind him.

It's still bright out, and there's plenty of time before we need to return to our sleeping chamber, so we sit with our backs against the wall.

We watch in silence as the men and women Lystra had shown us earlier train. They're closer than before, and it feels strangely uncomfortable to be sitting doing nothing while they work so hard.

'It's like they're dancing,' observes Fianna, pulling her knees up to her chest, resting her chin on her knees.

Such a clear, pure voice seems out of place in this harsh environment. Fianna also looks like she sounds. There's a kindness to her features, no sharp lines, just soft, gentle curves and a natural upturn of her lips that give her a perpetual smile. Her blond hair catches the sun and shimmers as if on fire.

'You couldn't have put it better,' Lotane murmurs.

They're all training with long staves. In an old man's hands, it's nothing but an instrument of support as he hobbles along a path. In the hands of those before us, they're a deadly weapon. It's a breathtaking display of agility, balance, and coordination, and I'm mesmerised.

There's an instructor amongst them, and yet he doesn't shout. He carries a stave too, and occasionally he steps in to correct a move or suggest an alternative as the men and women face each other and practice.

'Do you think what Lystra told us is true?' Lotane asks, starting the conversation we'd all been itching to have since we started our exploration.

'She believed it; you could tell,' says Fianna, leaning forward intently. 'To serve a king. What was it she titled him? The Once and Future King. Who would that be?'

I shake my head.

'I've no idea. There are so many kings, and they all have their grandiose titles. Maybe it's that figure carved into the wall of the eating chamber? I expect he's the king of this island.'

'Perhaps. We'll find out in due course.' Lotane scratches his chin. 'It's such a strange title. Not that it really matters one way or another. We're being trained to serve a king. A king!'

He sounds excited, and it matches the butterflies in my stomach. From the look on Fianna's face, she's experiencing it too.

'So, what are we training to become?'

'After studying those plants and herbs, I think we'll be food tasters!' Lotane laughs, and his joke lightens the moment as we laugh with him.

'Probably that and cooks!' I add, and we laugh a little more.

Yet the smile slowly slips from Fianna's face, and she tries unsuccessfully to wind her blond hair around her finger. Now it's so short she's unable to do what was obviously a comforting habit.

'Did you pick up on what Lystra said? There'll be more purges. Do you really want to face more tests like those we survived?' she asks.

It's a sobering thought, and as I look at the other two, I wonder who will still be alive a week or month from now.

'How worthy can a king be who demands the death of so many, so the survivors might serve?' I mutter.

Fianna picks at the stone ground.

'All kings are like that, aren't they?'

I nod sadly in agreement.

'It's true. People die every day of starvation or due to wars. To live in any kingdom is to know death.'

'So, what are we now? We're not exactly servants.' Lotane muses.

Fianna's laughter rings out as if it's a silly question, but her face takes a thoughtful look.

'I was sold at auction. I'm not sure exactly who owns me, but we're still slaves,' she says, but with a hint of uncertainty in her voice.

'I don't feel like a slave,' Lotane responds. 'I was sold at auction too, I guess we all were?' his voice raises slightly at the end as he looks at me.

I nod.

'I've never been fed like this, clothed like this.' He plucks at his shirt for emphasis. 'Nor can I remember having an afternoon to myself, where I can sit outside and watch other people work while I do nothing but talk.'

He's right, and his thoughts mirror mine. From the moment we awoke in the orphanage, there was never a moment we weren't put to work either within the orphanage itself or hired out to some merchant or another who wanted the cheapest labour money could get.

'I don't think there'll be many days like today ahead of us, but as long as there are no more days like when we arrived, we should be ok,' I say.

'By the gods, I hope you're right.' Fianna shudders at the memory and hugs my arm.

Lotane raises an eyebrow at her affection and rubs his chin, thinking carefully about his next words. He takes a deep breath, having obviously made up his mind about what he has to say.

'The strange thing is, those horrific days seem so long ago, and they don't seem to matter to me anymore. I so wanted to escape from here. I've never been so terrified in my life than those first days. But now, they're like a distant memory and no longer bother me as much.'

'That's exactly how I feel,' Fianna exclaims. 'It must be due to all the days we've slept. I don't know how I feel about being asleep for so long, but I've never felt stronger. So how can it be wrong if it makes us better?'

'So, what are we now while we train?' Lotane repeats his earlier question again.

Then the answer comes to me, Lotane and Fianna together, for we answer in unison.

'We're the Chosen.'

Tingling courses through my body.

Silence descends as we consider the words and the sense of kinship and belonging it engenders.

'What about this Revelation and the Serpent's Order that Lystra mentioned?' I ask.

The names intrigue me.

'We'll find out soon enough,' reassures Lotane, 'and we'll know what to do when that happens. I don't know about you two, but I'll keep my options open. Escape is still one, but if we can survive, we'll stand alongside a king! It doesn't matter in what capacity. It's a higher station than I've ever dreamed possible.'

Fianna nods, and to my surprise, I find myself agreeing too.

The light is fading, and the older Chosen at the circle's far side finish their training. We need to hurry and bathe, change then eat dinner before retiring to bed.

As we return in silence, I wonder at the wealth of this place. Magic is evident everywhere. Moon globes adorn ceilings and walls, negating the need for torches, lanterns, or candles. Yet only one race practises magic, and they charge a fortune for even the smallest trinket. With such wealth, why does this Serpent Order train children and not just hire the best men and women money can buy?

A whisper in my mind warns me all isn't as it seems.

I wonder when we'll find out what that is.

***

'I swear on my life we saw some!' Nestor places his hand over his heart.

Larn nods emphatically beside him, convincingly animated.

We're sitting around the table in our sleeping chamber, having all recently returned.

The rest of us can scarce believe our ears, but a strange chill runs down my spine. I knew this place would hold more unpleasant surprises, but this?

'Ssythlans,' growls Kralgen, brushing two fingers across his lips in a sign to avert evil. 'Everyone knows they rarely journey forth from the Sea of Sand; it's too cold anywhere else. You must be mistaken!'

'I'm telling you, there were two,' Nestor explains. 'We were exploring the passages below that balcony, and they turned a corner just ahead of us. We hurried to get a better look, but they just disappeared.'

'Gah. Disappeared. How convenient!' Bardel waves his hand dismissively. 'How do you even know what one looks like? I've never seen one, and I doubt anyone of us have!' His eyes look around, daring anyone to challenge his logic.

Ssythlans. Their name is used to scare children to stay in bed at night, but they keep themselves to themselves, only venturing from their desert to sell moon globes or trade gems.

That Nestor and Larn believe they're telling the truth is obvious, and it warrants further discussion, yet not wishing to invoke Bardel's scorn, I choose my words with care.

'If ssythlans lived here, it would explain those.' I point to the moon globe above us. 'This mountain is full of them. No one could afford to buy so many, surely?'

'Then there's the name of the Order.' Fianna's voice, however light, doesn't brighten the mood. 'Ssythlans are serpents, hence the Serpent Order.'

Lotane leans forward, tapping his blunt dinner knife on the table. 'Everyone knows they're eaters of babies, soulless, cold-blooded, and untrustworthy. If they're here, I wonder if those who died might have gotten off lightly.'

'You can join them if you wish!'

Lystra's cold voice causes us to freeze. I raise my eyes to see her crossing the chamber toward us. She spins a dagger into the air and, as she catches it, throws it hard to hammer into the edge of the table where Lotane is sitting.

My thundering heartbeat seems to be the only sound as Lystra holds out her hand.

Lotane wrestles the unadorned but razored dagger free and, with eyes lowered, passes it back to Lystra.

The threat of death lingers in the ensuing silence before she moves to the head of the table.

'I suggest you choose your words more carefully in the future. Only weak people fear the unknown or the unusual, and their ignorance can spread fear like cancer.

'Are you weak, Lotane?'

'No!'

Lystra points the dagger at each of us in turn.

'Yes, the Serpent Order are ssythlans, but never forget they're also our masters. I've found them nothing but fair and generous. Consider this. If it weren't for them, your future could have been lying on your back with a fat sweating man on top of you,' she says, looking at me and the other girls. 'As for you boys, it would have been a death at a slave ship's oars or fodder for the armies that fight across the lands.

'It's the ssythlans who give us everything here, not some human benefactor. The only human charity you've ever received saw you sold on the auction block to repay it. So, I suggest if you want to stay alive, you never again insult the hand that feeds and shelters you!

'Finally, let me assure you, they serve a king who cares nothing for the colour of their skin, nor yours, or that you're of peasant stock. It's following his orders that sees the ssythlans' extend their help to those who need it the most.'

Her eyes rove over us, and we squirm under the restrained fury they contain. Then without a further word, she turns and leaves the room.

There's an audible sigh of relief, and Lotane sits there shaking.

'Were you scared,' laughs Bardel unpleasantly, looking scornfully at Lotane while leaning back in his chair.

Lotane lunges across the table and slams his hand hard onto the surface.

Bardel leans back even further to avoid what he thinks is a blow aimed at him. The next moment the chair topples, spilling him to the floor.

Lotane sits back down, a broad smile on his face.

'Damned right I was,' Lotane grins as Bardel picks himself up off the floor. 'But perhaps not as much as you just were!'

Bardel is red-faced, fists clenched. A vein pulses on his temple, his eyes almost popping from his head. There's murder in his eyes.

'Brother!'

Bardel grabs Kralgen's shirt, who rises reluctantly at the summons. Together they stalk around the table.

Lotane stands, stepping back quickly. Whilst strong for his age, Lotane won't come off well in this encounter against two such big opponents.

With shaking legs and my insides like water, I stand beside him, trying to appear fierce. I'd had so many fights I'd lost count, but I'd also stayed alive by avoiding the ones I'd lose ... until now.

I can tell both brothers are indifferent to my interference as they prepare to attack.

Then Alyssa steps in between us.

'I was scared too, and I have the balls to admit it. What about you?' Alyssa says, grabbing the front of Kralgen's trousers.

Kralgen groans, unable to pull away.

'Too bloody right,' he gasps, putting his hand on Bardel's shoulder for support, eyes pleading.

'Can we call a truce?' he begs.

'You're pathetic!' Bardel hisses.

Whether his hurtful comment is aimed at Kralgen, Lotane or I, it's hard to tell. Irrespective, he returns to his seat, the fury draining from his face.

Kralgen looks down at Alyssa's hand.

'Now you know I have some balls; perhaps you can let them go?'

Everyone laughs as Alyssa wipes her hands on her trousers, and to my relief, dinner is resumed.

'There's enough danger without fighting amongst ourselves,' Larn attempts to say quietly, although his voice rolls like thunder. 'Let's keep our strength up and not get injured over something so trivial.'

I agree entirely, yet the food no longer tastes so good because Bardel keeps flicking dark glances my way. It seems I've earned his ire by standing beside Lotane. He obviously doesn't forgive or forget, so I'll have to watch out for him. I need a plan, and it comes to mind quickly.

I will have to become stronger. Stronger than Bardel and the others if I'm to survive.

***

CHAPTER IV

Days turn into weeks, weeks into months, and months eventually turn into a year. Yet, it seems far less than that. Frequently weeks are stolen from me, and I awaken rested, with any wounds healed after a particularly arduous week of training.

To start, thoughts of escape often consumed me, but those diminished, especially following a long sleep. In fact, everyone around me has changed, embracing this life, whereas before, we'd have done anything to escape it.

Every day we train. Our motivation? To stay alive, but more importantly, to serve The Once and Future King. Who he is doesn't seem to matter. I'm filled with a sense of purpose like I've never felt before, for I've a destiny to fulfil. Every day I strive, my overriding desire to grow and become a better version of myself, safe in the embrace of this place.

I still have questions. How long is our training? When will we see our king? Where does he rule, or is he in line to a throne? But it's not my place to ask them, not yet.

It doesn't matter what we learn; physical exercise is always a core part of our day. Climbing, running, jumping, swimming, dancing, gymnastics, and even throwing and juggling are disciplines we're expected to excel at.

I look at the ceiling, warm under a blanket, the mattress soft beneath me, waiting for the infusion of dream leaf to take effect. Every night, our water is mixed with the leaf to ensure we sleep soundly and awake strong and rested. Before falling asleep, I re-live the day, burning into my mind every detail I can remember to help me excel at what I do.

Today we'd been immersed in the Astorian culture, an ostracised and fiercely independent warlike nation perched on the northeast border of Delnor. From their greeting of a raised palm while the other grips the hilt of a weapon, to only eating with one hand, this military culture is intricate and new yet strangely familiar.

In fact, everything we do is familiar, and after this time, as a group, we've come to the same conclusion. Whether it's learning new dialects, a new skill such as tending wounds or even understanding the stars, it's initially taught to us during the long periods of sleep.

The infusion of dream leaf is more potent tonight, and once I succumb, a week will pass, maybe more, perhaps less. My dreams will be vivid but not disturbing, just comforting.

Then, when I awake, I'll feel rested and ready to take on all that's asked of me.

Nestor, Larn and Dyowne come back from the toilet, yawning, and nod or smile at me as they catch my eye.

I nod back. We'd all got to know one another well over this last year, finding similar stories that ended with everyone on an auction block before our journey here.

We'd all changed dramatically since then.

If we stood next to ourselves of yesteryear, we'd be unrecognisable. Strenuous daily exercise, allied with good food and undisturbed sleep, has been transformational. Even Larn, who'd been so thin and effeminate on arrival, looks like a walking heroic sculpture, and he's still the slightest of us.

Kralgen and Bardel are powerhouses, but all of us are strong, supple, looking healthier than any noble or wealthy merchant I'd ever seen.

I never could have believed I'd feel so good.

Yet despite surviving this last year together and working toward a common goal, three subtle groups have emerged.

Kralgen and Bardel stay together. What dark deeds led them to the auction blocks remains untold. Bardel always has something unpleasant to say, while Kralgen, the larger of the two, is quieter, deferring to his older brother. Strangely, despite Bardel not liking girls, they've gotten close to Orphea. But then again, her shoulders are broad, and she's almost as strong as they. Her head is now shaved and seen from behind; she's shaped like a man.

Nestor, Larn, and Dyowne have formed a bond. They always sit close in classes and talk amongst themselves. Maybe it's because they're from Suria and Rolantria, perched on the east coast of the Delnorian empire. These neighbouring kingdoms export freshwater fish raised in shared lakes. I get on well with them, even if I'm not part of their inner circle, perhaps because I'd opened up to them about my late father's trade.

Lastly, there's Alyssa, Fianna, Lotane and me.

Alyssa has changed from being shy and nervous to become headstrong and confident. It suits her look. Black-skinned with a dazzling smile, she's from southern Tars, where the sun burns hot like a furnace.

Fianna. She still attaches herself to me, staying close whenever she can. We're both Hastians, but that isn't the reason behind our bond. We share something else, a loss of a sibling we'd both held dear.

Then there's Lotane. Tousled blond hair and cleft chin identify him as Astorian, although he'd been brought up the son of a slave on the Isle of Sins. Do the looks we share mean something? I'm not yet sure. Then again, he gets on well with everyone, so perhaps they see them too.

My lids flutter, but deep sleep eludes me. Instead, I hover in a halfway place.

I realise with alarm that the dream leaf infused water I'd drunk has been mostly ejected through vomiting. Being my time of the moon, I'd been ill following dinner. Sufficient still remains that I'm still semi-conscious, but I'm unable to get up and drink more to remedy the situation.

The sound of snoring and deep breathing fills my ears, my hearing strangely magnified. I've no idea how long I lie here, but I sense the approach of many feet and carts. The moon globe still glows softly, and my open eyes stare at the ceiling as a hooded figure suddenly looms over me, snapping fingers close to my eyes.

It seems to happen in slow motion, and the sound is so loud in my ears that I'm sure I'll wince, shy away, or at least blink, yet I do nothing.

'Are they all under?' A hissing voice cuts through me like a knife.

No one responds, and the next moment, I find myself being lifted from my bed onto a cart.

It's nauseating, being wheeled along on my back, watching the ceiling rush by. I try to say something to let them know I'm not entirely asleep, but I can't.

Over the last year, I've come to understand just how vast this underground complex is. It might be called The Mountain of Souls, but it's built inside an extinct volcano. Even after a year, there are many parts I haven't seen, for some areas remain off-limits, yet there are leagues of passages and numerous entrances. It reminds me of a fire ant mound.

We enter corridors I've never encountered, the ceilings smooth above me, polished; such extravagance. I pass through a cavern, then onto a second, the roof pulsing with a comforting red glow.

The sound of buckles and a feeling of immobility make it obvious I'm being restrained. Straps are pulled tight around my chest, arms, legs, and forehead. My anxiety begins to diminish, to be replaced by excitement. I'm going to see first-hand the training that happens when we're asleep.

Suddenly everything shifts as the slatted hand cart I'm lying on is tilted upright. I'm supported vertically, facing inward with everyone from my cell around me in a semi-circle.

A robed ssythlan, a circlet ornamented with a snake on his brow, comes to stand in front of us, leaning on a polished black staff. Others move around, but it isn't them that draw my immediate interest. Behind is an enormous, red, multifaceted crystal. It sits on a tripod, standing tall. A light inside pulses slowly, and my heart beats in perfect time to the light.

I feel ... connected.

There's also a large mirror, but it's of little interest.

'We live to serve,' the ssythlan intones with a hypnotic hiss, cracking its staff against the ground to punctuate his words.

'We serve to live,' I hear myself replying, echoed by the others around me.

It's surreal. I've no control over what I say and observe myself responding to something I'd never heard before, although it's now apparent I have.

'Let the lessons commence,' the ssythlan orders.

He moves from my line of vision to be replaced by a broad-shouldered man. People of all nations speak the common tongue, but two still practise their own language. He speaks in Icelandian, followed by the common tongue equivalent, and I repeat it back, right down to the accent.

It's amazing to observe, listen, and feel myself absorb. The crystal pulses, my heart seems to respond, and my sense of well-being swells.

After Icelandian, we switch to High Delnorian. I understand it perfectly, even without the translation. I'm becoming fluent.

The ssythlan comes to stand in front of us once again after the instructor leaves.

It nods, and others come forward bearing goblets which they hold carefully to our lips. My mind informs me it's a further infusion of dream leaf as it slowly trickles into my mouth. This is how they keep us asleep for however long they need.

'We live to serve,' the ssythlan with the circlet intones again as my consciousness fades.

'We serve to live,' the response rings out.

Nothing I've ever said in my life seems to make more sense than those words. As sleep descends, I feel a smile on my face and happiness in my heart.

***

'That confirms what we thought,' Larn booms.

I wince as his voice echoes out. Perhaps I should have just told Lotane and Fianna. However, I'd been too impatient and excited to share this revelation to consider there being any harm in telling everyone. Now I regret it when heads turn our way as we break fast in the eating chamber.

'Let's take a vote. Raise your hands if you believe we should ask the ssythlans to teach Larn sign language as a priority,' Lotane asks with a half-grimace, shaking his head in mock despair.

Fianna's laughter is joined by Alyssa's and Orphea's as everyone raises their hands.

'Larn would do that loudly too. He's as subtle as a fart. Let's have them cut his tongue out instead,' Bardel sneers.

Bardel is so foul, but his unpleasant comment has Larn looking into his breakfast without saying another word.

'I don't know about the rest of you, but I'm glad we learn so much while asleep. It gives me more time to train these while I'm awake,' Bardel adds, flexing his arms.

'Looking good, Bard,' Orphea offers, earning a rare smile for her compliment.

'I've never heard of anything like this before,' Nestor muses, pushing his food around on the plate as if by rearranging it, he can make sense of my disclosure. 'You say there's a red crystal in the room and a mirror?'

'Typical vain girl. Did you check if your hair looked good?' Bardel interrupts, scoffing. 'I bet you were disappointed you're still pale as a corpse with eyes like someone pissed in them.'

'I wonder if the ssythlans would add your tongue to Larns if we asked them?' Fianna's clear voice can be as soft as silk, but now it's as cold as ice. Bardel's face starts to mottle red, but Fianna carries on. 'You might be rather handsome if you didn't say such foul things!'

I know Fianna doesn't mean that in the least, but Bardel's mouth opens and closes like a fish out of water, his anger disappearing at this perceived compliment, not knowing he's being mocked.

Fianna has defeated her opponent without blood being spilt, and I smile my thanks at her.

Nestor clears his throat.

'You felt connected to this crystal, you say?' Noting my nod in affirmation, he continues. 'Well, best everyone keeps this to ourselves. I doubt Malina will get in trouble, but they haven't shared this with us for a reason. But I'd love to see how this crystal works.'

Lotane smiles.

'So would I. But as you say, they haven't shared this with us, nor the room's location. If you wander off to investigate, you might not come back!'

Nestor looks thoughtful, his eyebrows knitting together. Then with a sad sigh, he taps his temple in agreement.

Lystra approaches our table, and all conversation ceases.

It's time to train!

***

For the last month, we've focussed on hunting and surviving in the wilderness. At this, the beginning of our second year, we're to be tested, thrown into the jaws of nature.

This will be another purge, but not by human hand.

The island we're on is large and mostly uninhabited. There's a small port on the northwest coast, and the population of the Mountain of Souls must be in the hundreds, but the areas south of the range of volcanoes called the Serpent's Spines remain wild, full of wildlife, both predator and prey.

The most dangerous indigenous animal on the island is the red wolf, and we learn this creature has been responsible for the deaths of many Chosen over the years. It isn't furred; instead, it has rusty-looking scales that provide protection and allow it to blend into the multi-hued undergrowth exceptionally well.

We've assimilated every morsel of knowledge about them, studied a caged one closely, and they are death incarnate.

To avoid being purged, we must survive by living off the land, avoid becoming a meal for these superlative predators, and then return within two weeks.

The first purge was terrifying, but this time, I'm excited despite the danger. I can't see how I can fail to survive. However, I'm sure that sentiment was shared by the Chosen who'd failed this test in years past.

If ... no. *When* I survive this purge, I'll be a step closer to serving The Once and Future King.

I carefully lower myself over the varnished edge of the rowing boat that's taken me close to shore. As I slip into the cool water, a pack is passed to me by an oarsman. Tightly bound in oiled skins, it should keep the water away from the contents inside. If not, I'm in trouble, and I'll only have myself to blame.

Why? Because I packed it.

It's a dark night, but the white crests of the rolling waves guide me.

With a looped tether around my wrist, keeping the pack bobbing behind, I swim. Fortunately, the tide is going in, and I make it to the sandy beach without exhausting myself.

It's strange to be totally alone. Insecurity, which is barely recognisable after so long, shows itself briefly. I dislike being away from home. I don't know when the Mountain of Souls became that, but it's the only place I feel safe now. Safe in a place where hundreds died so that a few of us might live. There's peace to be found amongst the spirits of the dead.

I move out of the surf's reach and untie the skin, shaking it dry. Under the bright stars, I gather my bearings, brushing my wet, salty hair away from my face. I'm glad it's short. It isn't just for hygiene or convenience. Long hair can diminish peripheral vision, hearing, and be used against you in a fight, reducing the chance of survival. These words sound in my head; information gained when asleep or awake, it doesn't matter.

The others are being dropped off separately all along the southern coastline throughout the night. At sunrise, my journey north through the wolves' hunting grounds will start.

I move about a dozen paces inside the tree line. I'm naked, and even if the weather is mild during the day, the night-time air is chilling after being immersed in the sea.

It's dark under the trees, but the darkness is my friend. In my childhood, it was full of danger, but for me, now it's like a warm embrace, keeping me safe and hidden.

The clothes from my pack are dry, the boots reassuring on my feet. I strap a belt with pouches and a dagger to my waist, fold the oiled skin tightly and stow it in the pack. I have enough food to last two days, so I take a small food parcel and eat. Body temperature is raised while digesting food, which will help me through this first night.

I close my eyes but not to sleep; instead, I attune myself to the sounds of the beach.

Whilst I'm on friendly soil, the most vulnerable time is when you come ashore, so sleeping this first night won't be prudent. The surf is hard to filter out, but there's always a moment where the noise diminishes between every wave that crashes to shore. This short space of near silence is when the forest's rhythm can be heard, and I sense its heartbeat. It's settled, nothing disturbs it, and I allow myself to relax into a trance, alert but allowing my body to rest.

I'm not used to having time alone with my own thoughts, for my thoughts are rarely my own.

Twice more this year, I've been in that semi trance-like state at night, briefly aware of what transpires under the light of the red crystal, the Heart Stone. First, it was because of my time of the moon, but then, I wanted to experience it, curiosity or concern driving my decision. So, when I detected the sleep infusion was stronger, I made myself discreetly sick after drinking it, reducing its effects.

Alongside the learning of various disciplines, we're taught mantras. I'm fascinated. Obey without question, live to serve, strive for perfection ... the list goes on, and the Heart Stone rewards our acceptance with a feeling of such attunement that I find it hard to question the righteousness of our teaching. If only I could witness more, but the infusion is regularly administered to keep us unconscious.

Suddenly, a new mantra comes to mind. Have I been taught it, or is it something of my own making?

I live to kill.

As I repeat it to myself, I see what I must do. It isn't enough to survive and return. I must slay the beast.

'I live to kill,' I say quietly, enjoying the sound of the words as they roll off my tongue. Then as some strange primordial feeling grows inside me, I stand, throw my head back and shout it into the darkness.

'I LIVE TO KILL.'

I settle down again and re-enter my trance, gathering strength. Meanwhile, my mind dances back and forth over how I can achieve this feat, and eventually, it calms; decided.

The distant horizon to the east starts to brighten, dawn is arriving without me even being aware of time passing, and I feel rested.

It's nearly time to start the hunt.

***

Nine days later, I remain empty-handed.

I resemble a forest creature now. Mud and mulch cover my skin, while my clothes are covered by animal skins, disguising my scent as much as possible. The long dagger at my hip is now complemented by four stone-tipped spears that I've crafted, and I carry them at all times.

I've found signs of a large wolf on several game trails and laid traps, yet the only thing I've caught are deer, rabbits and other small animals. Eating them along with roots and fruit has kept me strong, yet however much I bait my traps with bloody leftovers, the red wolf I'm hunting has yet to show itself.

There have been frequent fresh tracks very near where I camp under the shadow of a volcano. I've attempted to follow them to discover the wolf's lair, but my tracking skills are insufficient to distinguish them over the rocky slopes.

The Mountain of Souls is only three days away. Since landing, I've travelled slowly north, ensuring I'm closer to home for when I slay a beast.

All I need to do is stay alive for another five days, which I've no doubt I can do, then return to the mountain, having survived the purge. Yet that isn't what I want. I don't know what drives me to kill this wolf, but if I return without its head, I'll deem myself a failure. That concept is unacceptable to me now. This is my mission, and I have to complete it.

Is that another mantra?

It's hard to know what my thoughts are and what's been placed in my mind.

Yet, I can't understand why this wolf is always one step ahead of me. These beasts are notorious for hunting humans and killing dozens of Chosen, so why is this one …

I stop. To catch this red wolf, I need to be the prey, not the predator.

The fact that the one I'm tracking is always one step ahead is not because it fears or is avoiding me. No. It's because it recognises that I'm a hunter too and is waiting to catch me off guard. A strange cold chill runs down my back as I finally realise the truth.

It's gauging my strength and weaknesses. I'm being hunted even as I hunt.

Due to its instability, there's little foliage on this side of the volcano, and vast swathes of rock have slid down, stripping it bare. A large boulder stands before me, and I climb atop, making myself comfortable.

I'm not weak, and the wolf knows this. It has likely witnessed me bring down numerous prey, recognises a consummate reaper of souls like itself, and now bides its time, wondering if I'm worth the risk.

The problem is, I don't have time, nor do I want the wolf to choose when and if our battle takes place.

I lay the spears across my legs.

How to outfox a wolf?

I smile at my wordplay, then realise with surprise that this is the first time I've smiled in a while. Usually, happiness manifests itself when completing a task exceptionally well or when … when I'm with Lotane. I roll his name around my mind, enjoying the gentle flush of warmth that banishes the cool of the shade.

Lotane always seems to have the energy to try and make me smile.

Gah. This is not the time for idle thoughts, however pleasant.

Now, what draws a wolf?

The scent of blood.

Yet all the bloody meat I've laid as bait for my traps has not coerced this one to an easy meal and a quick death.

The solution is obvious but not pleasant.

I need to give it the scent of my blood, enough of it so it believes me injured and weak. Then I'll lay traps around my camp instead of on game trails … have it come to me.

I draw my knife, looking at my reflection in the polished blade, studying myself. The face looking back at me is one I recognise and yet seems older than its years. I bring my face closer. Maybe not older, perhaps just darker. Yes. My eyes are beginning to acquire the coldness that Lystra's and all the other instructors hold.

I shake my head, taking a breath. Consciously cutting myself could open me to infection, but I need to bleed for some time. I bring the knife up to my scalp. Head wounds bleed profusely, but I pause. If my head bleeds, it won't drop onto the ground; it will soak my shoulders. Sighing, I cut the back of my left forearm deep enough so it won't stop bleeding too soon.

I grimace as I jump down from the rock, keeping the spears in my right hand so the blood doesn't render them slippery. It's time to find a place to camp and lay those traps.

The sun is descending, and I need to hurry. To the volcano's west is thick woodland, yet setting a new camp there will ensure I enjoy daylight for a little longer instead of being in early shadow to the east.

Nonetheless, I take my time, drag my feet, take uneven footsteps, and allow my blood to drip to the ground, leaving a trail the wolf will be unable to resist.

In time I come to a hangman's tree. These are so named for the horizontal branches that grow strong from their side, allowing victims to be easily strung up. Its wide trunk will protect my back.

Around it are various other, less robust saplings, but this is good. I'd enjoyed learning how to make sprung traps; small, sharpened stakes attached to bent, restrained saplings can be devastating. I'd caught almost all of the animals so far by using this method.

It doesn't take me long to prepare my first circle of traps on a wide perimeter, seven in all. However, I won't take chances. Behind them, overlapping gaps, I make another seven, closer together. Throughout, I re-open my wound, ensuring sufficient blood drips across the leaves and mulch. Nothing can come through in a straight line without setting one or even two off.

I check and recheck my work.

Even though darkness is rapidly falling, I won't light a fire yet, as it will keep the beast at bay. Nonetheless, I prepare wood and tinder under the dim light of the two moons, ready for when the beast is slain.

Satisfied, I sit with my back to the hangman's tree and bandage my arm. I'd had to pack light, but these bindings had been a compulsory item. The spears are by my right hand, ready to grasp, and ten small, unused stakes lie to my left. My dagger remains at my hip.

The traps are unlikely to kill the beast immediately, but once wounded, whilst still dangerous, it will be unable to escape, and I'll need to get close to finish it off.

It's vital to stay alert, so I fashion a vambrace of sorts with the remaining stakes, tying them around my left forearm. It's rudimentary armour, and I doubt I'll need it, but it passes the time as all around me, darkness creeps across the land like the hand of death.

There's no saying when the wolf will come, and I need to rest. Closing my eyes, I allow my body to relax into semi-consciousness. This way, I can regain strength and still be aware of the beast's approach.

In my mind, I rehearse what might happen. It may get sufficiently impaled upon a trap so I can simply spear it from a safe distance. Just as likely, it'll be badly injured and slink off into the undergrowth, in which case I'll wait until dawn, follow the trail of blood and find it either dead or too weak to defend itself, as again I finish it with a spear.

Of course, it may not approach at all, but I'm sure it will. It's been stalking me all this time, and my blood is too much of a stimulant for it to resist. Beasts are predictable, just like humans.

The forest sounds at night are loud, for many animals prefer the dark's comfort and safety. The human fear of darkness is primarily due to tales of old. I smile. Thoughts of my mother come to mind, for she often told me those tales before bedtime, and her ethereal looks in the candlelight were enough to give me the shivers and have me squealing in fear. I wonder if I ever have children, my looks and words will scare them too.

I've allowed myself to be distracted, and suddenly I notice something different; the absence of sound ... the forest is holding its breath.

I open my eyes, and there approaching me is a red wolf. Its eyes glow green in the semi-darkness, and I feel its throaty growl reverberate in the pit of my stomach. How it got past the traps is beyond me, but I'm moments from a grisly death. I should have been more alert. This creature owns the forest, and I'm but a foolish trespasser in its home.

I'm still lying down, and the spears are thus useless. My hand edges toward the dagger at my waist and hasn't even gotten close when the wolf leaps.

My left arm has the vambrace on, so I thrust it into the beast's maw as it lands on top of me, pinning me to the ground. It savages my arm, some fangs sinking between the thin wooden stakes into my flesh. The pain is excruciating, and I scream, but at least it can't close its jaws fully as it shakes its massive head left and right.

Desperately I grab the dagger from my waist, wrenching it free from its sheath with my right hand and thrust blindly upwards again and again. Then, finally, one of my strikes hits deep, and the wolf yelps as hot blood rains upon me.

It's a savage life-or-death fight for us both. I manage to shift my weight, twisting, unbalancing the wolf. It tries to roll away, releasing its grip on my left arm. I roll with it, pushing my bleeding but armoured arm into its thrashing jaws to foil its attempts to bite my head and neck.

Its scales have deflected many of my blows, but now that I manage to get on top, my strikes have more weight, and they start to bite as deep as the wolf's fangs.

'Die!' I scream in frustration. How many wounds can this beast sustain without succumbing? Yet, almost as if to answer my cry, the fight is suddenly over. The creature lies still beneath me.

I haven't the strength to move, so I lie on top of its warm body, allowing my hammering heart to settle. The forest is coming back to life now our titanic struggle is over; birds call out, yet their melody seems out of place after the death they just witnessed.

My arm needs attention. It's bleeding, and the wolf's fangs will cause an infection if I don't cleanse the wound thoroughly before I bind it.

With a groan, I slowly push myself back off the wolf's body. My face is wet with tears, blood and dirt, a sticky mask that pulls on my skin. I kneel, take a deep breath, and mentally prepare myself to stand when the forest goes deathly silent again from one heartbeat to the next.

***

I lift my head to see another red wolf standing before me, eyes glowing with hunger. Was it the dead wolf's mate or another random predator smelling an easy kill?

Why those thoughts cross my mind, I don't know.

I'm unarmed and badly hurt. My knife is still hilt deep in the chest of the other dead beast, and as my wide eyes take in this new adversary, it runs and leaps.

I cast aside the notion of trying to block its jaws with my left arm again as I have no weapon to kill it with, and if I do, it will end up savaging me to death. So instead, I drop and roll under the wolf's leap, not toward it, but after, so that as it lands, I kick out with both feet.

Caught off balance, it rolls away into the bushes, then recovering itself, begins to circle, gums drawn back in a snarl, saliva dripping from its jaws.

I'd managed to kick the wolf outside the rings of traps, and there's a swoosh as it triggers a snare. The yelps of shock and pain as one of the wooden stakes punctures its chest smother my own sobs.

Chest heaving, I turn, snatch up a spear, and while it struggles to free itself, step in and thrust. Unfortunately, I'm weak, it's dark, and I can only grasp the spear with one arm, so it takes at least five strikes before the wolf falls silent. Its yelps are as heart-wrenching as any cry for mercy I've heard.

A cacophony of hoots and trills marks my second victory, but I can barely stand as I stagger back to my belongings, soaked in blood, sweat and tears.

My pack's contents are strewn around from the struggle, forcing me to scrabble amongst the mulch in the semi-darkness. Fortunately, I find the pouch containing flint and steel, so I kneel alongside the small pile of tinder and firewood I'd prepared earlier.

Blood covers my left hand. I wipe my fingers in the soil and dirt, removing the sticky wetness that will spoil any chance of lighting a fire if it runs onto the flint.

My whole body shakes from pain and exhaustion. My left hand can barely hold the flint, forcing me to support it with my knee as I strike it repeatedly. The fifth time the spark takes, I blow onto the ember that offers salvation.

The smell of smoke is heavenly, even though it threatens to make me cough. As flames begin to greedily consume the dry wood, I force myself to ignore the pain, my need to close my eyes, to build it up. I have to search outside the circle of snares, dragging fallen branches back to the fire. I curse myself with every step; I should have gathered more earlier.

Flames leap. The comforting crackles and warmth threaten to send me to sleep, but I can't, not yet.

With my back against the tree and legs stretched before me, I cut the broken vambrace free. Unfortunately, I'd already used the bandage I'd brought to bind my self-inflicted wound earlier, and it's now useless, soaked in blood, wolf saliva, and general filth.

Even unwrapping it almost causes me to pass out as it's partially stuck to my earlier wound, and when it's finally free, I look with dismay at my arm.

Pieces of wood are embedded in my flesh, and I sob as I pull them out with filthy fingers. Even with the light of the fire, it's hard to see, and the tears in my eyes blur my vision, making a tough job even worse.

As I inspect my forearm, it looks like some of the cheeses served at breakfast, full of holes. But these holes are leaking blood.

If it were daylight or I had the strength, I'd find herbs and leaves to make a poultice, but I'm nearing the end of whatever resolve I have left. Ripping away my left sleeve to the shoulder, I tear the material into strips before wadding the pieces and stuffing them into the wounds. It's a rush job, and I just manage to secure them in place with the rotten bandage before I feel my head start to swim.

With my dying strength, I toss the last couple of branches onto the fire.

I should ensure the snares are all set, just in case, but even as the flames roar and flicker higher, it's getting darker, much …

***

I wake to the light of dawn, my throat parched, sweating profusely.

Moaning, I roll toward the fire, intending to blow the embers into flame, only to find it dead, the ashes cold with no hint of warmth.

I've been unconscious for at least a full day and two nights.

Through bleary eyes, I spy my waterskin next to the tree. Thankfully, it's full. Unstoppering it, I force myself to slowly sip half of the contents. Never has water tasted so good, and I feel a little better.

I'm reluctant to look at my arm, so decide not to until I'm in a better position to do something about it. I crawl over to my backpack, not trusting myself to stand, and am relieved to find a food parcel inside, wrapped in leaves. Some ants have started making a meal of the meat and fruit within. Bringing it to my nose, I'm relieved to detect no hint of rot.

Thank the gods.

I make my way back to the tree. The food is tough, but the water washes it down, allowing some strength and clarity of vision to return.

As I sit, I gaze at the two dead wolves.

I shake my head. One is slightly larger than the other, a male and female likely mated. Despite my injured arm, I'm lucky to be alive.

Hand against the rough tree bark, I slowly lever myself upright. Sweat forms on my brow, and I wait for a moment, considering my situation. I must return to the Mountain of Souls within four days to pass and survive. Even if I was healthy, I'd take three days ... so there's no time to waste.

'Get moving, Malina,' I mutter, gathering my belongings and stuffing them into the pack. My arm I'll attend to when I come across a water source. Now, all that's left is the trophy I need to bring back. In my state, I should just take the female's smaller head. Unfortunately, pride, or stupidity, has me hacking the heads from both animals.

It's grisly work, but my knife has a serrated back to the blade. Initially, the scales prove a problem, but once past them and the boney spine, the rest is easy, just flesh and blood. But now the severed heads are lying on the ground before me, I realise I can't carry them in my hands; they'll have to squeeze into my pack.

I empty everything onto the ground, resolving only to take the waterskin and the flints.

To my annoyance, only the female wolf's head fits in the pack; there isn't enough room for both. I smile as a barbaric thought comes to mind and put my knife to work again.

Half an hour later, I'm heading north, keeping a slow, measured pace. My choice to bring my trophies home is rash. I need every ounce of stamina, and my fever isn't abating, but I can't bring myself to leave them behind.

Evening finds me only as far as the northern slopes of the volcano I'd started my day upon, yet this is a conscious decision. There's sure to be water somewhere at its rocky base.

Sure enough, I see a tell-tale shimmer at the bottom of the slope and pick up the pace.

My mouth is parched. I'd emptied my waterskin several hours before, and my skin is burning hot. Thank the gods, this will see me through. I can cleanse my wound, fill my waterskin, and it will be enough to get me back to the Mountain of Souls.

Feverish laughter spills from my lips as I approach. It's a small pool, but it will be enough.

Then the laughter turns to a sob.

Half in, half out of the pool is an old, half-eaten carcass of a small deer, and it's been dead for some time. The water is corrupted by its rotting flesh, and I can't use it.

I feel like sitting down on the rock and crying, but inside my head, mantras suddenly form, strengthening me, filling me with resolve even as my body wants to quit.

Looking down into the pool, I smile at my hideous reflection, the wolf head perched on my own, the bottom jaw and neck carved away.

This mountain is mine.

My throat is dry, and my limbs are shaking, yet nonetheless, I tilt my head back and laugh.

I live to kill.

***

How many days I wander northward, I don't know.

Every step is a victory; every step is a curse. My body is cold one moment, then burning hot the next. I've survived by licking the dew from leaves in the morning, and there'd been a night's rainfall that allowed me to drink water from muddy puddles that briefly formed on the ground.

When was that? Last night, the night before? I don't know.

Every rock tries to trip me, every vine sets out to snare my feet as I stumble and stagger north, ever north, the Mountain of Souls now so close that I can almost touch it.

Even with my eyes closed, I can sense it. It calls to me. I can sense its beating heart, steady and comforting, whereas mine is ragged.

My backpack broke ... when I don't know, but I carry the female wolf's head in my arms while the other remains on my head. It's foolish. I've lost my footing several times, and so encumbered, I've been unable to break my fall. I gasp as my knees twinge. Just one more complaint from a body that wanted to give up days ago, yet with a mind that refuses to listen.

As I weave through the trees, I hear sobbing and crying. My torment brings back memories of the first purge, and I relive the horror. They've been absent for so long, removed from memory by my training, and now I'm stunned again by the brutality.

Just as quickly as they come, they go. Mantras replace them, soothing the trauma away, helping to make sense of it all.

Death is as natural as life. Only the strong survive. Some must die so others may live.

It isn't my voice I hear as they sound in my head, but it doesn't matter.

My legs give way, and I hit my head against a tree. Fortunately, the wolf's skull acts like a helm, yet the blow leaves me dazed. My last dregs of strength desert me like grains of sand through a timeglass.

Complete your mission!

The words enter my head with such force that it shocks me from the blackness that threatens to pull me under. Yet, however forceful the command of those words, my body doesn't respond.

Complete your mission!

I want to; I need to. It isn't dying that fills me with fear. It's the fear of failure, not doing my duty. Yet I can't. Death is coming for me. I can feel its touch as the chills make my body shudder uncontrollably.

My little brother appears from nowhere and sits in front of me.

I'm confused.

'Why are you lying down, Alina?'

I smile tiredly. All these years, and he still can't pronounce the M.

'It's my time to die,' I whisper back.

Tears well in his eyes, then flow down his cheeks. He flings his arms around me, holding me tight, and I can feel their warmth.

'No! You can't die. You can't. Live Alina, live for me!'

He lets go and walks a few steps, turning back with his hand outstretched.

I moan as I push myself upright, grab the fallen wolf's head and stumble after his figure.

Those big eyes of his draw me onward as he looks back. I can't let him down, not like I did when he died in the orphanage.

'Just a little further, Alina,' his voice chirrups as he skips into a concealed tunnel entrance behind a rockfall.

There's a guard stationed there who looks shocked as I stumble toward him.

I'm afraid he'll hurt Karson, but the guard ignores my brother and stands by as I hobble past in pursuit.

'Almost there, Alina,' Karson cries, spinning around, his arms a blur.

He used to do this to make himself dizzy and fall over. I'd laugh so much that my sides hurt. This time when I laugh, everything hurts, but it doesn't matter. My little brother is here, and I love and miss him so much.

He leads me through endless tunnels, and we pass several people who step out of my way, eyes incredulous at my appearance.

A closed wooden door with a grate appears, and Karson disappears through it, his hand waving me to follow.

'Wait,' I cry, pushing the door open.

But he's gone.

Blinding light brings me to a standstill as if I've walked into a wall. As my eyes adjust, I find myself at the edge of the training circle.

Lystra is there, along with my fellow Chosen, who are going through some exercises. Even in my delirious state, it's obvious they've been here for days.

Eyes turn toward me in amazement.

I must look quite a sight; dressed in filthy animal skins, a wolf's head in one hand, another perched on my head, and I'm covered head to toe in dried blood.

I laugh and howl, baring my teeth.

Returning late will mean my death.

Yet it doesn't matter. I've completed my mission and felt my brother's arms around me again.

I sink to my knees, howling, and the world goes black.

***

CHAPTER V

I dream and dream.

If I'm dreaming, then I can't be dead. Or is this what being dead is like?

Irrespective, dream replaces dream faster and faster.

I'm falling because I can't hold on. My brother falls because I cannot hold on to him. I keep coming last in races and tests, followed by the agony of a sword or dagger piercing my body.

Sometimes the sword is so hot that it scalds me; other times, it's the ice-cold of the grave.

I hear voices, but they're not to do with my dreams, or perhaps they're causing them.

'She should be purged.'

'I disagree.'

'She failed to return in the allotted time.'

'She returned with the heads of two red wolves she'd killed by hand. Who else has accomplished such a feat and survived?'

'She's near dead, so just kill her anyway. Only the strong survive. That's our way.'

'But she *IS* strong. She's beating the poison in her blood without our assistance; her heart still beats!'

The voices fade to be replaced by more dreams.

I walk with my little brother. The sky is bright, the sun warm. Gentle hills surround us, white clouds fill the sky, and birds sing while circling high above.

It's Idyllic.

He runs, spinning around, his laughter flowing like a mountain stream. Yet suddenly, he stops, grabbing my hand, his eyebrows almost knitted together.

'They're changing you, Alina,' he says, holding my hand, his eyes now wise, all-seeing but tearful, worried. *'Don't forget the cost of your happiness!'*

Suddenly, he points to our trail behind us, and instead of lush grass, a bed of children's corpses lie, stretching off into the distance. The hills become mounds of bodies, and the birds; carrion crows, eyes fierce, cawing in hunger. The sky boils red, and the clouds start to rain blood in a torrent.

I cry out in horror, pulling Karson to me, but he disappears, the warmth of his body fading to be replaced by strangely familiar whispered mantras.

Live to serve. Obey without question. Live to kill. Complete your mission.

There are so many, and they bring comfort and surety to my jumbled thoughts. Order now reigns over chaos, and suddenly the blood feels warm and soothing upon my skin, easing my angst.

'Let the Heart Stone decide. If she lives, it's because she's still worthy of being a Chosen.'

'Agreed. The Heart Stone will decide.'

***

I awake to the brightening of the moon globe. The Heart Stone, it seems, has decided to let me live.

My legs tremble under my weight as I roll out of bed, and I'm troubled by my physical state.

Over the last year, I've eaten well, trained hard, and become the epitome of strength and conditioning, yet now my muscles have started to atrophy, and I struggle to stand.

'Welcome back, stranger,' says a soft voice, and I turn to find Fianna standing before me.

She pulls me into a brief, warm embrace before stepping back.

The others are starting to rise.

'How long has it been since I returned?'

My voice sounds strange to my ears after so long.

'Almost four weeks. You were only brought in here last night just before we went to sleep.'

Lotane, Larn, Nestor and Alyssa also came over to greet me.

'The return of the Wolf Slayer,' Lotane smiles, his strange eyes twinkling.

'It's good to see you!' Nestor and Larn echo.

Alyssa grips my shoulders and looks deep into my eyes.

'You completed your mission. Well done.'

I'm about to laugh at her formality, but I can tell she's serious. It reminds me of how important that had been to me before I returned.

I note Kralgen, Bardel and Orphea readying themselves. They seemed to be pointedly ignoring me, which is fine.

'Where's Dyowne?' I ask, noting her absence.

'She never made it back,' Fianna says with a surprisingly indifferent shrug.

'Only the strong survive.'

I hear the words and am shocked to realise that I've spoken and meant them.

'Indeed. Only the strong survive,' Fianna says as if in prayer.

'If that's the case, then what's she still doing here?' laughs Bardel pointedly, sneering at my weakened state.

'Hah. She killed two wolves, whereas you almost became dinner for just one,' Lotane says, intervening before Bardel says more. 'If it wasn't for your brother, there'd be even more room at the table!'

Laughter echoes around the room, and Bardel, knowing when to quit, throws a final dark look my way, then growls at Lotane.

Lotane just shrugs off Bardel's rancour.

We put our boots on, then half run, half swing to the eating cavern. Even getting there is a competition. Lystra isn't always around to tell us to climb along the walls or swing from straps that hang from the ceiling; we just do.

I'm ravenous by the time we arrive and feel shaky. Lystra is there waiting, and she beckons us all over to join her at a long table.

Older Chosen and instructors sit around, and the whispered conversations fade as people catch sight of us. A strange silence settles around the chamber, which is typically filled with the soothing hum of voices and the chink of plates and goblets.

'Ooowwww,' someone howls softly and subdued laughter ripples around the chamber.

Lystra's head whips around, her eyes searching.

My cheeks blush as my anger rises, yet Lotane holds my arm to calm me.

'OOOWWWW,' several more howl.

'They aren't mocking you,' Lotane says in my ear. 'What you did has been the topic of many conversations since you returned. Feel proud.'

Suddenly, the whole chamber erupts, and Lotane throws back his head and joins in beside me.

'Come on!' Lotane shouts, pausing to draw breath.

Suddenly I'm swept up in this most uncharacteristic display, and my howl joins the rest.

Robed figures appear bearing our breakfast, and two carry the wolves' heads on enormous platters. The eyes have been replaced by red crystals, the teeth polished, shining brightly.

Applause replaces the howls, and slowly silence descends but not normality, far from it.

Lystra actually smiles at me, and for the first time, there's the briefest hint of genuine warmth and respect in her eyes.

'Welcome back, Chosen one. Welcome back, Wolf Slayer.'

Lystra stands, and every eye in the room is on her.

'WE LIVE TO KILL,' she shouts.

'WE KILL TO LIVE,' we roar in response.

It's the best day of my life, and my heart beats fervently, yet I hear a small voice in the back of my mind, trying to be heard.

They're changing you, Alina.'

***

I was given one week to regain my strength. Yet, strength wasn't the main issue. I'd missed a month of weapon training.

Despite having mostly caught up in the following months, Lystra's full attention is on me.

Everything we've done over the last year has prepared us for this, our training for strength, flexibility, and agility, all geared toward the moment such instruments of death are placed in our hands.

Growing up, I'd seen swords, daggers, spears, and bows on soldiers and guardsmen. Since then, I've seen other Chosen training with staves and the guards carrying weapons.

The last purge we'd endured had seen us armed with a basic dagger, the first time we'd been allowed to hold a weapon since our arrival and a sign of growing trust.

What I hadn't appreciated was the myriad of variations to these weapons, and the dozens of others I'd never conceived could exist.

Yet now they seem familiar, even if I've never seen or handled them before.

Some we're expected to become competent with, others to master.

I stand opposite Bardel, and whilst his face remains impassive, I perceive his dislike for me and the enjoyment he'll take from humbling the Wolf-Slayer. Until I'd returned, he'd spun a tale of bravery, of him fighting a wolf until Kralgen stupidly scared it away. He bears the scars with pride and takes it personally that my accomplishment diminished his.

We're both in thick, padded, cloth armour designed to absorb the blows of the wooden weapons we wield. Whilst we practise form with steel weapons, sparring with them is deemed too dangerous until we gain further skill.

Bardel has the advantage in everything. He's taller, has a longer reach, and is far stronger. Added to that, he wields a longer wooden sword and shield.

I back away, circling as he steps forward, listening to Lystra's instructions but also hearing words and seeing images in my mind of how to offset such disadvantages.

I hold two wooden swords, one long, one short.

A foolish observer might think two swords give me the advantage over a sword and shield bearer, but Bardel knows how to use his shield as a weapon.

He tries a right-to-left cut, but instead of parrying, I move sideways. *Try not to cross swords against a more powerful opponent with a heavier weapon.* I know this like I know so many other things.

'Well done,' Lystra shouts.

My eyes remain fixed on Bardel, but I also pay attention to Lystra as she gives advice. She's still cold, still a killer, yet she's not uttered a threat for so long and instead puts all her energy into our training. Not that she's softened; it's us who have changed, becoming what is needed to survive.

Bardel attacks again, cut after cut, the air whooshing as the wooden blade passes, and he successfully drives me back.

A painful thwack across my shoulders as Lystra's stave finds its mark is my reward.

I can see Bardel's pleasure in the narrowing of his eyes at me being the object of her disappointment.

'In combat, you'll not always know what's behind you or at your feet,' she hisses. 'A single misstep, a stumble over uneven ground, and your life will end. Circle your opponent where possible, learn your ground fully, and kill him swiftly before ...'

Bardel lunges at my left leg.

I bring my short sword down, deflecting his to my side, while my other weapon smacks his wrist, causing him to drop his sword.

I roll past him, spinning as I come to my feet in a crouch, my long sword lashing out for the back of his legs. A blow that would have cut them away had the blade been real.

Instead, before the blow lands, he shield-bashes me, knocking me off my feet, then kneels astride my chest. Smiling broadly, he brings the shield's edge crashing into the ground, just above my head, with enough force to crush my skull had it landed.

'Only the strong should survive,' Bardel growls, his teeth white against his dark stubble and complexion.

Pain from the shield's initial impact has sent lights flashing across my vision. His shield had not only numbed my right arm but crashed into my temple. Yet even as my head spins, I hear those words.

We live to kill.

We're learning to fight; weapons are used to kill. Does this phrase bother me or bring comfort?

Lystra glowers with disappointment as I glance at her through the pain. Disappointing her causes me anguish. It's so important to please her.

Bardel gets to his feet, stepping aside, but as he does, he draws his foot back to give me a vicious kick, to literally stamp his authority.

I spin, twisting on the floor and sweep his legs from under him. As he falls to his back, the air explodes from his lungs, and his head hits the ground with a satisfying smack.

When I come to my feet, Bardel stays on the ground. Blood runs freely from his nose, and then suddenly, his legs twitch uncontrollably. I back away as he thrashes around in a frenzy, foamy saliva flying from his mouth before, with a final gasp, he stills.

For a moment, I feel horrified, as surely I should, but then that emotion is swept aside, and the air I breathe is as fresh as I've ever known.

Lystra is watching me, and I turn to her. Will she kill me for causing Bardel's death, even if it was by accident? Yet even that thought doesn't petrify me as it once would have.

Lystra stares at me long and hard, almost expectantly.

'I live to kill,' I hear myself say.

She nods, and her smile couldn't be brighter.

***

Lotane, Alyssa and Fianna sit with me in the giant eating hall. The others sit at different tables nearby, but not so close that we can hear them.

'How did it feel to kill Bardel?' Fianna asks, her head resting briefly on my shoulder.

I'm about to say, *'it felt awful'*, a reflex response, to pretend to show remorse. But it's so far from the truth I can't bring myself to. The moment I acknowledge the fact to myself, I feel warm.

'It felt good. It still feels good.' Speaking the words out loud surprises me. Surely this isn't me. How have I changed so much?

Fianna nods. 'I thought it would. Bardel didn't like you, or any of us girls, perhaps except Orphea. He won't be missed by anyone except Kralgen. Irrespective of the rules that bind us here, be careful of him from hereon, just in case.'

It's true. Kralgen's roar of anguish at watching his brother die had echoed around the training circle. It was strange to hear such emotion when we'd all learned to suppress it for so long. A part of me hoped Lystra would kill him for this outburst. Instead, she'd rendered him briefly unconscious, and when he came around, he was in control again. I'm still unclear if he holds me to blame for Bardel's demise.

Lotane nudges my knee under the table with his. 'I'll watch your back,' he says, a concerned look in his eye.

'*We'll* watch your back,' Fianna frowns, rapping Lotane on the knuckles with her knife before putting her arm around my shoulder.

'Ouch! That's exactly what I was going to say next,' he laughs, rubbing his hand, eyes twinkling.

Alyssa smiles. 'We've all got each other's backs.'

I'm warmed. There are times like this when, despite the desire to always be first, there are moments when friendship seems almost as important.

I return to my eating, occasionally looking at the others.

Alyssa, her skin dark like polished wood, shining with such a deep lustre that it appears she's always slightly wet. Serious, honest, steadfast, and as strong as steel. What you see is what she is.

Fianna is fair of skin and hair with perpetually upturned lips. She looks so kind, and there's a softness to her that I'm so grateful for. Yet, beneath that exterior is a granite resolve and deadly skills. She could kill someone and still look innocent as she licked the blood from her knife.

Lotane. As I study him, I can't help but smile softly. Even as he eats, his features somehow have an amused look. It's as though he finds entertainment from everything and everyone around him. He's strong, broad, and muscled, yet he doesn't act like this makes him superior. There's a self-deprecating humbleness about him that's appealing.

A sobering thought enters my mind. These are friends, yet will this only last until such time as we're pitted against one another again. To survive a purge and complete our training matters more than anything. It felt good when I killed Bardel, even by accident. How would it feel if I had to kill someone else ... someone I liked?

Only the strong survive.

This simple mantra puts my mind at ease.

We finish our food together. Whatever we now do always seems to be done with coordinated efficiency.

Fianna carefully dabs the corners of her mouth with a cloth while Alyssa uses her sleeve.

Lystra has been sitting separately with some of the other instructors. Even when they talk amongst themselves, there's no softening of their demeanour as if it's inefficient to show emotion.

She comes over, two men shadowing her and stops in front of our table.

'Ranged weapon practice,' she informs us, then moves on to the next table. We get to our feet and follow an instructor who beckons and strides away. He doesn't look back to check if we're behind him. It seems as natural to follow Lystra's orders or his command as breathing. I know that obeying instructions is the right thing for me to do.

We're heading toward my favourite chamber, one of dozens within the Mountain of Souls. The use of ranged weapons is a discipline we have to excel in. Size, speed, agility, and coordination all impact our ability to master certain weapon types whilst only becoming highly competent in others. However, it's impressed upon us how important this specific one is.

Today we're to practise throwing weapons, and there's almost nothing we don't throw.

We take a few minutes limbering up before starting our practice.

'Yes,' Alyssa crows with delight, her javelin thumping into the straw target, centre mass. Mine is a handspan wide of the middle, and I grimace. It was a good throw, but I want it to be perfect.

'Well done,' applauds Fianna, hefting hers, testing the balance before she takes two quick steps and launches with a ferocity that doesn't seem to match her smiling demeanour.

Fianna's javelin smacks into the target alongside Alyssa's.

Lotane's follows immediately after. They've all hit the centre but not me.

'Rotate your shoulders back further to generate more power,' the instructor advises me, 'and bring your hand higher as you release,' and he demonstrates the motion.

After a few more throws, my javelins are finding the centre mark too.

Next, it's heavy spears. There are many static targets in the chamber, both large and small. However, we're now instructed to hit moving targets, pulled across the floor by rope and pulley.

The spear is Lotane's favourite weapon. It can be used to deadly effect in hand-to-hand combat if there's space to wield it and can be thrown if required.

I gauge the speed of a round, shield-sized target and lead the rapidly moving object before exhaling as I throw and manage to hit the centre.

'Yes!' Fist clenched, euphoria floods through me.

'Beautiful,' Lotane remarks, and I flash a look at him. 'Beautiful throw is what I meant,' he laughs, then turns back to the target he's practising on with Alyssa.

I hear him use the same compliment to her, and I feel strangely disappointed.

'Your throw was just luck,' Fianna teases me, then grunts, her own weapon flashing to join mine. She makes it look so easy, and I wonder if I exhibit the same competency.

We must make every target five times in succession, and we don't fail. Not now.

There are also obstacles, and we're expected to run, jump and throw while moving.

Alyssa and Lotane are something to behold. They're powerful, and as they move around the course together, I cannot help but admire them. They work well as a team.

'They look good together. Don't you think?' Fianna asks next to me, hugging my arm briefly as we await our turn.

I nod, my stomach churning.

We train for several hours, then after a break, move on to daggers and stars. We wear harnesses holding a dozen at a time and throw them all within a matter of heartbeats, aiming for targets all around.

After that, it's axes and swords. Throwing an unbalanced weapon such as a sword and being able to hit the target requires endless practice.

We're still too young in terms of experience to have achieved complete mastery yet, but oh, how we strive, seeking excellence and receiving nothing but encouragement from the instructor.

The disappointment I feel when the session is over is tangible. Working hard and achieving goals seems inordinately important to me, and I know the others feel the same.

'You've done well,' the instructor informs us as Alyssa replaces the final javelin in the rack. 'The day's training is over,' and he holds up four blindfolds for us to take.

We don't need to be told to keep them on. Not now.

Alyssa heads off first, followed by Lotane, Fianna third, while I'm held till last.

Pausing for a moment, I visualise the possible ways back. There's quite a distance to walk, and we are two levels down. I decide to challenge myself and set off on an indirect route. The chambers and passageways are a warren, but in my mind's eye, I can see where I need to go.

I tread softly, my fingertips tracing the walls, counting the steps between one junction and the next. Silence is crucial as it attunes your hearing to the slightest noise and can be the greatest sense of all. A foe hidden from sight can still be detected if you're quieter than them.

So, as I tread softly, I'm aware of footsteps as they approach and pass, and I try to discern their weight and sex from the fall of their feet.

I see everything now as a game, a challenge to expand my mind and body, helping me become a better version of myself. If I am diligent enough, I will become a queen amongst the Chosen; perfection itself.

I shuffle to a halt.

Where did that come from?

I'd never had ambitions or dreams while growing up other than to avoid being punished in the orphanage. Now I have two. To be the perfect Chosen and serve The Once and Future King.

A soft scuff of a carefully placed foot sounds just in front of me. I freeze. Had the step not been stealthy, it wouldn't have bothered me, but this had been a misstep by someone trying to be quiet.

I wait, controlling my breathing, and can sense the subtlest tell of someone drawing breath nearby.

Is it an instructor? Lystra perhaps? No, they wouldn't waste time observing a Chosen going about a task. I'm tempted to remove the blindfold, but rigid discipline stops me from doing so.

The soft placement of footsteps draw closer, and I know the hidden person is standing right before me.

'Malina?' whispers Lotane's voice, so softly I can barely hear it.

'Put your blindfold on,' I hiss quietly. 'You will get in trouble if you're found without it should anyone know of our task.'

Trouble leads to punishment, and the punishment here can be deadly.

'It is on. It's your scent; it gives you away. You smell like sun fruit.'

My heart starts beating furiously.

'Have you noticed that every other sense is heightened when we can't see?' he asks. 'For example, the sense of touch.'

I can sense movement and hold my breath as his hand finds my arm and gently drops to hold my hand, his fingers sliding between mine.

'Then there's the sense of smell.'

His breath is warm upon my face and neck as he leans in. The heat of his body is palpable.

'What about taste, I wonder,' he murmurs next to my ear.

The next moment his lips brush against mine.

For a moment, I give in, but then step away, my head spinning.

'You presume too much,' I say abruptly, then push past his questing hands and down the corridor, my heart beating louder than my own hasty footsteps.

Damn him.

Why did he have to do that?

I vanquish him from my thoughts and concentrate on returning to the sleeping chamber.

It's some time before his footsteps follow mine.

***

As is often the case when I have a moment, my thoughts wander over recent months.

We train amongst ourselves, with Lystra, various instructors and even some ssythlan warriors.

If Lystra exudes violence, cold, indifference or even disappointment, the ssythlans show absolutely nothing. They don't hold back whenever we cross weapons in the training circle, whereas we're trained to, so we often suffer injuries without inflicting any. Their reflexes are fast, and their movements so sudden that they're incredibly tough opponents.

Kralgen, who prides himself on being the best of us, is the only one currently coming close to beating one. He's changed for the better after his brother's death, as if a shadow has been removed. On losing, he smiles, bows, and then goes away to practice even more.

I'm confident Lystra could beat a ssythlan, but we're constantly improving.

To start, our weapons training is entirely within the training circle. Shortly thereafter, we practice in the forests, upon the shifting stones of extinct volcanoes, down steps, everywhere. Even aboard small fishing boats.

We're given the knowledge of generations in months. We train during the day, and the instruction continues at night during our sleep.

Training in many different environments allows us to understand how the same weapon can function differently depending on where it's utilised. New footwork patterns and stances for swordsmanship or archery are shown, allowing us to adjust to a small vessel rolling upon the sea or shoot an arrow from horseback.

A gentle sea breeze cools my face, bringing my thoughts to the present.

I lean forward, scratching the gelding's neck I'm riding, and it whickers softly in appreciation. It's breathing hard, and so am I, despite it undertaking the wolf's share of the work.

'Come on, handsome. One more time,' I say, guiding the horse with my knees.

We're on a sandy beach, safely north of the Serpent's Spines. The sun is warm, and the seawater sparkles like a thousand gemstones. It's idyllic, yet nothing touches my soul more than centring my arrow into the targets and receiving Lystra's praise.

Alongside me on his own mount is Lotane.

Nowadays, the group is often split to train in pairs or threes.

'Are you talking to me or the horse?' he asks, flashing that broken grin.

I feel confused about him.

There's been a bond between us since we saved each other's lives when we arrived, and I knew he was someone I could trust and rely on. Yet, I'd thought that had been the sole basis behind the glances we exchanged.

Then, after that encounter in the passageway, I was worried it might make things awkward between us. Yet, he doesn't mention it and acts like it never happened. Perhaps he's put it behind him after my rebuttal and wants to remain friends.

On the other hand, I often think of that moment, and sometimes, when I close my eyes before sleep, I can feel his touch on my hand, my lips.

Damn him.

Now I find it hard to look directly at him when he speaks to me.

Instead of answering, I dig my heels into my horse's flanks and send it across the wet sand nearest the surf. Our targets float upon the waves, sinking and rising even as we lift and fall to the beat of our horses' hooves.

Lotane whoops as we fire arrow after arrow across the waves. He stands tall in his stirrups, as am I. The quivers are attached to our legs, and it takes as much practice to pick and nock one as it does to release it accurately once drawn.

His exuberance makes me laugh. He can be such a likeable fool at times. So much of the time, we are serious beyond our years, yet somehow, he manages to retain a part of his old self. I don't know whether I'm jealous or disappointed with him.

I hit six out of seven of the targets and Lotane five. It's still an incredible feat, but Lystra's face shows she disagrees with my unspoken sentiment as we haul on our reins to stop before her.

'Your foolery caused you to miss three targets between you.' Lystra's voice is cold, disapproving.

Even though we tower above her on horseback, I feel small.

'Imagine those targets are archers who are here to assassinate our king. He now has three arrows in his chest!'

If there had been any remnants of joviality in Lotane's eyes, it flees instantly.

'You'll attempt this a final time. For every target you miss, you'll have an arrow in *your* chest!'

It's no false promise, and I look down at my hands to see them shaking slightly. I cannot remember the last time nerves affected me so. Yet quickly, they cease. There's a comforting whisper in the back of my mind, telling me everything is possible, for I'm one of the Chosen.

Likewise, whilst Lotane's face had turned pale, there's a steely resolve in his eye, no sign of fear.

He heels his horse around.

'Hah!' he urges it forward. This time, he holds the bow in his right hand, as we've trained equally on both sides, and his arrows fly true.

I follow suit, and it's as if I will the arrows to their mark; such is my self-belief.

'That was fun,' Lotane laughs softly. 'Something to spice up the day!'

I glare at him, but it causes him to smile even more, and I avert my gaze.

We return to Lystra, and she nods, her look still stern but also satisfied.

She motions for us to dismount, then swings herself into my horse's saddle and takes the reins of Lotane's mount, motioning us to hand our bows over.

Her eyes have lost their deadly glint as she leans forward in the saddle.

'Every action you ever make, even one as small as a laugh or a smile, can have consequences far beyond what you might believe possible. You won't always get a second chance to remedy a mistake. Do things right the first time, every time. Now, there are about two hours of daylight left, and it's a good hour and a half through the woods to get home if you run. I suggest you start now.'

Lystra rides off, the horses' hooves flicking up sand behind them.

'You could have got us killed!' I growl.

'It was worth it, just to see her get angry. She's rather beautiful when she's angry.'

I snort in surprise but feel a strange flutter of disappointment in my stomach, like when I don't perform at my best in an exercise.

'Come on,' I call over my shoulder as I break into a run, wondering about my reaction. 'Let's not make Lystra angry a second time by returning late, as your heart might not be able to take it.'

It's hard going on the sand, so we run amongst the trees beside the beach. There's the comforting wash of the surf and the gulls calling joyously overhead, but above it all, I hear the rhythm of my heart. Lotane is behind me by several strides, and I feel like a deer being chased by a wolf, yet instead of fear, a power resides inside of me that can turn the tables easily if I so choose. It's a heady moment, and I feel alive.

'Are you upset with me and what I said about Lystra?' Lotane prompts, his voice ragged as we twist and turn through the undergrowth, leaping over fallen trees and ducking under grasping vines.

'Why would I be? She's a perfect Chosen and beautiful too, and you both seem to get on so well,' I tease. 'A perfect match!' It hurts despite me saying it so nonchalantly.

Lotane grabs my hand and pulls me to a halt.

'I do think she's good looking, but you know she's not the one I'm interested in.'

'Is it Fianna?' I ask, my breath rapid.

'No.'

'Alyssa, perhaps. She's so strong, and you wish to be close with one of the best amongst us. She would be a perfect choice,' I reply.

Nothing but the symphony of nature can be heard for a while. Such chatter isn't usually for us, although it might have been once before we arrived here. Still, I find it hard to remember.

'No. It's not her either,' Lotane says, lowering his eyes.

'Then that only leaves Orphea. I think Nestor might be upset. I have a feeling he likes her.' My voice stays steady and strong, but I feel weak inside.

He's looking straight at me, those strange eyes boring into mine, tousled hair moving gently in the breeze. He hasn't let go of my hand, and it feels ... good.

'You saved my life, and because of you, the sun still rises for me each day,' he says shyly.

It's the most beautiful thing anyone has ever said to me, and my heart beats incredibly fast.

Alarms sound in my mind. What if it's forbidden to get close to another Chosen?

Yet when he gently pulls me toward him, I ignore them, remembering how his hand closed over mine to save my life when we first arrived and again when we were in the tunnels. His other hand brushes my face, and like some choreographed move, my hand does the same to him.

The world falls away for that moment. Nothing exists as we teeter on the verge of discovering something we've never known.

Yet suddenly, the sound of hoofbeats coming closer jolts us back to reality.

There could be severe consequences if we break unspoken rules and get caught.

'We need to get back,' I say wistfully, reluctant to let go of his hand.

The foliage is thick, and the horse passes by without us being seen.

'We have to go now; we mustn't be late,' I insist, gently pulling my hand away.

Lotane nods.

'I made a promise to myself,' he says, ever so softly, as I start to move away.

I turn back.

'What promise?'

He steps forward, pulling me to him, and his mouth closes softly on mine, lingering. His lips are moist, his breath sweet, and I moan as the moment stretches.

When he finally steps away, I can scarcely breathe.

'What was the promise?' I ask. My mind is so flustered I don't know what else to say.

'To find out whether you tasted as sweet as sun fruit. The thing is, you don't.'

'What?'

My shock makes him laugh, and he pulls me in.

'You taste sweeter,' he murmurs, and his lips meet mine once more.

***

CHAPTER VI

Two years have passed since our arrival on the island.

Lystra greets us as the moon globe brightens, and the moment I awake, I recognise the signs of a long training sleep.

First is the immense sense of well-being, a soul-deep feeling of completeness, of being one with the world surrounding us. Second is the feeling of mental growth. My head is full, almost bursting. I'm not sure with what exactly, but I'll get glimpses, and when the right time comes, the knowledge will be revealed.

I rise from the crisp bed linen and ease the stiffness from my muscles as I go through a series of stretches, and my movements are mirrored by everyone around me.

Lotane assists Alyssa, and me help Fianna, yet his eyes often meet mine, and I feel that familiar tingle in my veins. We snatch what opportunities we dare to get close physically but studiously avoid making it obvious. We haven't actually had alone time since our kiss by the beach, and there's a pent-up energy between us, and it's all the more exciting because it's our secret.

'Your turn,' instructs Fianna, and she moves behind to gently ease my arms back until my fingertips touch, then helps me through a few more routines.

Breakfast awaits on the table, and we go as one to eat.

They must feed us when we're asleep, but we're always ravenous when we wake up from a long one.

Out of habit, we scent the food, passing it around quickly. It takes moments, but it's routine and one that will keep us alive. Likewise, our first taste of the food is just that. The smallest amount, barely a crumb, just to be sure there's no hint of something untoward. It's been so long since we've had to put aside a bowl, but I'll continue doing this till the day I die.

We set about devouring the food, and as this is our first solid meal for a while, we don't waste time speaking.

Someone's foot rests upon mine, and I'm about to pull away when Lotane smiles furtively at me, his eyes narrowing slightly under the tousle of his messy hair, and I realise it's his.

The moment is exquisite, and my heart quickens. Here we are, hidden in plain sight, gently touching. I want to hold his hand and have everyone know, but no one can. There's a bittersweetness about this situation. To be gifted at finding something so special but cursed by being unable to openly explore it.

I recall my mother and father before Karson came along. They'd been happy and in love and had often talked about their younger years. Had they felt something like this?

Breakfast is finished quietly, efficiently, and as we finish pulling our boots on, footsteps approaching have us standing at the end of our beds; straight, tall, heads and shoulders back.

Lystra strides into the chamber, and she exudes a sense of pent-up excitement, so different from the violence we've learned to read. Behind her are two guards holding bundles of clothing.

Her gaze travels over us, judging, and she nods, seemingly satisfied with what she sees and draws breath, her eyebrows arching, eyes gleaming.

'Chosen. Today marks the midpoint of your training. For two years, you've remained strong, succeeding where others failed and surviving when others perished. In recognition, you're to be honoured like never before in your life. The memory of what you'll shortly experience will stay with you as long as you live.

'Till now, you've heard me tell of who you'll serve; you've had to believe, hold faith. Today, that faith will be rewarded and strengthened to bind you like armour, fortifying you for the trials to come.

'Today, you see The Once and Future King!'

Joy, happiness, excitement. We rarely publicly share these things, keeping our emotions private, but at this announcement, the discipline that holds us so rigidly is, for a moment, forgotten.

We turn and hug one another. Lotane's lasts the longest and holding him in front of everyone only fuels my euphoria more. Even Kralgen picks me up and swings me around, almost unaware of his actions.

Lystra snaps her fingers, and discipline immediately returns, although the smiles on our faces are hard to remove. I'm grinning like an idiot, and it's hard to not look at the others around me to continue sharing this moment.

Yet the snap was also an instruction for the guards to step forward. In their arms are black clothes.

'You've also earned the right to wear black while you're here, to recognise your commitment, your bond to those around you.' Lystra informs us.

'Who are you?' she shouts, the sound in the small chamber deafening.

'The Chosen,' we reply in unison.

Taking the new clothes, we replace the brown with black and lift our hoods.

'When the time comes, you'll know what to do,' Lystra says, then strides from the room, beckoning.

We follow after. I struggle to contain my excitement and briefly clasp Lotane's hand as he hurries along next to me. I have the urge to make haste, even to run, if only I knew where. We come to a chamber used for climbing, which is usually a dead-end, yet now a previously unseen passageway leads off.

Lystra turns to look at us but says nothing. However, her demeanour and the gravity of the moment descend upon us, and we settle down.

My legs tremble.

From within the gloomy passageway, a heavily cowled ssythlan motions us to follow. No words are spoken, and as the entrance is only wide enough for two abreast, we pair up. Fianna ends up beside me, and whilst my heart yearns to share the moment with Lotane, he's but a few steps ahead.

As we follow the silent robe-clad figure, the quiet is broken only by our breathing and the occasional scuff of our footsteps. Up ahead, a pulsating, gentle red glow begins to appear, and I find my heart following its rhythm.

This is the chamber where we're brought whilst asleep.

Sure enough, before us, the Heart Stone appears. It's the only light source in the room, as no moon globes are illuminated. It bathes everything in its red embrace, and the sense of anticipation rises.

Beside the Heart Stone is the mirror I'd caught sight of when I was previously brought here. At the time, I hadn't considered it worthy of note, yet as we're guided by Lystra to stand before its frame, I realise my mistake.

There's strangely no reflection of us, yet there must be glass, for I clearly see the mirror image of our chamber. However, the image within the frame is brightly lit, whereas we stand in semi-darkness. It's a replica of where I'm standing, but somehow in a different place.

The ssythlan who'd beckoned us in turns away and leans forward to place its hands into palm-shaped indentations on the frame, almost as if he is attempting to push it over.

Silence reigns as we wait, yet the sense of anticipation only rises, and I hold my breath. At the back of the brightly lit chamber in the frame, there's a dark passageway like the one we entered, and from within, I can see movement as a light approaches.

Then *he* strides into view.

The aura around him is so bright that I shield my eyes. Gradually, it ebbs away until it's a gentle glow, and our king is revealed. Two green-robed retainers who'd accompanied him stand back as he approaches.

He's tall, black-haired, fair of skin, with piercing violet eyes gazing from a strong, angular face. He's dressed comfortably in an open-necked white shirt, brown leggings, and boots lined with silver thread. There's an agelessness about him, wisdom beyond years etched in the finest of lines around his eyes. Upon his head is a thin circlet of gold. It seems superfluous, for he's already so regal, and clasped at his neck is a cloak of the deepest blue.

He's not heavily muscled, yet he exudes immense strength in his every move.

My heart begins to beat faster.

He opens his arms as if to embrace us, and I wonder if he were able to do so, whether just his mere touch would make me weep with joy. I fall to my knees at his majesty, as all around me, the others do the same.

Tears fall from my eyes at his beauty.

At that moment, everything we've suffered fades into an insignificant speck of nothingness.

'My children,' he begins, his voice reverberating in my chest, soul-deep, and I'm sure even the mountain hears his voice. 'You've endured so much to arrive at this moment. Regretfully, even more will be asked of you in the coming days. You are my Chosen, and I favour you all. Don't let my faith in you be misplaced. I'm relying on you to pave the way for my return, for without you, that isn't possible. All you need to do is follow the guidance of my ssythlan clerics. Just remember; only the strong survive. Be strong, and soon you'll stand at my side, the mightiest of heroes!'

My heart aches. He needs me, and I'll do everything in my power to help.

'Remove your hoods so I may see you, my children. Show me your faces and approach as instructed to receive my blessing.'

Kral is beckoned forward first and, under the guiding hands of the ssythlan, presses his forehead against the mirror.

The Once and Future King reaches out and rests his fingertips gently against Kral's forehead and whispers something quietly.

We all hold our breath. Kral replies too quietly to hear, and as he's guided back to kneel in line, his eyes shine with an inner light.

Lotane follows, then Orphea and Nestor.

Then it's my turn.

My legs tremble as the ssythlan cleric beckons me over. I'm ashamed. Does my king want to see a pathetic, nervous wreck or a Chosen?

I stand proud and gaze steadily into those violet eyes. Let *him* see my strength, my fortitude, a Chosen he can be proud of.

His head tilts to one side, eyes widening ever so slightly. Have I impressed or perhaps insulted him? We stare for a few seconds or perhaps an eternity, then he leans forward, and I can no longer bear the weight of his scrutiny. I drop my head, resting it against the cold glass.

Then it happens. A sense of bonding, unity, love, and devotion. Everything feels magnified a thousand times.

'Promise that one day when our mission is over, we'll sit down and remember the long road we travelled,' he says softly.

'I promise.' I've never said anything so sincere in my life.

A hand takes my shoulder, and I don't even register that I've been brought back to the line until Fianna briefly clasps my hand before moving to stand before the mirror.

I lose all sense of time as I kneel, watching the others approach one by one, jealous of their time before *him*. Then it's over. Darkness descends, and once again, the Heart Stone provides the only light and brings our heartbeats back to normal.

Lystra was right. I've never been honoured like this before in my life.

***

We wear the black, we've met the king, and having survived two years of training, now receive even further privilege. Having just finished our evening meal, we followed Lystra up a guarded stairwell to be shown our new accommodation.

Looking around my small, private sleeping chamber, I'm not sure I'm happy with the change. I'll miss Lotane and the others when I go to sleep. They're such firm friends, or, in Kralgen and Orphea's cases, comrades. Irrespective, having them all around was comforting.

Squeals of delight sound next door, and I console myself that I'm far from alone. Orphea, Fianna and Alyssa's rooms are along the same corridor as mine, and from the high-pitched note, Fianna is delighted with the new arrangement.

I snort in amusement. This should be a dream come true for a peasant girl like me.

A thick fur rug under my booted feet is as blue as the clearest sky. On either side of the bed's headboard, small chests are placed. Over the arch to the toilet area, the two wolf skulls have been mounted while a large wardrobe stands near the doorway. Finally, a table and chair sit in a corner. The furniture, unsurprisingly, is plain and functional, no embellishments whatsoever.

The strangest thing is that the chests and wardrobe are all empty. We receive clean clothes daily, so there's nothing to store.

I sit on the bed. Even if it's not my old one, it's familiar and comfortable.

'No more horrible smells when the boys use the toilet,' Fianna squeals as she runs into my room. She promptly proceeds to inspect everything.

'Empty too,' she says, closing a chest lid in disappointment. 'Ah well.'

Alyssa follows with Orphea in tow.

Like me, Orphea seems less than happy. She's been close to Kralgen and must undoubtedly feel his absence like I mourn Lotane's.

For a moment, sympathy wells with me, and I get up to console her. But then she looks at me with such dispassionate eyes that I realise it would be a wasted gesture. I berate myself. Sympathy is a weak trait; she's right not to need it.

'I can't believe we're further from the food hall,' groans Alyssa. 'Come. Why don't we see the boys' rooms, then go and find something to eat?'

We follow Alyssa from the room and don't have to go far; just down the end of the corridor, followed by a left turn to find the others gathered in Kralgen's room.

'Do you know Lystra's room is at the end of the passageway along with the other instructors?' Larn tries to whisper.

As ever, he's so loud that we wince. He shrugs in apology. It's a good thing he doesn't say much.

'How exactly do you know it's hers?' Orphea asks. 'Every room looks the same down to the rugs unless you've got a couple of rat skulls nailed to the wall like pale face here,' she says, looking at me.

'Lystra's sitting in it! It's full of weird stuff, books and the like.' Larn's voice echoes out down the corridor.

Lotane pokes his forefingers into both ears, rolls his eyes, and receives such a scowl from Larn that everyone laughs together.

'Come.' Kralgen stretches his arms out wide as though to enfold us all. He likes to take every opportunity to show off his growing frame. 'There's a breeze up here coming from somewhere. Let's go find out where it comes from.'

Sure enough, he's right. The air had always been a little stale in the level below, but it's noticeably fresher up here.

I dislike following Kralgen. It might be unfair, as his brother was the malicious one, but he's of the same blood. Nevertheless, he's come up with the idea and thus takes the lead, trusting his nose and intuition. Sure enough, he leads us unerringly despite not having been on this level before, and as we turn a corner, we come to a halt.

The passageway opens onto a large terrace carved out of the north side of the mountain face. As we hesitantly wander forward in disbelief, the view over the beaches and forest all the way north to the small port is breathtaking.

We've all climbed the peaks here and seen the views before, but to have this at our fingertips is something else. Benches and lounges are scattered over the terrace, and it's obviously a place to relax.

'The view of the sunrise and sunset from here can be breathtaking.' Lystra's voice makes us all jump, and we turn to find her standing behind us. 'I often looked at them and wondered if the arrival of our king could eclipse their beauty. I came to the conclusion that it will.' Lystra's voice trails away wistfully before her face becomes stern and unyielding again.

'Harder challenges wait before you, and to survive, you must believe in something more than just yourself. Every day brings you closer to enlightenment when you'll learn exactly what the future holds for you and how to serve our king. Do not fail and die before you've earned that honour!

'When you look at the sunset tonight, it will be because you've earned the pleasure with your blood, sweat and tears. Now, it's time to train, so follow me!'

***

I'm spending more and more time away from the Mountain of Souls, my home. I only feel safe there now. Safe in a place where hundreds die so a few of us might live. This is how it should be. It's nature's way. The lambs must die so the wolves can live.

When we're away, whatever the distance, the Heart Stone pulls on us, calling us back, creating a sense of longing that can't be ignored.

Sometimes it's just for a day here and there as my fellow Chosen and I hone our survival skills in the wilderness south of the Serpent's Spines. Other times it's surviving on the waves out at sea as we learn the art of sailing on the island's small fishing boats. Yet, however exciting our task is, the relief we feel when we walk under The Mountain of Soul's comforting shadow is tangible.

But today, we are somewhere new, and as usual, I cannot wait to face whatever challenge awaits.

The eight of us stand before a tower on a small island off the east coast. Like the mainland, it's lushly forested, full of bright colours, lively animals, and would be considered a paradise were it not for the red wolves which roam the place.

We've followed a path from a tiny dock to the tower along a beaten path lined with volcanic rock.

The large, circular tower in front of us is also made from volcanic rock, and there's something strange beyond it being the only building on the island.

There's no door.

Lystra turns to look at us, her eyes measuring.

'How would you enter?' she asks Kralgen.

Kralgen leans back, staring upward.

'I'd climb. The blocks are loosely fitted, so the entrance must be at the top.'

Lystra nods, but it's obvious it's not the answer she wants, and Kralgen's face shows his disappointment.

'What about you, Larn? Would you follow Kralgen's lead?'

It's a rhetorical question, as Lystra is looking for something more.

'There must be a hidden door triggered by a latch. Given time, I'd find it.'

Larn's voice sounds confident, but it's false confidence. He's merely clutching at the next logical approach to gaining entry.

Lystra smiles briefly. Yet, it isn't a sign of warmth nor approval, just of acknowledgement.

Her eyes raise to meet mine. She has such a piercing gaze. It might be cold and dispassionate, yet there's no hatred there. She demands an answer from me, even without vocalising it.

'I believe Larn is correct about a hidden door, but perhaps rather than search for it, I'd stay concealed, then observe and follow anyone who enters.'

'Anyone else?' Lystra asks, and my heart sinks as my answer isn't what she's looking for.

Orphea looks smug as she steps forward.

'There must be a tunnel, and this path is a diversion to misdirect attention from where the entrance truly lies.'

Damn, she's probably right. It's a good answer, and it frustrates me that I hadn't thought of it. No jealousy exists between us; at least, I don't believe so. Instead, it's just the desire to succeed the first time, every time.

'No!'

Unbelievable. Orphea is wrong, and no one else can come up with an alternative.

'Malina and Larn were the closest, yet only Malina's plan had a chance of success,' Lystra explains to my joy. 'But what if the need to access is urgent, and no one comes along for days or weeks? Waiting indefinitely isn't good enough, and soon won't even be necessary for some of you.

'Every year you survive improves your worth, as do the gifts that The Once and Future King wishes to bestow upon you.'

A pleasant shiver runs through me. To have pleased *him* is what I strive for ... what we all strive for. The memory of seeing our king is indelibly etched in our minds. Surprisingly, we don't talk about it by unspoken agreement, as no words could ever do the moment justice.

'Watch.'

Lystra rolls up the sleeves of her robe. In the two years I've been here, I can't recall seeing her arms, only her face and hands. Yet now, my eyes are irresistibly drawn to them.

She's olive-skinned, which fits perfectly with her black hair and brown eyes; thus, the glyphs and runes on her forearms aren't as apparent as they might otherwise be.

Reaching out, Lystra places her hands against the wall. Her face twists, snarling in pain as the runes slither to her wrists and fingers like worms, twisting and coiling in a frenzy. Between her snarls, I hear whispered words. They seem strangely ill-fitting because I'm sure some are of endearment.

There's something grotesque, even obscene, about the runes' movements, and whilst I'm mesmerised, I feel slightly repulsed.

Nonetheless, I gasp, astonished at what's happening before my eyes.

The wall before Lystra folds back as if made of wet clay, and there is our entrance into the tower.

I'm beyond shocked. Everyone knows ssythlans are the only race able to wield magic.

'This is where you'll learn to use magic, something denied to humans for time immemorial,' she says, her voice strained.

Stepping aside, Lystra motions us through, and we enter a comfortably furnished chamber. Bookcases line the walls with row upon row of tomes crammed alongside each other. Sumptuous armchairs are dotted around, and moon globes give it a cool light despite the fact there are no windows.

An interior wall adjacent to where we stand melts aside to create another entrance, and five robe-clad forms step through, then throw back the cowls of their robes.

They are ssythlan clerics from the Serpent Order. Their skin, made of tiny scales, catches the room's light, and they shine. A thin, forked tongue flickers between their lips, and their eyes are as black as night. Something about them reminds me of the red wolves.

Lystra bows to them in deference, but when she turns back to us, her eyes are as commanding as her voice.

'What you've just witnessed is earth magic, the ability to influence the very nature of the land around us. This was the magic used to shape our home in the Mountain of Souls. Here you'll learn of the five magics and, if you're strong enough, learn to wield one.

'You may ask questions.'

Nestor coughs politely.

'How can we learn to use magic if only ssythlan mages can wield it?'

Had we not seen Lystra's demonstration, it would have been a sensible question, but now it borders on stupidity.

Lystra's disparaging look negates the need for any answer.

Lotane lifts his head, eyes seeking Lystra's approval, and she nods.

'I can only assume becoming a mage takes decades? Is that what we're to become?'

A strange hissing fills the air; it's the ssythlans' laughing.

Lystra looks briefly at the ssythlans, to see if they wish to say something, but they return to silence.

'You're right,' she says. 'It does take decades to become a mage, but you're not here for that. I said, you're here to learn how to use magic, which is entirely different, and until very recently, impossible.'

'Aren't there just four magics?' Kralgen sounds unsure, despite his rasping growl.

It's a prudent question I'd also considered asking. Stories tell of the ssythlans controlling earth, air, fire and water.

Lystra rubs the runes on her forearms absently. 'So tales would have us believe. But, no. There are, in fact, five. It's the fifth that will act as the catalyst to allow you to use one of the other four at a rudimentary level. Only our benefactors possess the ability to use the fifth as they're favoured by the gods,' and she bows briefly to the ssythlans.

'What's the fifth magic called?' Fianna asks, her voice ringing clear as a bell. Even if we can't use it, the pursuit of knowledge drives her question.

Lystra smiles, perhaps enjoying the words that spill from her lips. 'Blood Magic!'

***

Magic. The ability to control the elements.

The stories I was told by my mother in childhood had always held my imagination. Scorching walls of fire, lightning strikes, Golems rising from the ground and armies being washed away by the sea's fury. Unstoppable and elemental in its furious power.

As I grew older, I sadly realised the reality was far less exciting. The high point of magic in my youth was seeing a moon globe shine from a noble's window.

Thanks to the ongoing tutelage of the ssythlan clerics, I know it's more than that, but sadly not much more.

We've been taught the limits and uses of the four elemental magics for the last week. The limit of projection is, with few exceptions, to what can be touched. Fire magic can create fire but requires a direct transfer of the flame from the wielder's hand to the object being consumed or crafted. Earth magic again requires contact to effect change. Water and air offer some influence over a surrounding area but are more subtle than seismic.

It transpires that on top of these restrictions, there are physical and mental ones.

Being an adept mage requires years of dedicated study and practice. Magic surrounds everything, remaining invisible and intangible to the uninitiated. A trained mage can see, absorb, and subsequently channel it through force of will. However, this quickly depletes not only the magic absorbed but the mind and body of the mage.

Now I understand why the mages here take turns to mentor us, for their demonstrations require them to rest and replenish. Whilst amazing and useful, no elemental mage, through magic alone, can conquer realms or slay heroes and monsters if there are such things.

The gods have decisively ensured that no one can challenge them in their halls of plenty.

It's been fascinating to learn, and there's the usual sense of well-being when I apply myself. It's also mesmerising to witness the ssythlans summon fire into the palms of their hand, draw water from the trunk of a tree or create a breeze to send a small boat skimming across the waves.

They don't wield their powers like Lystra did, and there's no sign of any markings on their skin that I can perceive. Their lifelong studies allow them to manipulate their magic with whispered words and expressive gestures. It's almost as if they're forming something invisible within their hands or moulding the force they summon before it manifests itself.

Every day, I endure the touch of their softly scaled hands upon my forehead as they perform *The Seeing,* a ritual of joining mind, body, and spirit to open our Spirit Eye. Once complete, I'll have the power to exert control over the element I'll shortly be imbued with.

Even now, when entering the meditative trance I've been taught, I can perceive my heart pumping, the blood flowing, and life force pulsing. By all accounts, I'll soon be able to see the colour of magic that will shortly reside within me.

Yet, I itch to *do* something. We're usually so active, and I miss our physical training.

I note Larn smiling, sharing a secret joke with Orphea as he whispers softly behind his hand, feigning to brush something from his face. For some reason, he hasn't been captured by what's being taught, and it's a serious lapse.

However disciplined we are, sometimes it slips ever so slightly, but only if Lystra isn't around.

Yet, even while Lotane is next to me, and occasionally our shoulders touch as if by accident, I'd never dare talk during instruction.

It's still strange to listen to the ssythlans and their soft lisping way of speaking, courtesy of their forked tongues. Larn says something again, and I stare hard at him.

Malina, Stop! If I'm seen to be distracted, it won't be good.

I focus again, listening intently to every word. It's what I usually do; it's what everyone does. To learn as best we can, to obey without question. The more I listen, the more it sounds familiar, and I smile. Yes, I've heard this before in my dreams. Listening to the ssythlan reinforces what has somehow been placed in my subconscious already.

A ssythlan mage flicks its head in annoyance toward Larn.

'Do you wish to say something?' it hisses, tongue flicking.

We're all seated in a wooded clearing on trees shaped by earth magic to grow horizontally from where they exit the ground.

Larn's face turns white, having been caught not paying attention.

'Why learn how a mage controls magic when we're not going to become mages, just magic users?' Larn blusters in that intensely deep voice of his.

Knowledge is everything and leads to power. It's a stupid question, bordering on insolent.

The ssythlan's face is similar to ours except for the forked tongue, skin and eyes. They smile as we do, so it obviously appreciates something as its lips curve upward.

'Stand. Approach,' it commands.

Another mage steps forward.

Larn complies immediately. There's no, *why?* We do as we're told.

Yet as he moves toward the instructor, the ssythlan motions quickly with his hands, and Larn stumbles and falls. Suddenly he's sinking and is up to his waist in mud, which quickly reverts back to hard-packed earth, trapping him.

The second ssythlan steps forward, reaching out his hand as if to somehow pull Larn from the ground, and as he grasps Larn's wrist … Larn screams.

We flinch but daren't move as flame and smoke engulf Larn's arm where the mage grasps him. As the ssythlan releases Larn and steps back, the fire continues to burn.

Larn twists about like he's been cut in half, yet he's still trapped, and the fire magic voraciously consumes him. It's been a long time since I've heard one of us cry so piteously, and it's through no weakness on Larn's part.

It's not just the flesh being consumed; his arm is disintegrating. Even the bone turns to ash, and the fire is now reaching his shoulder.

Orphea retches, throwing up her breakfast. The smoke and ashes from Larn blow over her, and the stench of burning flesh is revolting. It's all I can do to stop my stomach contents from following hers.

'Magic, despite limitations, can be deadly,' the second ssythlan fire mage hisses loudly, ensuring it's heard. 'Fire magic can light a candle but is almost sentient. If given purpose, it can control moon globe light or consume a disrespectful Chosen!'

Larn stops struggling and making noise unless the crackle and pop of his flesh counts. Thankfully for him, he's passed on to the next life if such a thing is to be believed.

It's strangely hard to drag my morbid gaze away from Larn, whereas it should have been easy. Yet I return my attention to the ssythlan, my trembling body calming as half-heard words soothe away my angst. *Only the strong survive. Death is the only certainty of life. Learn to live. Live to obey.*

'You now have enough knowledge of elemental magics to understand their use, as long as you see past the restraints of your imagination. From the morrow, we start putting that knowledge to the test. First, however, a magical element will be forced to choose you as its host. For that, we'll use blood magic to circumvent the need for a decade of training and bind it to you forever.'

I catch Orphea's gaze. Her eyes are damp, and perhaps not just from the smoke. Are there tears in her eyes? No, that can't be the case.

The ssythlans continue their lecture, and we don't even stop for anything to eat. As the sun sets, the smoke slowly dissipates from Larn's ashes, and a gentle breeze comes along to scatter them.

I'm just grateful his remains are blown away into the undergrowth.

'Today's session is over,' one hisses. 'Tonight, you'll be called, so be ready.'

Should I feel anger or resentment about Larn? Maybe. Yet already, it's as if it no longer matters. Yes, it doesn't matter to me at all. Why would it?

I search the others' faces too. Except for Orphea, no one even glances at where Larn died. Instead, the chatter turns to the binding. What it will entail, and which magic will choose us as its host.

A host?

Something doesn't sound too savoury with that wording, but it doesn't matter.

Soon I'll be a magic user and thus a better Chosen.

That is what matters.

***

'Malina, come.'

Lystra stands by my bed, hand firm on my shoulder. There's no hint of camaraderie on her face. In fact, it's colder than usual in the darkness, but this doesn't bother me.

The room where we're sleeping is within the mage tower itself, and she beckons me to follow as I rise from bed, readily clothed.

We sleep in fresh clothes that we wear throughout the following day. These are replaced every evening after we cleanse. That way, we're always ready to face whatever is required with minimal preparation.

I tread lightly, following Lystra across the flagstone floor. I haven't put my boots on, for Lystra is also barefoot. I follow her lead unconsciously without even realising it most of the time.

The floors in the tower are always slightly warm, and no doubt, some magic infuses them to maintain such a comfortable temperature.

Sometimes I find it strange that we endure such incredible hardships throughout our days, yet once the toil is over, we cleanse, eat well, and then have a soft bed to sleep in ... and now warm floors. It's as if once the rigours of the day are behind us, these are the rewards we can come to expect.

Yes. That's it.

Everything about this place is based on a reward system. If you obey and survive, you thrive.

We make our way down a long, spiral staircase. Down and down it goes, lit every so often with the cool light of a moon globe. We must be far below ground, and only magic could have carved such a structure out of bedrock.

'Everything we do is to attain strength, to harness power, so that when the time comes, we can serve the king like no other,' advises Lystra softly. 'Yet as with all we learn, all we endure, there's no easy path, at least not for us. Our path is lined with pain, and the more we suffer, the stronger we become. This forges us into a weapon to do the will of the gods!'

There's a fervour to her voice as she announces the last, an unshakeable belief in what she says. It matters not whether the part about the gods is true; everything else most definitely is.

'As you know, the power of a mage is limited by mental and physical strength, but you're not to be a mage,' she continues as we descend, 'but instead a magic user. The binding of an element to your body will be your hardest test so far. The more pain you can withstand in the process, the more powerful you'll be in the element that chooses you. Earth magic chose me, and it has served me well.'

We reach the bottom step and enter a round, low-ceilinged chamber. There are no flagstones or pillars, no wall blocks; everything is smooth, without a crack or flaw in the stonework. The light here is provided by flickering torches affixed to the walls by brackets as opposed to the steady luminescence of moon globes.

The five ssythlan mages are robed in black. When aren't they? Where the light catches their strange skin, it shines in a thousand subtle hues. On the contrary, their eyes never seem to reflect light; instead, they absorb it.

Beyond them is a large workbench upon which are blank parchments, long quills, strange metal instruments, black orbs, and sundry items I've no idea about. There's also something akin to a raised bed but without a mattress.

I'm motioned over by a cowled figure. It's strange. Nowadays, I rarely feel trepidation or fear, but when I do, such as now, it doesn't seem to affect how I respond. My body, or perhaps my mind, makes the decision subconsciously without me being aware, and I instantly obey.

Buckles are tightened, and it feels familiar.

A ssythlan bends over me.

Can it taste my fear? I've learnt about so many creatures, and if they're anything like snakes, it definitely can.

Its tongue actually flicks out across my face before it speaks. 'Endure. You cannot avoid the pain but embrace it until it pulls you under. The longer you endure, the more magic you absorb. If you awaken, you will host an element to better serve our king.'

The mages move to the bench, and I lift my head, studying what they're doing, learning even now.

They each write upon a scroll, and I begin to relax. So far, even though pain has been mentioned, it doesn't seem imminent.

The murmur of words reaches my ears, and now they're waving their hands over the parchments. Every time I'd previously seen them work magic, their movements had been subtle, smooth and graceful, as if crafting and cajoling the elements to their will. However, this time, their actions are frenzied, their fingers bent like claws, and they grasp at something unseen in the very air itself.

As I strain to watch, rising from the parchment, the inked runes arise, glistening. They twist and writhe in the air between the mages' hands as if tortured, seeking escape at any cost.

The ssythlans turn with great care as if afraid of what they carry. Nervousness takes hold of me.

Discipline or conditioning, I don't know what, keeps me from struggling or desperately trying to escape. I remember the runes and glyphs that wriggled upon Lystra's arms when she opened the wall, and I know these *things* will be placed upon me.

The ssythlans chant in their native tongue. Whereas before, it had sounded soft, now the hissing takes on a menacing note. Chills run up and down my spine. My instincts scream at me to do anything to prevent this from happening, yet circumstance prevents it even If I'd tried.

Lystra grabs my shirt, ripping it asunder, leaving me bare from the waist up. There's no avarice in anyone's eyes as they gaze upon my semi-nakedness, just religious fervour.

Their chanting reaches a crescendo. This is why the chamber is deep underground, so the others who still sleep can't hear their voices.

One by one, they open their hands, allowing the wet runes to fall upon my skin.

They're cold, and I flinch. It's as if someone has just dropped a fish on me. I watch through wide eyes while they flounder as if lost across my stomach toward my navel, and as they reach it, they start to burrow.

Suddenly the chamber echoes with the loudest scream, and it's a moment before I realise it's mine. The pain is excruciating beyond anything I've ever experienced, and images of Larn come to mind, burning to death. This is perhaps what he went through.

My body twists and shakes as if that will help repel these monstrosities forcing an entrance, tearing through my skin, feeding, yet becoming part of me.

'Look at me!' Lystra shouts above my screams, and her hand grips mine in a rare show of support.

I stare through the pain, noting the ssythlans arguing behind Lystra, their hands waving around in confusion, darting glances at me.

'The binding, something isn't right. Focus on one element in your mind; help it choose!' Lystra urges.

Waves of pain engulf me, and my throat is raw as I scream, yet I don't pass out, nor does my heart stop. I can't believe my body isn't shutting down, but the pain keeps me conscious, and it just grows and grows until every nerve ending is on fire.

I can't do what Lystra asks, however much I want this to end. From moment to moment, images symbolising fire, earth, air, and water cascade through my thoughts, getting faster and faster.

The ssythlans are around me again, holding my legs, arms and head, chanting frantically.

The noise, the images, everything is coming together, my heartbeat crashing in my chest, threatening to burst. I cannot breathe.

Then ... the pain is gone as if it never was.

My nerves, which felt like they'd been dipped in acid, thrum gently, and I can feel the breath from Lystra's mouth as she demands to know what's happened from the five mages.

Strange. With the pain gone, only now does blackness start to gently take hold, but I'm not afraid.

This is not the approach of death, and I feel safe and warm in its embrace.

***

CHAPTER VII

The following days pass quickly, even if the memory of the pain we all endured doesn't.

I'm under constant scrutiny because, for the first time in so long, I've broken every rule in the book; the magic book. Breaking rules typically leads to punishment or death, yet in this instance, no one is sure how the rules were broken.

The elemental magics don't exist in harmony. Some have direct counterpoints, like fire against water and earth against air, but irrespective, they all repel each other. This means a mage can only absorb one element, and when a binding takes place, a host can only accept one elemental magic into their body.

Somehow, I have all four.

I don't know whether to be honoured or horrified, but everyone, including Lotane, Kralgen, and the others, looks upon me with emotions ranging from jealousy to concern.

Yet whatever elements have chosen us, we all bear their mark, and I more than any.

Each of the others has runes and glyphs scattered across their forearms. They're strangely unpleasant to the eye even before the summoning of magic brings them to life.

By contrast, my entire body is marked, but instead of separate runes, mine have joined together in a series of swirls that loop around my limbs in a multitude of hues. It's as though an artist has taken a paintbrush to my body, for I'm alive with subtly coloured swathes of orange, blue, green and white. My face is the only area where the colour is uniform, a gentle light green.

It isn't unpleasant to look at, and after being the pallor of a corpse my whole life, I'm not averse to the change.

'You looked lovely before and even more so now,' Lotane whispers reassuringly, somehow reading my thoughts as we stand listening to a fire mage.

'She looks more ssythlan than human. I wonder if she got a forked tongue too?' Kralgen asks with a smirk after overhearing the comment.

I bristle at Kralgen's choice of words. Perhaps he didn't mean it nastily, and I'm just overly sensitive; after all, his brother was the spiteful one. I still wonder if he holds me responsible for his brother's death and is taking this opportunity to put me down.

An appropriate barbed response evades me. How frustrating that I'm not good at insults, but then I realise perhaps that's no bad thing after all.

Maybe I'm just frustrated that I now have to practice four times as hard as the others who only need to master the single element they've been gifted with. A gift? Perhaps not if it's misused, like when Larn was burned alive. Larn, poor Larn. I must hold on to the memories of the bad things that happen here, remember them.

We spend the morning focusing on creating a bond between our mind, body, spirit, and the elemental magic imbued within us so that it responds to our calling. By the end of it, Lotane and Kralgen establish a connection, yet I can't.

I'm jealous, for they manage to summon a small flame into the palm of their hands.

They're both sweating, although not from the flames they've summoned, but from the price of pain required to summon it.

I just have a headache from failing.

All this time, I've excelled at everything. First, it was just so I could stay alive, but lately, it's to ensure I can serve The Once and Future King to the best of my ability. Yet now, the multiple elemental magics inside confuse my summoning. I find it so difficult to call upon one when I'm blinded by the swirling colours of four.

'Only the strong survive; remember that, Malina,' Kralgen smiles, waving his flame about.

Even if he isn't being mean on purpose, I can't help myself.

'Perhaps that's why your brother's dead with maggots for eyes,' I hiss.

Kralgen's face turns white.

The ssythlan's head snaps around, and its hiss of irritation at our lack of focus manages to stop Kralgen from taking my comment any further, and the instruction continues.

I'm not proud. It was a horrible thing to say. Our emotions are always held so tightly in check that when they do find release, it can be quite surprising.

We break for lunch. Despite being provided with some, we also forage in the forest. There's so much here to sustain us; now we know where to look. Fruits are reasonably abundant, but there are also mushrooms, roots and edible flowers to balance our diet, and it keeps us honing our skills even when we're at rest. Red wolves inhabit this island, so we never let our guard down. Ever.

I can only respect how they train us with barely a pause.

Lotane walks between Kralgen and me to ensure the peace is kept and the uneasy truce remains. I know it's also so that our fingertips occasionally snag on the others. Every opportunity we get, we take, even with Kralgen frowning alongside.

We return to the small clearing to eat our findings and await the ssythlan instructor's return. The others are elsewhere with their respective mages; for the moment, it's just the three of us.

If only Kralgen had been chosen by water magic, it would be just Lotane and me. I wonder what heat we could generate if it were just us. The thought makes me tingle.

Having finished their lunch, both Lotane and Kralgen practice their summoning again.

I want to tell Kralgen he looks like he's suffering from constipation but swallow the comment and close my eyes. We might be on a break, but we're too conditioned to lie on the floor and do nothing. I need to practice.

Reach for the red, the warmth, I tell myself. Call for it, demand its presence. Feel it grow within you, rising like a flame.

Nothing.

'Gah,' I say. 'This is so damn frustrating.'

Lotane opens his eyes and smiles. I swear I can never get used to his eyes, and his smile is genuine, even if it's tinged with pain.

'Let me assure you, it's none too pleasant succeeding. I can only imagine how unpleasant it gets when we learn to summon more than just a paltry flame in our hand.' He leans in close, whispering. 'You do realise you're already as hot as a flame even if you can't conjure it.'

He steps away and closes his eyes again to refocus.

My cheeks warm, pleasure briefly driving away my frustration before worrisome thoughts push his compliment aside. What punishment awaits if I can't succeed in this? Thoughts of failure make my blood boil, and I know I have a frown etched deep into my forehead.

Kralgen, on the other hand, grins like a hungry wolf.

'Be careful, or that ssythlan mage will torch you like he did with Larn!'

Damn. I don't know if Kralgen is mocking me or just warning me!

I close my eyes again, anger growing in my heart. That anger starts to burn brighter, and I visualise Kralgen burning as Larn had. Surprisingly like a serpent awakening, I immediately feel the fire magic unwind inside me. I discern its primitive instinct to fulfil my wish and recoil in horror from the thought.

What if I'd unleashed the magic in anger? Just because I don't like Kralgen doesn't mean this is the way to resolve the issue.

I steel myself, expecting pain now I've made a successful connection. Strangely, I detect a willingness to obey from the fire magic, a desire to please. This is all wrong. There should be a violent struggle with a raging beast that demands to be fed by my suffering before it concedes control, allowing itself to be harnessed.

To create a flame, as had Lotane and Kralgen, I'm supposed to visualise forcing the magic through my body to form something akin to a candle in my hands. When I try, I can see it flowing there of its own accord, without restraint.

How much should I ask for, and for how long? Typically, pain would limit what I receive, but with none controlling the flow, it just keeps coming, wave upon wave. The colour is mesmerising, the warmth I feel as it rushes through me intoxicating … just like Lotane's touch.

I hear a noise and open my eyes to find that everything around me is on fire. My clothes have burnt away, and I'm standing there naked, my skin untouched, whereas the very ground I stand upon is glowing fiercely.

Lotane and Kralgen shield their faces as they back away from the conflagration. Lotane is shouting, or at least I see his lips move, but I can't hear above the fierce crackle of the flames.

It's surreal. My eyes are open, but I feel no panic, just the warmth of the fire's embrace caressing my skin with a gentle touch. The flickering, dancing tongues of fire are beautiful. I just want to see more of it, see how high it can reach, and the flames leap upward to consume the trees above me in response to my desire.

I laugh, and fire spews from my mouth like a blossoming red rose.

It's ecstasy.

Then suddenly, the sky goes dark, and so does the world around me.

***

I amble through the forest surrounding the tower.

The grass tickles my bare toes, pleasantly cool to offset the sun's gentle heat, which filters through the canopy. A thousand wings hum, from insects to birds, their excited movements comforting. I feel so alive, perfectly attuned to nature. I've never been more content, and I don't want this to end.

'Your happiness means everything to me, Alina,' chirrups Karson next to me.

I don't know how long he's been there, but his little hand is clasped in mine. I can feel his warmth, his love, and my heart swells with joy.

'Whatever it takes, I don't mind. As long as you're happy.'

His voice cracks a little as he says it, and I turn to see smoke pouring from his hand where I grip it. It's thick and dark, and as I let go to see what happens, he bursts into flame.

'NO!'

I frantically try to pat the flames out, but more rise every time I touch him.

'It's ok,' he bubbles, skin peeling from his face. *'Whatever it takes to make you happy.'*

Recoiling in horror, I stumble backwards as he's consumed, his ashes swept away by a howling wind.

I flee from where he died, and with every step, I feel better again. Yes, the grass tickles my bare toes, pleasantly cool to offset the sun's gentle heat, which filters through the canopy. I feel so alive, perfectly attuned to nature. I've never been more content, and I don't want this to end.

My steps falter, for there in a clearing before me is Karson.

'Alina,' he shouts, spinning around and around, laughing.

I laugh too, yet my laugh erupts as a gust from my mouth, and he's swept screaming into the air, to be flung far away.

'NO!' I cry, sinking to my knees, my head in my hands.

'Don't worry, Alina. It doesn't matter; it really doesn't. You see, you're already happy again!'

It's true. The pain has disappeared, and I'm on my feet, the grass cool beneath me.

'I love you, Alina,' Karson says, slipping his hand into mine once more. *'I'll always love you. I just wish it wasn't so cold.'* He shivers.

It's true; his skin is freezing, and suddenly his hand breaks like glass beneath my touch. White mist comes from his mouth. He takes a step, and his leg snaps at the ankle, and even as he puts that down, it shatters, sending him to the floor where he fragments into a thousand frozen pieces, except for his head.

'Does it make you happy, killing me?'

Frosted eyes fix mine, and my tears freeze.

'Yes! No! Of course not,' I cry desperately as his head melts into a puddle to be swallowed by the thirsty soil.

'So, if it doesn't make you happy, why do you kill me again and again?'

I spin around to see him whole before me. His little hand points over my shoulder, and where just moments before had been grass, there are mounds of his corpses. They're all burned, frozen, or turned to stone.

'Is it because only the strong survive, and I'm not strong enough?'

My heart feels like it's breaking; the agony is overwhelming.

'It's a mistake. I'll never do this again. I promise!'

'Have you considered the future, Alina? Have you? If you serve blindly, what might it hold?'

Suddenly, mountains of bodies rise from the earth around me, twisted limbs, gaping wounds, and staring eyes. Then they shift, the bloated arms begin to pull, the legs to kick, and the next moment the mountains collapse, burying me in a suffocating pile of rotting flesh.

Then just as suddenly, they're gone, and so is Karson.

Yet I hear his voice as if a whisper.

'Look to your heart, Alina. Look to your heart.'

I kneel there without the strength to move.

Yet before long, the grass tickles my bare toes, pleasantly cool to offset the sun's gentle heat, which filters through the canopy.

***

'She should be destroyed.'

'No.'

'But look at what's happened.'

'We know, but this isn't our decision. *He* demands that she live.'

Silence.

How long have I been in this darkness? I sense it's a long time, for I've had so many dreams, but it might just be moments or days or weeks; I've no idea.

I want to open my eyes, to sit up, yet whilst my mind is awake, my body isn't, that damned dream leaf.

Then the ssythlan language fills my ears, the soft hisses and clicks they make soothing on the one hand, and yet on the other, I feel they could be discussing having me for dinner. If only I knew.

Since my arrival, I've been taught many things whilst I sleep, including languages. Surely that must have been done with the assistance of magic.

Yet, no elemental magic can do that.

However, we've been told briefly that blood magic binds the body or spirit to objects or others, creating resonance, singularity and understanding.

The ssythlans have told us very little else about it, and this is because it's their magic. No humans possess the jealously guarded secret of how it's used or manifests itself.

Yet I have the strangest feeling...

Look to your heart, Alina; my earlier dream reminds me.

I'd thought the underlying message had been reminding me to not die inside, but perhaps there is more. I turn my spirit eye inwards, shutting out the ssythlans' noise.

It's easy to identify the four elemental magics, for my mind and body swirl with their unmistakable energy. It's as if I'm filled with a maelstrom of thunderous clouds, each vying for supremacy, crashing against and then from the other.

Fire is a blindingly bright, flickering orange that constantly changes its hue. Earth maintains a steady, pulsating green, and I sense a bitter taste akin to iron. Water is a giddying vortex of different blues, whereas air is white, full of deafening, howling sounds.

Yet of blood magic, there's no sign. Perhaps my instinct was wrong. To host four magics is unheard of. I should be satisfied with such if only I could control them.

Karson's words echo again in my head.

Look to your heart, Alina.

My heart. I've searched my mind, my spirit, but now I look deeper, finding my heart, and there, saturating it, is a dark red mist, so dark as to be borderline black, hiding just under the surface.

It notices my attention and recoils as I reach out with my thoughts, afraid of being discovered. Is it hiding from me or the fury of the elemental magics that fight, constrained within my mortal body?

Something about its vulnerability reminds me of Karson. He always responded to kindness, never threats or violence. So, I whisper sweet nothings, patient and relaxed, eventually coaxing it into sight with feelings of love.

There it is.

My whole body resonates as the blood magic comes forth, sensing kinship and unity.

'Help me find peace,' I intuitively ask of it.

Like a blossoming flower spreading its petals, the blood magic reaches out tendrils to caress the other elements. Then, as I observe, the elemental storm settles as the aeons old adversaries listen to my entreaty.

'We are one,' I project, knowing they'll hear me and understand my intent.

Suddenly, the elemental magics are vying for my attention, no longer full of anger and resentment but inquisitive and playful.

I laugh, for like children, they wish to be held.

What mother can ignore her children?

So, in turn, I embrace them even as they swirl around me, coming to understand the possibility of their uses. It amazes me the amount of power vested in my body. Despite exhausting myself earlier, already I'm replenished.

We are joined; we are one. There's no conflict within me, only harmony. The next time I call for help, I know they'll answer without hesitation.

I'm not some god, far from it, and I chuckle at the thought when it enters my mind. The weapon skills I've learned have made me far deadlier, yet not every adversary can be overcome, or a problem solved with brute force.

Now I'm at peace, the ssythlans talking in their whispering tongue catch my attention.

I cannot understand them yet, but in time I will.
In time.

**

'Always sleeping while the rest of us train,' Kralgen mutters.

Everyone is limbering up on the mountainside terrace, the horizon glowing brightly.

Having just awoken in my sleeping chamber, I knew they'd be here.

Fianna's smile is radiant and of genuine relief. She's as beautiful as she is deadly.

'You disappeared for a week,' she offers the answer to my unspoken question. 'Don't worry, Kralgen's just grumpy because you singed his eyebrows off and spoiled his good looks!'

'If he's grumpy, how do you think I feel?' Lotane demands, coming to hug me. He points at his nearly bald head, then runs his fingers over the bristles and laughs. 'My hair was crisped, so I had a new haircut. Do you like it?' His lopsided grin always demands one in return.

I tilt my head to one side and then burst out laughing.

'It'll take some getting used to!'

After everyone greets me in a different fashion, I start exercising and take a few moments to study the others.

Nestor is looking glum. Never the brightest soul, I think the dark earth magic runes on his arm suit his demeanour. Orphea, likewise. She seems distant, distracted by something.

Alyssa looks fierce, and with her water runes barely noticeable on her skin, she's hardly changed.

Fianna groans slightly.

I turn as she whispers something, and her shoulder-length hair starts blowing in the breeze she's summoned around her head.

'I do this to wind up Lotane,' she winks. 'It's worth the pain,' and goes to stand next to him, so when he turns about, aware of her presence, he's face to face with her streaming locks.

He goes to cuff her gently, but she ducks away, squealing, and I can't help but smile. The moments like this are so few, and thus so precious.

I continue through my stretching exercises, and as the sun crests the horizon in a breathtaking display, bathing the terrace in its orange glow, we head to the eating chamber.

Even Kralgen's dark demeanour lifts a little as we swing from straps or climb along walls. It's a friendly competition to start the day, and we arrive at the lower level a little out of breath.

Lystra awaits. Sometimes I wonder if she ever sleeps, but she never looks tired.

Both the food and the conversation over breakfast are light. Lystra looks over us like a disapproving mother wolf. She never joins in, and we know how far we can push without being reprimanded.

Alyssa is always teased about her appetite. She eats enough for three, and it's incredible to watch her shovel food into her mouth. She takes the jests well. There isn't an ounce of fat on her, nor any of us, for that matter.

Lotane is often the instigator of the jokes. He speaks quietly so as not to upset Lystra.

'Here,' he says to Kralgen, holding up two curved pieces of crusty bread, 'I think I found something to replace your singed eyebrows.'

Soft laughter sounds around the table, and even Lystra's lips twitch upward momentarily.

Kralgen says nothing, just munches away on a garnal fruit, then picks up the peeled skin and drapes it over Lotane's head.

'Much better,' Kralgen growls, and Orphea slaps him on the back in approval.

'Enough,' Lystra's clipped voice stills the moment, and we switch modes instantly. 'There's much to do, and every moment that goes by without training is a moment lost. Now, finish your food.'

We set to work devouring what's in front of us. It's rare now that food is put to one side. Our senses are so attuned to corrupted food that I think they no longer wish to waste good resources on us.

It's not long before we're following Lystra, her stride purposeful yet graceful. I catch Lotane admiring her form and elbow him jealously in the ribs. Having been caught in the act, he smiles, and I briefly mimic Lystra's walk. Fianna snorts back some laughter before Lystra's sharp look over her shoulder settles us down again.

The passageways we travel are familiar, and we're heading toward the waterfall room or the training circle. It's too early for a shower, so the training circle it is.

Yet I'm wrong.

We stop at the junction which turns left to the circle or right to the waterfall room, but instead, Lystra puts her hands on the wall directly ahead. As with the tower, after a moment of concentration and evident pain, the stone folds back, and steps leading down appear before us.

A hidden passageway. Just how many are there, and where might others lead?

She motions us through before closing the passage behind us, then leads the way.

Down we go, step after step, until we enter a tall cavern with a pool in one corner. Smooth-walled, I can't discern its purpose, but Lystra doesn't take long to reveal what we're doing in her usual no-nonsense fashion.

'Watch,' she instructs and steps up to the wall. There are no flaws, no handholds, just smooth, impenetrable rock. Her face screws up in concentration.

I can sense by a tingling that she's summoning her earth magic, and the runes on her arms flow to her hands, turning them black.

Then she starts to climb.

It's amazing. The wall softens like wet clay; her hands and feet pushing into what was solid rock only moments ago. She climbs higher and higher before slowly retracing her steps. Even as we watch, the holes close as if the rock heals itself.

Sweat beads her brow, and her skin is pale from pain, but it's an awe-inspiring demonstration.

'We can make permanent change with earth magic,' she gasps, before composing herself, then carries on in her usual tone. 'Or the change can be temporary. You need to consider wisely which. Remember, every action you choose has repercussions. Create a cavern here, and what you displace might create a rockfall elsewhere.'

'As long as it's on someone else's head. What matter?' asks Nestor.

He half-smiles as he poses the question, yet it's well-asked.

'If you're climbing the outside of a wall, it's possible someone on the inside might notice,' Lystra explains.

'So, those of you with earth as your element, you can practice what I've demonstrated, but don't go higher than twice your height. That includes you, Malina,' and she nods at me.

'Fire, you'll accomplish the same, but instead, you'll endeavour to melt the rock to create holes with which to climb. As Malina demonstrated on the island, what fire is created by you cannot harm you. Just try to keep your clothes on!'

Everyone laughs, just as much out of shock as from humour.

Lystra has actually made a joke, and even if it's at my expense, I laugh with the others.

'Alyssa, I'll deal with you in a moment,' advises Lystra, nodding to the pool.

'What about me?' asks Fianna. My element is air, so what can I do?'

'You're going to learn how to slow our earth and fire users when they fall,' Lystra nods with a serious look on her face, 'because if you don't, they'll be fewer for dinner tonight.'

This time no one laughs ... because this is no joke.

In this place, failure and death walk hand in hand.

***

My arms ache as I sit with the others in the eating chamber. I'm exhausted, and it's only midday.

The others are in similar shape, although the pain lines on their faces are deeper etched. Food is brought over to us, and I detect the faint aroma of flare seed. Others have noted it too, yet it isn't harmful. Instead, it gives a short-term energy boost, which is precisely what we need.

Even Lystra, who has endless energy, looks somewhat drawn. This is the cost of using elemental magic.

Our break is over all too soon, and we head back, pausing at the solid rock junction wall.

'Nestor!' Lystra snaps, and he steps forward to place his hands on the wall.

'Aarrghh,' he groans, sweat running off his face, which is contorted in pain. The wall starts to slump, almost as if it will turn into a puddle on the floor, and we step back.

He stops for a moment, eyes glazed and looks at Lystra, who returns it. Her stare is unforgiving, and there's no need for words.

The rest of us stand there, and I wonder what they're thinking. No one dares say anything to break Nestor's concentration or to invoke Lystra's ire. The unspoken thought is; if he fails, will this lead to a punishment or death?

Wiping the sweat from his brow Nestor tries again and fails as the wall ripples and sags before returning to solid rock. He falls to his knees, breathing deeply, not from despair nor from fright, but instead from anger.

I can hear him growl deep in his throat, and the next moment he pushes his arms into the rock face and tears it asunder as if ripping through parchment. Soon there's a hole in the wall and chunks of rock hanging off as if some creature has burst forth.

The hole might not be a doorway, but he's created an entry.

Nestor slumps, unconscious, and Fianna, standing next to me, bites her lip so hard that a bead of blood forms.

Lystra moves swiftly, bending down, her hands going to Nestor's head.

This is it. She's going to snap his neck.

Yes, only the strong survive, but Nestor tried so hard.

Instead, Lystra checks his pulse before standing upright. Pushing her hands against it, she talks softly but firmly, and the opening appears, the chunks smoothing to become part of the wall again.

'Carry him,' she orders, looking at Kralgen and Lotane, then motions us down the steps and closes the opening before following.

'Lean him against that wall,' Lystra motions.

Lotane takes Nestor from Kralgen, props him up, and then returns to us as we wait.

'There's a lesson over there,' Lystra points at Nestor. 'He didn't give up despite the pain. He completed the mission I gave to him, and that's what you must all do when the time comes. His approach might have lacked finesse, but sometimes what will be asked of you won't always require it.

'Now, Malina, create a platform that Fianna can stand on halfway up the wall.'

I pause, thinking, before stepping forward.

Till now, I'd pushed my hands into the wall, creating indents to climb up, but having just seen Nestor's dramatic attempt to create an opening, I have another idea.

Instead, I reach for the earth magic inside of me and find it almost leaping to answer. There's no resistance or pain, yet I close my eyes, twist my face, and growl, hissing under my breath. By contrast, all the time, I imagine pulling the warmth of my magic into a soft embrace, asking for its help.

I place my hands upon the wall, visualising steps to protrude, and when I open my eyes, there they are, five steps perfectly spaced, moving diagonally up the wall. They're as wide as my shoulders, just as I imagined them, and I step onto the first, finding it as unyielding as I'd expect.

I step to the top, then repeat it over. I don't know if I could have projected my will to create them all at once, but I'm wary of trying. I'm not constrained by pain for whatever reason, but I want to stay conscious and understand my limits. I'm not sure falling unconscious while draining every drop of magical strength will endear me to Lystra.

Finally, I visualise the platform, like a mattress standing proudly from the wall, and as with the steps, the rock responds to my will. I look on in disbelief at what I've created, then sing my thanks in my mind as loud as I can, knowing on some level that I'm heard.

I turn and carefully descend to see looks of admiration and perhaps even envy on the faces of those looking at me. Whilst I'd had to pretend to feel pain while completing my task, there's no faking how exhausted I am. My legs barely support me, and I'm hollow inside as if I need to eat.

Lystra shakes her head, the corners of her lips lifted in a wry smile.

'Your control and power is laudable. As you've such command over earth magic, you'll practice with air.

'Fianna. Climb to the platform. It's time for you to put your life in Malina's hands.'

Kralgen chuckles. 'Hey, Fianna. I'll miss you when you're gone.'

'A new volunteer to go first,' Lystra snaps at Kralgen.

I yawn hugely on purpose, enjoying the worry in his eyes.

However, despite my tease, I'm genuinely exhausted, feel faint, and as I catch sight of Nestor unconscious against the wall, I realise I'm nearing my limits. Lystra will want me to slow everyone's fall before she's satisfied, and I don't think I have it in me.

I catch Lotane staring at me from the corner of my eye.

Unlike the others, who are worried I'll fail them, I know instinctively he's worried for a different reason, and the warmth that thought generates gives me more strength and resolve than any threat.

Kralgen has reached the top. His slate-grey eyes narrow as he looks down. I look inside, find the whisper of the magic remaining within, and breathe deeply, coaxing it to my aid. '*Sing with me?*' I ask, and the hairs all over my body stand on end as it responds to my call.

***

How often have I sat here, bathed in red from the sunset as we all relax at day's end? Usually, I'm entranced by the view, surrounded by familiar patterns in the rock.

Now, thanks to Nestor, those familiar patterns are gone.

We're taught to seek perfection in everything we do. Now Nestor seeks to imprint that perfection on his surroundings.

Even as everyone sits on stone benches, chatting or reclining after eating the dinner that's now brought up to us, fighting fatigue from the day's activities, he practices his earth magic. It's almost as if even the tiniest flaw offends his eye, and he works to smooth everything out.

He's never someone to truly take note of amongst the rest of us. He isn't tall, overly muscular, and neither bright nor fair. He's plain looking, with a face you'd forget, and initially, I wondered how he'd got this far. Yet he shares with those of us who survive some essential traits; tenacity, strength of will, and apparently, his capacity to endure pain.

Even Kralgen, who considers himself superior to everyone, looks at Nestor with grudging respect and perhaps even wariness.

Unlike magic users, true mages only suffer fatigue, not pain, during summoning. The pain for the Chosen is excruciating and draining. For that reason, magic users will never have a mage's power. That I don't experience pain like a mage is a detail I keep firmly to myself.

For the others, I know summoning is the least favourite of all the training we do for that very reason. Yet there is Nestor, visage twisted in agony as he faces the rock wall, palms against it, willing every tiny imperfection to disappear.

What would happen if I used my earth magic to try and thwart him?

If I tried to cause imperfections in the same rock at the same time, would the strongest will prevail, or would the elemental magic refuse to combat itself?

Maybe one day I'll find out.

As the sun drops below the horizon, we return to the mountain's bosom, to our sleeping chambers. I manage to linger behind, so I briefly accompany Lotane, our hands brushing, hidden.

Bidding each other goodnight, I'm shortly sitting on my bed.

There, on a bedside chest, is my night's sleeping infusion. One of the rules we abide by is to drink this every night. I'm positive it isn't just the pain of punishment or death that makes us follow this rule, nor the lure of perfect sleep, awakening refreshed without side effects.

No.

We're compelled to obey whatever instructions we're given by more than just conditioning. To drink an infusion, to live to kill. It doesn't matter; we do exactly as we're told.

This lack of choice doesn't bother me, for it's the way of the world, but what does is not knowing exactly how our free will is stripped from us. The thirst for knowledge and to gain more power with its acquisition now drives me to find out.

I dutifully drain the goblet. I've no other choice. It's stronger tonight, indicating that we'll train whilst asleep. Yet despite having obeyed this compulsion, I intend to remain awake long enough to briefly observe proceedings before I succumb.

The ssythlan mages impress the need to force the elements, manipulating and coercing them to do one's bidding; it works for them, and indeed the other Chosen follow this lead.

Instead, I treat them as favoured children, showing affection, appreciation, and love.

Focussing on my breathing, I direct my thoughts inwards, addressing the magic within, and I'm met by a welcome feeling of comfort, warmth and eagerness.

I wish my heart to slow, delay the dream leaf's impact, and convey that feeling to the red mist of blood magic that understands my intent, and my body responds.

The other magics are there too, observing, swirling together, individual, yet united, content to wait their turn whenever that may be. I reach out, mentally holding them close, and they shimmer in response.

The sound of wheeled carts draws my attention.

My eyes remain open, and there's a brief flash of reptilian faces looking down, checking I'm unresponsive before I'm lifted to a cart and wheeled out. Moon globes flash by overhead as we travel down passageways and ramps.

Eventually, we arrive at the Heart Stone chamber, and as the cart bed swings upright, with me strapped firmly inside, I gaze upon the mirror, wondering if I'll see *him.*

Unsurprisingly it's blank. I'm disappointed, but the Heart Stone pulses hypnotically, and my heart soon beats happily with the same slow cadence. This place is home, the centre of my world. Everything feels right here, as it should be.

The other Chosen have yet to arrive, although the rattle of approaching carts grows louder.

Five ssythlan mages enter my field of view in their black robes, quietly conversing in the shadows. Darkness encroaches on my vision and starts to pull me under, yet I fight against it.

I desperately want to learn something, indeed anything of note, before I succumb to sleep, especially about how we're controlled.

A tugging inside me, insistent, impossible to ignore; my magic vying for attention.

'*Hush. Be still*,' I project. However, it's to no avail as the intensity increases.

It's so distracting.

Opening my spirit eye, I gaze inward to find the red mist of blood magic coiled and waiting. As it senses my gaze, it explodes toward me in a terrifying blur, too quick to avoid. A flashing kaleidoscopic multitude of reds flashes through my thoughts as if seeking to escape. Subconsciously, I cry out, anticipating pain ... yet there's none.

Darkness.

No colours, no magic, just complete silence, and darkness. I'm not unconscious and remain in my meditative state, waiting, wondering what's happened.

Time seems to have little meaning, and I don't know how long I wait until ...

Creaking, like a ship's timbers moving in a swell, break the nothingness.

Consequently, a thousand cracks appear around me, and like a breaking mirror, the darkness shatters, letting in the glorious light.

The resulting glare isn't painful, and I relax as it begins to fade, then marvel as everything is laid bare like never before.

Surrounding me, streams of faint colours intermingle as magic elements waft on an ethereal breeze. Whether or not they have a purpose is hard to tell, but they twist around one another like people in a crowded marketplace.

Somehow, the blood magic understood my desire and opened my spirit eye beyond my inner self to uncover everything in this chamber.

Incredible and unbelievably beautiful.

I'm sure it's the same everywhere. The world must be full of magic, unseen by everyone. I don't know why I hadn't appreciated that before, nor had the ssythlan mages mentioned it.

However, despite being mesmerising, I don't know how this will help, so I'm about to close my spirit eye when that now-familiar tugging occurs.

What now?

I steel myself for something dramatic as the swirling elemental magics fade away.

Replacing the different colours, the room is crisscrossed with subtle red lines, like a spiderweb. It's fascinating and intricate, and the more I focus, the brighter they become.

Like veins carrying blood, these red lines aren't just random.

I'm connected to the mages, the Heart Stone, and the mirror, while several others disappear through the rock walls linking me to others unseen.

Blood Magic!

The happy wriggling confirms what I had suspected or perhaps somehow even knew.

I'm fascinated.

If I'm linked to the mages and probably Lystra with blood magic, this would explain the compulsion to obey, hang on every word and seek their praise.

Compared to the others, blood magic is subtler, for it's unseen.

Compared to the others, it's more powerful, for it cannot be disobeyed.

I wonder if Lystra is bound. She must be.

Movement brings my fading attention back to the mages.

I wish I could hear what they're saying.

There's a gentle subconscious nudging, my magic vying for attention, and as soon as I turn my thoughts toward it, it acts almost of its own volition. Moments later, the hissing language is a whisper, brought to me on the subtlest breeze.

My magic coalesces into a cloud of warmth and contentment as it feels my delight.

We live to learn.

The blood magic helps me focus on the hissing language even if I can't yet understand it.

The conditioning I've been exposed to drives me to learn, follow orders and obey.

We must be perfect and do everything in our power to attain more power.

I'm only doing as my training demands, and thus my sense of well-being increases.

Sleep finally pulls me under, but I smile inside.

For I'm learning the language of the ssythlans.

***

CHAPTER VIII

Three years I've been here. I'm seventeen years old, as are those around me.

Had my father still lived, I might well be married by now, perhaps with a child. At the very least, I'd be helping him on his fishing boat.

The thought shocks me.

Instead, I'm here. Would that alternative version of me look at this one with distaste, loathing, or perhaps envy?

Lotane nudges me as we stand in line, waiting at the centre of the training circle, perhaps aware that I'm drifting, or maybe just because we share the slightest touch at every opportunity. A casual brush of a hand, a rub of a shoulder. Nothing obvious, completely innocuous. Absolutely delicious.

We continue to train daily, vying to be the best we can be.

Yet, we're not blinded by conceit concerning our abilities. Well, perhaps Kralgen is and in some ways, rightfully so.

But however hard we train, three years of swordsmanship won't make us untouchable to someone who has trained extensively for a decade. Lystra remains unbeatable whenever she steps in to spar with us.

We practice survival in the wilderness but won't be as accomplished as a hunter who lives on a wild mountainside his whole life. And our sailing skills will never come close to someone battling the sea every day from dawn to dusk.

Yet, every day we strive to improve, and we have a range of skills that are unbelievable when I consider them.

To serve The Once and Future King.

The thought drives me ever onward, yet my intermittent dreams of Karson sometimes make me question what would otherwise be blind obedience, albeit not for long.

I wonder how we're to serve when we're grandmasters at nothing but excel in everything.

We would all be worthy bodyguards, hunters, and soldiers, but not the absolute best.

If we solely trained martial arts, it would be easy to see how we might serve as we master that one skill, but whilst it remains our highest priority, it's one of many.

I shake my head as if the physical movement will help order my jumbled thoughts.

Unanswered questions like this frustrate me, and even worse, I know asking will not be well received. Maybe in an hour, these questions won't matter to me anymore.

Why?

Today is another purge. A celebration like no other to mark our further passage into adulthood. A dozen guards armed with crossbows stand ready, yet they're not here for us. The need for that is long gone, for conditioning and blood magic bind us here securely and obediently.

We're dressed in leather armour: cuirass, greaves, kilt, forearm bracers, gorget. There's no embellishment on these items, just plain, hardened leather stained by years of sweat and scored by constant combat.

It's sturdy and offers good protection without being cumbersome. It's also easier to conceal, makes no noise, doesn't reflect light, and if the worst happens, can be swum in for a short while, unlike its metal counterparts.

Not that there'll be any swimming today. Unless in blood.

Lystra walks along our line, then moves to stand a few paces in front before turning to face us, hands on hips, eyes bright. She's dressed in armour like us and makes a striking figure, bronzed from the sun, with long muscled legs, supple and graceful. A warrior born.

'Those who will soon stand before you are not worthy,' she shouts. 'They're murderers and rapists, men without honour who have somehow escaped righteous judgement. Today the gods will decide their fate, and you will be the means by which that judgement is delivered. Yet even the damned can find redemption. If they kill you, then they earn the right to live. Only the strong survive.

'To live, you must kill!'

'We live to kill!' we roar, swords smacking against our shields. The sound echoes back from the mountainside like thunder.

Karson's voice whispers in my head, but I push it to one side. Now is not the time.

Movement catches my eye, and ssythlans crowd on the balcony above the training circle, come to see their prodigy perform.

They're conversing, and my magic brings their voices to me so I can hear their whispered hissing.

After all this time, their language is beginning to make sense, yet they're saying nothing of note, merely celebrating the bloodletting to come, eager to watch us.

A door to the training circle opens, and in walk our adversaries.

I'm shocked.

Lystra's words had painted a picture in my head of bedraggled figures, starved, beaten, maltreated, having been locked in a ship's hold for weeks following a lengthy incarceration. I'd expected this to be an execution of humanity's dregs, empty-eyed, accepting of their fate, knowing they deserve it.

Instead, in front of us stand a dozen healthy men, one of whom is enormous.

They're all outfitted in a variety of armours, and a further surprise is that it's from our stores. It's apparent from how they stand, comfortable and sure, that the men before us are trained, and their gaze is measuring, full of hope and determination.

Why not. Before them stand only young men and women, barely into adulthood, even if we exude an easy confidence.

Three large carts creak as they're wheeled across the circle. One is burdened by the weight of weapons. The others are empty but won't remain that way for long. They stop a dozen paces away.

Lystra steps forward to address the convicted men, yet her voice is loud and carries to us all.

'In this circle, you'll be judged by the gods. Win, and you'll live on the islands. Lose, and you'll be buried on them. You'll fight one at a time, and no mercy will be offered or expected from you.'

Nods meet her announcement. There's no fear in their eyes.

I'm also judging how they stand and which foot they favour, trying to ascertain whether they're right or left-handed based on musculature. Are they thick of waist under their armour? Are there battle scars on the right or left side of their body?

My mind automatically accumulates this trove of information with barely a conscious thought.

'You,' Lystra points to a grizzled man with a series of scars on his right forearm, indicating his dominant side. 'Choose your weapons!'

The man rolls forward like a boulder, short and powerful, with thick wrists and a bull neck. He chooses a tower shield and a short sword.

It's a telling choice, and I'm sure he's used to fighting in a close formation. His calves are muscled, and I nod to myself. He's used to marching and was undoubtedly in one of the many armies dotted across the warring kingdoms.

'Nestor!' Lystra shouts without turning her head.

Dutifully, Nestor steps forward. He doesn't look back or anywhere but at the man before him.

It's hard to fathom the age of Nestor's opponent, but he looks to be in his forties and is heavier, stronger, and likely far more experienced than Nestor.

Lystra raises her hand, then brings it sharply down.

'FIGHT!' she commands.

Both men circle, and while Nestor is lighter of step, the older man's footwork is sound, and he peers over the top of his shield that protects him from face to feet. They exchange probing thrusts, gauging each other's reactions, seeing whether the blow is met with a shield or sword.

Maybe it's because of Nestor's youthful stamina that he attacks more. He isn't rash, yet lands twice as many blows against his opponent's shield as he receives in return. Before too long, I can see a slight wince from the stocky warrior every time one of Nestor's blows land. The tower shield is heavy, and the constant impacts are taking their toll.

Everyone's eyes are glued to the contest, and shouts of encouragement rise above the combat.

Lotane leans in close to me. 'It's too early for that man to tire. Look at the breadth of his shoulders. That shield weighs nothing to him. He's trying to lure Nestor into something rash.'

He's right. The weakness he's showing is no weakness at all.

Nestor continues to cautiously attack the tower shield, slowly chopping it away. Each time the man moves his shield to the left to meet the blow, it's slower to recover.

'Be careful, Nestor,' I whisper.

Even if he'd heard my warning, I'm not sure he'd have listened.

The man's shield drops away prematurely, anticipating a blow coming to his left side, but Nestor thrusts instead. It's true, straight, and perfectly executed.

I know what's going to happen before it does.

The man whips his shield back, deflecting the sword thrust to his right, and pushes forward in the same instant, trapping Nestor's sword arm briefly between the two shields. With a war cry, he slams the shield edge down onto Nestor's front foot, crushing it, before knocking our fellow Chosen to the ground with a mighty shield bash.

Nestor slams onto his back, arms spread, shield off to the left, sword to the right, defenceless.

'No!' I cry and feel something respond within me.

As the man steps forward, leaning down to thrust his blade into Nestor's chest, he stumbles, and Nestor frantically brings his shield between them, deflecting the man's sword to strike the ground by his side. As the man struggles to retain his balance, Nestor brings his sword up, thrusting it into that bullish neck.

The man stands there, shocked, blood spewing from his mouth, then sinks to his knees alongside Nestor. Despite the horrific wound, the man still grips his sword and places the point under Nestor's chin.

To my amazement, instead of making a killing thrust in his dying moments, he lowers the weapon and then reaches out to pat Nestor on the chest, almost as if to say, '*it's all right.*'

With a jingle of mail, the man falls face-first onto the ground. Nestor lies there, eyes open, face white with pain, incomprehension, and relief.

Was this an evil man's desperate final act of seeking redemption or something else?

'Get up!' hisses Lystra at Nestor.

He gets painfully to his feet, his face composed, although sweating profusely.

Guards run forward to drag the dead warrior's body away to be thrown on one of the empty carts.

Lystra indicates for Nestor to stand back in line.

'You're a disgrace,' she snarls, her fingers twitching near her sword, her face an inch from Nestor's as he stares straight ahead.

Death awaits a fresh soul, but in the next moment, she steps back.

'Kralgen!'

Kralgen beams, eyes gleaming.

'I want the big one,' he demands, pointing at the hugely muscled behemoth.

'I never thought I'd be thankful to Kralgen for anything,' mutters Lotane, and I can only agree.

Kralgen's opponent also looks to be from Icelandia, that bitter desert of ice way to the far north. White braided hair tied together hangs down the back of his tree trunk of a neck. Bright blue tattoos mark his face, and I'm reminded of the elemental runes we all bear.

He stretches his arms out wide and laughs loudly. His teeth are horribly black against his pale skin, stained by the squid ink liquor he's imbibed to keep warm in the coldest months.

He walks to the weapon cart and picks up a war mallet.

These are enormous, two-handed weapons and can fell a knight in plate armour with a single blow. He holds it in one meaty fist and doesn't even bother with another weapon as his enormous strides take him back to stand opposite Kralgen, who has thrown his shield to one side.

It's a prudent move. If he tries to block the mallet, it will shatter his arm.

'Come, little brother,' booms the Icelandian, recognising Kralgen for one of his own. The common tongue he speaks carries the guttural twist of his native tongue. He bangs his deep chest with the head of the mallet. 'It is only right we show the Southlanders how to fight!'

I've no idea how Kralgen will fight this monster and his weapon. This truly is a purge. Nestor might have prevailed, but I'm wondering whether he'll be made to fight again, and if Kralgen dies to this brute, then the rest of us will need to fight three opponents or even more.

Will any of us survive?

Kralgen looks to Lystra and nods.

'FIGHT!'

Kralgen charges. He's extremely big for seventeen years, heavily muscled, strong and tall. Compared to the Icelandian, he still looks like a child.

I watch in awe as the war mallet sweeps around in a blur, waist height. It's going to fling Kralgen broken halfway across the training circle.

Instead, Kralgen drops and rolls under its arc, comes smoothly to his feet, rams his blade up into the Icelandian's stomach, and then rolls away, leaving the sword behind.

I don't know whether Kralgen expected the blow would kill the Icelandian, but he was quickly disappointed if he did.

'Shakrala!' the Icelandian screams, invoking his god of the frozen seas, and even with the sword buried deep in his guts, leaps, the mallet smashing down.

Kralgen spins aside at the last moment, and shards of rock hiss through the air as he ducks under his foe's outstretched arms, and as he moves away, the sword is in his grasp once more.

'By the gods, Kralgen's way better than I realised,' Fianna gasps, leaning close to me as blood pours from the horrific open wound in the Icelandian's stomach.

There's a clatter as the mallet handle falls to the floor, and the next moment, a flash as Kralgen launches his sword. It crosses the distance in the blink of an eye, and the Icelandian falls, dead, the weapon having almost split his skull in two like an overripe fruit.

Kralgen roars, arms spread, looking up to the heavens as if the very gods have just witnessed this extraordinary display.

It takes four guards to remove the giant body.

'Lotane!' Lystra calls, her face now glowing.

I can't help it. I squeeze his hand briefly before he steps forward. It's foolish; he needs to be focused, not distracted. But I need him to know I care.

His opponent is selected, and the man chooses two swords. It requires incredible proficiency to dual-wield two offensive weapons.

'FIGHT!'

***

Karson sits in front of me, little legs crossed, arms folded, and with a critical look.

How can I sit in front of my little brother and feel so judged?

I lean forward to hug him, but he raises his palms, forestalling the motion.

We're in a field, although I don't recognise where. The grass isn't lush nor sparse, just grass.

The wind blows, not hot nor cold. It isn't fetid or fresh, just air.

I open my hands, showing my empty palms.

'Do you see,' I say. 'I'm not wielding magic. You're safe with me now.'

He doesn't seem convinced.

'Why, Alina? Why did you kill those men?'

'You don't understand; they were evil, murderers and worse ...' I begin to explain.

'How do you know that, Alina? Did you see them commit heinous deeds, witness their trial, and agree with the evidence? Or did you just believe because you were told? Did you just kill them because you were ordered to?'

He's too young to ask such questions. He *sounds* like my brother, yet he has the wisdom of one much older.

'I live to kill,' I respond automatically.

'You're not alive, Alina,' Karson laughs, and suddenly a mirror like the one in the Heart Stone chamber is before me. *'Look!'*

'What are you talking about?' I laugh, admiring my reflection as it appears. 'I look better than ever!'

'Don't trust everything you see in a mirror. Look closer.'

I step nearer. It's true; under closer inspection, everything changes.

Now my reflection looks back at me, dead-eyed. Torn clothes droop over a skeletal frame from which flesh hangs and maggots feast.

'If you walk in the dark, Alina, you cannot see who you are, and you'll soon become worse!'

'Worse. How can it become worse?' I hear myself croak through putrid lips, my swollen tongue barely shaping the words.

'It's because soon you'll only see what you want to see. What THEY want you to see.'

My image in the mirror shimmers, and there is the me I recognise. Strong, a bold look in my eyes. Or is it a cold, dead look?

'You must remember. Don't trust everything you see in a mirror. Promise me you won't forget,' pleads Karson, his hands pressed together as if in prayer.

I go to take him in my arms, but he backs away, shaking his head, fading with every step.

Then his voice is but a fading memory as I sleep without further dreams.

***

Darkness still holds me firmly in its warm embrace. The moon globe is dim, and I can sense it's still early morning. My nightmare has awoken me before my sleep infusion was ready to relinquish its hold. It's rare for me to experience such troubled sleep, for usually, it's deep, uninterrupted, and filled with a feeling of contentment.

This latest nightmare with Karson has affected me badly. I blink back tears. It shocks me, for none have fallen other than through physical pain for so long.

Thankfully, mantras ring in my mind, pushing back against this moment of weakness.

Only the strong survive.

How true.

In fact, of all the mantras we've learned, this is the truest of them all.

Yet tonight it doesn't offer the solace it usually does.

There are still about another two hours until it's time to rise, but I don't wish to go back to sleep to find the mountains of bodies waiting to smother and suffocate me. To suffer Karson's accusing eyes and judgmental comments.

I miss my brother, his loving arms and cheeky smile, and loneliness, something I haven't felt in the longest time, tugs at my heart. A crazy thought comes to mind. However hard I push it away, it comes back, each time stronger than before, until it's irresistible in its intensity.

My mind made up, I swing my legs out of bed. My heartbeat threatens to rise, but I quash it. I've never dreamed of doing something like this in the years I've been here.

I step barefoot into the corridor, soundless as I tread softly but with purpose along their empty lengths. Never once have I stepped outside of my sleeping chamber this early. Surprisingly, there's peace to be found beneath the mountain before everyone arises. I sense it slumbers like those harboured within it.

As I pass the chambers where Nestor, Orphea, Fianna and Lotane should be, I can't help but pause, looking at their empty beds, and my heart aches anew.

Fight to live. Yes, that couldn't be more appropriate.

I falter as I near Lystra's chamber.

'Complete your mission,' I whisper, and my resolve firms as if made of steel.

I'd never considered manipulating my conditioning to further my own agenda.

I glance inside as I creep past. It's abnormal to see Lystra as vulnerable, but there she is, fast asleep, features uncharacteristically soft and peaceful. Her chamber always surprises me, for it's full of books. She's as much a scholar as a killer.

As I progress, I unconsciously brush my fingers along the rocky walls and hum a lullaby that comes to mind from my childhood. Thanks to my magic, I'll be aware of the vibration of someone approaching, like a spider with its leg on a web.

Eventually, I arrive at my destination without meeting anyone. At this hour, it appears no one wanders the mountain. The Chosen are sleeping soundly under the influence of their infusions, and whilst I'm sure the numerous entrances to the mountain remain guarded, those within are no longer considered a threat.

Before me is blank rock, yet I step forward and don't even need to go through the charade of placing my hands on the wall. My desire alone is sufficient to evoke my magic to act. The rock parts before me, and I project thoughts of gratitude as I step into the short passageway beyond.

Doubt suddenly grips me.

What will be the repercussions if I'm found here? Only the strong survive, whereas my action might be perceived as a weakness.

I push forward, resolute.

A chamber opens before me, and there in the middle sits the Heart Stone, and the angst I experienced recedes as my heart responds to its rhythmic beat. Alongside it, the mirror of no reflection stands.

I'm not alone.

There, on three small carts, lie Fianna, Nestor, and Lotane. They're fast asleep, breathing evenly, and their colour is good, a far cry from when I'd last seen them.

Nonetheless, they're swaddled in bandages, but at least there's no sign of blood soaking through the pristine wrappings.

Nestor had been made to fight again with a broken foot. Only his incredible capacity for pain had seen him through. There'd been no finesse in his next fight. He'd simply thrown himself at his confident opponent in a surprise move. His foe, a Surian, had thrust, his sword lancing into Nestor's side. Nestor, teeth gritted, had pushed forward, and I'd watched it exit his back. With the sword trapped inside him, Nestor grabbed the shocked Surian, then plunged his dagger repeatedly into the man's neck until they both fell, a bloodied mess.

Fianna. I'd trained with her countless times, yet perhaps never really appreciated her skill. Her first opponent had underestimated the fair-haired beauty and died swiftly. Unfortunately, the next one had been strong and fought with a spear as if born with it in his hand. Fianna had been pierced a half dozen times before twisting past the weapon's deadly point to deliver a killing blow.

Lotane had fought two stocky soldiers from Hastia. He'd taken some deep sword wounds from the first, then some nasty gashes from a spiked flail after. They were numerous enough to warrant his stay here due to blood loss.

Orphea was the biggest surprise of all. She'd fallen to a willow-lean Tarsian who'd chosen a rapier and a dagger as his weapons. She'd fought almost indifferently as if the outcome was preordained in her favour and had paid for her hubris. The Tarsian was the only one to survive from the prisoners, and I wonder briefly where he is now. Was his life spared as promised? I wish I knew.

Stepping forward, I lean over Lotane. His face, which has taken on a more serious look over the last few years, has relaxed, and he's more like that boy who saved my life.

I warm at the memory and lean down, unable to resist, for this is what I need. Taking Lotane's hand in mine, I brush my lips against his. How have my feelings suddenly grown so strong that I couldn't wait to see him?

Everything is exquisite being here. Lotane beside me with the Heart Stone pulsing and my heart beating with its rhythm. I know Lotane's and the others do too. This is why they're here, because its presence helps their recovery.

I smooth back Lotane's unruly hair, my fingers caressing his face, entranced by the fullness of his lips. It still amazes me that someone so attractive can be drawn to me. Until him, no one had looked my way because they found me beautiful; it was always a morbid fascination at my ghostly complexion and yellow eyes.

A tugging on my mind brings me alert. Softly placed footsteps accompanied by the gentle hiss of muted conversation whisper in my ear. I shouldn't be surprised that Lotane and the others would be checked on throughout the night, but I hadn't been thinking straight.

Fortunately, the ssythlans will enter the Heart Stone chamber from the passages on their side of the mountain, so my escape route is clear.

Without my magic, I'd have been discovered. I hasten down the corridor, retracing my steps.

Lotane will recover, and my heart thumps happy again.

When I return to sleep, my dreams will be full of him.

***

'Only two more years before *he* walks amongst us,' Nestor muses.

He's just returned somewhat sheepishly from his long sojourn with Fianna and Lotane.

Alyssa finishes chewing some food and grins.

'Two years seems like a long time, yet I'm sure we'll be kept busy in the interim.'

Fianna sits next to me, occasionally resting her head on my shoulder.

Lotane's foot gently rests on mine under the table. I know he's a little envious, and so am I. We keep our feelings a closely guarded secret. If only we were allowed to *be together* out in the open. This is a constant source of frustration for me. I should be happy, and in general, I am. But as my love for Lotane grows, I feel conflicted.

Love. I smile to myself. This is the first time I've admitted that my feelings have grown to such an extent.

Kralgen drops a bone on the plate he's been gnawing on like a wolf. Often, when he speaks, there's a statement to draw people's attention. After years of silently deferring to his brother, it's as though he thinks no one will listen otherwise.

'One thing that puzzles me is where he's coming from? I'm positive he isn't going to step through that mirror. So, will he arrive by ship, and where does he currently live? Is he in exile somewhere?'

Fianna's laughter peels out, and Kralgen's glare is ferocious at what he perceives as mockery.

'It was so quiet here when you weren't around,' he grumbles. 'Perhaps you can get chopped up again, and we can have some peace back!'

'Oh, don't be so grumpy, Kralgen,' Fianna teases. 'I am laughing because I've been wondering the same thing. He's The Once and Future King, so he must have ruled before ... but when and where? We've learned so much history since we've been here. I know the royal houses' names stretching back decades across the kingdoms, yet he's never been mentioned. There are so many things I wish I'd felt able to ask him when we first saw him, and that's at the top of my list.'

Kralgen grunts, smiles briefly at Fianna, and then returns to eating.

Lotane taps a spoon against his bowl and then waves it toward Fianna and Kralgen.

'I agree. I now have so many questions, all in a similar vein.'

'What about you, Malina? What do you think?' Kralgen asks, eyebrow raised.

Kralgen's change of attitude toward me is refreshing. Having emerged unscratched from my bouts at the last purge, he's displaying a newfound respect for my skills and opinion.

After a moment's consideration, I shake my head.

'I may as well wonder why the sun rises in the east and sets in the west every day. It does, and that's all that matters. Does it matter from where he comes? That is just to quench our idle curiosity. What matters is that he's coming, and we'll be here waiting.'

'Well said,' says Kralgen, thumping his hand on the table.

Lotane grins.

'Just think. One more year to the Revelation, and we'll find out what our roles will be. I already have a good idea of what they are. Malina here will hunt fresh meat for his table. Kralgen will butcher it, and Alyssa will cook it. Then Nestor will fashion flawless dishes for the food that Fianna serves to the king, and thus we all have our place.'

We laugh, for these are happy days because the king is coming.

'What about you, Lotane?' I ask, tapping his foot. 'What will you be?'

Before he can answer, Kralgen looks up, raising a greasy hand.

'I can tell you that. He'll be the jester, the court fool,' and he tosses some food at Lotane, who catches it in his mouth.

Lotane stretches out, arms spread, a huge grin on his face.

'I like that idea, Kralgen. I'll ask Lystra to put a friendly word in for me. See if she can get me the job. Now, watch this!' Lotane grimaces in concentration and small flames appear, dancing on his fingertips. When he pops them one by one into his mouth as if to hide them, flames grow from his ears.

Such moments are rare, and I smile, yet something is niggling me, and it slowly fades.

Here we are, around a table, laughing and joking. There's so much space with just the six of us where once there were ten.

Who were the others? I struggle to remember them.

Of course, there was Orphea, but the other's faces and names have faded. I look around as if that will help me picture them.

'What are you looking for?' asks Nestor, seeing my questing stare.

'I was trying to remember the others.'

'The others?' asks Kralgen. 'Other than Bardel, what others?'

He's genuinely perplexed, and that same look is shared by everyone.

'Orphea, your brother, and then there was ...' Yet for the life of me, I can't remember.

Alyssa nods slowly. 'Orphea and Bardel. Yes, of course.'

'Only the strong survive,' Kralgen growls. 'Orphea was weak, but we are strong. That's why we won't be forgotten. Look at Malina there; she's strong. She took a man's head clean off with a single blow. That's no mean feat.'

Kralgen raises his cup to me, and I gratefully return the salute. More so because the memory of my opponent's death is tinged with a golden glow. It was a glorious, crowning moment. I'm also relieved that mentioning Bardel's name hadn't soured our bonding.

Having finished our food with the setting sun casting long shadows across the terrace, we drink our sleep infusion and head back to our respective chambers.

Before long, I'm lying on my bed, a sense of well-being warming me.

Inside I sense my magic. As Kralgen had pointed out, I'd easily won both my bouts, bringing back to mind how I'd used it.

Unknown to everyone, I'd summoned its aid against my opponents.

Like when I'd helped Nestor survive, my magic had hindered their footsteps, but it hadn't stopped there. Hair and dirt were blown into eyes, and my opponents' sweat had run onto their sword grips before we even exchanged blows.

We hadn't been told not to use all the skills at our disposal, so I'd simply ensured my victory.

Only the strong survive, and not all strength is found in muscle and sinew; it's also in the mind, heart and soul.

A Soul. Do I even have one anymore?

Yes, I'm sure I do. I strive to serve one who would bring peace to this world. Whilst I may have taken lives, they were evil men. Although the one who had allowed Nestor to live ... was he evil? And if he wasn't, what about the others?

With such a troublesome thought in mind, I fall asleep.

***

CHAPTER IX

Lotane's hands gently hold my face as we lie under the protective cover of a whirl tree's branches. These beautiful giants of nature look like someone has spun them, so their limbs circle around the trunk. They're evergreen, yet some fallen fronds have created a soft blanket for us to relax on. In the near distance, the surf crashes on the beach, its rhythmic pounding matching our hearts.

We're south of the Mountain of Souls, but few come this way. As we're considerably north of the Serpent's Spines, we're safe from the red wolves, but considering what we're doing, we're still in dangerous territory.

Who'd have thought that we'd be given Suntarg, the seventh day off, to do as we please as long as we return before sunset. Lystra had told us that our privileges would grow over time, and they have continued to do so.

Kralgen uses his free time to hone his martial skills like any other day, and Alyssa often follows suit. Nestor practices his earth magic incessantly, and Fianna, I think, flits between them all.

I wonder what Lystra would do if she suspected something was growing between me and Lotane.

His lips are soft, in direct contrast to the hardness of his body which I pull tight against me. All the times we had to restrain, to hold back, and now we indulge in each other.

But only so far.

There's no doubt I'd give myself to Lotane and join with him, but by unspoken assent, we deny ourselves this pleasure. We can't jeopardise being discovered by taking the final step from which there'd be no return.

I know some infusions prevent pregnancy, yet it's not something we've been taught, and I can't just ask. Until such time as it's safe to couple, we take pleasure in finding other ways to bring each other to release. Lotane's lips are moving slowly up my arm, lingering in the crook of my elbow, sending shivers throughout my body before moving up to my neck and ear. It's ecstasy.

'We have time,' Lotane moans huskily. The soft warmth of his breath alone almost melts my resistance, but instead, I untangle myself from his enfolding arms.

For one so muscled and powerful, his touch can be as gentle as a summer breeze. It's a delightful contrast.

I smile, softening my rejection.

'I think we both need to cool down. We can't have Lystra seeing you limping back in such a state,' and I wink, for his arousal is plain to see despite his loose clothing.

'You're right,' he reluctantly nods, levering himself to his feet. 'I hate that you're always right, but I love it too.'

He's said that word. We haven't said it directly to one another. Perhaps we're both waiting for the right time. Yet it matters not when we feel it in each other's arms.

Reaching down, Lotane pulls me effortlessly to my feet. I'm at least his equal in most things and better than him in many others, yet he makes me feel safe with his physical strength. His hugs alone could make arrows shy away from us.

'Want a race to the beach?' he asks.

The twinkle in his eye makes the challenge more of a game. If anyone else asked me that, I'd do everything to beat them and more. But our races aren't a competition; they're almost a mating ritual, like a bird showing off its coloured feathers.

'Mind that you don't catch it on a tree,' I laugh with a grin and head off.

'Oh gods, I hadn't thought of that,' I hear him mutter as I leave him behind.

Laughing so hard, I can barely breathe, I run toward the western coastline.

I'm exhilarated, my heart beating happily, laughter loud in my ears. Lotane is so far behind, but I'm hot and can't wait to cool down in the sea, so I increase my speed some more. Being slight, I weave through the foliage like a dance. I duck, roll, twist and turn, avoiding every grasping vine or drooping leaf. It's something I gain pleasure from, outwitting nature and its many obstacles, and also part of our training. Leaving a trail that a foe can easily follow is to invite danger. I barely leave a mark.

Nonetheless, despite my self-imposed urgency, I keep looking over my shoulder, but Lotane is nowhere to be seen. I smile, feeling a tingle inside me, happy my charms have a long-lasting effect.

I turn my attention forward and sprint through the last bit of foliage onto the beach. The tops of the waves greet me, glistening like a thousand stars, but then I stumble to a halt, briefly incredulous at the sight marring the perfect vista.

Just offshore are two galleys.

The furthest boasts a sleek, shark-like silhouette and is a pristine Delnorian war galley.

The closest burns furiously from bow to stern with a gaping hole in its side. From the top of its single mast flutters a smoking flag of Tars, a black hawk holding a red arrow on a yellow background. I watch, astonished, as it lists and starts to slip beneath the waves. As the angle increases, flaming crates on the stricken ship's deck break free of their lashings. This merchant galley is doomed.

Crawling or collapsed on the beach are perhaps a dozen survivors and in the waves between the shore and the ship are maybe a half dozen more, some hanging on to flotsam, others splashing helplessly amongst the waves. It amazes me how few sailors can actually swim, but then neither could I until I'd come here.

I'm frozen for a moment. This island is forbidden to those who don't live on it. But then, my father comes to mind, dying in a watery grave, and I can't stand by when those struggling to survive could be a father, mother, son or daughter.

Kicking my boots off, I rush past those who've found the sanctuary of land. I fight against the crashing surf, wading until the water reaches my chest, then dive under the next roller. There's a tranquillity below the surface despite the turbulence of the incoming tide, and I use the undertow of water to carry me out. As I rise to catch my breath, I can hear the cries for help above the crashing waves.

I set off, swimming powerfully, wondering if my magic can help, and in tune with my thoughts, it responds immediately. It feels as if the undertow rises and carries me along. I no longer fight the incoming tide on the surface, and my strokes bring me effortlessly to the nearest splashing figure.

It's dangerous to approach a bad swimmer, for they can push you under in a panic, so I swim below the surface and come up behind the man. Fortunately, he's weak and on the verge of giving up, so when I put my arm around his neck and order him to lean back and kick, he responds without incident.

I head for shore, the man's weight a burden, but the tide helps. I don't know if my magic does too, but I'm reticent to call upon it constantly in case I'm tired out when I need my strength the most.

As I reach shallow water, Lotane is there, and stepping forward, he helps with the sailor. Together we drag him onto the sand, away from the clutching sea that sought to claim him, then drop him next to some of his crewmates. They're all in terrible shape and unable to help.

Lotane points to a head bobbing in the water, and we both run back into the crashing surf. This woman isn't too far; the tide is bringing her in. Grateful, bloodshot eyes show relief as we arrive before her strength gives out.

Lotane and I make easy progress back to the shore, yet I'm gasping for air by the time we reunite her with the ship's other crew.

Having taken a moment to briefly catch our breath, we're about to head back out when one of the Tarsians struggles to his knees and then stands up.

'Stop,' he croaks. After licking his lips, he says it with a hint of command in his tired voice. 'Stop!'

'Why? There are more of your crew we could help.'

My glare adds weight to my words, but the man stands firm. After all, I'm just a young woman, and he, it would seem, from the braid on his jacket, might well have been the captain of the sinking vessel.

'There's no point. We're all dead anyway. Those bastard Delnorians are coming to finish the job.'

He points over my shoulder.

I've no idea how it escaped my notice, but at the end of the beach, the Delnorian war galley has beached, and dozens of leather-armoured soldiers are swarming down a gangplank.

The bedraggled captain comes to stand at my shoulder, accepting my strange appearance with nothing more than a blink.

'Thank you, girl. Not many would have done what you did. You've a good heart. Now, you and your man need to run and save yourselves. I'll stay with my crew. They don't have the strength to escape or fight, and I won't leave them.'

'See if they have any weapons,' I command Lotane.

While I keep an eye on the Delnorians, he hurries to the shivering, moaning sailors, frisks them, and returns shortly with two long, sheathed daggers.

The captain shrugs as if in apology.

'We were a merchant vessel. All my crew ever carried were daggers, and my sword is on the seabed out there.'

'Give them to me.' I reach out my hand.

Lotane hands them over, accompanied by a quizzical expression.

'You won't need one, as you'll get help.'

I reach behind, pushing them out of sight under my trousers' drawstring.

'Tell Lystra what's going on and get back bloody quickly. If you stay, there'll definitely be a fight, and you'll die.'

'Girl,' the captain interrupts. 'Those Delnorians could do worse than just kill you. Both of you should go now! Our lives aren't worth yours.'

I ignore the captain. I can't let these men be slaughtered on the beach. This is not Delnorian land; this is ssythlan territory, Chosen territory, and these survivors are now under my protection. If only someone had been there to save my father.

'Lotane. You said earlier how I'm always right. Well, this is one of those times. Now, don't let me down. Run like the wind!'

He holds my gaze with those blue-green eyes as he gives me the briefest kiss, then turns and sprints for the woods.

I watch him go, then turn to see twenty Delnorian marines spreading out in line formation. A galley the size of the one beached can carry up to fifty fighting men, but the captain is prudent, leaving slightly more than half to guard his vessel. Their leather armour is dyed a pale cream with blue highlights, and the blue feather of their crested helms wave in the sea breeze. Round shields with a bronze boss are raised defensively at the front of their line, swords held at the ready. Four archers walk just behind, arrows nocked, prepared to draw. The Delnorian captain, with a red plume to denote his position, advances at the centre, leading by example.

I'm tempted to run. The Delnorians are too far away to stop me, but I await their approach, and a plan starts to take shape in my mind.

Yet as they get closer, a chill runs down my spine.

There's no escaping the look of dark intent in the soldiers' eyes.

They intend to kill everyone.

***

It will take Lotane an hour to reach the mountain, then who knows how long for Lystra to be found and help to be rallied, perhaps an hour. Add another to return, and three hours will have passed.

I certainly can't fight twenty trained marines and prevail, so I'll likely be dead in the next five minutes.

Magic swells within me, almost as if demanding release; fire to burn them, earth to swallow them, wind to hurl them away like leaves on the wind, and water to have the seas rise up to wash them away.

Is it my thoughts that conjure these images or those of the sentient magic residing within me?

Irrespective, no one has such power, yet perhaps my lesser magic and cunning can help me overcome the odds instead.

With fists clenched behind me, conditioning takes over, and calm replaces the nerves.

The merchant captain stands silently beside me, and his crew only have the strength to sit up or roll onto their sides to see their death approaching. They appear resigned to their fate.

'Stay back, say nothing and do nothing,' I hiss from the corner of my mouth to the Tarsian.

The Delnorians are perhaps twenty paces distant. They move slowly, eyes scanning the treeline. They're cautious on foreign soil, showing how experienced they are. No rushing to simply slaughter a waiting, helpless prey.

Stepping forward, chin held high, I cross half the distance towards them, arms held wide.

'Welcome, Captain.'

I speak High Delnorian, not the common tongue. It's used solely by nobility, denoting their rank. The captain will have a rudimentary understanding, as his training for command will have included basic instruction on how to greet the upper echelons of his superiors.

Surprise flashes across his eyes. It's hard to read more because of the helm, but the fact he bangs his sword twice against his shield, instructing the advance to stop, shows I've made an impact.

It's time to press my small advantage.

'Remove your helm when I'm addressing you.' Again. I use High Delnorian.

This time he looks nonplussed, which isn't surprising. He understands greetings but can't converse.

I switch to the common tongue.

'My apologies, captain,' I say with a warm smile. 'It's been too long since I spoke my mother tongue. Is it no longer customary to remove your helm when addressing a superior?'

I wait as his mind tries to come to grips with a scenario he wasn't anticipating. His rigid military training and respect for authority are stifling his judgement.

'Well?' I snap. 'Has my father passed a law changing a tradition that has remained in place since time immemorial?'

It's a huge gamble I'm playing. The High King himself is the only person able to change such a law, and here I am, pretending to be his daughter. Yet if I positioned myself as minor nobility, I would have very little authority, and my knowledge of Delnor is limited to the central royal family and isn't that extensive.

The captain slowly removes his helm and steps forward from the line. His sunburnt and scarred face is etched with confusion and a heavy dose of disbelief.

I look pointedly at his sword, and he reluctantly sheaths it, but I note he doesn't order his men to do the same.

'Forgive me, highness,' he says, but his voice lacks the deference I'd hoped for. 'I'm unaware of me noble king, Arndel, 'aving any children other than his son, Sarndel. He looks askew at me, his fingers lingering near his sword hilt.

Whispers in my mind point out not all isn't it should be. The training I've received spots the trap before it's sprung. 'Well, captain. Firstly, when you pronounce my poor dead brother's name, at least have the decency to do so properly. *Serndel* was, of course, heir to the throne. As his illegitimate sister, I'm not common knowledge to the wider population for obvious reasons!'

'You don't bear no resemblance to the king nor any Delnorian I've ever laid me eyes on,' presses the captain, reluctant to believe I am who I pretend to be. 'What ya doing on this beach dressed like a peasant if you is who you say you is?'

It's true. My light green face, multi-hued arms, and yellow eyes mark me as different to any race I could bring to mind. These are a far cry from the traditional olive skin, dark hair, and brown eyes these people have, and my plain black clothes are hardly fit for a princess.

'Do you think I'd be exiled here if my heritage was obvious?' I snap angrily. 'Nor do we stand in the Hall of Ancients where I'd be measured by my bejewelled hair!'

I don't give him time to frame a response.

'Now, enough of your impertinence. What are you and your men doing on this island? These are ssythlan lands, and they've been neutral for a reason since the war began!'

'Ain't it obvious? I'm 'ere to finish the job I started out there!' The captain jerks his head toward the sea. 'We've chased 'em for nigh on a week, the slippery bastards. Now, if yer highness will stand aside, I'll do so and be on me way!'

I'm pleased to note the eyes of his men are darting back and forth between us; their resolve shaken. Unfortunately, the captain's appears to be firm. I've obviously read him wrong, and my challenging tone has irked him into intransigence.

'Really? You intend to commit an act of aggression and war on a neutral country's soil to simply satisfy your bloodlust, killing your enemies? You ... a mere captain of the navy, are going to risk this escalating? No. You will do no such thing!'

'If you is who you say you is, then they is *your enemies* too,' growls the Delnorian captain. 'There's none lower than a godless Tarsian to a noble like yourself, even if you is a bastard. So, princess, let us kill 'em, and we'll take the bodies with us. No one will know. Problem solved.'

He's caught me in my own trap. The Tarsians are perceived as heathens, godless people, and are, of course, enemies of Delnor in the great war. There's no reason I wouldn't do as he suggests unless ...

'The *problem* with your otherwise perfect plan, captain, is that you won't be going anywhere for the next few hours. You've beached your galley with the tide coming in and the unpredictable wind that accompanies it blowing to shore. I suggest you wait another hour or two for the danger of these gusts to die, and then, yes, you have my blessing to rid the world of these stinking Tarsians and be on your way. But NOT before we know you're unseen and can do this without being discovered.

'For all we know, there's a ssythlan delegation coming any moment now. My bodyguard is already on its way!'

'Wind. What wind?' There's nowt but a gentle sea breeze.' The Delnorian captain's eyes have narrowed, full of distrust. His hand is openly gripping the hilt of his sword. 'You're making this all up, and the only reason is ...'

I don't let him finish his accusation, for I'm already releasing the magic within me, calling upon its assistance. I imagine gusts that buffet the Delnorians, something that would make getting their galley back out to sea a tremendously difficult endeavour.

With a roar, a gust confined to the stretch of beach occupied by the Delnorians picks up a cloud of sand that hits hard enough to sweep half the soldiers off their feet.

The wind hasn't come near me, the Tarsian captain, or his sailors, but even so, I stagger as my energy is instantly drained to feed this potent display. I curse, promising myself to be more precise with my thoughts.

'Do not doubt my word again, captain!' I say, moving over to him, ensuring I maintain an aura of superiority. I stand tall, despite wanting to curl up and fall asleep. My magical display has left me exhausted.

'You men,' I snap, looking at the Delnorian marines as they pick themselves up, shaking off sand and blinking it from their eyes. 'Guard these captives, and let no harm come to them until I return with your captain!'

The marines jump to do my bidding, moving around the Tarsians, kicking them into a huddle.

Despite having little strength left, I want to ensure the wide-eyed Delnorian captain has no doubts remaining. I raise my hand.

'Listen. You can hear the wind approaching before it arrives if you can filter out the sound of the surf and the forest. Another gust will be arriving ...'

It hits at my request, far less forceful, yet still enough that everyone turns their heads from the stinging sand.

'In all me years at sea, I ain't never come across this before,' he shakes his head in wonder. 'I apologise, yer highness, for doubting you.'

Thank the gods, my bluff has held true. Now I just need to play for time until Lotane returns.

'You're forgiven, Captain. Now, walk with me and tell me how our forces are faring. The tide turns in about two hours, as will the wind. If we remain undisturbed till then, you can do with these Tarsians as you will.'

I set off along the beach, managing to catch the Tarsian captain's eye as I do. He sits with his sailors on a dune, looking dejected, surrounded by a ring of Delnorian marines. I nod reassuringly and see relief and hope blossom in his eyes.

The Tarsians' lives are in my hands.

I will save them all.

***

Lystra and her fellow instructors keep us informed about the conflicts besetting the wider world. I'm well versed in the evil and greed of the Delnorian empire that once stretched west to Sea Hold, north to the Frozen Sea, east to Suria and south to Tars.

War had sundered the empire ten years ago when Suria, Rolantria, Hastia and Tars decided to throw off the yoke of the High King's tyrannical rule. Since then, despite supposed attempts to end the War of Independence, armies continued to clash across the lands and seas. The only realms to remain neutral are Icelandia, which remains friendly with Delnor, Ssythla, and surprisingly, Astoria.

Brief truces are sundered by assassinations, raids or skirmishes as immoral generals seek to take advantage of temporary ceasefires. In truth, we're told no one side is righteous, with atrocities committed by all.

However, after so long, the strength of the Delnorian military is finally starting to tell. According to Lystra, it won't be long before Delnor grips the rebel kingdoms tightly in its mailed fist once more.

Thankfully, The Once and Future King's arrival will end this tyranny, bringing peace and prosperity.

'So, tell me, captain,' I open the conversation as he catches up, 'this is the first time I've seen one of our galleys this far south. What brings you reaving this way?'

'Well, we've managed to thrust an army south into Tars, sundering their country down the middle. Despite 'em being godless heathens, I 'ave to admit they've put up a good fight these last years. One of their main forces is holed up in their damned coastal fortress town of Tarsala, and we're starving 'em into submission. We're blockading the port so they can't get supplies from the Hastians. Occasionally some ships slip out during the night, but we hunt 'em down. We've warned them good enough that if they surrender, we'll spare 'em, but they just keep on fighting.

'Your father even offered 'em full clemency. All they 'ave to do is lay down their arms, return to their 'omes and promise to stay out of the fight, but so far, they're fighting tooth n claw. They're adamant Delnor sent assassins to kill their royal family, and you know how they is when it comes to the royal bloodline. Without gods, that's all they 'ave. So, royal blood spilt must be answered by royal blood spilt. Considering that, you best keep yer identity closely guarded.'

He looks pointedly at me, tapping his hooked nose for emphasis as if to say my secret will stay safe with him.

'The thing is,' he continues, 'if we can get the godless Tarsians outta the fight, then Hastia will surrender straight away 'cause we can attack 'em from the south and north. They know they're doomed if that happens.'

'Getting Rolantria and Suria to surrender might be a step closer then. Gods, it'll be a blessing to see this damned war done. Too many good men and women 'ave been lost on both sides, and that ain't counting the civilians. I ain't seen me wife or children in three months. Yet least they're safe, unlike so many poor souls.

'I admit I'm worn out by this killing. Would you believe I was a trading galley captain, plying me wares all the way to Astoria before this? May those days come again soon.'

We walk in silence, and I'm shocked by his words, for they're like nothing I expected to hear. The High King of Delnor offering clemency to the Tarsians if they surrender, a Delnorian galley captain tired of killing, wanting to see the end of the war. The Delnorians are ruthless warmongers, empire builders and oppressors!

This flies in the face of what I've learned. He must be lying, but the captain speaks with belief and assurance.

Maybe I can convince him to let the Tarsians live. Then he and his galley can be on their way.

'You're right, captain,' I soothe. 'This killing has been going on far too long. Why don't we take the first step and stop it here? Let these Tarsians live. They can't go anywhere now their ship is sunk.'

The captain looks sharply at me from under bushy eyebrows.

'You know I can't. I'm under direct orders, and even you don't have the authority to contradict 'em. Don't ask again. However, you was right about not killing 'em 'ere on neutral soil. The last thing we need is a diplomatic incident and 'ave the lizzies in a hissing fury.'

Shielding his face, he looks skyward, gauging the time. 'The tide will turn in an hour. We'll bring 'em to the galley, then dispose of the bodies at sea when we're done. No sailor likes the idea of drowning, but the sea is a mistress for life, however capricious she may be. Their souls will find peace in the depths even without a god to greet 'em when they die.'

Even while ordering their death, he's trying to do the right thing. There's genuine regret in his voice, certainly no fervour, like when Lystra speaks about The Once and Future King. Here's a man undertaking a distasteful duty out of necessity, with free will and regret.

Free will. I wonder if I have that anymore.

Shouts of alarm make us turn to see the guards overseeing the Tarsian sailors, pointing further along the beach to where figures have appeared.

My heart leaps, for Lotane has returned with Lystra, my fellow Chosen, and a host of guards. In total, they number about thirty, a sizeable force that the captain will have to take seriously.

'Damn it,' the Delnorian captain growls as he jogs back up the beach toward his men.

I run alongside, happy that the Delnorians will now be forced to leave the Tarsians alive, averting further bloodshed.

'Don't worry, Captain,' I assure him. 'The Tarsians will be held securely when you depart. No word of their survival will reach other Tarsian ears. The main thing is you sunk their ship, denying their army further supplies. You can be proud of what you've accomplished. I'll go talk to Commander Lystra. She leads my mercenary guard and will ensure no one speaks of what they've witnessed here.'

It seems lying comes easily to me. First, I'm a princess, and now Lystra is a commander. Maybe I'll introduce Lotane as a chef.

The captain halts just shy of his men and looks at me as I stop alongside.

'My name's Drakal, Captain Drakal, yer highness. It's been an honour. Please introduce Commander Lystra so we can exchange pleasantries, and then we'll make ready to depart. Thankfully, that devilish wind seems to have disappeared.'

Smiling, I jog off, relief washing over me. My life had been in peril when this all started, let alone the lives of the Tarsians. Now, with my friends approaching, the situation has been saved.

Despite the soft sand, I make swift progress, moving lightly across the beach to stand before Lystra. She's encased in sweat-stained leather armour, armed with a sword, dagger and shield. Those behind are similarly armed and armoured, although I spy a few spears and bows.

Lystra's eyes are full of fire, but there's the subtlest softening of her features as she surveys me. Behind her, Lotane and Fianna's broad smiles warm my heart. Nestor, Alyssa and Kralgen also nod in recognition. I want to run and feel Lotane's arms around me, but this isn't the time or place.

'I expected to find your body covered in flies.' Lystra shakes her head. 'However, I shouldn't be surprised by now, should I, Wolf Slayer? What happened after you sent Lotane to get us? How did you survive?'

I quickly retell my story as we move at a slower pace toward the waiting Delnorians.

'The illegitimate daughter of the High King of Delnor. That's the most outrageous lie I've ever heard.' Lystra's laughter peels out. 'Did the crew hear this or just the captain?'

'They all heard and believed it. There's no doubt in their minds,' I reassure her.

'I applaud your bravery,' Lystra says, taking my arm, pausing briefly, 'but the risk you took was unnecessary and unwise. You put yourself in danger, not for another Chosen, not for a mission, but for strangers to whom we know no allegiance and who have no value.'

She turns and marches on, the gap closing between us and the waiting Delnorians and Tarsians.

I want to argue; tell her that every life has value, and for that reason alone, it was worth the risk, but I don't wish to invoke her ire. Not once have I disagreed with Lystra in all these years, for to argue is to die.

All the Tarsians are sitting up, having recovered from their near drowning. The Tarsian captain raises his hand, and a wide grin settles on his face. I nod back, feeling touched by the gratitude in his eyes.

Captain Drakal steps cautiously forward whilst behind him, his men stand ready. Thankfully, their weapons are sheathed, but their hands linger near hilts or are poised, prepared to nock, and draw an arrow.

Lystra drops her shield to the ground in a gesture of trust and steps forward, extending her hand in greeting, her expression warm.

'Welcome to the Islands, Captain. Our royal charge,' and she nods to me, 'advises that you're of good intent and will be leaving on the tide. We expected trouble and only brought weapons when we should have brought wine, so please forgive my lack of courtesy.'

Captain Drakal's relief is evident. His force is currently outnumbered, even though he probably has another thirty men in the galley.

They grip forearm to forearm, then Lystra briefly embraces him before slowly walking away with the captain by her side.

Can this really be Lystra talking? I'm astounded by her demeanour and smiles. This is nothing like the Lystra I know. She is hard and unyielding. She is death.

I edge closer to Lotane and the others, keen to be close to my friends.

Kralgen and the rest of those around me follow Lystra's lead, drop their shields and step forward, extending arms in friendly greeting. The Delnorians follow suit, and the tension disappears as the threat of death dissipates like smoke on a breeze.

The Tarsians remain at our feet, looking up in bewilderment as men and women of war begin laughing in relief at the avoidance of bloodshed.

'Be ready,' Lotane whispers as he walks past to grip the hand of a Delnorian marine.

Be ready. The words are chilling, and Lystra's uncharacteristic behaviour suddenly makes sense.

A skilled warrior is no threat if completely disarmed.

'Delnorian marines.' The voice of Drakal cuts through the conversation, commanding everyone's attention. 'Commander Lystra has asked for the privilege to address you all.'

It's no coincidence every Delnorian marine now has a Chosen or a guard by their side.

Lystra's smile is radiant. She can be as beautiful as the rising sun. The leather kilt and greaves accentuate her bronzed-toned legs; the vambraces on her arms help define the lithe musculature, the cuirass and helm, her neck's gentle sweep.

She is a devil dressed as a goddess.

'Delnorians,' she begins, her voice carrying easily over the roar of the surf. 'Speeches are for politicians, not warriors, so I'll keep what I have to say short and to the point. Amongst those who stand beside you, we have a saying.'

She puts a hand around Captain Drakal's shoulder, drawing breath, creating an expectant pause.

'Only the strong survive!'

No hint of dark intent is revealed as her other hand moves smoothly past her waist, drawing her dagger, and in the same motion, drives it up into the neck of the unsuspecting captain.

Almost every Delnorian marine is slaughtered in the next heartbeat, and only one manages to pull free in time to draw his sword. He backs away, eyes wide, terror etched upon his face.

An arrow whistles past my ear and takes him in the eye.

I expect him to fall dead instantly, but his hand grasps the shaft, his jaw hanging open, mewling like a cat. Then slowly, he sinks to his knees and falls face down in the sand.

My heart pumps furiously before slowing a beat later. I haven't even drawn my daggers as I wasn't aware of the plan, but nor do I need to.

Whimpering catches my attention, and I look around to see the frightened Tarsian sailors looking up at us.

Lystra walks over to me.

'Complete the mission; kill them. The ssythlans have taken care of the others on the ship.'

Along the beach, the galley burns furiously, consumed by elemental fire. Figures jump from its decks, but they cannot escape the flames.

The Tarsian captain is on his knees, incredulous.

'Why? Why would you do this? You saved my crew from the sea and the Delnorians!'

I reach out, gently smoothing thick black hair from his tanned face with my fingers.

'To obey is to live,' I explain, as my reservations are pushed aside by my training and conditioning. 'Now, close your eyes, and hold on to the sound of the sea.'

My other hand holds the hilt of one of the daggers pushed into my trousers.

The captain shakes uncontrollably, the piteous cries of his crew being slaughtered adding to the drawn-out agony of the moment.

For his sake, I end it swiftly.

***

Why? The Tarsian captain's question plagues my mind.

Today's bloodshed had been unnecessary, or so I'd thought, yet it had happened nonetheless, and it seems to matter to no one but me.

Nonetheless, when the order was given, my doubts had faded, duty and conditioning had won, and the killing had been too easy. Surely, taking lives and ending dreams should never be easy. I struggle to hold on to my remorse, but it slips through my fingers like grains of sand.

'Why didn't we just let those Delnorians get back on their ship? There was no danger anymore once you arrived.' I pose the question to the whole table as we sit eating dinner on the terrace.

Kralgen shrugs. I don't think killing bothers him any more than sneezing.

'What matter?' he grunts, stabbing some meat with a knife as if it were still alive and needed dispatching before bringing it to his mouth.

That, for him, is the end of the conversation.

'What about the rest of you?'

'Only the strong survive. You know that!' Alyssa waves dismissively. 'They weren't Chosen, and if they're not with us, they're part of this world's problems.'

Nestor nods emphatically. 'We can't be distracted from our mission. Keeping those Tarsians alive and under guard would have taken resources and time. The ssythlans might pose as neutral, but we're at war with the world until The Once and Future King brings peace under his rule.'

'Well said!' Lotane slaps his hand down on the table, and I'm both shocked and disappointed.

His half-smile of apology eases the hurt somewhat, and the gentle pressure of his foot on mine makes me return the smile. He's allowed his own perspective, but I thought him a gentler soul. He was once. We all were.

Only Fianna raises her voice in agreement. 'I can't see what harm it would have done to allow them to live. The Delnorians were going to leave, and the Tarsians could have been set to work on the fishing boats. They'd have definitely chosen that over death. However, Nestor also has it right. The killing will only stop when The Once and Future King takes his throne. We can't be distracted from our mission nor risk its nature being discovered.'

Those last words ring like a bell in my head, o*ur mission.*

The importance of duty, obeying orders, unquestioning allegiance and completing missions have been drilled into us when awake and asleep. Whatever the cost, it's justified.

Why does my faith waver? Am I worthy to serve the king if I doubt what's asked of me?

The thought makes me sick with worry. I must strive to put my doubts aside.

Everyone is finishing their food. As is customary, our evening water is infused with dream leaf. It is always the same. In all the years I've been here, the only change has been the strength. Tonight, it's stronger, and we'll be transported to the Heart Stone chamber.

Will it be to learn something new, or will it be to help us forget what happened today? It's as if our conscience is wiped clean, so memories of unpleasantness fade into nothingness.

I return to my chamber, bidding goodnight to the others as they stop off at theirs. I prepare for bed, clean, use the toilet, going through my pre-sleep routine. As I climb into bed, my boots are neatly at the end.

I know this will be reflected in every other room.

Fatigue pulls heavily on me.

I plump the pillow, elevating my head. I miss being able to look at Lotane as I go to sleep. I'd always keep my eyes half-closed, so it wasn't obvious.

My consciousness fades, and as it does, I see the Tarsian captain's face.

'Why?' he asks.

I hope this sleep is long, and I forget everything, so I don't have to answer that question.

***

CHAPTER X

You can't escape. We'll find and capture you. You think you can evade us; you're wrong!'

Lystra's last shouted words ring in my ears as I hunker down, observing the rocky landscape of the small and unpopulated hellhole of Skyle Island from my shady position. It takes only a day and a half to traverse from north to south and only half a day from east to west. Unlike Furness, full of bountiful wildlife, this place is devoid of life other than insects and lizards.

Rocks like broken teeth stick up from the surf surrounding the shoreline. What few trees that manage to grow here resemble skeletal arms, the bony fingers of the branches and twigs reaching to the sky. The leaves are grey as opposed to green, and droop like rotting skin, soon to decay and fall.

I half expected the air to smell putrid when I swam ashore at the one safe bay, but fortunately, the sea's fresh air sweeps across the landscape.

I've been alone here for two days, but now my pursuers have landed, and in the interim, I've discovered there are very few places to hide, and surely, they know them all already.

At the island's north end, small caves riddle the cliffs. The rocky beach at their base is hard to access, and the caves are unreachable when the tide is in. Had I stayed there, I'd have remained safe only so long as it was dark, and the sea lapped at their entrance.

A short journey west along the coast, the rocky ground is split by massive fissures as though some great beast has riven the island with claws the size of trees. These would be decent hiding places, but they're hardly innocuous.

Then finally, there's the peak of the island's small hill in the centre. It offers a good vantage point from which to spy pursuers, and that intelligence could be used to initially evade them. That would have been the best option.

Instead, I'm huddled in a sparse copse of trees overlooking the small cove where my pursuers have just landed. It's nearly useless as a hiding place, offering scant protection from the sun and no place for concealment other than behind the narrow trunks.

The distant but excited barking of wolfhounds tells me they've picked up my scent. There's been little I could use to disguise it, even though I tried. Foul-smelling and rotting seaweed hangs from my clothes, but the hounds aren't fooled.

A sharp screech has me tilt my head upward. A sin-hawk is scouring the island, acting as the eyes for the search party.

They think they'll catch me.

I could have used my magic, created a new cavern, and sealed myself in bar some air holes. The weakness with that plan is fresh water and food. This island has next to none, and I've no provisions. So far, puddles and shellfish have sustained me, but it's not enough. I'd have to come out eventually or die in the darkness. I'm already dehydrated and hungry.

No.

My plan is more audacious, and I just need a little luck for it to work.

'Come on. Take the bait,' I whisper.

A well-aimed throw with a rock earlier in the day had injured one of the few gulls that had come here to rest. That bird is now restrained, tied to a dead tree on the far side of the hilltop with strings of seaweed keeping its beak clamped shut so it can't peck free. I'd felt cruel leaving it thus, to die a slow death.

'Yes. There you go!'

The sin-hawk screeches, its piercing call discernible even from this distance.

As I hoped, the gull's attempts to fly with a broken wing have attracted the sin-hawk. Now the bird of prey circles above this irresistible sight, forgetting to hunt for the human prey it was supposed to.

I've ensured my scent trail runs strongly from the cove to the hilltop, having traversed the landscape there several times. Now with the hounds following my scent and the sure sign of the sin- hawk circling its prey, my pursuers set off at a run, north of my position, heading west.

'Fools!'

I smile, waiting for them to near the peak. Once over the ridge, they'll see my lure, but it will be too late.

I wait, biding my time, then set off at a run, stooped low.

No shouts of alarm sound. My pursuers are focused on making the peak, believing they're almost upon me, and I make it to the rise above the cove to find their boat tied to the small jetty, bobbing on the waves.

They haven't left a guard! How foolish to commit everyone to the search. But I'm a Chosen, and even unarmed, I'm dangerous.

A small pile of wooden crates sit on the beach, and I descend cautiously despite my instincts urging me to speed. Time might be on my side, but I want to be well gone from here before my ruse is discovered. Opening a crate, I find some drinking skins and dozens of food parcels inside.

'Thank you!' The gods approve of my plan and earn my gratitude.

Now I have the means to escape with a bounty of supplies. My pursuers have certainly come prepared, expecting me to hide in a cavern of my making. They'd have remained well-fed while I starved to death.

I heft a crate and carry it along the jetty, looking at the boat as I do so.

It has a single mast, a rudder at the back, and some oar hooks along the side. Big enough for eight men and four dogs, this craft isn't ideal. I'll struggle to manoeuvre it alone … however, I'm not truly alone.

My magic will save me, making the difficult task of getting this vessel into open water as easy as wishing for it.

I'll escape against all the odds and Lystra's prediction.

Two days without a good drink has left me light-headed, so I set the crate down, removing a skin.

Damn!

It's full of harsh-smelling wine. The others are all the same. Amongst the crates on the beach, there must be some water. The hounds can't drink wine.

Taking a few gulps to quench my immediate thirst, I throw the skin into the bottom of the boat and jog along the jetty. If I don't find water with the following two crates, I'll leave anyway. I can moor on another island and find fresh water there.

I pry open the lid of the next crate as nausea grips me in an iron fist.

How did I end up on my knees?

They've laced the bloody wine, the scent and taste obscuring the drug.

Damn them. Damn them all.

***

A hood is pulled roughly from my head, and I open my eyes, squinting into the guttering lantern light to find myself in a small cell with a robed captor.

I struggle to stand but can't move. My arms are bound behind me, and I'm secured to a sturdy wooden chair that seems bolted to the ground. My feet are also chained, thick steel bands around each ankle. I call upon my magic to see if I can release the manacles, but to no avail. When metal items have been so heavily fashioned, magic has little effect on them.

Nonetheless, I could use fire to kill this individual. However, he's too far away to have removed my hood. There must be someone else standing behind me. Even if I get lucky and kill them, I can't free myself and will die of starvation.

There's a wooden table on which an ominous wrapped bundle lies. The stained leather looks supple and creased from years of use.

'Tell me your name.'

The voice of the hooded figure is male, but his features are obscured by the shadow of his cowl. He's standing in the far corner of the room, a shadow within the shadows. Into the opposite corner, another figure moves to stand silently, confirming my suspicions.

'Malina. Malina Darksun.'

It's been so long since I've spoken my last name that it takes a moment to remember it. The birthname passed from mother to daughter. There's no point in lying. He can gain no advantage from knowing my name ... I've no family left to be threatened.

'Well, Malina. Who are you spying for?'

The voice is soft, even kind. I detect a hint of Surian. It's information I might be able to use later. He's straight to the point, sure in his line of questioning. There will be no games played here, no attempt to trick me. Just a direct interrogation and whatever else follows.

'I'm not a spy, sir.'

'Oh, Malina. Let me tell you how this will go. If you tell me the truth, I'll know, and we'll get along just fine. You'll be given food and water, and if you tell me everything, you'll be released and see the light of day again. You have my word.'

His voice is sincere and persuasive.

'So, let me ask you again. For whom do you spy?'

'I'm no spy, sir. I'm crew on a trading galley from the Isle of Sin.' I keep my voice low, allowing it to tremble a little. I bow submissively, then look up, eyes beseeching, pleading to be believed.

'What's the name of your vessel?'

'The Widow,' I reply promptly. The island ships are all named to reflect sadness, to remind everyone of the pain its people once faced.

'What's your position on board?'

'Oarswoman. Fourth bench on the port side.'

'You're lying!'

He moves across the room like a wraith from the afterworld.

'Bitch!'

He hits me across the face, the stinging slap making my eyes blur. Sobs shake my body. It's crucial to project weakness, so he won't believe I've the resolve to resist or lie.

'I'm not lying. I've been a crew member since my father died. He was a Surian fisherman, and once he was gone, I had to support my mother.' There, I've managed to create a link between this man and me. If he has any pride in his heritage, it might bring us closer together.

'Your father was a Surian?'

'Yes. He was banished to the Isle of Sin when I was five and took me and my mother with him. He died of the fever.'

This time when he hits me, the tears are real. I'm not sure if he's broken my nose, but blood streams over my lips into my mouth as I blink furiously.

'Let's start again. Who is it you're spying for?' He turns to the bundle on the table and slowly unrolls it to reveal strange-looking tools. He looks over his shoulder as he holds up an object that looks like a spoon.

'This is my favourite instrument. It hasn't been specially made or designed to inflict pain, yet it's perfectly formed and adequate for the task I have in mind. It is, as you'll have noticed, an eating spoon. I use this particular one for taking eyeballs out when I don't get the answers I want.

'Of course, we don't start there. That would be far too messy and unfortunate, especially if you change your mind and want to talk.

'Do you want to talk and tell me everything? Who you serve, and where you trained? Who your companions are? I promise that no further harm will come to you if you do.'

'I'm an oarswoman,' I begin, but stop as he waves his finger in front of my face.

'I admire your courage, I really do,' he says, pushing back his hood to reveal a gaunt face with a knife-like nose, pockmarks and full lips. 'Many people I've had the pleasure of questioning shit themselves at this point. They tell me everything. A brave few get through some of what's going to happen next. Fingernails are pulled out to start, and then toenails. The injuries at that point aren't life-changing; nails can grow back, and the pain isn't permanent.

'After that, however, the hot irons will leave terrible burns that may or may not heal. Sometimes I get impatient and forgo the other subtle tortures like spiking your eardrums and go straight for the eyes. No one holds out once an eye is removed, and the spoon comes for the other eye. However, even though you'll tell me everything, I'll be enjoying myself too much to stop at that stage.

'So, before we begin such an ugly journey, why don't you tell me the answers to my questions, and then we can discuss your release instead.'

'I have nothing to tell you,' I whimper, and this time the fear creeping into my voice is authentic.

His hand reaches for the tools, all neatly lined up, glinting an evil yellow in the lantern light.

'Wait, wait!'

'Why? I'm actually just as happy to torture the innocent as someone guilty. However, I'll give you a final chance? Just tell me who you serve, who your lord or king is.'

My resolve wavers. I could say I serve The Once and Future King. He won't have heard of him, and who knows, it might buy me some time. All I need is to get him or his hidden accomplice to release my hands, then I can kill them both and make my escape assuming I can get my legs free.

Yet all the training we've undertaken over the last month screams at me to say nothing. The secret of my king mustn't be disclosed.

I silently bow my head.

My captor sighs, but with pleasure, not disappointment.

'It takes years to truly master the craft of torture, yet even a novice can often get results at the early stages. I think it's only good practice to let an apprentice learn from experience. So, I hope you don't mind if I observe his initial attempts.'

The other figure, broad and tall, steps forward, and I know even before he throws the hood back who it is.

Lotane.

'Take the fingernails from her right hand,' instructs the torturer with glee.

I can't help but watch with morbid fascination as Lotane picks a small handgrip from the roll and moves behind me.

'Forgive me,' he whispers, as his hands take mine. His touch is soft and gentle, a final caress to show he cares.

There's fumbling but then a firm pressure on my small fingernail.

I resolve not to scream, but when the time comes, it echoes around the small chamber until my throat is raw.

Only the strong survive.

***

I sit up in bed, lifting my right hand.

My fingers had been bandaged before I went to sleep, but not now. Now the only physical sign of what I'd endured are the missing nails. They'll grow back soon enough, and the painful memories are already fading.

As I look around, I fight the urge to lie down with Lotane in his room, and for him to wake in my arms, knowing everything is fine between us. He'd carried out his mission on me, crying silently the entire time. There'd been no chance to talk after our ordeal. We'd all eaten separately and gone to sleep at different times.

I'm glad I'd been one of the first to try and escape. Had I instead been a torturer and known what awaited me when my escape attempt failed, I think that would have been worse. I just hope Nestor forgives me for what I did to his hands. My own had been so clumsy, having had four nails removed, that it had taken three attempts to yank his first nail free. Despite his high pain threshold, his screams had cut me deeply. Yet there was never a moment that I'd thought about stopping. I'd been ordered to do it. What other course of action was there?

Fortunately, the threats of hot irons, perforated eardrums and spoons had remained just that, preparing us for what might await if we fail at whatever we are asked to do.

Who are you spying for?

Those words echo in my head. Will I be required to spy? The Revelation is rapidly approaching, and the interrogation training we'd received now adds another possibility to the long list of many.

Bodyguard, Diplomat, Advisor, Spy, and of course, cook or court joker.

I smile, thinking of Lotane. He's my joker, and whilst I've given my loyalty to The Once and Future King, my heart belongs to Lotane.

The moon globe brightens ever so slightly, and I rise swiftly from bed. The sooner I get to the terrace, the sooner I'll speak with Lotane.

Frustratingly the other girls are in the corridor before me, yet we remain silent.

The three of us reach the terrace first. Yet we don't exercise; rather, we move quietly apart, deep in our individual thoughts.

Movement catches my eye. Through the archway, Kralgen looms, followed by Nestor and Lotane. Lotane has his head lowered. When he looks up and our gazes lock, there are tears in his eyes. I'm shocked, and it's too much for my heart to take.

Throwing caution and secrecy to the wind, I run over and fling my arms around his neck, pulling him into a tight embrace in front of the others.

'I'm sorry, I'm sorry,' he moans, burying his head into my shoulder, shaking as sobs silently rack his body. His arms are around my waist, and for that moment, despite the heartbreak he's suffering, my heart leaps with bittersweet emotions. To be held in Lotane's arms every morning is everything I desire. I just wish he wasn't in such torment over what he'd done to me.

Shocked silence interrupts the moment, and I slowly release him, stepping back to look around. The others are staring, eyes wide in disbelief at this public display of affection.

Kralgen steps forward, and I steel myself for the mockery that will pour from his lips.

He comes to stand in front of Lotane, who raises his head, eyes red, to stare back in defiance.

'Only the strong survive,' growls Kralgen, his voice gruff.

There's a moment's pause during which my heart seems to stop, but then he grabs Lotane around the shoulders and pulls him into an unexpected hug, slapping him on the back in a show of comfort.

'It took strength to do what you did to Malina. I'm not as slow as you seem to think, so while you might try hard to keep it secret, I know you've feelings for her. I had to do the same thing to Alyssa, and it's the hardest thing I've ever done.'

As Kralgen says this, he steps away from Lotane, his own eyes red, and turns to Alyssa.

'Will you forgive me?' he asks, a lone tear racing down his cheek as if afraid to be seen.

The next moment, she's in his arms, and Nestor is suddenly holding Fianna, and we cry in front of one another, unashamed.

I'd never felt closer to everyone than at this moment, nor happier to have suffered so much pain since it was the catalyst that allowed us to show our feelings, albeit briefly amongst ourselves.

Yet we regain our composure quickly, for it's a secret that can never be shared.

***

Several months have passed, and it appears our secret remains intact. The winter we'd experienced was much like every other season. This far south, the weather remains warm throughout. The only difference is the rain. At times we were drenched between dawn and dusk.

I'm glad spring is approaching, for that way, when Suntarg comes around, it won't seem too strange for Lotane and I to head off into the forest to find some time for ourselves. Our training has been relentless, yet it never seems to wear us down. That we're so happy to be pushed beyond mortal limits every day without complaint never fails to amaze me.

'Thankfully, there's still just the three of them,' Fianna murmurs interrupting my thoughts. Her observation is followed by a soft yawn as I look north from our terrace to see the small trio of black ships moored off the coast.

Each of the ships is huge, with three large masts upon which the sails are now furled. When we'd initially seen them as we ate dinner the night before, we'd run to find Lystra, thinking the island was about to be invaded. We were wrong, but not as much as we'd thought.

These are ssythlan ships, and throughout the day, each one had disgorged two hundred reptilian engineers, their supplies, and tools.

How do I know this?

Because Fianna and I had been seconded to assist at the small dock, which was utterly inadequate to handle anything much larger than a large fishing boat. Along with the ssythlan mages, she and I had used our magic to coax these large vessels into place one by one. Then, once they were unloaded, we turned them around and sent them on their way, assisted by several rowing boats. Once clear, the next ship was brought in.

It was exhausting work, all the more because I feigned being in pain much of the time. For whatever reason, I still feel the need to hide the ease with which I summon. Yet, as ever, the exhaustion I experience is entirely real.

Now, as I gaze upon the scene below, my eyelids are heavy even without my nightly infusion. Fianna rests her head upon my shoulder, half-asleep herself.

The others had spent the day weapons training, and Kralgen takes great relish in sharing how he defeated them all. With weapons, he's the best of us, and despite his delivery being somewhat gleeful, he offers insight and advice on how everyone could improve.

Nestor is the exception. As usual, he stands aside, focusing on the stone walls of the terrace that nestle against the mountainside. Grimacing with pain, sweat beads his brow as he brings forth his elemental power. Every evening he works these stones, seeking imperfections, sculpting the wall as if it were a blank canvas. He has created a perfect replica of the view we see from the terrace, but with the arrival of the ships, he has to make changes.

'So, what's going on with the new arrivals. Did you get any insight?' Alyssa asks, beckoning Fianna and I to join them at the table.

It's an effort to move over, but we do. It gives me a reason to sit next to Lotane. Our feet touch, but we'll never show more than this again, just in case Lystra visits as she often does.

'Very little,' Fianna offers by way of response. 'They were all engineers and crafters, that's for sure. The number of tools and equipment they unloaded looks like they'll be doing a lot of construction. They only spoke ssythlan amongst themselves, so I guess we'll find out exactly what they're here for in due course.'

Despite nodding in agreement, I could add more but don't want to let on that I'm learning ssythlan using blood magic. I'd picked up some information from idle chatter and worked out the rest. They're going to build docks to the north of the island for a fleet.

Unfortunately, there'd been no chance to listen in on individual conversations for long, as once their gear was unloaded, the ssythlans headed off to a rallying point slightly outside the port.

'I think I know why they're here.' Lotane's look is sobering, his frown deep. 'I'm quite sure they're here to construct the world's largest bed so Kralgen and his enormous ego can fit inside and sleep soundly at night!'

Roars of laughter meet his announcement, and even Kralgen shakes his head with a wry smile.

It's only Fianna's look that quietens everyone as she gazes open-eyed toward Nestor.

We turn in unison to see Nestor peeling back the rock wall from a concealed passage entrance, having uncovered it during his sculpting.

'Who wants to go first?' he asks, noticing our attention.

Although I'm sure everyone is intrigued, we shake our heads. We don't go where we're not supposed to. We follow orders and routines. Exploring something that's sealed off isn't going to get us any kind of praise. The passage entrance is lit by the sunset, but darkness awaits beyond the first dozen steps. Dust is thick on the ground, but there are recent bootprints.

Surprisingly Kralgen stands up.

'I'll have a quick look.'

Once the decision has been made, there's no hesitation. Kralgen is a Chosen, and now he's given himself a mission, he applies himself.

Crossing the terrace, he pauses briefly, but only to summon a large flame into the palm of his hand, and then he strides inside the same way he enters the training circle, without hesitation or fear. He's visible until he turns a corner, then the flickering light of his flame fades and disappears.

We sit there in something approaching nervous silence for a while. The sun is setting, and we should retire to our bed chambers. If Lystra visits, this could lead to problems. It surprises me to realise that I care for Kralgen. He might be boorish at times, but I've warmed to him lately, and he's a Chosen like me.

I'm about to tell Nestor to call into the passageway when Kralgen reappears, smiling. It's the same smile he wears when he's beaten us in the circle.

'Nestor. Seal it back up!' Lotane calls softly as Kralgen rejoins us.

A few moments later, having done as Lotane directed, Nestor sits at the table too.

'Well?' Nestor asks impatiently.

'It's a well-used passageway, that's for sure,' Kralgen answers. 'There are bootprints in the dust as far as I walked before I turned back. I don't know where the passage goes, but I found something surprising. The bootprints paused at regular intervals along the walls. I couldn't see why for a while, but then, I had an idea.'

'By the gods, we're all doomed. Kralgen's evolving. He can now think!' Lotane chuckles. We all smile but are too interested in the tale to laugh in case we interrupt Kralgen's flow.

'I let my flame die.' Kralgen continues. 'As soon as it was dark, I saw the light.'

Lotane bites his lip. He wants to make another joke, but with an effort, he holds back.

'The light came from spy holes looking into our sleeping chambers. We're being observed.'

The statement isn't met with disbelief, far from it, and Alyssa sums it up well.

'What's new? We're always under scrutiny, and much of our training is done when we're asleep.'

Shadows creep across the terrace. It's time to sleep, and maybe we'll be watched, maybe not. No one seems that bothered except Nestor.

He appears thoughtful as we file back into the mountain. He's likely upset that he has yet to finish adding the ships to the wall.

Lotane gives me a gentle nudge and smiles as he turns off toward his chamber, and my heart warms.

I'd do anything to spend a night in his arms.

Anything.

***

It's a cool morning as we stretch on the terrace before heading down to break fast. The air is fresh, the sky a deep blue that almost matches the empty sea now the ships have gone. It's hard to distinguish where one finishes and the other starts.

Alyssa assists me. Usually, this is a peaceful time when we ready ourselves mentally for the day ahead. We revel in the challenge and often danger, knowing that every day makes us stronger and better equipped to serve.

Yet this morning, we're pensive.

Fianna runs onto the terrace, and we pause expectantly.

'He's not in his chamber. I think Nestor's done something stupid.' Fianna's voice is low, barely above a whisper, yet it carries on the still morning air, and I shiver.

'What should we do?' Lotane asks, looking around. He usually has an answer for everything, so to see him at a loss is not a good sign.

In all our years of training, no one has simply disappeared. They've been killed in front of us or during a purge. None of us has ever been ill, and for Nestor to simply be absent is unheard of. There's no way we can cover for him should he decide to return later.

'We need to tell Lystra,' I say, 'and we need to do it before the day's training begins.'

Fianna is pale. I can only imagine how she's feeling.

'I'll go,' she says, starting to turn away.

'No!' I'll go,' I state firmly. 'Lystra will see your feelings if you tell her. It had best be me.'

'Malina's right,' Kralgen nods. 'Let the Wolf Slayer bring the news. After Lotane, she's Lystra's favourite.'

I scowl at Kralgen, who beams happily at his joke, but then hurry into the mountain, heading for Lystra's quarters. She's rarely there, going to sleep later than us and rising earlier. Today is no different. Her bed is made to perfection, the sheets and blanket sharply creased. Even her books are stacked evenly, aligned to the edge of their shelf.

How to find her in this enormous mountain? My only choice is to randomly search, but I also know time is of the essence.

Pausing, I turn my focus and thoughts inward, expressing my desire to the magic that slumbers within. My magic responds, and as I hurry to the eating chamber, conversations are brought to my mind like leaves rustling in a tree.

Despite its subtlety, using magic like this is powerful beyond what I'd envisioned. With no guidance, it seeks down passageways into chambers and caverns a hundred times faster than my feet could ever take me. Never would I have realised that its reach could be so vast. I'd hoped it would sharpen my senses as I ran through the mountain, but it's doing all the searching for me.

There! Lystra is talking with another instructor. Having just duelled, they're heading for the waterfall room to cleanse.

I run.

I'm already fast, but sensing my urgency, my magic comes to my aid of its own accord. A personal breeze pushes me along at speeds I'd never usually be able to reach. Despite my urgency, I wonder why I haven't experimented more with my magical gifts.

Down passageways, ramps, through chambers, dashing past surprised guards, I follow the whispered directions and arrive at the waterfall room as Lystra is about to enter.

She takes one look at me, notes my dishevelment, and takes my arm, leading me back outside.

Her grip is vicelike. There's no kindness to her eyes, no softness to her mouth, just that aura of controlled violence. Yet, where once that scared me, it doesn't bother me any longer. Death is so familiar, and I'm confident in who I am.

Perhaps sensing this, she lets go, and her demeanour becomes more inquisitive.

'What brings you to me this early, Wolf Slayer? In all these years, you've never broken routine. So, tell me quickly, what's wrong?'

This is not the time for anything but direct conversation.

'Nestor has gone missing. Last night, after our evening meal, he discovered a hidden passageway behind the terrace wall that leads behind our sleeping chambers. He resealed it, but I believe he must have investigated, for this morning, he's not to be found.'

I curse inwardly. Having used magic to find Lystra, why, by the gods, hadn't I used it to find Nestor first? Even as the thought comes to mind, my magic sets to work again. I'm tiring, for it drains me, yet as I watch Lystra's frown deepen, I let it have free rein.

'A hidden passageway?' she muses.

I can tell from her voice she's unaware of its existence, but this is the ssythlan's mountain to do with as they please.

'If the ssythlans discovered him, they have every right to dispose of him, not just for encroaching where he shouldn't go, but for stupidity.

However, they might be lenient as he's so far into his training. There's no precedent for this, so expect him to die.'

For a moment, anger rises inside of me, driven by burning resentment that life can be taken for simply satisfying curiosity. Yet just as quickly, it's replaced by familiar mantras, and the fire disappears like mist on a hot day.

'Take the others to the training circle. Practise with staves until I come, however long I am!'

I turn away. My magic hasn't discovered his whereabouts. If he isn't speaking, then it will never find him. I whisper my thanks, willing the search to stop. I'm drained, and the day's training has yet to commence. Lystra is already angry; if she sees me struggling, I won't enjoy the experience.

Enough time has passed that I meet with the others in the eating chamber. Fianna looks at me expectantly when I walk in, but I keep my face impassive as I sit amongst them.

'Lystra is going to investigate. She isn't hopeful,' I say softly.

Lotane gently puts his arms around Fianna's shoulder as her face briefly turns white, but she shrugs it off.

'Only the strong survive,' Fianna intones, and we all repeat it like a prayer. The gods must have answered, for it brings peace and acceptance to our souls.

I look at Lotane to find him gazing back at me. Do his thoughts mirror mine? Could I put aside his possible loss so quickly? I know I could. The thought saddens me, for we've all been indelibly changed, conditioned, and forged into something hard and unforgiving.

I barely taste my breakfast, and as a group, we eat quietly, each lost in our own thoughts. That doesn't mean we dally, far from it. We finish quickly and head to the training circle via the armoury.

This far south, the sky is almost always blue. Yet dark clouds are gathering on the horizon, and their appearance matches Fianna's mood. She throws herself into her training with such ferocity that even Kralgen takes a step back when he faces her.

We train without pause. The polished wood is somewhat sensual in my hand, reminding me of how Lotane feels when we pleasure one another, yet this is only a giver of pain. It's a weapon concealed in plain sight, for it appears no more than a traveller's aid. But, when used by a trained warrior, a stave can easily break bones, shatter joints and crack skulls.

Lystra joins us mid-morning.

We don't pause or gather around to ask about Nestor; that isn't our way. We're training, for that is today's mission. It isn't until the noon break that Lystra addresses us all.

'Nestor will rejoin you in due course. It transpires he trespassed into a holy area. Fortunately for him, our ssythlan masters are merciful, and he's not being punished. Rather he's being encouraged to forget things they consider sacred to them.

'Personally, I'd have seen his heart cut out for stupidity, but I'm less forgiving. I doubt the ssythlans will be again. Now, it's not long until your final purge. So, let's train and ensure you're worthy to serve our king.'

'We live to serve,' I say, and my voice is echoed by the other four. Then stave in hand, I turn to face Kralgen.

He's the best of us, but one day I'll be better.

**

CHAPTER XI

My head thumps when I open my eyes, and my body is stiff from inactivity.

It's been a long sleep, a strange way to prepare for our final purge.

I usually feel refreshed despite the stiffness, and often my head feels full to bursting with hidden knowledge waiting to be unlocked. Yet not today. The moon globe is dazzling, and I close my eyes, momentarily delaying the inevitable. Physical and mental lethargy is something I'm not used to, and this is the first time I haven't leapt out of bed in years.

Serve the king; complete your mission; to live is to obey. Mantras echo inside my head so forcefully that facing the glare is the better option. I rise and swiftly head to the terrace for our early morning stretching routine while the sun rises.

To the north, campfires flicker. The ssythlan engineers are up early as well.

As the others gather, I note that the usual morning energy is absent from everyone.

'To live is to obey,' grimaces Lotane, rubbing his temples. 'As if we didn't know that already. Good morning, Alina,' he adds, forcing a smile to replace his frown.

'Don't forget; live to kill and a hundred others,' grumbles Nestor, shuffling over.

Fianna brightens at Nestor's arrival.

'What happened?' she asks. 'You had me worried for a while. Are you alright?'

Nestor looks non-plussed, his eyebrows knitting together.

'What are you talking about?'

Lotane laughs softly, although he still appears pained.

'The passage you went into. According to Lystra, you ended up in a ssythlan holy place. They weren't too happy.'

This time it's Nestor's turn to laugh.

'I'm pretty sure I'd remember that! You must be mistaken.'

We exchange glances and start our routine. Lystra had said they'd make him forget, and it's apparent he's forgotten the entire episode.

Kralgen looks darker than usual when he joins us, while Alyssa's bright smile is absent.

We all feel the effects of this last training session.

Nonetheless, discipline and conditioning don't allow us to linger. We go through our stretching, helping each other where required.

As we're about to leave, Nestor pauses at the wall where all his sculptures are. The rest of us stop, looking at one another. Has he remembered? He walks along the wall past the blank section where he's sealed the passageway to his first work of art. It's the image of The Once and Future King with the ssythlans and humans at his side.

He rocks backwards and forward, grabs his head with both hands and starts squeezing hard.

'Are you in pain?' Fianna asks nervously as Nestor moans loudly.

'It's wrong. It's wrong. It's wrong,' Nestor groans over and over.

Kralgen steps forward, takes Nestor's arm and pulls him forcefully into the passageway.

Nestor returns to his usual self and, perplexed, looks at Kralgen.

'I'm fine. Leave me be,' he grumbles and heads off, the rest of us following the well-trod path to the eating chamber.

Nestor is a strange one. His infatuation with imperfection is borderline madness at times. I don't dwell on it, for thoughts of the final purge come to the forefront of my mind.

Upon arriving, we sit together, and food is brought. There's never a choice in what we receive, any more than in what we do. Our lives are so tightly controlled. Yet the food is nutritious, and my childhood memories of going hungry day after day in the orphanage never fade. I'm sure it's the same for the others, for no scrap is left on the plates once we finish.

Several guards and instructors sit in pairs dotted around the chamber, otherwise, it's empty. This place could seat hundreds, but there are always so few here.

Nestor seems agitated and snatches glances at the carving of The Once and Future King on the walls.

'Wrong, wrong, wrong,' he mutters.

'I'll tell you what's wrong,' growls Kralgen menacingly. 'Your head facing backwards once I twist it around. It's the day of our final purge, damn it. It's not the time to go play with the rocks. Get your priorities straight!' and he cuffs Nestor around the head.

Although Fianna frowns, none of us can disagree with Kralgen's handling of the situation. Nestor had survived his recent stupid actions through good fortune. However, good fortune will never be enough to survive a purge.

It isn't long before Lystra appears.

'As you know, today will be your final purge,' Lystra advises as she strides toward us, saying the words we've waited to hear since we arrived.

Silence greets this announcement as we control our excitement. What demands will be made of us? What mighty deeds will we have to undertake? Surely this final purge will test us like never before.

Lystra stands there, hands on hips, watching our reaction and seems satisfied, for she nods and carries on.

'To survive, you simply need to do what you have been trained to do. You need to kill.'

'We live to kill!' we shout in unison, and Lystra smiles.

I know that winning her approval means as much to me as it does to everyone in the room, and I want to see her smile again. It's so rare.

There's not a hint of worry on anyone's face. How far we've come. Is our confidence misplaced, or is it blind arrogance? No. I trust myself to do whatever needs to be done, everyone around me is as proficient as I am, and we have every right to feel as we do.

'Lotane, pair with Malina. Kralgen with Alyssa. Nestor with Fianna,' Lystra commands. 'Now follow me.'

Lystra's stride is brisk and purposeful. I can read we're to stay in step with her, not to climb the walls or swing from the ceiling. Such an understanding of what's required is entirely intuitive by now. The tethered energy and sense of expectation of those around me is almost palpable.

I intend to keep my happiness at being partnered with Lotane from my face, but he smiles briefly as we walk along, and I can't help but respond in kind.

Lystra leads us to the armoury, and we outfit ourselves in leather kilts, greaves, cuirass and vambraces. A flashback of the last purge comes to mind. It seems we're to face trial by combat again. Perhaps because some of the group hadn't fared so well last time, we're to face more skilled opponents again.

But why are we paired?

Perhaps no criminals or soldiers are awaiting. Maybe we will have to face each other?

The thought shakes me to the core. Could I kill Lotane if ordered, or for that matter, any of the others?

'Don those robes.' Lystra's voice interrupts my chaotic thoughts as she points toward a pile of neatly folded garments, and we remain silent as we do as we're told.

Next, it's our weapons.

'Take this,' Lystra commands, handing me a crossbow before turning to the others to issue crossbows and daggers. Like everything here, mine is functional. There are no embellishments, no subtle carvings in the wood, or tooled metalwork. It's simple and deadly. I'm given half a dozen bolts in a belt holster.

These are not duelling weapons, and a wave of relief washes over me.

Our attention is entirely on Lystra before she even begins to talk.

'You'll know what to do when the time comes. Stay close to your instructor and follow their commands without hesitation.'

We nod in unison. There's nothing unusual about following instructions. What *is* unusual is being reminded to do so at this final stage of our training. Purge or no, we follow without question and have done since we arrived, never more so than now.

For a while we stand, waiting. I want to get on with whatever awaits.

Lotane shifts from one foot to the other, exuding restrained energy, Kralgen paces like a caged wolf, Alyssa stands to one side, weaving the dagger she's been given through intricate patterns. Fianna and Nestor shadow box, loosening their shoulders. There's no fear, only eagerness.

To live is to obey. Complete the mission.

Once I know what the mission is, nothing will stop me.

Several instructors enter. Lotane and I are tasked to follow one by the name of Ardwich. He comes from the Sea of Sand, and his face has the same amazing sheen as Alyssa's.

We follow him briskly through the tunnels and enter the training circle. The sky is unusually dark today, with heavy clouds threatening to rain. As the thought crosses my mind, bloated drops fall from the sky and splash heavily on the ground.

The others, in turn, take positions around the circle alongside their instructors.

The wind howls softly, but something rises above its cry that catches my keen hearing. Despite Lotane looking away from me, I can see from his head's subtle tilt that he's also straining to hear more above the splash of water and the wind's cry.

Whatever is making the sound is getting closer, and then the door through which we entered the training circle a short time ago is thrown open and in stumble dozens of hollow-eyed urchins. My heart starts to beat erratically as I look at the tear-streaked faces and smell the stench of fear. Images of my first horrific day flash before my eyes, and for a moment, I fear I'll pass out, but suddenly, voices fill my head, and my heart starts to slow.

Only the strong survive. Obey without hesitation. Kill without remorse! Complete the mission!

I catch Lotane's gaze. There's a conflict going on there too, but suddenly his features calm, and just like me, he stands impassive, looking down at these frail creatures that are herded to our feet.

Today is indeed a purge, our last and their first. A new levy of orphans has been brought to be baptised in blood.

A skinny, dark-haired boy screams, pawing at my legs. It's incredible ... the range of emotions that eyes can convey; bowel clenching fear, frantic desperation, unfounded hope. He should have saved this energy for what lies ahead; he might even have survived.

Am I really only three years older than him? It seems more like a lifetime, for there's no resemblance to that which I once was.

I glimpse Ardwich motion from the corner of my eye and turn to him.

'Only the strong survive,' Ardwich states, his voice deep and commanding, not a flicker of emotion marring the smoothness of his ebony face.

Of course, that makes sense. This is how nature decides what lives and dies; I'm just an instrument of nature.

I'm holding my crossbow. When I cocked it and loaded a bolt, I simply don't remember. Such things are done without conscious thought. It feels solid, comfortable in my hand, an extension of my body.

I look down at the boy. His brown eyes are overflowing with tears, his nose running, and the rain is washing clean furrows down his face. Something tugs at my heart, and briefly, the mist that clouds my judgement parts to let me see what I am about to do.

No! I shout in my mind. *I'll not be a party to this butchery. Surely this is not what the king wants! This is NOT what I want!*

Yet seemingly of its own violation, the crossbow points at his face.

The next moment the boy's eyes close, and he collapses. It happens so slowly, as if the world holds its breath. Every raindrop appears to hang in the air before suddenly crashing to earth as time returns to normal. The look on his dying face changes from fear to confusion and finally, relief.

Relief.

Yes. I must have done the right thing to have brought him relief.

All around the training circle, I hear children's screams and the bellowing of various instructors. One moment it sounds like I'm in the underworld, and the next, it's as if the music of the gods is being played for me alone.

'Come,' instructs Ardwich, beckoning to me and Lotane. 'It's time to sort the wheat from the chaff!'

***

'Why, Alina? Why did you kill me?'

I gaze with horror at Karson. It's been so long since I've seen him.

He stands before me, his body riven in a dozen places, face ghostly white, dark rings around his eyes. Blood is everywhere, and a puddle of thick red gore at his feet just seems to grow and grow.

'What happened?' I cry in anguish.

Karson's eyes convey what he's about to say.

'You killed me; you killed us all!' Blood bubbles from his horrific wounds.

His little arm extends behind me, finger shaking to point at hundreds of his corpses.

All those disfigured and broken little bodies stare at me with wide, accusing eyes. A foul-smelling breeze blows smoke over the landscape, and when it clears, I'm standing in the training circle, strewn with the bodies of dead children. They're not Karson, but they're someone's son, brother or sister.

Why does it look so familiar? This is not a dream, I realise. This is a memory, and suddenly the purge I participated in comes rushing back to me: the screams, the pleas, the blood, and the complete lack of mercy.

'I'll never harm you again. Please, little brother, forgive me!'

Karson stumbles forward. My arms enfold him, and his head drops onto my shoulder, the warmth of his breath tickling my ear. Suddenly, he gasps, stiffening, and there's a dagger in my right hand sunk deep into his back!

'No,' I scream, realising with horror that my other hand grasps a dagger too.

'Break free, Alina. Break free. Look to your heart!'

A last sigh escapes his lips, and I don't want to let him go, but a searing pain causes me to cry out in agony, and I drop his tiny body to fall amongst so many others I don't recognise.

Again, the sharp pain, and I tear my shirt aside and look at my chest. There's a huge hole, and I can see my heart beating. It's black and swollen, covered in mould, with maggots wriggling over the surface.

I steel myself, reach into the sucking, wet cavity, and grasp my heart. With a scream, I grip it tightly and rip it from my body and cast it aside.

Then everything goes black.

Yet the blackness is slowly replaced by light, and I open my eyes to the subtle glow of the moon globe. My face is sticky, and I reach up to find it wet from tears. My head pounds, unlike anything I've ever felt before, and the memories come flooding back as fresh as ever.

Our final purge had been nigh on two weeks ago. It had been as horrific, if not more than our first. There'd been no glory, no honour, just two days of slaughter, the ground soaked in blood, tears and shit. Inside I'd screamed as loud as the children around me, but like theirs, it was to no avail. Despite wanting nothing more than to leave the circle, I'd obediently stayed, carrying out my gruesome duty without hesitation or mistake.

Every day since I'd trained under Lystra's watchful eye, then every night, I'd greedily drunk the dream leaf infusion before falling into bed, hoping to forget what I'd done, but I can't.

Why couldn't *they* have put us into a long healing sleep so that we could wake up without enduring weeks of suffering and regret?

Is this a final test of our conditioning?

Even our evenings, which are a time for relaxing and conversation, are unusually subdued. We hadn't spoken more than a handful of words between us, and I'd found it hard to look anyone in the eye. Even Lotane had kept his distance, knowing any sign of affection after such an event was utterly inappropriate.

Now, having awoken so early, my tiredness remains overwhelming. I know I should attempt to go back to sleep, but I've no wish to revisit those dreams.

Nearby whimpering in the quietness of the mountain makes my pulse jump briefly, and I leave my room, tiptoeing to the adjacent sleeping chamber.

Fianna twists and turns in her bed, cheeks glistening with tears in the weak light.

Are the dreams she's having like mine?

I'm determined to fight the need to sleep and hold on to my senses. For the first time in so long, my dreams make me question what I'm doing and who I'm serving. If I fall back to sleep, will I forget these feelings and this nagging desire ...?

The desire for what?

I can't quite grasp what it is. It's an itch I can't scratch.

The face of the first boy I'd killed comes to mind, and there'd been others. How could I want to stay now? They've forced me to kill children. The blood of innocents is now on my hands.

All this time, I'd be training to serve The Once and Future King. But I thought my skills would be used to protect, to face his enemies. Would the king want a child killer serving him?

I'm a child killer.

Sweat runs down my face, and my stomach convulses as the reality of my actions hits me hard. I rush to Fianna's toilet area and kneel, retching for what seems an age. My body is wracked with stomach cramps as I bring up bile, shaking uncontrollably.

'Malina?'

My heart almost stops at being discovered in this moment of weakness, and I turn to see Fianna coming toward me. I sit back, trying to control myself. I'm about to lie, make something up, anything to explain my presence in her quarters, when she crumples to the floor next to me.

'I was having the most terrible dreams,' she whispers. 'I keep seeing ...'

The next moment we're holding each other, sobbing as hot tears run unchecked. A memory of me plunging a dagger into Karson's back worryingly crosses my mind, and I hold my hands up briefly to ensure they're empty.

Fianna composes herself, sitting back a little, smiling in apology as she wipes he nose and eyes.

'The things I did during that purge,' she starts off, her voice cracking. 'I didn't want to, but they happened anyway. I know the memory will fade quickly, they always do, but I hate myself. I don't want to be the monster I was today ever again.

'I'm torn. I want to stay for this is home, and I want to serve. Yet, despite my feelings for our king and his cause, I feel like running away. I haven't wanted to escape since we first arrived, but now I'm finding it hard to think of anything else.'

Her face suddenly takes on a frightened look, so unlike the strength we typically portray. 'Please, please, don't say anything about this to the others, will you?' she entreats, grasping my hands, eyes wide, pleading.

I'm shocked. Not just because Fianna mentioned escape but because I realise that's exactly the itch I'd been unable to scratch. The feeling had been buried for so long under conditioning, discipline, training, and camaraderie.

'I feel the same, so don't worry, your secret's safe with me,' I whisper, my confession putting her at ease.

We hold each other briefly, finding strength in friendship before picking ourselves off the cold floor.

'Sunrise is still a way off. I'm sure a little more sleep and this will all be a distant memory,' she reassures me, wiping her face. 'Can you believe tomorrow is the Revelation?'

I shake my head.

'We've come so far.'

Fianna pulls me gently to the chamber entrance. 'Sleep well,' she whispers in my ear, planting a kiss on my cheek as we part. 'I'm sure whatever awaits us will make all this worthwhile. Tonight was just a rare moment of weakness.'

My chamber is only a few steps away, and with the dream leaf infusion still in my bloodstream, drowsiness comes at me in waves.

Yet, the long-buried seed of thought that Fianna shed light on is now growing.

Escape.

Even the resulting headache doesn't stop me from mulling over the idea. There'd been a time when that had been my dream. But it had been foolish, for life is now good here. Not forgetting, I've been chosen to serve a king who will bring peace and stability to the world.

My heart is at war with my mind over this.

Escape. It doesn't seem appealing in the least until another word and a face come to mind.

Lotane.

***

'We're within touching distance of serving The Once and Future King,' Alyssa says, her voice tinged with reverence.

I hope she's right because if we're ordered to kill another Chosen as further proof of our readiness, I now know that none of us would be able to refuse. My earlier thoughts of shame and escape still linger, but the jolt of nervous excitement running through me as Alyssa's words hit home pushes them aside.

'YES!' Kralgen shouts skyward. His face contorts, tongues of fire lancing upwards from his hands in celebration. His face reflects the light, shining red and then orange, giving him a manic, possessed demeanour.

Caught up in the enthusiasm, Lotane follows suit.

Excitement and conditioning sweep aside everyone's dark thoughts, and we embrace, overcome by the magnitude of what awaits.

Today is the Revelation.

Lightning flashes out at sea, and thunder rolls across the island.

Years of rigid discipline ensure we undertake our stretching, but afterwards, we run like fools to the eating chamber. We take a seat at our usual table, a little breathless, and once food is delivered, we set to eating.

The conversation this morning is minimal. However, much can be said without words. I notice Alyssa lean toward Kralgen to pass him some bread, and their fingers touch lightly, innocently ... but it's far from innocent. Nestor stretches past Fianna to get some meat, putting his hand on her shoulder to steady himself, even though he's perfectly balanced.

How I'd previously missed these acts of intimacy when Lotane and I had been practising them for so long, I don't know. However, the art of being affectionate in plain sight whilst not drawing attention to ourselves is something we've all mastered, just like everything we've set our minds to. Even as I consider this, Lotane's foot rests on mine, and he raises an eyebrow, looking askew at the others, smiling.

He notices it too.

After feeling so distant these last two weeks, my heart swells.

Glancing beyond our table, I study the group of younger Chosen on the far side of the chamber. The memory of reaping their fellows during their first purge makes me flinch with guilt and remorse. Yet, I also recognise the beginning of their transformation. A healthy glow is beginning to replace the hollow eyes and skinny limbs.

They've yet to face so much more, and I briefly reminisce and remember with pride my success in killing the two red wolves. The purges I survived are shining beacons of light as I think back. If only they hadn't involved horrific deaths, killing others ... killing children.

Lystra appears as if from nowhere, standing at the head of our table.

We pay attention as she clears her throat, and to my surprise, a hint of warmth is evident as she surveys us.

'Today is a momentous day, the day of the Revelation. You've earned this opportunity, this honour, with your blood, sweat and tears. You are superlative warriors and magic users. As the strongest, you survived, and as the Chosen, you'll go on to accomplish the greatest of deeds.

Her delivery and choice of words make Lystra's speech all the more forceful, for this is the first time she's ever complimented us without reservation.

Lotane applies further pressure with his foot. His amazing eyes shine with pride, and I know mine do too. I hate some things I've been party to, but I can recognise my achievement in making it to this day when I doubted I'd ever survive the first.

Breakfast is finished. Today we'll find out what the Revelation is.

Lystra eats at a leisurely pace, measuring us with her stare. Our iron discipline is tested in those few moments like never before, but eventually, she rises to her feet, and we follow in smooth unison.

'Come,' is all she says.

We follow her from the chamber and out into the training circle.

As we stroll across, I'm warmed, not just by the air but by the love I feel for this place. So many joyful moments I've spent here. Yes, there's been pain, horror and events that will stain my soul forever, yet I've exulted in my training. I've become something I never thought I'd be. As Lystra said, I am a survivor, warrior, magic user, and Chosen one.

We pass to the other side, exiting the circle and again into the mountain. We pause at a junction, and Lystra indicates for Nestor to step forward.

'Open an entrance here,' she commands, pointing.

Nestor places his hand on the wall, the runes and glyphs writhing over his hands as he briefly closes his eyes, grimacing, and the entrance to a hidden passageway opens before him.

We move inside, up a gentle slope, the ground, walls, and ceiling polished smooth by magic.

As we reach the top, it opens into a chamber. A huge, circular wooden table intricately carved with mythical creatures takes centre stage. Maps and scrolls are scattered across it, a rare piece of chaos amongst the regimen of order we're used to. Chairs are positioned around the table, and plush lounges rest along two walls. Several sin-hawks sit on perches, hoods covering their heads.

One wall shows The Once and Future King flanked by ssythlans and humans as a horde of defeated beasts pleads for mercy at his feet. Nestor's attention seems to be immediately drawn to it, and a twitch appears under one eye.

Four ssythlans await, arms folded beneath the rune-covered sleeves of their robes, black eyes staring from within their cowls. Beyond them is the balcony that can be seen from the training circle. It's from here that they often measure our worth.

Lystra motions for us to stand abreast, facing them.

A stone wall peels back, and another ssythlan glides in. Unlike the others, its hood is down, and a thin golden circlet sits upon its brow, twisted and fashioned in front to form a serpent's head. Yet, that remains the only difference.

I kneel alongside the other Chosen.

'This is Prince Sylnar of the royal family of Ssythla,' Lystra makes the introduction. 'There's no higher-ranked ssythlan outside of their capital.'

So, this is the ssythlan who rules over this island and all that happens here. Yet, that matters little at this moment. What does, is whether I'll be chosen as a soldier or a bodyguard? Perhaps my magic skills will see me ensconced as an advisor or used as a diplomat ... maybe even a spy. Anything, as long as it doesn't blacken my already charred soul.

'Chosen ones,' the prince hisses. 'The gods have smiled on you all. Not only have you survived where hundreds have died, but the greatest of privileges awaits you all; to actually live in the time of our king.

'In two years, he'll return to these lands to rule over them all. Upon his ascension, the greed of nations will come to an end. Poverty will fade away, inequality will vanish, and slavery will be abolished. The people of this world will know freedom and will owe you a debt of gratitude for your part in making this happen.

'However, dark forces stand in the way of this happening. From the lowliest cutpurse to the self-proclaimed noble families, evil infests this world. By his will, your task is to lance this festering boil that blights humanity.

'Henceforth, you'll go out into the world using the skills you've acquired. Take the lives of those beyond redemption and weaken evil's grasp. Then, when the time is ripe, you'll be directed to strike the most powerful. When they fall, chaos will reign, paving the way for our king to return with his enemies in disarray.

'You are to be life takers, assassins, soul stealers. You are to be the divine justice of our king!'

The ssythlan's tongue flicks out, perhaps tasting the atmosphere. Its thin lips draw back in a smile, and the scales on its face shimmer in greens, blues, and gold.

I hold my breath. Is it possible it can sense my despair? An assassin? Where's the honour in that?

However, the atmosphere in the room is so charged; it's surprising lightning doesn't crackle between us all, and without further pause, it continues.

'A final test of your worthiness awaits on foreign shores. Should you return successful, further missions await. Our king depends on you, don't disappoint him!'

Silence descends, stretching painfully, but we daren't move, for our discipline binds us tighter than chains. Preceded by clicks, hisses, and several long blinks, the ssythlan speaks again.

'Lystra, you know what awaits. Make the necessary preparations! You may leave.'

We smoothly rise, and as Lystra shepherds us out, the ssythlans whisper amongst themselves. After all this time, their hissing tongue is so familiar that I don't even hear it as another language.

'These are the finest Chosen ever trained,' one observes.

'Making them magic users was the right thing to do. They will succeed where others have failed.' hisses another.

'They will definitely serve our Lord Nogoth well.'

Nogoth?

I've just learned the name of The Once and Future King.

***

Following our dismissal, we'd been given the rest of the day off to do as we wanted. I'd kept quiet as we returned briefly to our quarters, keeping my thoughts private. Everyone else had never appeared happier, in direct contrast to how I felt inside.

Shortly though, our final test awaits us, although we've yet to be told what shape it will take; undoubtedly, it will involve more killing. No further ships have docked at the small port, but they must be on their way. We've no idea whether we'll travel as a group or individually or where we'll be heading.

'I don't feel good about what we've been told,' I whisper, holding Lotane's hand as we wander through the forest just south of the mountain.

Despite being alone, such words are dangerous to say aloud wherever we are.

'We're to be assassins!' I say. 'There are no heroic stories or fables told of such creatures of the night. They've no honour, no code save to kill their target for gold. Isn't that just what a thief does when he kills his mark?'

My mind is in turmoil, and whereas I usually traverse the undergrowth without hindrance, every single vine or branch snags or attempts to trip me.

Lotane's hand steadies me, but I find it hard to take much pleasure from his touch, especially as I sense him stiffen at my words.

'What do you mean? I've never felt so good about something in my life. Everything we've gone through now makes sense.'

Lotane's voice is tinged with the religious fervour I hear whenever Lystra talks.

Now it's my turn to bristle at his words.

'Are you saying that what we have isn't as good as this news then?'

'You know that's not what I'm saying!' Lotane pulls me to a halt, his eyes imploring. 'It worries me when you talk like this. It's dangerous as well.'

I sit down beneath a whirl tree, and almost reluctantly, Lotane joins me a few steps away.

'This is not the future I hoped for,' I admit. 'I would rather be a hunter than an assassin, and I'd rather you be a court jester.' I smile softly, looking at him through misty eyes. 'Don't get me wrong, I want to serve, but you do realise we're controlled by blood magic and don't always see straight because of it?'

Lotane snorts. 'Don't be silly now. No one can coerce me into doing something I don't want to do. Yes, we're used to following orders, but if I really disagreed with …'

'Killing children?' I interrupt.

'It was a dark deed.' Lotane acknowledges. 'But we had to go through that ourselves!'

'But that doesn't make it right. Those who fail shouldn't have to die.' It's impossible to hide the exasperation in my voice. Lotane rarely ever frowns. His face has a perpetual lopsided grin, but now that's absent.

'In the greater scheme of things, it doesn't really matter,' Lotane says. 'The vision for a future where countries are not wracked by war, where children are not sold and poverty is extinguished, that's what truly matters. You're focussing on the minor details. The greater plan is something no one can criticise.'

'I don't disagree with the vision, my love.' It's the first time I've addressed him this way, and I'm glad I've done so. The cold aura surrounding him drops, and he moves closer, pulling me into his arms. 'It's just the dark things we've had to do, and now what awaits us. I meant it when I said I'd rather be a hunter. We're going to be tasked with taking lives by stealth.

'I knew plenty of thieves and beggars as a child. Many had no choice and only stole from the wealthy to keep themselves alive. Do they really deserve a dagger in their back or poison in their food?

'I don't want to be an assassin. If I'm to fight, I want it to be honourably, face to face.'

Lotane smiles reassuringly, believing he's found the solution.

'Then, if that's how you feel, don't kill your target with a knife in the dark. Be who you want to be. We've been trained as warriors, so fight as one!'

I shake my head, easing myself from his embrace and turning to face him. I'm sitting cross-legged and reach out, taking his hand in mine to soften any unintended hurt.

'You're missing the point. Yes, we've been trained to kill, but deep down, that doesn't mean I want to. Do you really want to be a killer of men, women, and more children if that's your mission? People who haven't been trained, who stand no chance, and who'd have chosen another path had they been born into wealth?

'Don't answer blithely now. Don't tell me; only the strong survive.'

Lotane shrugs. 'What choice do we really have? If I'd been bought by the army and ordered to kill, what do you think would happen if I refused? You know I'd be executed. It's no different here and no worse. If we want to live, we've no option but to obey orders like we've done since day one!'

Trembling with suppressed emotion, I hold his gaze firmly with my own.

'I'd have agreed until today, but after all these years, we're going to actually leave this place. The ssythlan prince said: *Should we return, further missions await.* So, what if we fight our training and conditioning and choose not to return?

'So now there are two options, and you must choose one. A life soaked in blood as a Chosen, or life in my arms if we can escape!'

Lotane shakes while I gaze into his amazing eyes, perceiving the inner conflict.

'One moment, what you say makes sense ... I can't believe what we've suffered and been made to do. Now you've painted such a vivid picture, I also don't want to be an assassin. As you said, I knew good thieves too. In fact, in the past, I stole to survive. But the next moment, I want to repay what we've been given because I hear our king's voice, and his truth is the one that matters.

'How is it you challenge what we've been taught, what we all see as right?'

I consider my answer carefully. I can't lie to Lotane, nor is this time to hold back truths.

'In my dreams, my brother talks to me. He makes me question our teachings and shows me things I'd never have otherwise seen. Without his words, I'd follow blindly, but he forces me to face the consequences of my actions and question what I'm taught to believe.'

'Your brother died in the orphanage.' Lotane's voice is worried, softly spoken, and full of concern. 'He can't talk to you, Alina.'

I smile.

'Do you know, that's exactly what he always calls me. But, whether he's real, a figment of my imagination, or simply my own conscience, it doesn't matter. He has shown me the truth of things.'

'Do you know what I see in my dreams?' Lotane asks.

His face has darkened, eyebrows drawn together by a deep frown. My heart falters, for I know he only desires a life at the king's side.

My lips remain sealed, dread eating away at my nerves.

Then that smile, that beautiful, mischievous smile, spreads across his face like the sun shining after a storm.

'I see you naked underneath me, your limbs entwined with mine, giving yourself to me and I to you, time after time after time! Then you lie in my arms, your head on my chest while we watch the sunset. So, to answer your question. Yes, I'd rather be a jester if I could have a life in your arms. But how do we make that happen?'

I can almost hear Karson's happy laughter, but it's obscured by mine.

The kiss Lotane and I share brings everything he outlined in his dream and more to the forefront of my mind, and it's hard to let him go. Reluctantly I remove my hands from his neck and sit back, a little breathless.

'We make a pact,' I say. 'We're about to go on our first mission, and whether it's together or apart, we escape. We've been taught so much about the world and have the skills to survive.'

Lotane rubs his chin. He always does this when deep in thought.

'You're right. If we're together, it doesn't matter where we go; we can pick and choose our time and head in any direction we want. If our missions are separate, let's choose Astoria. I've have such a desire to go there!' he says, eyes shining.

'Astoria it is,' I agree. 'Whoever gets there first waits every Suntarg on the trade road as it enters the capital Ast until the other arrives.'

'What about the rest?' Lotane muses.

My heart warms. He's concerned about the other Chosen. However, sadness quickly replaces the warmth.

'It's too great a risk to mention this to anybody else. Kralgen clearly embraces this life, and Alyssa is so close to him now. Fianna might come with us, but she wouldn't leave Nestor, and he's never opened up about how he feels. If we're discovered, we won't be shown any mercy.'

Lotane shrugs.

'They have to choose their own destiny,' he says. 'I have chosen mine, and it's the one I always wanted but couldn't see for the promise of greatness in front of my eyes.

'I will choose the one I love.'

***

CHAPTER XII

'Only the strong survive. Complete the mission. Kill to live. Obey without question. Kill without hesitation.' The chanting ssythlan voices merge into one so powerful that I fear my eardrums will burst.

Am I asleep or awake? Is this a nightmare, or is this real?

The relentless assault of chanted mantras are joined by flashing images and excruciating pain. I cry out, feeling my sanity slipping away.

'Enough,' I plead. 'Enough.'

'Who survives?'

'Only the strong!' I answer immediately.

Suddenly the pain is replaced with euphoria, and the relief is so instant I weep with gratitude.

'Why are you here?'

'To live to serve!'

'Why do you live?'

'I live to kill!'

'Who do you serve?'

'The Once and Future King!'

They start again. Is this the second, hundredth or thousandth time, or have these questions been asked for all eternity?

'My king, please, save me,' I cry out.

The voice recedes. There is silence, tranquillity, and euphoria.

I serve The Once and Future King. The gentle mantra swims around my head, but now I hear another familiar voice, the voice of my Karson.

'Escape, Malina. Escape, escape.'

It's such a simple mantra that it's impossible to forget. I won't forget!

'It's time!'

...

...

'Wake up, Malina.'

A goblet of cool water is pressed against my lips as I open my eyes. I have a headache, yet it recedes as I drink, along with the memory of my dreams.

I'm in my sleeping chamber, the moon globe is dim, yet it sheds enough light to see a dark shape.

'It's time!'

Lystra's voice emanates from shadow. Her face is hidden, her voice a whisper, and I momentarily feel uneasy.

'Time for what?' I ask softly, confused, yet I'm already swinging my legs out of bed and pulling my boots on. Obeying orders ensures my safety and is the right and natural thing to do. I wonder briefly if the others are still asleep.

'It is time for your first mission. Soon you'll begin to believe and put all your misgivings and doubts behind you! Now, follow me.'

Without another word, Lystra turns, and I follow as she sets a brisk pace.

Her choice of words is somewhat unnerving, but I shrug it off. It must be late, the moon globes are dim, and there's no sign of movement from the sleeping chambers I pass. My muscles are stiff, but they loosen quickly enough. I feel rested and full of energy despite the hour. I've been in a longer sleep again. This will stand me in good stead for my escape, I only wish I'd had a further chance to discuss things with Lotane, but we already know what we'll do.

We hurry along corridors, occasionally passing guards who don't even blink as we pass. Then, we come to a wide spiral stairwell, the walls and steps unnaturally smooth, and begin to ascend.

'Aren't we going to the docks?' I ask as if it's of little consequence.

Lystra's chuckle isn't too reassuring.

'The ssythlans are the closest race to the gods,' she begins. 'As the oldest race to walk our world, they alone hold many secrets of magic. Moreover, they have a way of travel from ancient times that doesn't require a ship or horse!'

This dramatic announcement leads to silence as we save our breath for what seems like an endless climb. Step follows torturous step. Various landings and passageways beckon, but we continue upwards. Just as I wonder if it's possible to climb to the moons, we exit the stairwell onto a terrace excavated from the mountainside. It's not far below the mountain's majestic peak and gives breathtaking views of the starlit sky in all its glory.

That this is a special place is immediately apparent.

Under the gentle light of several moon globes, I discern Ssythlan guards standing at the four corners of the terrace, wearing wide leather straps that crisscross their bodies. They could almost pass for humans when clothed, but, semi-naked, their skin shimmers like a thousand mirrors. I'm surprised by a short stubby tail no longer than my forearm emanating from their lower spine. I can't tell which gender they are, for there's nothing to indicate their sex.

Set into the wall to my right, another guarded passageway leads off. The Mountain of Souls reminds me of a fire ant nest; the leagues of passages and chambers are so complex. However, there are no ants, just ssythlans and humans.

Lystra leads the way across the terrace to a waist-height wall that, during daylight, would offer unparalleled views across the whole island.

'You may look around, but don't leave here. As you know, there are some holy places the ssythlans don't want you wandering into!' Lystra's words leave no room for misinterpretation.

I watch as she heads toward the guards, then bring my attention back to the terrace.

Cautiously I inspect the walls, drawn to the carvings, wanting to take a closer look. It's apparent they're different from what we're used to seeing in the eating hall and throughout the mountain.

In addition to the usual humans and ssythlans shielded beneath the king's arms, fantastical and hideous creatures kneel and cower at his feet. Some have torn wings, others tusks, sharp fangs, or claws. Fearsome each and every one, they bow down, pleading for mercy before our king who radiates goodness, forgiveness and love.

The craftsmanship of the carvings here is beyond compare; every figure is smooth and polished, with no hint of flaws, cracks, or imperfections.

Nestor would approve. However, now I know what had upset him despite the memory having been removed. Amongst the other things he shouldn't have witnessed, he must have seen these carvings and recognised his were not only incomplete but inferior.

No doubt, once he's returned here after completing his mission, he'll go throughout the mountain correcting them all. I won't be here to see it, yet I smile at the thought nonetheless.

Two vast polished lenses held steady on an intricate stand steal my attention. From the number of shining cogs and gears, this is some kind of telescopic instrument. My curiosity is piqued, so I wander over to inspect it. As I peer through the lens, the blue and the white moons are magnified in all their glory. The detail is incredible, and I wonder what the ssythlans hope to learn.

I'm about to move on when something catches my eye. A third black moon nestled between them! I lean back, but it isn't visible without the lens. I never knew there were three moons.

Ssythlans pass by, paying me little heed. There's no sign of hostility, let alone interest in me. I'm here because I belong here, as do they.

Do I belong here?

No.

I'm here to escape; this place is not for me. No more purges, no more witnessing the deaths of those around me. No becoming an assassin, a killer, a taker of lives. I'm happy to trade the promises of glory for a life with Lotane, where death isn't around every corner.

A robed ssythlan cleric approaches the lens, and I give way, moving around the terrace toward another eye-catching feature, an enormous mirror. I walk up several stone steps onto the dais over which it looms. It's wider than my arm span and several hands higher than a tall man.

Like the one next to the Heart Stone, I wonder if this allows communication with the king.

However, this frame is of rough stone, etched with arcane runes. Something akin to crystal dagger handles protrude from the back. Shiny, black, unreflective glass finishes this slightly disquieting piece.

The hairs on the back of my neck rise as I detect something moving in the mirror.

Mist swirls within. But no, it isn't mist, but clouds of ethereal faces. The closer I look, the more I see. There are hundreds, maybe thousands. Every one is twisted in indescribable torment.

'Don't touch it!' a voice snaps from behind, and I pull myself away.

I turn to find a man, maybe four years my senior, measuring me with grey eyes that seem tired beyond his years. He's wearing black woollen trousers and a loose black shirt that doesn't quite conceal his muscled physique. Two empty sheathes hang from his belt, but in his hand is a wooden staff.

'That is the Soul Gate,' he continues. 'I believe it's the most powerful artefact the ssythlan's possess. Using it, we can travel anywhere we wish to administer the justice of The Once and Future King. Tonight, you'll see the evil the carvings warn us of and the fight that awaits you.'

No, I think to myself. Tonight, after all these years, I'll disappear, never to be seen by the likes of you or Lystra again. But what's this rubbish about using a mirror to travel anywhere?

'I'm Darul,' he continues. 'Like you, I am Chosen. Lystra has appointed me as the guide on your first mission. Have you ever been to High Delnor?'

I shake my head while he pulls two daggers from the back of the frame. They have a strange crystal blade, thick and blunt. He pushes them into the sheathes at his waist.

'Then now is the time to show you!'

With a no-nonsense grip, Darul takes my hand firmly and pulls me toward the mirror.

I stumble after him and watch as he steps into the glass, disappearing before my eyes, and even as I try to resist, his strength drags me forward.

The moment my hand touches the glass, I'm sucked in, and for a moment, the blood-curdling screams of the damned tear away at my sanity. The cries speak of eternal suffering, of pain beyond mortal endurance, and just when my mind is about to slip into darkness, I'm through.

***

I stumble, crashing to my knees as lightning flashes and thunder shakes my core.

Suddenly, I'm puking my stomach contents everywhere, and my strength deserts me. I feel lightheaded and detached. Something isn't right. I feel … different.

A scream pierces my ears, and Darul's strong hand clamps firmly over my mouth, stifling the sound as he pulls me upright, kicking and struggling weakly against him.

Rain is falling in sheets, and I'm drenched in moments. The wind howls around, shrieking and buffeting while thick angry clouds race across the sky. Have I been tricked and sent to one of the lower plains of hell?

Darul is shouting at me, and gradually his words find a way through the maelstrom and my confused mind.

'We're in High Delnor. It's just a storm. Settle down!'

He relaxes his grip, letting me go, and I stagger like a newly birthed lamb, turning unsteadily in all directions. Sure enough, when the lightning flashes, a city is revealed, stretched out around me. My vantage point is a broad, flat rooftop, ankle-deep in water, while a few steps away, something akin to a small temple stands proud.

A familiar-looking building catches my eye in the distance. I'd seen pictures of this in one of the few books my orphanage had possessed. It's the High King's citadel in Delnor. It shines brightly, despite the darkness, with hundreds of lights illuminating its walls even when the lightning isn't splitting the sky.

We really are in High Delnor!

Darul retrieves the staff he'd dropped in our struggle, before half-carrying me to the pillared temple porch and out of the downpour.

'This is the roof of the Grand Library in High Delnor,' he explains loudly, water running down his face. 'I want you to remember every detail you can, then describe it to me. It's imperative you do so.'

I nod weakly. Where has my strength gone?

Glancing around, I take in the carved columns, the heroic figures carved into the plinths, and what looks like an altar stone.

'We are ...'

His ringing slap makes my head spin.

I step back, raising my hands defensively as a blood rush sharpens my senses briefly.

'Good.' Darul smiles, apparently pleased at my reaction. 'Remember every detail, every one!'

He pushes me out into the rain again.

Surprised tears mix with rainwater as I shuffle around the rooftop, conscious of Darul's fierce gaze. Had I not been so disorientated, I'd have not only seen his strike coming but would have answered it with my own!

Gods, I can't wait to escape.

Yet currently, I can barely stand, let alone run, so I'll do what Darul asks of me.

Rainwater drips into my eyes and soaks me thoroughly, but I don't allow it to distract me. Instead, I take my time, studying everything from some cracked roof stones to the carved parapet, the view and, of course, the small temple. Of the Soul Gate that we'd passed through, there's no sign.

As I return, soaked to the bone, Darul points to a grey stone bench. Interestingly, everything here is grey, white, or black; it's colourless. Not that I'd expect to perceive colour at night, but without a light source, I wouldn't expect to see much of anything either. So how can I see so clearly?

'Wait there,' Darul commands. 'You're too weak at present. I'll be back in two hours once you've found your strength. Everyone struggles their first time through.'

A weak smile of acknowledgement is all it takes, and he heads off, leaping from rooftop to rooftop, before vanishing into the storm.

Shivers and chattering teeth have me calling upon my magic to warm me through, but although I'm aware of its presence, it seems unsure and doesn't respond.

I've never felt this strange, this disconnected. Something is wrong beyond just being exhausted.

I hold up my hands. They're grey in the moonlight, except there's no moonlight … just occasional lightning and the distant glow of white streetlights dotted around the city. A strange, black mist rises from my fingers and hands, and then I notice everything, from the altar to the bench I'm on, appears to be smoking.

If only Darul was here to tell me what's going on, but he won't be back for some time.

Despite being drenched, having thrown my guts up, being hit in the face and seeing everything smoking in shades of grey, I smile.

It's time to escape.

***

As I'd studied the rooftop, I'd also noted possible routes down to the street. The library roof is terraced, and I quickly head in the direction opposite to what Darul had taken, lowering myself to the next level.

I'm unusually fatigued, especially considering how I'd felt before entering the gate, and it's hard going. Still, after scraping my knees and elbows through the wet fabric of my black clothes, I jump to the cobbled streets.

My ankle twists on a smooth cobblestone, and I end up on my backside in a puddle.

Damn.

Gingerly, I wriggle my foot. My ankle is sore, but not enough to cause concern. Grabbing a drainpipe, I pull myself upright and take a few tentative steps, then pick up the pace, putting some distance between myself and the library.

The sky brightens as dawn approaches, the storm thankfully abating. Despite being lost in a city that I've never been to, in a country hostile to my own, for the first time since before my mother died, I'm finally free.

'Lotane, I'm coming,' I whisper.

The thought lends me a little strength. I'm pretty sure I'm the first through the Soul Gate, but I can't afford to linger. I don't know whether Lotane will appear on the library roof or elsewhere. The only certainty is where we'll meet.

First, however, I need to ensure Darul doesn't find me. Like any Chosen, he's well trained in tracking, but this city is vast, and only the main streets are lit. There'll be nothing to indicate my route, and I'll be safe as soon as I'm out of sight of the library rooftop.

I need shelter and somewhere to sleep. Once daylight arrives and I've recovered my strength, I'll need to sort out supplies and equipment. I've come through with no money, no weapons, nothing but my clothes. But I have skills beyond most mortals, and if I have to acquire what I need through nefarious means, then so be it.

My feet squish inside my boots as I jog through the puddles littering the cobbled streets. The city isn't as quiet as I thought now I'm at street level. Occasionally I pass houses from which the stirrings of life can be heard. Several have lanterns on either side of their front doors, burning with a strange white light. Again, there's no colour, just the bright white flame and the shades of grey and black around it. I keep expecting to see fires burning, for that mysterious smoke rises from anything and everything.

Occasional sounds of drunken laughter echo on the night air, yet it isn't comforting.

An alley looms ahead, offering sanctuary, and I slip into the shadows. Yet bizarrely, I can still see clearly. Has travelling through the Soul Gate somehow affected my vision? I just wish everything wasn't so grey and stark.

The rain finally stops, but as it does so, from a doorway to my left, three figures move to block my route.

I stagger to the far side of the alley in disbelief, shocked at what stands before me. I can make out they're men, but their faces twist and shift, one moment normal, the next hideous, eyes bulging, teeth elongating. A dark light emanates from their core, pulsing.

The carvings on the terrace back at the mountain come to mind. The horrific beasts that grovelled at the king's feet are here in front of my very eyes!

Horrified, I skirt around them. I'm in no fit state to fight.

My vision blurs momentarily as I stagger along. Behind me, I'm aware of the grotesque trio spreading across the alley, following. Fortunately, they don't seem intent on closing in.

However, I hear a low whistle, and as I struggle to pick up my pace, two men and a woman step out in front of me. Like the others, their faces constantly twist between normality and hideous caricatures.

Knives and cudgels are in their hands as they approach.

I'm unarmed, weak, with no magic to call upon. This situation won't end well.

'You shouldn't be 'ere,' the woman cackles. 'This ain't yer patch. I dunno where yer from, but yer ain't going back now.'

An impossibly long black tongue lolls from her mouth, then disappears. The man to her right has horns or snakes pushing from his head, while the one on the left has worms falling from his eyes. A moment later, they flicker back to the nasty-looking humans they are.

Dizziness has me reaching for the wall as I desperately try to steady myself. I need to run, or my life will end here. The thought sickens me; I'm not used to running.

It hadn't made sense until this very moment, but it's to fight this evil that I've been trained.

Footsteps quickly close in, and I turn, ducking under the cudgel swung at my head. As my assailant overbalances, I snap my fist out, hearing a satisfying whoosh of expelled air as it sinks into his soft gut. I step past, stamping backwards into the side of his knee, and his screams sound shrill on the night air.

The blood rush that accompanies combat which I'd hoped would give me strength, doesn't arrive. I stumble off-balance, shying away from some grasping fingers. This time the palm of my hand connects with the bridge of a nose, and a loud snap precedes the howl of pain that satisfyingly joins the screams.

Yet my lungs are heaving, my vision dims, and the kicks and punches I manage to land no longer have any weight and only sap my strength further.

Suddenly a foul-smelling sack is dropped over my head from behind, and I'm struck hard.

'Let's have some fun before we kills her,' a thick voice made harsh by years of drinking says, followed by a wicked laugh. 'After the hurt she's done, we deserve some payback.'

Another blow to my head, and I'm falling into blackness.

***

The scrape of rough fabric as the sack is pulled off my head brings me around, and a thumping headache awaits. Considering what's before me, I wish it had stayed on.

A frustrated groan at my weakness and failure forces itself past the filthy gag stuffed into my mouth. My arms are restrained behind me, and my legs secured. I can't move more than my head, but even that causes dizziness.

It's early morning - the light coming through filthy windows. Yet this sunrise is unlike any I've ever known. The sun is a dirty white; the city over which it shines, shades of grey and black. Dark clouds fill the sky, and there's no hint of colour anywhere. Has my eyesight been permanently damaged by travelling through the gate? Not that it will matter for much longer.

On several dilapidated sofas beneath the window, three men lie half asleep. Their faces twist and blur, making it hard to determine what they look like.

At my feet is a filthy straw mattress. Upon it, a further two men and a woman entwine in a mound of slapping, grinding, wobbling naked flesh. I'm morbidly fascinated by their bodies changing from the hideous to the horrific before my eyes.

Whilst in human form, the woman's body is a mass of rashes and sores, but she flickers, and the next moment is like a bloated slug, glistening, with excretions dribbling from a dozen sucking holes.

The men are just as bad. Blackened limbs, rotting flesh, maggots falling from their mouths one moment, just pale fat bellies, filthy nails, and skinny limbs the next.

To my right is a rickety wooden table covered in sharp, wicked-looking metal instruments. Against a wall stands a mirror, reflecting my drawn face back at me. To my left is a wooden door, beyond which is freedom, life … something I'll never see again.

Tears run down my face, but not from self-pity or despair; I'm furious. I've not only failed in my mission to escape but apparently made a terrible decision to do so. The selfishness of putting my happiness over and above what I'd been trained for is laid bare before me.

The grunts and groans cease, and the absence of sound makes me glance down.

'She woke.' The woman grins, peering around a broken nose and swollen eyes. 'Don't yer worry gal. The boys is all ready for yer. Warmed up, so to speak. After they 'ave their fun, I'll 'ave some for meself.' She points to the instruments on the table, making her meaning clear.

The three of them laugh. I'd happily kill them, but I don't have the strength even if I was free, nor can I get a response from my magic.

I attempt to talk through the thick gag, pulling a piteous look.

One of the naked men stands up. 'I fink she wants to beg for mercy,' he chuckles, pulling my gag down roughly. 'What ya wanna say?'

I whisper soft words, sniffling, my head down, a beaten, defeated prisoner.

'Was that?' he asks, leaning closer.

I sink my teeth into his ear, clamping my jaw shut as he howls, trying to pull away. He only succeeds once I've torn most of it off.

'You bitch!' he screams, blood pouring down his neck.

He slaps me hard again and again across the face. My vision darkens, but I laugh weakly, my chin covered in blood as I spit his ear onto the floor. I hope I pass out, never to wake up, but I'm not that lucky. The pain is dull, barely felt, as if he's striking someone else.

Despite the man's pain, I can see lust push it aside.

My bonds are cut. I feebly kick, scratch, and claw, but I can barely lift my arms. They must have drugged me, for I've no strength to fight. No wonder my magic feels beyond reach. If it wasn't, I'd have set them on fire, watched them burn, and died happily alongside them.

'You sure knocked the stuffing outta 'er. She's got nuffin left, mores da pity. She looks 'alf dead. Why ya look so green n orange?' asks the woman, grabbing my chin, turning my face to look at her, intrigued by my coloured skin.

Maybe they'll kill me quickly if they think I'm ill so I don't suffer the ignominy of what will happen before I die.

'I'm horribly diseased,' I mumble.

'Hah. So's dem boys. Yer in good company!'

Suddenly there's a thump, and the door to my left crashes inwards to slam against the wall.

Darul flows into the room, wooden staff in hand, and while my three captors lunge for weapons, he's upon them. The crack of the wooden staff as he brings it down upon the woman's skull leaves no doubt she's dead. *One ear* manages to grab a wicked-looking dagger, but he drops it with a cry of pain as the staff breaks his wrist, sending the blade skidding across the floorboards.

The trio on the sofas scramble to their feet, bearing cudgels and knives.

The two naked men back away with hate-filled eyes toward their three friends as Darul turns to me. He doesn't say a word, simply pushes me roughly off the chair. As I fall to the floor, he closes the door and jams the chair under the handle, wedging it closed.

He says nothing as he looks from the woman dead at his feet, black blood pooling around her head, to me, back to the five men who begin to circle him.

In silence, Darul lowers his head, breathing slowly, the staff held vertically in front of him. His booted feet are slightly more than shoulder-width apart. To an untrained observer, it appears a suicidal approach. But I know he won't die because I'd be doing the same thing in his boots. We are Chosen, and we live to kill.

From the stillness comes motion, so sudden to my foggy mind as I lie on my side that I'm unsure what I'm seeing.

The staff blurs as Darul leaps forward, felling the apparition before him with a blow to the side of the head that leaves an eyeball hanging from the socket as the man collapses lifeless to the floor.

He then leans back, using the staff as a brace while a knife flashes through the air to thunk, quivering into a wooden window frame. Quickly he spins and kicks another thug in the chest, sending him crashing into the wall.

Two down in a matter of heartbeats, and there's no slowing of the fight as the men shout in fear and fury, crowding each other as they try to overwhelm Darul.

The staff sweeps up between another's legs, eliciting a high-pitched scream that makes me wince.

Only the original two naked men are left standing.

Darul moves toward them while they cry out in fear and pain under the barrage of his blows. The staff smacks loudly into knees and elbows, shattering bones and joints, incapacitating them until they're mewling, crying wrecks upon the floor.

Darul dispatches the other men, then looks at me with a half-smile.

'I knew you'd try and run,' he says, his voice flat, indifferent. 'Long ago, I tried to run. Some or maybe all of your friends will try and run. Yet, there's no escape from death if you do. Even if you'd escaped me, avoided these scum, and then found sanctuary … you'd still die.

'Your soul was taken from you as payment for passage through the Soul Gate. Your body will die quickly without it, and that's why you're so weak and disorientated. You won't last till the end of the day unless you reclaim it by returning home. After all this time of using the gate, I can live for maybe a month before I succumb, but as this is your first trip, you'll definitely die soon.

'In your heart, you know what I say is true. Without our souls, everything is shades of grey, black, and white, and everyone we look upon shows glimpses of their true inner evil. Had you tried to eat, there'd be no taste. Had you smelled a flower, there'd have been no scent. You're currently soulless and dying, but it needn't be that way.'

Pulling one of the strange crystal daggers from his belt, he kneels above the man who'd been fornicating on the mattress and who can't even raise his arms in self-defence.

'This is a Soul Blade,' Darul says to me, spinning the weapon by its blunt tip on his finger. It shimmers, catching the pale light of the morning sun. 'You'd be hard-pressed to cut butter with it, and it's impossible to cut ourselves with.'

So saying, he draws the edge across his hand, but as expected, it leaves no mark.

'That's because we have no soul. For those who still have theirs, however dark, well …'

Darul brings the weapon down, barely holding it between thumb and forefinger until it hovers above his wide-eyed victim's heart.

The blade is so blunt, yet as he lets it slip from his grasp, I watch incredulously as the crystal disappears into the man's body until only the crossguard and hilt show. Even water would have offered more resistance than flesh.

'Please, no,' whispers the man, then dies.

Darul fixes me with his intense gaze.

'A Soul Blade can kill instantly. Plunge it into your victim's vitals, and it will have the same effect as a normal weapon, but with one big difference.'

He pulls the blade free with as much ease as it went in, and there's no sign of a wound, no gaping hole, no leaking blood. However, the dagger blade now shines with colourful light. It's mesmerising in this world of greys.

'The other way is to have the weapon enter a non-vital part of the body. Then, just like us, your victim will die in time, separated from their soul, the world around them hideous to behold. This allows us to kill a target stealthily without anyone understanding what's happening until too late.

'Your turn,' Darul says, pulling the other dagger from its sheath.

'That scum will die anyway from the wounds you gave him,' I gasp. 'I would rather he die a slow death than kill him.' Yet even as I say the words, I realise they're untrue.

'Only the strong survive,' intones Darul. 'You have a choice. Kill, or die here. I won't kill you, but you'll still die.'

There's no misunderstanding Darul's meaning, and my doubts have already disappeared as I crawl over.

Darul has so effectively broken *one ear's* bones that he can do little more than wriggle as I sit astride his nakedness and take the proffered Soul Blade. His face flickers back and forth between his own and some twisted apparition, but the look they share is similar; bowel-wrenching fear.

'Is this what you imagined,' I hiss, my fury rising. 'Me on top while you thrust into me? Well, it hasn't quite worked out the way you planned, has it?'

The dagger's hilt fits snugly in my palm as if it was made for me.

Despite my weakness, I drive the blade down again and again. Finally, the screams stop as the dulled point pierces his heart. It's strange not to be covered in blood after such a savage attack.

Falling off the corpse, I retch, not at what I've done, but from general nausea.

Darul retrieves the dagger, picks me up effortlessly, and, after brushing the implements off the table, sits me down on the rough wood while holding me upright.

'This Soul Blade now contains the soul of this scum who was going to rape and kill you. Now, when you return through the gate, your soul will be returned to you in exchange for this offering.'

A sudden banging on the door makes my head snap around, inducing another wave of nausea.

'What's going on, Fletch?' a voice shouts, and the door handle rattles as someone attempts to open it. 'Get the lads, quickly,' I hear, and boots pound along the floorboards outside.

'I've no wish to die in this place,' I mutter. 'But I've no strength to get back to the library roof. You'd better go before more come back and you're overwhelmed.'

Darul smiles, even if his eyes remain hard.

'You've now seen evil for yourself. The Chosen's mission, as you know, is to rid the world of people like them,' and he nods at the corpses. 'But soon and more importantly, to remove those in power, so paving the way for our king's return.'

The door shudders as something heavy smashes against it from outside, and angry shouts sound through the wood.

'Will you come back to serve our king?'

There's no doubt in my mind, not now. Maybe if Lotane has yet to go on his mission, I can tell him of our folly. If he's already gone, he'll have failed at his escape as I had at mine and hopefully been given the same choice.

I nod, my steady gaze reassuring.

Darul presses the Soul Blade's hilt into my hand.

'We don't need to go back to the library. We have what we need right here. Push the dagger into the mirror!'

I stagger to the wall to do as instructed. When the blade touches the mirror, the glass ripples, there's a dark flash, a feeling of wetness and air whistling past my ears. A heartbeat later, I'm falling onto the dais beneath the Soul Gate.

I lie on my back, staring up at the morning sky. I've never seen a blue so deep; it's stunning. The yellow sun is rising, glorious in its brilliance, and birds circle high above, red plumage shining. I can't help but cry at the beauty of it all.

Darul moves to stand above me with Lystra alongside him. She kneels next to me, lifts my head and the sweetest water I've ever tasted trickles down my throat.

'Sleep, my Chosen,' she whispers. 'Welcome home.'

***

CHAPTER XIII

'Hello, Alina.'

'Karson! It's been too long!'

I run through a grassy field full of bright flowers and dancing butterflies and sweep him into my arms, enjoying his warm hug while I spin around.

His laughter is so infectious that before long, I collapse on the floor, unable to stand.

I'm so happy that I cry and cry. I sob so hard that my heartbeat struggles to stay steady, and I hold him so tight that I suddenly worry I might break his bones or do something terrible.

Reluctantly I release him, and he jumps up, skipping around, spinning, and laughing before sitting in front of me again.

'You've found love, Alina, and that's amazing, for in love lies the hope of redemption. Let love drive your decisions, not duty. Let your heart decide what's right or wrong, not orders or conditioning.'

I shake my head, and a frown replaces Karson's smile.

'It's true, I've found love, and that love drove me to try and escape. But Karson, it was the wrong thing to do! The things I've seen, the evil I've witnessed. To run away with Lotane would be an unforgivable act of selfishness when there is none better to fight against evil than I. It's what we've trained for; it's our mission. That must come first.'

He's serious again, the look judging.

'You can't always believe what you see in the mirror, nor with your own eyes, Alina. I've told you this before. Your soul is in jeopardy, Alina. It's at a crossroads. Look there!' and he points to his left.

There are more mounds of bodies.

'And there!'

Again, there are more.

Everywhere he points, death is prevalent, as far as my eye can see.

'Those are your possible futures, Alina. You're responsible for all of those lives taken.'

'Do you always have to judge me so harshly?' I reply, my joy at seeing Karson eroded by his words. 'Have you not been listening? I'm being tasked with destroying evil, and if my path is littered with corpses, then it's because I'm making the world a better place.'

Karson clenches his little fists and shakes them angrily.

'To have found love in your heart and then to lose your soul at the same time is a sad thing, Alina. You have to open your eyes and look closer to see the truth.'

Anger rises within me as I hold Karson's gaze with my own.

'Why can't you see that I've been chosen to help usher in a new golden age for this world? Is not sacrificing my soul selfless if it's for the greater good? Are taking the lives of wrongdoers not acceptable if tens of thousands of innocents are saved? I believe that's a price worth paying, and if I die in making this happen, then so be it. It will have been a worthy sacrifice!'

Karson's face turns whiter than usual, and the accusing look is replaced by something else.

Fear.

'No, Alina, you mustn't die! If you do, this is what the world will look like.'

Darkness falls, and suddenly we're standing in a city. Crumbling walls, broken doors, empty windows, and rats everywhere gnawing on piles of bleached bones.

The light returns, and we're in a field again with the bodies gone.

Yet Karson begins to fade away, and a cold wind blows.

'You've chosen your path, Alina. Now, what once was ... will soon be again. But don't forget, different futures await if you simply abandon the one you're heading toward. Don't always take the path of least resistance. It usually leads down to the darkness, whereas to struggle uphill brings you to the light!'

***

I awake to the semi-darkness of my chamber.

Never have I been so happy to awaken here, but that feeling swiftly vanishes. In moments, I'm wracked by guilt and a sense of unworthiness. All these years, I've doubted, and even led Lotane astray when he'd been walking the righteous path.

Who am I to question older and wiser minds than mine? Until I was brought here, I was nothing, and despite being given everything, I've been blind and ungrateful.

Why would The Once and Future King want someone like me to serve him? I want nothing else now, and I cry silently, hot tears running down my cheeks, soaking the pillow. I want another chance, but it isn't for me to decide that, nor was it Darul's. Only the king can offer me redemption, and if he demands my life for my cowardice or disloyalty, then so be it.

Yet that realisation causes me to pause. There's only one way to receive a verdict from the king: to see him again. However, I doubt the ssythlans will be accommodating to an approach. I can't lie, and an *'excuse me, can you please summon the king so I can tell him what a faithless Chosen I've been?'* probably won't get me very far.

There's only one thing for it.

With a sense of purpose, I leave my room without putting my boots on, quieter than a mouse.

The magic within me quests outwards, giving me a sense of security as I hurry through the mountain, and just like when I'd visited Lotane, I arrive at the Heart Stone chamber unaccosted.

Red light pulses hypnotically, and calm sweeps aside any misgivings I might have harboured over my actions.

Who knows how much time I'll have, so I approach the mirror and place my hands upon it as I'd seen the ssythlan do. I stare at the king's chamber through the glass. It's nigh on an exact replica of the one where I stand, except that with no Heart Stone, it's empty.

Where is he?

I shake my head with a wry smile. Had I really expected The Once and Future King to appear just by holding the frame or find him waiting for me, playing knucklebones to pass the time?

Think, Alina! How do I summon the king?

I feel a familiar tugging from within, not vying for my attention, just the blood magic making itself felt.

Smiling, I whisper my thanks. It's obvious. I'm linked by blood magic through the mirror to the king. It's this bond that fills me with the desire to serve, carrying out his wishes as if they are my own.

So, if the blood magic binds me to the king, then it also binds him to me. That is how the ssythlan cleric was able to summon him.

'My king,' I whisper in my mind, and I wait patiently, yet he doesn't come.

'My king.'

Once again, I call softly. This time the blood magic rises inside of me. Opening my spirit eye, I see it respond to my need by coiling around the thread that joins me to the mirror, making it thrum like an instrument's string.

I wait somewhat impatiently, and then I see a glow in the corridor.

He is coming. Nogoth. The Once and Future King.

I release the mirror, stepping back, watching his approach. As before, there's an aura around him, lighting his way. He looks as regal as before, in clothes that are a mixture of greens and browns, and if it weren't for his golden circlet, he might have just been hunting in a forest.

He pauses briefly as he catches sight of me, then continues in his confident walk.

'My child,' he says, and the rolling depth of his voice resonates in my very bones like thunder. 'Nothing has surprised me for centuries, yet today, I find myself somewhat at a loss. No one but my loyal ssythlans can request my presence, yet there you stand, alone.

'I don't know whether to be outraged or amused, demand your head for insolence, or reward you for your strength of resolve.' He rubs his chin, regarding me, considering his options, then shrugs his shoulders.

'Tell me, how long has it been since I last saw you?'

It seems a strange question, but who am I to wonder why, and I'm glad he hasn't demanded my head, although once I tell him my reason for being here, it wouldn't surprise me.

'Two years, my king,' I say, bowing.

He shakes his head. 'Do you know that for me, it's been about two months since I spoke to you? Time passes differently for us both. It's a paradox I'm unable to fathom, and there's little that I can't understand.

'So, to reward your courage, tell me, what has you seeking my audience?'

My mouth is suddenly dry, yet I gather my strength and take a deep breath. There can be no holding back on the truth; I will lay my soul bare.

'We are to serve you, and I feel humbled to have been Chosen, but ...' and despite my resolve, I stumble, struggling to admit my weakness.

'Tell me,' he sighs softly, kindly, as if with infinite patience. 'I will not judge you if you but speak your mind, for I have asked you to share it!'

Encouraged by his words, I recover my train of thought.

'My king. Whilst I've completed my training, I failed my final test. I lacked not only the courage and conviction at the last but led another astray too. I realise my mistake now, but I cannot forgive myself for what I've done. I truly wish to make amends and serve you with all my heart, but I feel unworthy. I'd rather die than live with this cancer hidden inside of me, so I come seeking your judgement.'

Never has my heart beaten so swiftly. Even as the words tumble from my mouth, I realise I've condemned myself to a grisly fate, yet it's nothing that I don't deserve.

But instead of righteous outrage, anger, and unmitigated fury, a smile appears.

'My child. Did you ever stop to consider that you didn't fail the final test, but instead passed? I know what you and the other Chosen face, and the final test is not passing through the gate or collecting a soul. It's the choice to return and serve with all your heart, having seen the evil you must face every day.

'You say you lack courage. Yet here you stand, expecting a death sentence for your perceived crimes. Now, as we're talking candidly ... what personally caused you to attempt an escape? Without addressing the cause, your doubts might, at some stage, resurface.'

My head is swimming. I can hear his question, but I'm almost overcome with euphoria at his words. I didn't fail! I blink back tears of happiness in case they're perceived as tears of relief.

Pull yourself together, Malina.

The king looks at me expectantly, and he's asked me to be honest.

'Why must hundreds of children die so a few like me are Chosen? We're told you're wise and just, and you're returning to rule a broken world, bringing peace and equality. Yet I also have the blood of innocents on my hands, and, and ...'

'And you questioned how can a king who demands such blood be worthy of your loyalty?'

'Yes!'

How can he fathom what's on my mind?

'No Chosen has ever dared question me thus!' and his tone is slightly deeper, a hint of annoyance flavouring his voice.

I tremble. Yet, I'm also resolute.

'Malina.'

He remembers my name!

'My ssythlan clerics told me you were different, but they still did you a disservice. It isn't just the magic that imbues you unlike any other that makes you stand out. It's that when everyone just follows, you're the only one to question the route being taken.'

I find myself unable to meet his eyes.

That sage head nods slowly, and to my amazement, he lowers himself to the floor, crosses his legs and indicates for me to do the same.

'I really should have a chair brought here,' he half mutters, shifting his weight to make himself comfortable, then looks at me with that heavy gaze.

With elbows upon his knees and that strong chin resting on his knuckles, he studies me for a moment longer.

'I could be glib and say that to appreciate the greatest view, you should not only climb the highest mountain but plumb the darkest depths first. However, I fear you'd simply ask; *What view will I see?* Before you agree to do anything.

'So first, I'll remind you why you climbed and why so many fell along the way. Then, you'll have to determine whether the price demanded was worth it.

'The lands you live in are fractured, broken, and corrupt. Kingdoms are at war, fighting one another, scheming to prosper at the expense of others. The nobility doesn't suffer, for the battlefields they fight upon are lined only with the bodies of the poor.

'Look back at yourself. You were sold, your life worth a few coppers, yet that is not your worth. Now, here you sit, educated and wise beyond your scholars, more skilful than most warriors and with such questions as you ask, more considerate than most kings.

'Yet what you attained all comes at a high cost, the foremost of which is secrecy, and that's why none who are weak can live to tell the tale. What happens in the Mountain of Souls must never be revealed. Imagine if the kings of your world were forewarned of my arrival by those who failed? They'd be forearmed, and the lives lost during training would pale into insignificance and be for nothing.

'I intend to unify your world by casting out the ruling class that sucks the blood of the poor like a parasite. For that to happen and to successfully reclaim what was once mine, I need my Chosen to share this vision and be willing to fight evil in whatever guise it takes. But first, you had to be strong enough to survive.'

I could listen to his voice for hours, yet I have more to say.

'But with such a vision, why not simply have us follow you out of love or at least free will? Why bind us using blood magic, so we're coerced into obedience?'

Nogoth removes his circlet, placing it on the stone floor beside him, and then runs his fingers through his long hair. I can tell from his look that he's relieved to take it off. It must be a heavy burden to rule.

'You're very astute to have determined the means by which you're bound … that is a good question, but one easily answered. When you arrived, you were a lamb, and now you've finished your training, you're a wolf. Now, not everyone has as strong a conscience as you and therein lies a great risk. Imagine the carnage if a Chosen such as Kralgen was seduced by the killing and went his own way? No. I must ensure that never happens; thus, all Chosen must be bound.'

I mull over his words, trying to put aside my awe to remain objective. I'm still uncomfortable with the death of so many, and I was right to question him, but his words have eased my doubts. He was not compelled to answer me, and his transparency has eased my mind.

My faraway gaze must have been noticeable as I considered his words, for his cough brings my attention back to him.

'You mentioned you led another astray. Was it for the same reason?'

If it had been painful sharing my doubts and concerns, then explaining my feelings for Lotane will be excruciating. Yet, I can't deny my king, not now, and never again.

'No, my king. The reason I led him astray was the other reason I sought to escape. Love. I wanted to be with him more than anything.'

'Love,' Nogoth muses. 'There is truly no greater magic, and more than anything else, that earns you my forgiveness if ever you needed it. Some lose their humanity during training, but I'm glad to see you're not one of those.

'Malina. I've waited nigh on a millennia to return to your world. Now, recognising your compassion, I'd ask for your help, over and above your coming duties as a Chosen.'

I gasp. 'You need my help? You? But you're a god. What god needs a human's help?'

He laughs, full of good humour, and it's as if music plays in my ears.

'A god? Perhaps I might seem that way. I've lived for years beyond recollection and walked upon both your world and mine. But a god, I'm not. So, will you help me? From the others, I demand it, but from you, I only ask.

'Will you serve me of your own free will and do everything and anything which needs to be done, in full understanding of the sacrifice some might be forced to make?'

My eyes shine with tears.

His vision is beyond my mortal critique. To unify a land riven by wars, to raise the poor from the gutters and finally deliver peace under one divine ruler.

I can only nod.

'Then, leave me to my plans. In just one of your years, I shall come back to claim what was mine, and between now and then, you must help with the preparations for my arrival. Obey without question, live to serve, and know my love.

'You are my favourite Chosen, Malina. As proof of my belief in you, I would ask you to grant me a wish. When I arrive, be my advisor, stand at my side and never be afraid to share your wisdom. Stay my hand if I'm too bold, counsel mercy if I'm too vengeful and help me see right from wrong.'

My eyes convey the answer. He doesn't need to hear my words or my gratitude.

Placing the circlet back upon his head, he rises smoothly to his feet as I lower my head in homage.

'One more thing, Malina. No one must know you've spoken to me. Keep this to yourself.'

My eyes follow his receding figure, holding on until the glow of his radiance disappears.

I'll not fail him.

***

I can barely bring myself to eat the sun fruit I'm holding, and as I look at my fellow Chosen, I'm relieved to see I'm not the only one. It's almost comical, for they're also examining the food as if it's their first-ever meal.

After witnessing the darkness of the outside world, we admire the colours and scents of various fruits. Freshly cooked bread becomes an item of fascination as we breathe in the aroma, our senses close to overload.

Kralgen has a childlike look of wonder, which likely matches my own. Nestor and Lotane gaze around wide-eyed, whereas Fianna constantly plays with her hair, fascinated by its brightness.

Usually, Lystra would set the pace of our breaking fast, and we'd finish together. But this morning, she allows us to savour the finest food we've ever tasted without hurrying us.

I can't help but stare at Lotane. His blue and green eyes are stunning, and my heart aches at the beauty of his gaze.

There's no doubt the others feel as I do. We are reborn, and everything is new. This island is our paradise whilst the world around us is overrun by the denizens of hell.

'My Chosen,' Lystra begins, drawing our attention as we eventually finish eating. 'Now you're beginning to understand. You've all seen the darkness of the world beyond these shores and the evil it holds. Here, this island we call home is the only place where the light shines. Only here do the pure reside, for doing the will of The Once and Future King absolves us of all guilt.

'He is the only one who can restore order and bring light to replace the darkness, and with every soul we take, we bring our king ever closer.

'Yes,' Lystra continues. 'The Soul Gate isn't just our means of travel; it's his! After hundreds of years, it's almost time. The ssythlan High Cleric tells me the gate now resonates with the power that generations of Chosen have fought and died for. Soon, the lunar constellations will align, and enough souls will have been gathered to open it!

'I know some of you have had your doubts,' Lystra continues without looking at anyone in particular.

Kralgen and Alyssa appear baffled. Apparently, not them.

'But now is not the time to tread carefully; it's the time for us to shake the world with the stamp of our feet! Evil will hear our approach and know the end is upon them.'

We're all swept up by Lystra's speech. Her belief is inspiring but also slightly scary.

'On the morrow, you'll return through the gate, and the day after, then the day after that. You will continue strengthening your bodies and minds, finding purity in cleansing the unclean. Then, when you're ready, you'll be given the honour of slaying the darkest of them all, the generals, the queens, and the kings. Even the High King himself!'

Only the iron discipline of years of training stops us from exclaiming at this news.

It all makes sense now. In a world divided by war, if the High King is killed, the Delnorian empire will crumble. Then if the lesser rulers of the warring nations are dispatched, Nogoth will fill the power vacuum with no cohesive force to oppose him. His ascension to power will be relatively bloodless. It is a masterstroke of genius and strategy, and the Chosen are the linchpin upon which this plan rests.

Lystra smiles, and I'm shocked. I've seen her smile before, most often when she kills, more rarely when we exceed her expectations, but never with true happiness.

'Then, everything we've suffered, for every wound that's bled, and Chosen that's been lost, we'll be repaid a thousandfold as our king arrives to heal the world with his love! However, you'll not have to wait until the king's arrival to receive his thanks. To those who serve him with unswerving loyalty, his love matches your own. Come with me.'

Lystra takes her time, leading us from the eating chamber, up through the mountain, past our quarters, and then upwards again.

I look across at Lotane. The last time we'd climbed this high had been when we'd gone through the Soul Gate. However, we only go up a further level before Lystra steps onto a landing and leads us along another passageway.

Soon we're on another beautiful terrace similar to the one we'd enjoyed below. To my surprise, Darul, the Chosen who'd first taken me through the gate, is here. A beautiful woman holds his arm, resting her head on his shoulder as they gaze over the balcony wall at the incredible vista. Two other Chosen, for who else can they be, sit on a stone bench. One man is leaning back, resting in the embrace of another, but they stand fluidly when they see us enter and move away to give us some space.

I cannot believe my eyes as there's no hint of worry on their faces at being discovered by Lystra, and in fact, she strides away to embrace Darul and his partner briefly before returning, leaving them to one another.

'The greatest gift our king bestows upon us is his love, and thereafter his blessing for us to love another. I'm not blind and have seen the affection growing between you. Yet strength attracts strength, and this is how it should be. There's no place for the weak amongst us, nor in the wider world.

'Henceforth, you need not hide your affection from me nor each other when you're alone or within the confines of this level. Your sleeping arrangements have also changed to reflect your relationships. Your rooms can be found through yonder passage, and it will be evident to whom each belongs. However, let's not waste the day. Just because your training days are behind you, it doesn't mean we shouldn't continue to strive for perfection.

'So come, prove to me a final time that you're worthy to serve our king.'

***

'I made it as far as the docks in Tarsala.'

Lotane speaks softly as we touch blades, circling one another in the training circle. On either side of us, a safe distance away, Kralgen spars with Alyssa and Fianna with Nestor. I'm breathing raggedly, having already faced Kralgen and Alyssa.

Never before have we trained so hard to celebrate and to prove we're worthy.

The ring of clashing steel muffles out his words. The blades everyone uses are blunted, but whilst not deadly, they can still cause serious harm. I'm wielding two short swords against Lotane's long sword, and neither of us can get the upper hand.

Lotane whirls his blade in a figure of eight, then, using the sweeping momentum, raises and brings it down in an overhand cut. Blunted edge or no, this strike would kill me, but if I can't parry this, I don't deserve to be here or receive the gifts our king bestows upon us.

His is the heavier weapon, so I cross mine, catching his blade between the two. We pit our strength briefly against the other as we face off.

'I was so weak and close to death when Ateus found me,' Lotane continues. 'He told me what had happened to my soul, explained why people looked as they did, and gave me a choice to kill, then return to serve the king or stay and die.'

With a grunt, Lotane shoves me, and rather than attempt to fight his superior strength, I use its power to roll smoothly away and then to my feet to counter his next attack.

'I hoped you'd be given the same choice,' he says between grunts.

Our blades clash rhythmically, creating something akin to a harmonious tune.

'Truth be told, it took that journey to truly understand the meaning of our mission. I had to kill a cutpurse Ateus caught to earn my passage back.'

I attack furiously, and Lotane is hard-pressed to counter the speed of my weapons. Blocking one, he steps inside the arc of my swing and catches my wrist with his free hand. It's a dangerous move, but he executes it perfectly.

'I was surprised Ateus let me live. Is your story near the same?' he asks.

I'm in a disadvantaged position. Lotane is using his height to push my arms back and down. Suddenly I remove all resistance, and as he overbalances slightly, I butt him on the chin, sending him stumbling back in shock as I break free of his grip.

I nod in reply as we circle again. My blow hadn't been pleasant for either of us, but Lystra mustn't sense anything but commitment to our training, now more than ever.

The sun's heat is blistering, and sweat trickles down my neck.

Lystra comes to observe Fianna and Alyssa nearby, and we return to silence except for the grunts of effort.

'Change!' shouts Lystra, and the chance for further conversation is over.

Every half an hour, we rotate. Each of us has a different weapon. In a battle, you cannot expect every opponent to be equipped the same way.

Nestor now faces me wielding a double-bladed staff, a fearsome weapon in the right hands. The slightly curved blades at the ends and its long reach make Nestor a difficult adversary. Without a shield or a longer weapon, I'm at a disadvantage.

He spins, twirling the weapon around, and it almost sings as it parts the air. Whatever he does, his eyebrows knit together in concentration, and he focusses entirely on the task at hand. I find it strange that someone who seems so dark and devoid of emotion is attached to Fianna, who is the exact opposite.

Something about that thought makes me pause, and in that instant, Nestor attacks. I barely have time to block his first strike, and I'm caught off balance and backstep rapidly as he presses forward, not giving me time to set my feet. He can be so deceptively fast, if only he were slower ... and then, the next moment, he is.

My magic twists and turns inside me, and I realise it's come to my aid at a time of perceived peril without me consciously requesting it.

Nestor stumbles briefly, losing his balance, and as he does so, I step aside from his weak thrust and bring the flat of my blade smacking against his extended right arm. With a cry, he drops the staff, nursing his elbow.

'You're dead!' shouts Lystra angrily.

Momentarily, my insides turn to ice. She knows I've used my magic! But she rages instead at Nestor.

'You've lost your arm and are bleeding out. You had her, or so it seemed. Is this how you demonstrate your worthiness to serve? Gah!'

Lystra turns away in disgust, and Nestor looks at the ground in shame.

I feel bad. There are no rules against using magic in combat, but that's only because it's utterly impractical for anyone to employ it in this fashion. It takes too much time, focus, and pain to be used in a combat situation, except, it seems, for me.

It will take a little while for Nestor to recover from his numb arm, so even without Lystra directing me, I join Fianna against Kralgen.

Kralgen is using a long polearm. It's unwieldy but can cut a man in two, and in Kralgen's meaty fists, could probably chop a horse in half as well.

It's not a good duelling weapon, for even blunted, it can crush skulls and shatter bones, yet nonetheless, it's important we understand its abilities, and only Kralgen has the brute strength to wield it adroitly for long.

Now he's facing two opponents, Fianna with a spear and shield and me with my short swords. Kralgen swirls his weapon in long arcs, keeping us both at bay as he alternatively gives ground, then advances, ensuring we are wary of the change in his reach.

However, once you're inside a polearm's weighted head, the weapon's deadliness is mostly negated. I cross behind Fianna.

'Can you block his sweep?' I ask, the question masked by distance and me being briefly behind her.

She nods, knowing what I intend.

On her own, using her shield and spear to block the polearm's arc would leave the spear splintered and the shield equally useless, but if I'm still in the fight, as long as I finish Kralgen off, we'll be victorious.

I circle behind him, and he's in trouble, sweeping the weapon in huge arcs to keep us away. Then as planned, Fianna stays within its arc.

Slamming the spear shaft into the ground and the large tower shield behind it, she angles the top of them toward her. For the briefest moment, the momentum of the impact is deflected upward, and some of its force dissipates. Then, the spear splinters and the polearm ploughs into the thick wooden shield.

While this is happening, I'm rolling forward. Kralgen turns, his eyes catching my movement. He can't reverse the huge weapon, and this will be an easy victory. I roll to my feet, raising my swords to give him a good whack with the flat of the blade.

I register Kralgen's smile while he yanks back on the shaft of his weapon, driving its base into my stomach, knocking the air from my lungs, and flinging me on my back.

The polearm rises over his head, and I roll frantically to the side as it crashes into the ground where I was lying. Stone splinters sting my cheek as he raises the weapon again.

The next moment, he releases one hand, allowing the heavy head to clang to the floor behind while twisting, avoiding Fianna's thrust, grabbing the broken spear behind the head, and wrenching it from her grasp.

She leaps back even as that horrendous polearm starts to swing again.

Kralgen's face splits in an almighty grin.

'You lose!' he laughs, raising the polearm above his head, roaring in delight.

'Good work, the three of you,' Lystra's voice echoes around the circle, and I realise everyone has stopped to watch our battle. 'Take an hour to drink, eat and rest before this afternoon's bouts!'

As I gingerly pick myself up off the floor, Kralgen moves over to me and slaps my back hard enough to rattle my teeth. 'Good plan, Wolf Slayer. How's the stomach?'

In response, I retch, and he leaps back, then laughs hard as I stand up straight, smiling.

'Thanks for going easy on me,' I say. 'Alyssa would have hit me much harder!'

'Kralgen's face darkens momentarily, then brightens again. 'That's a joke, right?

I nod.

'You're fast, Kralgen,' Lotane joins in. 'No one's faster than you!'

Kralgen beams, not understanding the gentle sarcasm.

'What do you think you're doing?' Lystra's voice barks out, and we all turn, but her eyes are on Nestor. 'Twenty laps of the circle before you rest!'

'I might go join him,' Fianna smiles brightly. 'I'm not tired yet,' and she runs alongside when he starts off at a steady pace, still rubbing his arm.

I help myself to a food platter and water jug, smile at Lotane, and move away from Alyssa and Kralgen. Lotane joins me, and we sit with our backs to the stone wall, watching Nestor and Fianna run together. Lystra keeps alongside, undoubtedly delivering a scathing summary of Nestor's performance.

It's hard not to reach for Lotane's hand, especially now our relationship has Lystra and the king's blessing.

'Forgive me,' I ask softly.

'What for?'

'For convincing you to escape. It was wrong, and I didn't see it then.'

Lotane rubs his chin, averting his gaze, a strange nervous gesture. It's so unlike him that I get slightly worried. However, he takes a deep breath and looks at me with resolve.

'Are you sure that's how you feel? I want to make sure. I had my doubts, as you know. But now, the biggest reason for leaving has been taken away. We get to be together! No more hiding our feelings, no more snatching moments here and there, and no more lying alone every night wishing you were next to me. We'll have our own chamber. I can't explain how much that matters.

'We've tried to escape and were caught. We weren't killed nor taken to task. Instead, we've been forgiven and offered everything we wanted. And what are we asked for in return?

'To help rid the world of evil. To help the oppressed. To help usher in a golden age under the rule of our king, who has given us our lives and a chance to love! These are noble pursuits. What more can we hope for?'

There's nothing but the truth in Lotane's words, and I'm relieved that we've arrived at the same point of view together.

'You're absolutely right,' I say softly.

I want to share my experience, how it changed me, and my meeting with the king, but I can't.

Lotane's relief is beautiful to behold.

'I love you, Alina.'

My heart feels like melting. I love him too, and it's a gift.

Nestor runs by with Fianna, reminding me of my earlier thought.

'Do you think they look good together?'

Lotane chuckles, a look of surprise on his face at my line of questioning.

'I think you know the answer to that. They couldn't be more dissimilar. Nestor would be better suited to mate with a statue. I don't know what Fianna sees in him, but maybe she likes the silent type. As for Kralgen, I sometimes wonder if his father was a root vegetable, whereas Alyssa is as smart as they come. There must be some kind of magic between them, just like we have. However, all that matters is that they're in love too.'

I snort with laughter and smile. Lotane and I do have something magical, but then a chill banishes the warmth his words had given rise to. *We do have something magical* ...

Scared by what I might find, I nonetheless need to know.

Concentrating, I look through my spirit eye. I haven't had to do this for so long, as my magic responds with barely a thought. Immediately I see the shifting patterns of colours within, a reflection of the markings that now cover my skin. However, that's not what I'm interested in.

When I shift my focus outward, the elements all around are faint and inconspicuous, but there's something that isn't.

As I previously saw in the Heart Stone chamber, red threads run from us. One leads to Lystra. The others I know connect us to various ssythlans and another through the mirror to The Once and Future King.

Now, however, a further red thread joins me and Lotane.

As Nestor and Fianna move away, I see they're bound too, and unsurprisingly, so are Kralgen and Alyssa.

'What's wrong?' Lotane whispers, seeing my face drop, where it had been glowing with happiness moments ago.

I shake my head, smiling wanly, unwilling to share my discovery.

Our falling in love has not been an accident; Blood Magic has been used to bind us. Now, on the very day of accepting my fate, finding happiness and everything we've ever wanted, I find myself trying to stop my heart from breaking into pieces.

***

'Are you happy now, Alina?' Karson asks, his eyes fierce. *'Surely, you have everything you want?'*

He's sitting on the end of the bed I share with Lotane. His eyes sweep the large room we've been given. Plush red rugs cover the floor, while the twin wolf heads are positioned on either side of a private balcony entrance. Chests and wardrobes abound, and they're filled with clothes, the like of which I'd only ever seen on nobles or wealthy merchants.

A cabinet sits next to my side of the bed, where I discovered small paper sachets of herbs. A small note advises that, when mixed with water and drunk once a month, I'll never conceive. Not that I'd allowed Lotane to join with me on our first night, much to his confusion and hurt.

'Hush. If you speak too loud, you'll wake him,' I admonish Karson.

'Well. Are you happy?'

Tears running down my face are the only answer I can give. I'd always comforted Karson when he was young, yet I now feel the need for his hugs.

Perhaps sensing that, he wraps his arms around me, but they aren't to soothe, for he turns me to look at him.

'It isn't so bad,' he says, glaring. *'You've everything that's needed for a perfect relationship. You and Lotane will be lovers by day and soulless killers by night. What's there to cry about?'*

'How can you be so cruel?' I cry, pushing him away, forgetting my warning to speak quietly.

Karson's demeanour stays dark.

'I've tried being kind. Perhaps this is the only way to get you to listen! A false love, a false happiness, and a false life. You'll become like the creatures our mother used to tell tales of, only they'd just drink blood, whereas you'll be stealing souls to replace your own!'

Stop it, stop it, stop it!' I cry, screaming, pushing him away. 'Lotane and I fell in love before they used Blood Magic to bind us. Our love is real; it isn't false. He's kind and gentle, thoughtful and loving.'

Karson's laughter is cruel and mocking.

'I'm sure that will comfort those who die screaming at his hands!'

'They'll be evil, so what matter?'

'Who are you to judge? Look at yourself. You were good once. Now you're about to become the very thing you seek to hunt. Perhaps it takes evil to recognise evil?'

I was upset, but now I'm getting furious. He's pushing me so much. Whereas once I heeded his words, finding wisdom in them, now they have the opposite effect.

'You never consider that what I'm doing is the right thing. Are you jealous that I love someone else now … is that it? Maybe that's what clouds your perspective. Everyone here believes in what they're doing. To help Nogoth return to make the world a better place!'

Karson shakes his head, the anger in his eyes matching my own.

'Have you ever considered that helping this Nogoth return and making the world a better place might be two entirely separate things?'

I've had enough. How could my brother, someone I love dearly, hurt me so much?

'I live to serve Nogoth. Now, just leave me ALONE!'

This time when Karson reaches out, there's regret in his eyes, but I thrust him away.

'Just leave me alone. You bring me nothing but sadness when I should be happy. You fill me with doubts when I should be full of conviction. Look at Lotane and the others. They're happy, and that's because they don't have to listen to you!'

Hands grab my shoulders, shaking me.

'Just leave me alone. Stop hurting me!'

'Alina! Alina.'

My eyes flutter open, and there's Lotane in the dim light of the moon globe, concern and love written all over his tired features.

Our eyes lock.

Lotane brushes the hair back from my face, soothing me.

'You were crying out in your sleep, saying so many things,' he whispers softly. 'Who were you talking to, and who is Nogoth?'

'I was dreaming of my brother. As for Nogoth … he's The Once and Future King. I overheard his name being spoken.'

Lotane's eyes register worry, shock, and wonder, followed perhaps by disappointment that I hadn't shared the king's name with him before.

I've never felt so alone, so lost, so unsure. I need to find something that feels real. It doesn't matter whether it's been created by magic or nature.

'Do you truly love me?'

Lotane nods, surprised, pupils wide in the semi-darkness, no doubt still dwelling on me speaking the name of the king in my sleep.

'Of course I do. With all my heart, body, and soul.'

I kiss him deeply on the mouth, and for a moment, he pulls away before surrendering to my hunger. My lips move down his neck, I bite his shoulder hard, and he moans with awakened desire.

'Then make love to me and let me feel how much,' I demand. 'Make me forget everything and everyone but you and I.'

Lotane is my Chosen one … and rises to my demands.

***

CHAPTER XIV

'Focus on the library rooftop. Visualise exactly where you wish us to go.' Darul guides me. 'Now, tell me everything you can remember.'

'It's fifty paces across, and the parapets are waist high. They're made of whyten stone and polished to a smooth sheen. The flat roof is covered in small stone tiles, a handspan square. Where we appear, those tiles have been cracked by the arrival of many Chosen over the years.'

I pause, bringing more details to mind, before continuing.

'The cracks look like a spider's web. The small temple has carvings of a battle depicting the victory of Delnor over the Astorians in years past. The bench we sit on has feet shaped like talons, and there's one claw closest to the entrance broken off. Set behind and into the outside of the temple is a small wooden door. Open that, and some steps lead down into the library.'

'Enough. Well done.'

Darul's voice doesn't show pleasure, but his praise matters. It's strange. I've seen him several times with his partner, Ranya, and with her, he seems happy. When he's with anyone else, he has gravestones for eyes.

'Arm yourself,' he orders.

Reaching out, I grasp the hilt of a Soul Blade and pull it smoothly free from the Soul Gate's frame. It's early morning, yet the crystal weapon doesn't catch or reflect the light but absorbs it. The only time it shines is when it contains a soul. Placing it in the empty sheath at my waist, I check my attire as Darul does the same. We're dressed as minor Delnorian nobility, and nothing is out of place. No metal can pass through the gate, so we're also armed with tall wooden staves.

Since our initial journey, I've been through the Soul Gate to the capitals of Astoria, Suria and Rolantria. However, this is my fourth trip to High Delnor during the day. Each time we're there, Darul leaves me at the library while he disappears to reap some souls to pay for our return. It would have been a struggle to do anything else in my weakened state, so my initial task was simple: study the roof, imprint every little detail in my mind, and then stay inconspicuous.

I'm not sure I'll get used to how everything seems to smoke and disintegrate. I've stopped looking at my hands now, worried I'll see myself fade away. However, there's one thing I'm getting used to, and that's staying alive without my soul.

'Now, take us through.'

At Darul's command, I grasp his hand and step forward, feeling the wetness of the gate wrap around me. The screams of the damned tear at my sanity for what seems like an eternity but, in reality, is just a few heartbeats, and then I'm standing steady on the library rooftop.

'Well done.' Darul nods approvingly, appearing beside me and pulling his hand free.

Pale sunlight washes over the rooftop as we reach the door at the temple's rear. Jumping from rooftops unnecessarily during the day would just draw attention. Darul carefully pushes a piece of wood through the gap in the warped door and lifts the locking bar.

Closing the door quietly behind us, we creep down the steps, then out from behind a curtain into a chamber. It's filled with dusty shelves bowing under the weight of the books and scrolls piled upon them and is apparently hardly visited.

'I will be back shortly,' he says softly, then heads off.

The other Chosen are acclimatising elsewhere within the city. One unfamiliar face goes easily unnoticed, whereas six together might draw attention. It makes sense to keep us apart until we're ready, which won't be long, as the magic in our bodies is helping us adjust faster than expected.

I'm happy to be left here awhile. Travelling through the Soul Gate is akin to stepping into a nightmare. I use this time to mentally prepare myself for the hideousness of many we'll meet. Darul says it gets easier over time, like the separation from my soul. The mind begins to see things how it used to, and thus while evil is still apparent, it's less horrific. In a rare moment of openness, he'd also mentioned it made Ranya look all the more radiant when he saw her after a mission. I couldn't agree more. The euphoria of returning to the Mountain of Souls and a world of colour must be equivalent to a blind man seeing for the first time.

Filthy windows abound, and the sun's rays spear across the chamber, yet I feel no warmth. Instead, the cold hand of death clutches me in its bony fingers as I walk along the shelves reading the spines of ancient tomes.

This section is about Icelandian history, and I pull a dust-covered tome down. It's heavy and leather-bound, with a brass clasp. Sitting down at a lonely wooden desk, I pry it open and peer at the faint writing within. Fortunately, the script is common tongue because, whilst I speak Icelandian, my training hasn't encompassed reading it. Pictures abound, and I'm sad that I can't see the colours that would bring this story of ancient kings to life.

Nonetheless, I turn the pages slowly, marvelling at the knowledge and history held within its covers. Our training to be Chosen is all about learning, and I apply myself, trying to memorise every fact I read.

The whisper of hesitant footsteps warns me of someone's approach. It isn't Darul, yet there's no threat, merely caution in their placement.

A wizened old man approaches, wagging a wrinkled finger that's as crooked as the staff he leans upon. He's dressed in white robes, for even in this world of greys, it stands out,

'Who are you, and what are you doing here?' His voice rises and falls, breaking like a teenage boy's. 'Well, are you going to tell me, or shall I call the guards?'

One of his eyebrows arches so high that it's close to migrating to his bald head, and I wonder how long he can keep it up there. Despite his age-related feebleness, he speaks with authority and is undoubtedly a librarian, perhaps even the head of this establishment. Considering I'll be coming through here frequently, there's no gain in provoking him.

What's also pleasantly surprising is that whilst his eyes flicker slightly red, he doesn't shift into some awful creature. Apparently, he's a decent soul, albeit a grumpy old one.

I smile disarmingly, tapping the open book.

'My name's Malina. As for what I'm doing here, well, I'm a student of history.'

The other eyebrow joins the first. They're so bushy that, temporarily, he almost has a good head of hair. I have to work hard not to laugh at the thought.

'You're probably looking to steal something,' he grumbles, looking closely, fascinated by my skin and eyes.

This time my smile is frosty. I am, after all, supposed to be a Delnorian noble and am dressed as one.

'Why bother stealing it when I could buy the whole library if I had the mind?'

'Hah,' he nods, gazing over my expensive robes. 'Fair enough. Still, I'm not sure I believe you're interested in history. More likely, you're having some kind of illicit liaison. Don't think I didn't see the young man leave a while ago. I can't allow that kind of thing to happen here!'

He has sharp eyes and a sharp mind despite his age. It's unlikely he'll ever be a threat, but I'll disarm him now, and there's no better way to cover a lie than by admitting guilt.

'You're right, I admit it. The young man and I are romantically linked, and this is a quiet place where we can find privacy. But I promise, nothing untoward happens here amongst these tomes, let me assure you!'

'Hmmm. I knew it,' grumbles the old librarian.

I can see he's ruminating over whether to ask me to leave, and I can't have that happen.

'But you're also wrong. I'm a student of history,' I press, bluffing. 'I'm here conducting research.'

A shrewd look spreads across his face, his nose and chin elongating slightly. I might have stumbled into a trap of sorts.

'So, tell me. What specifically are you researching? I'm the Head Librarian,' he says, confirming my suspicion. 'I also specialise in history. Perhaps I can help!'

I'm holding a tome on Icelandia, and it would seem logical to choose something from their history, but something else comes to mind.

'Perhaps you can, although I doubt it,' I sigh pessimistically.

'I can assure you, young lady, that I can point you to one of a hundred tomes instantly if you but share your quest for knowledge.'

His eyes flash red, impatience fuelling the change. There's no doubt I've piqued his interest, but the quest I'll pose him is an impossible one, although a part of me hopes not.

'I'm researching a king that was named on a scrap of parchment found in my forefather's catacombs. I've yet to find reference to him anywhere else, so I thought to travel to High Delnor, for is the library here not the greatest in the land?'

'It is, it is,' assures the old man, almost hopping from foot to foot in frustration. 'Tell me who you're looking for so I can help send you on your way.'

'The Once and Future King.' My voice is hushed, as I'm almost afraid to speak the words out loud. It's forbidden to mention his title, but it will be priceless if there's something in this library about him.

The librarian looks crestfallen, and I'm also disappointed. There'd been the smallest hope that this building of knowledge might hold something, even a reference to his previous reign, yet it seems that's not the case.

The librarian's eyebrows have returned to their normal position when marching footsteps echo through the stone hallways, and Darul shortly sweeps into the room. He nods formally to the Head Librarian, then extends his hand toward me.

'Malina, it's time to go.'

I replace the book as Darul approaches.

The old librarian nods in appreciation.

'Will you return?' he asks. His initial displeasure seems to have been replaced by fear of being left alone amongst the empty, quietness of the grave this place holds. He looks just like an old man should.

'High Delnor is my home now. You'll be sure to see me again, and I need to continue my research after all,' I reassure him as I move toward Darul.

'Until the next time,' I bid him farewell.

'Malina. One last thing.'

I look over my shoulder to see a knowing smile on the old man's face. 'My name is Arcan. Now, as we're properly introduced, feel free to use the front door next time you visit!'

***

'Come, stay close, and pay attention,' Darul instructs, leading me swiftly through the library.

I push myself to keep up. Back on the island, I can run for a day, yet here, despite acclimatising quickly, I'm shortly out of breath. The library doesn't appear to be a popular destination, and we don't encounter another person.

We pass down several grand staircases, their balustrades exquisitely carved and polished, to the columned entrance. I note Darul has a small money pouch tied to his belt. It would make sense to have resources to hand in the city.

High Delnor is a place where the extremely wealthy mingle with the poor. Here, the eyes of law-keepers and town guards are primarily drawn to the poor souls, so our guise is a good way to escape attention.

'Pull up your hood,' he whispers, and I lift the soft fabric around my head. There's little I can do about my multi-hued skin or eyes, but there's no point in flaunting them.

Darul pushes open a large blue wooden door. It creaks in protest as though offended that anyone might disturb its resting place, and we slip through.

The streets are already bustling with people. After so long in just the company of those inhabiting the Mountain of Souls, I feel assaulted by the noise. The sheer volume of people flooding by is unbelievable. Even market day back in Hastia when I was young had nothing on this.

Darul studies my reaction and nods toward the crowds when he sees me settle.

'Look closer.'

Direct daylight, or perhaps being far enough away at the top of a stone flight of steps, has given the scene a veneer of normality. But, when I do as instructed, I see peoples' faces twist and shift as they hurry about their business. To see the evil manifest itself in so many people at once is a harrowing thing, while all around the buildings let off smoke as if they're on fire with invisible flames. This is now an ugly world wherever the other Chosen or I travel.

Yet, I'm here to help end this. My mission is to usher in a new age where people are not consumed by avarice, jealousy, or lust for dominion. I've finally seen the light. There's no doubt in my mind any longer. I have everything I want, and now it's time to help the rest of the world find the same joy.

I look steadily into Darul's eyes.

'I'm ready.'

'Yes, you are.'

***

Throughout the afternoon, Darul shows me around High Delnor. Elsewhere, between the city walls, Lotane and the others are wandering the streets for the first time.

It's been so long since I've seen anything but the islands, and here I am in Delnor's bustling coastal capital. The harsh smell of saltwater and fish brings back memories of my youth before I was auctioned, and I long to explore, but my sense of duty pushes this rebellious thought aside.

Seagulls call noisily as Darul leads me purposely through the busy main streets. Perhaps he wants to test me a little more, and indeed, at times, it isn't easy. Having nigh on everyone around me shift from normal to unpleasant, or all the way to downright hideous, is hard to get used to. Yet, after a while, the shock begins to diminish, and despite the decaying look my dying eyes give to everything, I start to find a small measure of enjoyment in my surroundings.

Beautiful architecture is everywhere, the main streets dominated by white stone buildings for the upper class and high-end establishments. Where I'd grown up had nothing like this. Most of the buildings had been wooden and rickety, whereas almost everything here is made of stone. The wealthier the individual, the grander the house and the more intricate the carved exterior.

We pass through a marketplace packed with vendors' stalls, and they call us to inspect their wares. Darul ignores them, setting a fearsome pace, and I'm happy to move on. Every one of the vendors' faces is warped, shifting, evidencing greed.

Soon we're close to the seafront, walking toward some buildings covered in a smokey haze.

The docks are already busy, and the harbour is full of ships. Some are for trading, but the majority are war galleys. Several have large eyes painted on their prows, and these are getting ready to sail. Decks bustle with armed men and oars deftly manoeuvre the mighty vessels on the crowded waves.

Even in shades of grey, it's a captivating sight; the waves reflecting the sun, the clean, smooth lines of the ships and in the distance, on a hill, the citadel overlooking the harbour. High Delnor is not only the kingdom's capital but also the main port, and is heavily fortified. However, something is wrong with this perfect scene, and I spy what it is … a burnt-out ship, half-submerged next to a scorched length of the dock. Dozens of workers are swarming over that section, making repairs.

Darul brings us to a sudden halt in what was once a pleasant garden square but is now a field hospital. The stench of corrupted wounds lingers despite the sea breeze, and the sounds of despair rise above the seagulls' cries. Healers move amongst the crying soldiers who are, without exception, swathed in bloodied bandages. Rodents scurry everywhere, adding to the torment as their sharp teeth seek out the unwary.

'Just think,' Darul says quietly in my ear. 'One day, when The Once and Future King reigns, this world will know peace.'

I consider his words as I look at the carnage wrought upon these poor souls, many of whom won't survive. Yes. This is what we'll help bring an end to. All these men and women had hopes and dreams once, but thanks to the greed of kings and queens, they'll never see them come to fruition.

Leaving the sea of misery behind, Darul leads me to an eating establishment with tables and chairs scattered around a small courtyard set off to the side of a main thoroughfare.

'This place is called the Broken Arrow. The food won't taste good, but we still need to eat,' he says, as we move to a corner table where we can sit with our backs to a wall. 'Remove your hood. You'll be spending a lot of time here, and the best way we can operate clandestinely is to hide in plain sight.'

This seems contradictory, but I'm still learning, so I do as instructed.

A good-looking woman comes over, smiling happily. A bloated black tongue flops out of her mouth when she spies Darul, disappearing an instant later. As her gaze passes over me, her nose wrinkles like a wolf's muzzle.

'Good to see you, Lord Darul. It's been too long. Who's your painted lady friend?'

Darul pointedly ignores her.

'Forgive Ariane her rudeness, cousin Malina. She might serve the nobility, but she has yet to learn any of our graces. Fortunately for her, she serves the best pastries in the city, and thus must be tolerated even if not forgiven!'

He laughs disarmingly as he says this, stands to embrace Ariane, and plants a kiss on her cheek. I almost puke as grey saliva runs over her chin, her tongue wipes over Darul's face, and oversized black nipples poke through her blouse. An instant later, she's her usual smiley self.

'A platter of your finest and two root teas,' Darul orders, winking as she flounces away.

'I know, I know,' he says, grimacing. 'I felt the same way when I first arrived. I was shown the city by a Chosen called ...' Darul looks confused, shakes his head, and then continues. 'It doesn't matter. I'd been taught how to fight, survive, and everything you've gone through. I thought I knew everything, then realised I had to learn a whole lot more.'

'Are you and her?' I'm revolted at the thought.

'No. My heart belongs to Ranya.' Darul's eyes flare. 'It's been nearly a year since I've been here. Ranya and I usually hunt in Suria.'

Ariane returns, placing a pastry platter down while an assistant brings over two steaming cups.

'So where are you from, Malina?' she asks, black eyes running like open sores.

'From Highnor.'

It's a good ruse. Highnor is a small city astride the northern border with Icelandia, where those giants tattoo their skins.

'Really? Why would a Delnorian of noble blood ink their skin like a savage is beyond me!'

'Perhaps if you were a Delnorian noble from Highnor, you might understand,' I retort, and she turns away.

'I don't think she likes me.' I mutter. 'She suspects I'm more than just a cousin to you and is jealous because she wants you badly.'

Darul laughs. It's so unlike him that I'm a little shocked.

'You're right, and that shows you're already learning the most important lesson ... How do we choose who to reap when everyone around us can exhibit signs of evil? What we actually see is the manifestation of people's unsavoury subconscious thoughts. Just because she lusts after me, which is apparent when she shifts, doesn't mean she'd act upon it. However, how you judge what you see could mean the difference between your life and death.

'Look there.'

I shift my attention, following Darul's gaze to a nearby table where four men sit.

Their eyes are on one of the serving girls, and every one of them is horribly distorted as they laugh behind raised hands, muttering obscenities.

'As you can see, those four, given a chance, would likely act on their crudity. Such individuals can make selecting our targets much easier. Now, look at the serving girl. What do you perceive?'

'She's shifting, and her face is intermittently like that of a snapping dog.'

'What might that tell you?'

'She wants to just scare them off.'

'Exactly. Without their provocation, her thoughts wouldn't be so dark. Most people you'll see out during the day aren't that bad, with some exceptions,' he says, nodding toward the four men. 'Of course, maybe if they weren't drinking and were with their wives, they might not be so bad. Mind you, there are still plenty of cutpurses, child snatchers and swindlers about during the day. Then, as you know, most of the nobles here beat or even kill their slaves and, in their own ways, are far worse than the minor criminals I've just named. The High King is the worst of them all, for his dominion extends across the continent.'

Darul shakes his head.

'However, we tend to hunt at night, for those who are out … are out for no good. Now, let's eat.'

I turn my attention to the pastries in front of me. One moment they look edible, then like grey lumps of clay. Peering into the cup, the tea looks like the bathwater I used to share back at the orphanage.

Darul obviously picks up on my reluctance to eat, then catches sight of Ariane heading toward our table. He switches to High Delnorian, so she doesn't understand if we're overheard.

'You'll be relieved to know that as your body acclimatises to your soul's absence, you'll get used to everything. You'll still perceive the face of evil and the decay around you, but it will fade. In time, some colour might even return, making things easier.

'Remember, this is all about the show. We have to be consummate actors. We're nobles, part of this fine empire. That way, we'll never be suspected as the soul takers we are.

'Oh my, these are heavenly,' Darul gushes in the common tongue as he pops a lump of clay pastry into his mouth.

'Then let us enjoy heaven together, Cousin,' I reply, following suit, rolling my eyes in fake pleasure. The food is bland, and the tea that follows it is tepid and flavourless.

Ariane walks past, nodding in satisfaction as she catches my eye. It seems I've been accepted.

Darul leans back in his chair and suddenly looks surprised.

'Well, I've never ever seen that before,' he whispers in something approaching awe. 'Come, sit by me. See what I see.'

I slowly shift my chair around, ensuring I don't draw attention.

There, obscured by a pillar in a discrete corner, are a couple. They both appear to be middle-aged. Yet the man remains handsome, broad-shouldered and strong. In some ways, he reminds me of Lotane, for he has a ready smile. Opposite him is a beautiful woman, large-eyed and slim, graceful, and exotic, with something suggesting an inner strength that belies her physique.

They're holding hands across a table, eyes fixed on one another, oblivious to the world.

Yet what has captured Darul's attention is more than just their looks. In a world where everyone shows their dark side, these two shine with an inner light that's plain for us to see, and there's no hint of evil flickering on their faces. Even without being told, I know I'm witnessing love in its purest form.

'There's still good in this world then?' I whisper in awe. 'I was beginning to believe I'd never see a face here that didn't show the capacity for evil.'

Darul shakes his head, strangely reluctant to look away. 'I hope I look like that when I'm with Ranya,' he says softly before focussing on me. 'What? Yes, although not often, and never like that. Never like that. Now, let's finish this food and move on; there's much more to see.'

I don't have to exactly choke the pastries or tea down. That nothing has any taste just makes it like any other action, and soon, Darul is flipping a silver coin into the air to catch Ariane's attention. He leaves it on the table, and with a final glance at the lovestruck couple, we're off.

***

Behind the main wealthy thoroughfares, like a bloated underbelly, are the slums and alleys that house and attract the ne'er do wells like those I was attacked by my first night.

Wherever we travel, Darul names roads, points out drinking dens, shops, whorehouses, tailors, merchants, and carpenters, and then demands I repeat everything back and show him around. Some of the people we cross paths with here are often the stuff of nightmares.

Frequently we have to step aside for columns of Delnorian troops. Some look battle-hardened, and they should be, as the war has been raging for years. When they shift, horns erupt from their heads, and smoke rises from their nostrils. Others, however, have the fresh faces of youths recently conscripted and their fierce glares are simply to conceal the fear at what the future might hold. When they shift, their visage is far less fearsome.

Darul leans in close.

'In some ways, the war is like our own training. Only the strong will survive. However, not all of them, for the luck of the gods will also play a big hand.'

It's true. The men we'd fought in the training circle had been exceptional fighters.

We finally reach the smoke-covered buildings, and the clarion of hammer on metal rings loud above the buzz of conversation. This is the blacksmiths' quarter, and from the smell of manure on the air, there are stables around too. The streets to get here were busy, but this place is heaving with people, almost all from different parts of the military.

We stop at a smithy, and Darul greets the proprietor with a sneer. I'm surprised, but then I realise he's playing the part of a noble, and this man is but a blacksmith.

'My cousin, Malina, this is Arax.' Darul introduces me. 'He doesn't make the finest weapons, but then he's only half Delnorian. Only the gods know what the other half is. Because of that, he has to charge trade prices to pure-blood nobles. So, what's your favoured weapon when you train with that Icelandian heathen you call your guard?'

'Shortswords.' I keep my voice clipped. No niceties, just a hard, demanding stare.

Arax bows low, his face turning into something hideous as he no doubt considers trying to murder the two odious nobles before him.

He steps behind a curtain, returns to place a cloth-wrapped bundle on the counter, and then backs away with a bow.

Reaching forward, I untie the cord and pull back the expensive cloth to reveal two scabbarded shortswords with intricately tooled hilts. Darul had perhaps done this man a disservice. I pull them free, examining the blades, look down their length, and examine the edges. They appear to be finely crafted despite the smoke that rises from them.

I bring the flats of the blades ringing together, then hold them in turn to my ear. The one in my right hand I slam flat down against the wooden counter, and it shatters into a hundred pieces.

'His trade price just got cheaper, and even then, it will be too costly,' I sneer.

'My apprentice made those. He'll be punished,' Arax fumes, and smoke billows from eyes that flare black flames. 'One moment.'

The next weapons he returns with are simple, unembellished, and ring true, and shortly we're on our way, having also bought some leather armour of a type I hadn't seen before. Darul assures me he has what he needs in his room at Ariane's place.

It's a long afternoon, and we stop twice to eat something more substantial while exploring the city. Before long, I'm also laden with black clothing, shoes, leather straps, rope and sundry other items.

The sun is low in our eyes as Darul takes me toward the High King's citadel, which sits atop the hill overlooking the docks. It's kept separate from the city below behind earthworks and walls topped with barbed spikes. Delnor has a history soaked in the blood of war, and here's a reminder of its military power. Mighty walls and lofty towers, above which flags snap, emblazoned with crossed swords. Every twenty paces, guards stand to attention on the wide avenue that leads up the long hill to the gates. This is the only way to approach the castle other than across the killing ground surrounding it.

'Several times I tried to infiltrate this castle, yet it's too heavily guarded,' Darul sighs. 'Therein lives the greatest evil of our time. The High King! Now, come, we must return to the Broken Arrow and secure you a room before sunset. Lead the way.'

Unerringly I head off, setting a fast pace, testing my body. Only the strong survive, and I will be the strongest, yet I can feel my body weakening, but far slower than before. I'm positive I could stay at least another day or two.

It isn't long before we arrive back, and Darul talks to Ariane whilst I stand to one side, studying the people that go by. Already I'm starting to see past the horror, acknowledging it but not reacting as I first did.

I follow them upstairs.

'Here is your room, Malina,' Ariane gushes, opening the door with a dramatic sweep of her arm. 'It's fit for a lady such as yourself.'

My room is well-appointed, just down the hall from Darul's. Not that I appreciate any of the fineries. The bed and furnishings smoke as if about to catch fire, and everything from cushions to drapes are shades of grey.

There'd been a child in my orphanage who'd claimed that she couldn't see colours. We'd all laughed, believing it the most implausible lie or, if not, hardly worth mentioning. Now, I'm not so sure. If what I'm witnessing is something akin to the world she'd lived in, then I'd never understood the bleakness of her life till now. Just seeing the blue sky would lift my spirits, but no, it's just another shade of grey.

I make an effort to admire the furnishings, walk around the room a few times, and then nod my approval.

'It's perfect. Thank you!'

Darul starts counting out coins as I look around. My room is unsurprisingly on the top floor, and at the end of the corridor are some steps leading to a roof terrace. It really is perfect.

Ariane passes me keys for the room and front door, then skips away like a child with a fruit bun.

'I'll be right back,' Darul mutters, heading toward his room.

I take a few moments to test the door lock and window latch.

Darul returns carrying the gear we'd purchased, which he dumps unceremoniously onto the bed.

'Some money,' he says, holding up a small but full pouch. 'Don't carry all of it with you at any time. Cutpurses are as common as rats, so find a place to hide the rest. Now, get changed into the plain clothing we bought earlier, and this,' he holds up a small timepiece, 'has a small clockwork alarm. Quite the rage amongst the nobility. See if you can work out how to set it for five hours' time and get some sleep.'

'Why five hours?' I ask, although if I'd thought just a moment longer, maybe I could have arrived at the answer.

Darul smiles as if at a simpleton.

'For then, it will be dark, and it's the best time to collect souls!'

***

CHAPTER XV

The timepiece's gentle ping rouses me. I didn't think I'd be able to sleep but being soulless drains the body. I wonder if any Chosen stayed too long, fell asleep, and never awoke.

The clock face indicates it's just past midnight, and despite there being no light source, I can still see. Unfortunately, the feeling of decay at this time is even more oppressive. The night sky boils with heavy clouds while the curtains billow like angry spirits away from the open window.

I rise, pull on my boots, and then attend to my armour. It's dyed black, although most things look that way to me. Leather vambraces for my arms, greaves for my shins, thigh protectors, and then I lift the cuirass. I'd always trained in hardened leather, shaped to the body, yet this is very different. It's made of hundreds of leather pieces laced together. I lift it over my head, settling it on my shoulders before tying it in place. It's snug yet doesn't restrict movement whatsoever.

Amazing. I wonder how protective it is, but Darul wouldn't settle for anything less than perfect.

I hear something above the howl of the wind and recognise the sound of softly placed footsteps. The magic within me is awakening, yet it seems unsure, almost as if it's just coming to trust the soulless me.

'*Thank you,*' I project, accompanied by thoughts of love and reassurance, and my magic wriggles happily.

I step to the door and pull it open just as Darul's hand reaches for the handle.

With raised eyebrows and a nod, he steps through, silent.

In his arms, he carries my weapons, and now I know why he'd bought the leather straps, for he's fashioned a simple harness. I swing it around my shoulders, so the handles of the two swords lift on either side of my head. The Soul Blade I keep at my waist, just behind my right hip, out of sight.

Darul picks my cloak off a chair and clasps it around my neck, then steps back, nodding in approval, then looks over my shoulder through the window.

A brief flash is followed by a low rumble, and he grimaces.

'Let's hunt.'

Two lightly spoken words, yet they carry such a heavy price.

Softly closing and locking the door behind me, Darul takes the key and, moving down the hallway, conceals his own and the one for the front door behind a loose wooden panel.

'Best not use the front door at night,' he explains, then takes the steps that lead to the roof terrace. 'Now it's time for you to learn the other way around the city.'

As we step outside, the air is fresh in my lungs, and I shiver in expectation. My soul might have been stripped away, but that doesn't mean I can't feel the stirrings of excitement. I'm reminded of my wolf hunt, choosing to kill instead of simply survive.

Rain starts falling, yet I'm not bothered, not when I'm imbued with magic; instead, it's strangely comforting.

'Pay attention,' Darul instructs. 'There, due south, is the High King's citadel atop the hill. To our north, you can see the spire of the city temple. To our east, just there,' he points, 'is the library. I chose this inn because of its location and its convenient roof terrace. Fix its location in your mind.'

I do as instructed, noting other landmarks besides.

'When we use the Soul Gate, why don't we come right here? If your spare equipment is here, why not save time?'

Darul smiles at my question, his teeth white against the blackness of his face. 'Appearing on this roof when others might be using it would be hard to explain, and coming through the front door raises less suspicion. Also, who knows, one day, this place might be compromised. Even if we're doing them a favour, the town watch isn't happy with killers in their city. Now, follow me.'

Darul runs and leaps lightly from rooftop to rooftop. The city is so crowded that every building abuts another. I study Darul as he moves and see the surety of motion I'd expect of a Chosen, and he'd already proved his martial skills. As I pull myself up to a higher rooftop, I understand why Darul fashioned the harness for my weapons and why this supple leather armour is essential, as otherwise, I'd be truly hindered.

We arrive above a junction, Darul hunkers down, near invisible against the black sky, and I kneel beside him. Rain drips from our hoods, and puddles abound on the rooftops and the streets below.

He turns, hearing my laboured breathing, eyebrows raised.

'You're stronger than you have any right to be after such a short period here, so be honest, and let me know if you wish to return.'

'Let's hunt.'

His eyes bore into mine.

'Right. It's always prudent to collect a soul as early as we can. You never know when you might need to escape if you find yourself outnumbered or injured. Without capturing a soul, you'll not be able to use a mirror to return, and that's our only way. Fortunately, there's no shortage of evil people in this city able to pay for our passage. You only need to ask yourself this question. Do you want to go find evil or let it find you?'

While I'm impatient, I also remember what Darul said about not everyone being evil, despite their appearance. What if I choose an innocent victim looking like a beast simply because they're upset, angry or even afraid?

'Let's have it find us.'

Darul nods.

'In which case, we'll walk the streets below.'

With barely a sound, he slips over the edge of the building and climbs down, keeping to the shadows. Whilst he moved impressively over the rooftops, he's cautious during the descent. Time to show him what I can do.

I project my need and, conscious of the answering warmth within, step over the edge and descend to the ground below, the soft whistling of air the only sign of magic undertaking my bidding.

Thank you. Thank you for being here whenever I need you.

Darul shakes his head in wonder as I reach the slimy, cobbled streets.

'I am a little jealous,' he admits. 'Until your group, only Lystra had survived the binding. Every other Chosen who'd volunteered before you died during the process. It seems our ssythlan benefactors have finally mastered the ritual. Now, as we want trouble to find us, we can't have your sword hilts being so obvious.'

Darul steps forward and releases a harness buckle on my chest, allowing the weapons to slide down until they're settled at my hip.

'Ingenious,' I compliment him.

The thump of booted feet echoes above the splashing rain.

'It's the night watch,' Darul warns, scurrying off toward some side streets. 'They only patrol the main thoroughfares unless they hear trouble. We don't want to be challenged at this hour in case they ask questions we can't answer.'

As the stomping recedes behind us, we slow our pace. The rain is getting heavier, and so is the wind. The lightning and thunder are becoming more frequent, and it feels like this will be a bad storm.

The streets should be near pitch black, but instead, it's clear, thanks to my soulless vision. Steam emanates from sewers and drains, creating a hazy mist, yet it's more a distraction than a hindrance. Occasional streetlamps splutter above us, but they're few and far between, and the only real light comes from top-floor windows. The bottom ones are shuttered and barred. At night, darkness owns the streets. Fortunately, we own the darkness.

'We'll head toward the docks. That's where the real flotsam of the city congregates.'

It was the same as where I grew up. I wish at times like this that my sense of smell was as dead as my taste buds, for the stench of rotting fish and detritus is nigh on overwhelming despite the cleansing rain.

Illicit gambling dens, whorehouses, and vaguely legitimate taverns are scattered throughout this corner of the city, and it isn't long before we come across a naked, dead body in the street.

To my surprise, Darul draws his Soul Blade and attempts to push it into the corpse, but it doesn't penetrate. With a shrug, he sheathes it before turning to me, wiping water from his eyes.

After death, a soul can reside for a short while before it goes wherever it goes. A kill doesn't need to be made with a Soul Blade for it to harvest a soul. It just has to be soon after death. Always, always, harvest a soul as quickly as possible. In addition, as we walk, consider where your nearest escape route toward a mirror might be.

'Gambling dens always have fights, so there'll be no mirrors there, but whorehouses will likely have them in the rooms. Obviously, you don't want to travel in front of people if it can be avoided. The mirror must be wide and tall enough to fit through, or you might find yourself minus arms and legs on your return.'

'Really?' I breathe in horror.

Darul chuckles.

'No. I'm joking about losing limbs, but you do need a large enough mirror. Too small, and for whatever reason, you won't be able to pass, it will just remain a mirror, and you'll remain standing in front of it!'

We stroll on, the rain falling in sheets, muffling sounds, and even my enhanced eyesight struggles to penetrate it. We travel along a busy road, taverns on either side awash with light beckon in the brave or foolish.

Occasional, loud, raucous laughter pierces the night air, making me twist and turn, disorientated. Groups of off-duty soldiers stagger about, muttering angrily, having spent or lost their pay. Yet despite their grotesque shifting, none make any untoward advances in our direction.

I'm beginning to feel a little light-headed and know that despite my strength, I'll need to return soon. It's time to find trouble, not wait for it.

Lend me your help, I ask silently, and shortly after, angry voices filter through the rain.

'This way,' I say, taking the lead and head toward the docks as Darul hurries to keep up.

Cogs and galleys are moored here, and we splash through deepening puddles amongst the looming hulks toward the end of a quay, peering through the darkness. Ahead, dark figures appear, illuminated by some swaying lanterns. The noise of their argument rises above the storm.

'You've damaged the goods, you fools. You'll get eight gold coins!'

The voice is rough from too much liquor but holds a commanding tone.

'The deal was fifteen, and his black eyes will disappear by the time you get him to Suria,' hisses another. 'Don't mess with us! You've gotta be earning at least ten times what you're paying. Maybe we should just take him back!'

Darul places his hand on my arm.

'Way too many. We need to leave before we're seen!'

He's right. Five men are facing what seems to be a further ten from a galley, one of whom appears to be the captain from his pointed hat. Two sailors are armed with crossbows, whilst everyone else grips cutlasses or daggers. The gangplank is lowered behind the larger group, and bound on the wet planking is a captive, the price of whom they're bickering over.

I'd been bought for a handful of coppers. Who in the oceans is worth so much gold?

A whisper of warning sounds in my mind, and I spin, barely dodging the thrust of a dagger. I grab my attacker's wrist, pull him past, and toss him over the edge of the slippery quay into the water. Darul, warned by my sudden movement, deflects a sword with his forearm, then ducks under a wild swing before stepping forward and ramming his Soul Blade into the wielder's heart.

The fight is over in seconds, but it hasn't gone unnoticed.

As we turn around, all argument has ceased, and weapons are being raised. Fifteen men against us will not end well. Even in the downpour, the crossbows will prove our undoing, and they're aimed steadily at us.

Darul starts to back away.

'Taken another step, and it will be your last,' shouts the captain as the smaller group of kidnappers head toward us.

My stomach is in knots, not out of fear but because my magic demands release.

'Get ready,' I mutter at Darul from the corner of my mouth.

I fling my hands out, visualising my need, and water rises from the planking and hits those before us like a wave. A ferocious wind howls by, knocking some off their feet but, more importantly, extinguishing the lanterns.

Crossbows twang and bolts hiss into the sky, fired in a panic, as Darul and I charge.

Somehow, I push my exhaustion temporarily aside, although I know I'm slower than usual.

Nonetheless, my swords are light in my grasp as I roll at the last moment, coming to my feet amongst a disorganised and blinded foe. Thankfully, Darul and I can see perfectly and weave through them, swords cutting deep. Screams rise above the storm, and the captain shouts desperately for lanterns. Lightning flashes, and for those moments, Darul and I are illuminated, glistening in the rain, death incarnate.

In their panic, sailors swing blindly around them, injuring comrades, who, in turn, finding themselves under attack, fight back. It's carnage, and

I twist and twirl amongst the weaving steel like a dancer, lost in the passion of the music.

Thunder crashes, and it can be felt in the stomach, primordial, dwarfing anything human, yet I feel empowered, knowing that it's elemental, as am I.

Shouts announce the arrival of a dozen fresh sailors holding lanterns onto the galley's deck, but as they stare over the deck railings and behold the butchery, they retreat, slamming the hatches behind them.

Soon, only the captain is left standing, holding a long sword unsteadily before him.

'I, I have gold!' he stammers, holding out a heavy pouch. 'Take it!'

'We don't want your gold,' I hiss, my heart beating ecstatically.

'W-w-what do you want then?'

'Your soul!' I reply, knocking his blade aside as I spin and crash my elbow into his face. He staggers back, sword falling from his grasp, and I follow up with a heavy kick to his stomach that throws him onto his back. He lies there, black blood flowing freely across his face, which flickers from a snarling beast one moment to a terrified man the next.

My Soul Blade finds his heart and shimmers brightly as I pull it free, slamming it home in the sheath at my waist.

I survey the scene around me. The bloodied rainwater pours off the quay into the dock, and Darul moves amongst the fallen, using his Soul Blade to harvest as many souls as he can. His weapon shines like a beacon as he stands above the fallen captive, and he's about to drive it home …

'No!'

'Why not?' Darul frowns, water cascading off his shoulders as he crouches above the bound captive. 'He's a witness and filthy rich from the quality of his clothes. That makes him as bad, if not worse, than those we've killed!'

'He's too young. Look at him. He's not displaying evil.'

Darul shakes his head in disagreement yet leaves the wide-eyed lad alive, cowering at his feet and comes to stand opposite me.

'You don't need my help anymore. What I saw you do, shows you're stronger than I'll ever be. You know enough to find your way, and I'll let Lystra know. Good hunting, Wolf Slayer.'

Darul clasps my wrist, then turns, and within moments vanishes from sight into the pouring rain.

***

If only Darul knew how weak I felt, then maybe he'd stay, but pride and foolishness had kept my mouth firmly closed. I hadn't said anything about my magic draining me or how being separated from my soul had already left me weak.

Damn.

I look at the young lad, then, with a sigh, bend down, severing his bindings with my sword, and pull him roughly to his feet. I spy the pouch the captain had offered in exchange for his life and pick that up too.

'Follow me,' I instruct, then set off back toward the quayside, eyes scanning every shadow. Darul and I had missed those two sentries earlier, which almost cost us our lives.

I move slowly, conscious the lad has been tied for a while, and his circulation needs time to come back, plus he's in shock. I'm not much better as my strength is ebbing. This was too much too soon.

When we're a safe distance from the docks, I turn to face the lad. He's stopped shaking, and I take a moment to study him. His face flickers, yet I look past the gibbering monstrosity that briefly stands before me, recognising this is just fear and anxiety causing the transformation.

His clothes, while drenched and torn, are indeed finely made. Ruffled sleeves, intricate laced cuffs, an exquisitely tooled leather belt, and polished boots finish the look. Despite his scuffed and broken face, he fits the part of a wealthy noble's son that Darul had intimated he was.

'Where do you live, boy? We'd best get you home!'

He points over my shoulder, and I groan as I see where. The citadel on the hill. This is the last place I wish to go. Yet if I let him find his own way, dressed as he is, he'll attract predators like an injured rabbit. I wonder if I should have just let Darul kill him.

'Come.'

We keep to the shadows, and whenever I see someone coming, I pull the boy in deeper, letting people pass by, oblivious to our presence. I feel dizzy and nauseous and steady myself against a wall.

'Are you injured?' the boy asks.

He looks desperate. I'm sure he's more worried about being left alone than my state of health.

With my mouth open and facing the sky, I let the rainwater trickle down my throat.

I need a different approach. I'm taking too long, and skulking in the shadows might attract the attention I'm hoping to avoid if it's perceived as fear. I adjust my weapon harness so the sword hilts jut proudly above my shoulders. Instead of answering, I grab his arm and stride down the middle of the street, splashing purposefully through the puddles.

We make good progress and start to head uphill. Several unsavoury-looking types watch us approach but let us pass unmolested. One look at me dragging along this reluctant lad, and they probably think I'm a kidnapper or slaver. The boy's piteous complaints certainly add to the image, as he's crying at the merciless pace I'm setting.

My cloak and clothes are pulled by the wind, which also drives the rain sideways. On such a miserable night, the town watch seems to have given up patrolling the streets, perhaps believing they'd be washed clean of not just the dirt but the filth that wanders them. Sadly, that's not the case.

A group of five men lever themselves away from a wall. They've made their move, decided to confront me, confident in their numbers. Had I not been soulless, I might have paused, considering if they were do-gooders, intervening to save the boy from the hands of a criminal, yet my vision reassures me this isn't the case. Their faces shift from plain ugly to malevolent, ears pointing, lips and tongues bloating, reassuring me on my course of action.

'Stay close, boy,' I hiss menacingly, pushing my mouth close to his ear. 'Don't run because if I lose you, you're dead. Do you hear me?'

Shaking so hard his teeth chatter, he nods, eyes wide.

The five spread out across the street, about twenty paces distant. The leader, a tall, heavily bearded man, stands before the others. They've yet to draw weapons, a sure sign he'll talk first before taking action.

'Where ya going, pretty?' he calls loudly.

I don't answer or stop walking, just release my hold on the boy, leaving him standing behind me.

Another man laughs. 'I think she's coming to give you a kiss.'

Fifteen paces.

'Who is the boy? He doesn't seem to wanna be with ya?'

Ten paces.

The look of confidence begins to slip from the leader's face as he catches sight of my armour and the weapon hilts above my shoulders. His hand edges toward a long dirk fastened to his hip.

Five paces.

I leap and spin, drawing one of my swords. As I land in front of the bearded beast, his weapon clearing its sheath, I bring it down double-handed in a diagonal blow. My blade enters the side of his neck and exits below his armpit as I crouch before him, my blade glistening.

When such violence ensues, there can occasionally be moments of utter serenity, and this is one.

I crouch, the tip of my blade gently resting against the cobblestones as I look up, meeting the uncomprehending eyes of my victim. The storm pauses, holding its breath, for maybe two heartbeats, then as the leader's knees buckle, the top part of his torso slides off left as the rest falls right.

I'd never cut someone in two before, and a further heartbeat brings the rain lashing down again as I rise, drawing my other sword from its sheath.

The looks of terror and fear that replace the snide looks of cruelty and lust don't give me pause. I attack, severing the right leg of the next man as I duck under a whistling sword cut, then spin past, lancing the tip of my sword through the next one's eye even as he raises his cudgel. The third man hasn't even drawn his dagger, but that doesn't stop me from slashing his throat open.

The remaining one runs.

He's no longer a threat, but I'm here to do a job.

I'm the justice of the king.

Hefting my right sword, I take two swift steps forward and, with a grunt, fling it spinning through the rain.

Turning back, I draw my Soul Blade and touch it to the bodies of the fallen. For the briefest of moments, it shines so brightly that I squint.

The boy!

He's nowhere to be seen. Perhaps I should feel deflated, but I'm not. He chose his path, just like I've chosen mine, and I grin at my choice of words.

Splashing through the puddles, I retrieve my thrown sword and the soul from the corpse it's buried in.

This has been a successful mission, and it's time to return home!

***

CHAPTER XVI

Relaxing on the terrace, the north of the island laid out below me, I sigh contently, watching the sunset in the company of my fellow Chosen. It's Suntarg, and after a relaxing day, our sleeping chambers beckon. We no longer take a dream leaf infusion, for we travel at night, but our sleep remains perfect, undisturbed, untroubled.

In the distance, the ssythlan engineers have finished building their large encampment, yet it doesn't spoil the view. Docks and buildings are under construction, and it saddens me to think this paradise might soon be tarnished.

Nestor hums gently as he makes subtle changes to his wall carvings. It's bizarre; he spends time perfecting them whenever we're here, except for one; his initial carving of The Once and Future King. He mutters when he inspects it but hasn't changed it to include the monsters at the king's feet.

A cool sea breeze sends a lonely puffy cloud drifting across the red sky, and I reach for a goblet of watered wine, taking a sip, enjoying the fruity taste. Alcohol is now a further privilege, yet none of us partakes much; our work is too important.

Occasionally, at times like this, my thoughts go to the boy I saved.

Did he survive and return to the citadel, or did his blood stain the streets until the rain washed it away? Either way, three months have passed, and many more dark souls have been harvested since that night. All those lives taken, yet only one saved. I shake my head at my foolish thought. Many innocents have walked the streets unmolested because of the Chosen's work.

After all this time, I can survive my soul's absence for over two weeks before death's cold hand seeks to claim me. During the day, I frequent the library, picking random books to learn about the past. Arcan, the old head librarian, frequently keeps me company, sometimes just from a distance. He finally believes I'm the student of history I once pretended to be but have since become.

On my lap is an open tome he gifted me. Not being metal, I'd brought it back through the gate. The title has long since faded, and frequently the words are illegible, but it's a history of Delnor's kings. With twenty librarian scribes tasked with copying every ageing tome, this one had become surplus before becoming a gift. There's no mention of The Once and Future King, yet I devour it nonetheless.

'I remember a time when you had eyes only for me,' Lotane says, nuzzling my ear. 'Now, it's just that book!'

I lean back against him, his arms circling my chest and sigh in contentment. I close the tome, put it on the bench next to us and turn my head to receive a kiss.

'What about this morning when we joined?' I ask with a wink.

Lotane shakes his head.

'That doesn't count. Your eyes were closed almost all the time.'

'That's because she's finding you hideous with that scarred face of yours,' chuckles Kralgen, overhearing our comments.

'Oooof.' Kralgen moans as Alyssa elbows him hard in the ribs.

Lotane laughs good-naturedly, running a finger along the small, thin scar under his right eye.

'I think it makes me rather dashing.'

We all carry new scars except Kralgen. He's nigh on untouchable.

'Why do you find that stuff interesting?' Kralgen asks, looking confused.

I shrug. 'In some ways, I think this immortalises the dead. When I read their names and what they did, that surely gives them life again.'

'Hah. Maybe you should have been a scribe, not a Chosen,' Kralgen grins. 'I remember when your skin was all pale and pasty. You could easily have passed for someone who stayed hunched over books all day, hidden from the sun.'

In times past, I'd have bristled with anger at his comments, but I know he holds me in as high esteem as I do him. The fact this banter never upsets anyone shows just how close we've become.

'One day, I'll teach you how to write your name,' I retort. 'It's very easy. It's spelt A-S-S.'

Lotane guffaws, Fianna's laughter peals out, and Nestor comes over, drawn by the merriment.

Alyssa wraps her arms protectively around Kralgen.

'Leave my ass alone.' She winks.

I breathe deeply, experiencing a sense of completeness I'd once never known existed.

This is a perfect life, and I don't care that blood magic plays a part.

Nestor's face, which is never bright, takes on a darker tone. For whatever reason, ever since his trespass, he seems troubled whenever he looks upon certain sculptures or a ssythlan. Therefore, I know before looking over my shoulder that we have one as a visitor.

'My Chosen,' Lystra calls.

We stand, turning to face the archway through which she's entered. Sure enough, the ssythlan prince is there, his hood pulled back, ensuring he's instantly recognisable by the golden circlet on his brow. I'm sure it's for our benefit, as the ssythlans all look the same to us except for their build.

Lystra looks radiant, her face awash with the light of the setting sun, as well as from pure joy. I can't help but smile to see such unadulterated pleasure. I shiver, excitement suddenly making my body tingle.

Lotane's hand grasps mine, and I know he recognises this is a special moment, for we've never been visited here by a ssythlan before.

I kneel, bowing my head, as the other Chosen do the same.

'You may rise,' the ssythlan hisses. 'I bring the news you've been waiting for, and you're the first to hear it. The other Chosen will have to wait until their return on Durntarg.'

The ssythlans usually speak slowly. They find it hard to form the common language with their forked tongues, but tonight, its words tumble out. Even the prince is overcome with the importance of this moment.

'Till now, you've hunted the murderers, rapists, thieves and other dark souls that plague the lands. Yet from hereon, your prey will no longer be found in the alleyways and whorehouses of High Delnor. Instead, it will be found in its citadel!

'From hereon, you have one mission ... to kill the High King!'

Whilst we're too disciplined to react in excitement, the ssythlan gives us a moment before continuing.

'But be warned, other Chosen attempted and failed in the past. Yet none were magic users like you, none as well trained as you, and none have the motivation like you. Complete this mission, and the return of our king is assured! Lystra will lead you as always, so I leave you in her hands.'

The ssythlan turns away, whereas Lystra bounds forward. She might once have killed us without a second thought and overseen the death of hundreds of children. She might be the most ruthless killer I've ever met, but she's a fellow Chosen, one of us, and I love her dearly.

We all gather around and hug like the family we are.

Eventually, Lystra breaks free, helps herself to a goblet of wine and lifts it high.

We gather our own as she beckons us close.

'For our king to rise, not just one, but all must fall. We start with the High King, but our wrath will be felt by the kings and queens of darkness across our world! We are Chosen, we are soul stealers, and together we will usher in a new golden age!

'To The Once and Future King!'

I quaff my goblet of wine, revelling in the smiles and laughter. Lotane's arms are around me, and my heart beats furiously with love and hope for the future.

It's the kind of moment that I wish would last forever.

***

The stars and moons are obscured by thick clouds. For anyone without a lantern or torch, it would be pitch black. However, for me, it isn't. Everything is shades of grey, black and off-white, the benefit of being soulless, albeit temporarily.

The surf rolls onto the beach where I'm waiting, like a hand trying to pull me in. However, I sit just outside its grasp, at least for now.

There's a familiar tugging as my magic playfully asks for release. I'm sorely tempted, for over these many months since I was imbued with such power, I realise that it's only truly happy when free, just like a caged bird.

Therefore, when I can afford the tiredness that summoning it brings, I use it in whichever way possible. Whatever the task, I experience a shared sense of primordial joy in response to my request. Thus, it answers my call without hesitation whenever I direct my thoughts inward.

To date, all the souls I've gathered have been with magical assistance.

Whispered threats or distant cries are brought swiftly to my ears, while the scents of hidden wrongdoers are brought to my nose. Even the vibration of a murderer's soft step doesn't escape my magic's attention, and thus mine.

The crump of compacted sand warns me of someone approaching, and even without turning, I know who it is.

'Hey, Kral.'

'Wolf Slayer. I should have known you'd get here first.'

He sits beside me, a reassuring presence.

'I don't see why we need the help of a damn ssythlan,' he sighs.

It always surprises me how he dislikes them so much. I'm quite sure it's because the ssythlan warriors beat him in years past. There can be no other reason. They provide for us, feed us, and without them, we wouldn't have the honour of serving our king.

'Even Lystra agrees that damn citadel is impregnable to force.'

'Gah. Given time, I'm sure you and Nestor could tunnel under it with your magic. Once inside, we'd have our chance. Or maybe the High King would come out if we waited long enough.'

I laugh.

'Time is the one thing we don't have any longer. I think what we try next is the only way. Look at what happened last time. We were almost caught, and Alyssa is still pained by her arrow wound. That place is like an angry swarm of bees now. We've lost our chance to go in through the back door.'

If nothing else, reminding Kralgen about Alyssa's graze with death has him nod grudgingly in agreement.

'You were always the one with the brains, and as it's your plan, I'm good with it,' Kralgen grumbles, throwing handfuls of sand in some kind of frustrated statement as he digs a hole with his hands.

We sit quietly, awaiting the others. We'd all entered High Delnor separately through the Soul Gate the night before and are set to meet on the beach to try a completely different approach to infiltrating the palace.

We'd already failed nigh on a dozen times. Most attempts had seen us climb the cliffs on the coastal side, the least protected approach. For that reason, it was always easy to reach the castle walls themselves. Our magic had served us well, creating footholds where needed and giving us security should we fall. The problem was that beyond the curtain wall, from whichever direction we approached, was a large killing ground patrolled by dogs and guards. Large braziers left no areas in the dark.

The closest we'd come to success had involved the necessary deaths of several guards, whose uniforms we'd used for disguise. Alyssa had stayed at the wall, as there was no hiding her ebony skin, while the rest of us had approached the castle proper. As we reached the gate, things had gone from hopeful to bad so quickly that it was impossible to know what had gone wrong.

Thankfully, I'd overheard a whispered conversation between a guard sergeant and a private he was sending for reinforcements. We'd been recognised as infiltrators despite helms disguising our faces. The ensuing fight had left ten guards dead and some of us lightly wounded. As we'd fled across the open ground to the wall and the cliffs, Alyssa had stepped forward, bow in hand, to send our pursuers diving for cover, but she'd been hit by return.

Nothing else had come close. Bribes hadn't worked, and threats hadn't worked.

Reading the book gifted by the old librarian between our failures had given birth to our current plan as it often referred to monarchs giving court to visiting dignitaries and their helpers.

The crump of more footsteps interrupts my reverie.

Lystra and the others are approaching. It's time.

My boots are cast into the shallow hole Kralgen has dug, and the others follow suit. I ensure my Soul Blade is secure as I step barefoot but lightly dressed into the surf. Faint lights shine off the coast, highlighting our destination.

I could use magic to assist, but like the others, I'm a consummate swimmer, and I'll save my strength in case one of us gets into trouble. The water is cold enough to take my breath away, but I don't baulk. What is simple cold when we've faced so much worse in our years of training?

We set off at a steady pace toward the distant ssythlan ship. Aboard awaits Prince Sylnar, ostensibly on a mission to offer military aid to the High King.

It doesn't take long before the grey hulk of the ssythlan ship rises above us. It's so different from the sleek galleys used for trading and fighting that I'm used to, and there's something ominous about it.

Nets are lowered over the side, and I scramble up, clothes plastered to my body. A ssythlan soldier meets us on the deck and, without saying a word, leads us toward the ship's aft. Opening a door, it motions us in, pointing to some bunks where towels and dry robes are laid out.

'Female, there. Male, there,' it hisses, then leaves.

Lotane flashes me a smile over his shoulder as we strip and change, tossing our wet gear into a trunk. New boots fit snugly on my feet, and a belt with a money pouch and dagger cinches my robes neatly around my waist.

Everything might look grey, but we know the robes are forest green, far less menacing than black. It fits neatly with the ssythlan flag of a snake swallowing its own tail with a crown in the centre.

'That colour looks good on you,' Lotane whispers to Kralgen.

'You can see in colour?' asks Kralgen, his eyes widening.

'Of course I can. What do you mean?' Lotane scoffs. 'Why wouldn't I?'

'But everyone still sees in shades of grey, don't they?' Kralgen asks, a look of concern spreading across his face.

The rest of us shake our heads.

'There must be something wrong with your eyes,' Fianna trills. 'It was only on my first journey that things were grey. What about the rest of you?'

This time we all nod.

'Aly. Do you see in colour?' Kralgen asks, and his look is so childish and bewildered that Alyssa can't keep a straight face any longer.

'They're teasing you, Kral,' she says, going on tiptoes to kiss him on the cheek.

Kralgen smiles, his teeth bright. 'Hah, that's good, cause I asked for Lotane's robe to be the brightest pink they could find.'

We all laugh, even Lystra.

She might be our leader on this trip, but there's been a seismic shift in how she behaves. Of course, she's still serious and demanding, but she treats us as equals, and in many ways, we are.

'Here,' Lystra says, draping a corded silver necklace over my shoulders.

An ornate ring is attached that sits just above my breasts. Tucking it under my robes, I take my Soul Blade and drop it into the ring, so the blade nestles in my cleavage.

This had been Nestor's idea. We won't be allowed in the citadel with weapons, so the daggers on our hips are a distraction to be seen and removed. However, if we're successful in our mission, we need a means of escape. The Soul Blades, despite their hilt, have no sharp edges, no point, and hung around our necks, resemble a cumbersome religious symbol. They'll be found, but we hope we'll be allowed to keep them and find a mirror to make our exit, or our deaths will follow the High Kings.

The cabin door opens, admitting Prince Sylnar. Intricate swirls cover the sleeves of its robe. Tassels hang from the corded belt around its waist, while upon its brow sits a thick silver loop, twisted to form a serpent at the front with gemstones for eyes. Completing the ensemble, the prince carries an ornate staff, once again topped with a snake's head.

It casts those black eyes over us and hisses.

'The death of the High King is more important than your lives. I expect you to make the ultimate sacrifice if required to complete the mission.'

There's no hesitation. I nod along with the others. What better way to die than knowing your death ushers in a new era of peace and prosperity? Hopefully, that won't be the case, but if it is, so be it.

The rattle of the ship's anchor chain being drawn up reverberates through the hull.

'We will be in sight of High Delnor just after dawn, and if the gods smile upon us, we'll be allowed to dock. If so, I'll seek an audience with the High King immediately after. There's no plan we can rely on, so rely on your training and instincts to complete the mission.'

Complete the mission. I couldn't resist this order even if I wanted to, and I don't.

I've seen the darkness, and every time I hunt amongst the slums and alleyways, I feel infected as it seeps into my very pores. Only a malevolent king would allow evil such free reign to roam the streets of his own capital.

The same resolve shines in the eyes of those around me.

'Get some rest, and meet me on deck just before sunrise,' the prince hisses, turning away in a flowing movement, closing the door behind it.

We don't talk. Rest is too important. We climb into our bunks, and with a final smile at Lotane across the cabin, I close my eyes and dream of the death of kings.

***

The sea is becalmed as the sun crests the horizon. Not a breath of air feathers the tops of the lazy waves, and any other ship would have required oars to make headway, but not our one.

Its large sails are pulled taut, and the trail of our wash reaches behind us as we round the headland on which the mighty citadel of the High King sits.

Horns sound faintly on the morning air.

'They've seen us. See, they're running up flags,' Lotane observes.

Sweat causes me to blink, and a pulse throbs in my temple, the precursor to a headache and fatigue that will last the day. It's unpleasant to feel my strength and magical power being drained with every passing moment, to perceive a hollowness as I'm depleted from the inside. Fianna shares my distress, her hands moving, grasping, and pushing as she forces the power of her magic to fill the sails with wind. We look like we're dancing as I continue my charade alongside her.

'You can stop. Well done,' Lystra's voice cuts over the creaking timbers.

As I relax, breathing heavily, the oar ports bang open, and twelve giant oars rattle out. This is no galley, and the ship will make slow progress from hereon.

Nestor rests a hand on my shoulder and Fianna's.

'At times like this, I'm glad I use earth magic. That must have been excruciating,' he says in a rare show of companionship.

'Look, there!' Fianna's clear voice draws our attention.

We follow her outflung arm toward the harbour, where like sharks scenting blood, three Delnorian war galleys are skimming from the entrance. Their oars move in perfect unison, and Lotane's low whistle shows his appreciation of the crew's skill as the ships' prows turn toward us. The eyes on either side of the hull stare with malicious intent, and beneath the waves, a bronze-headed ram will bring death and destruction upon us if they choose to attack.

Hopefully, that won't be the case. Ssythla is neutral in the current war, keeping itself well away from the lands of men except for trade, and from every mast of our ship, the ssythlan flag flies. Even the sails are emblazoned with the snake and crown sigil.

On our ship's raised forecastle, Prince Sylnar stands stoically, grasping his staff, resplendent in his robes of office, easily visible to the closing crews of the Delnorian vessels.

Two of the galleys peel off to our starboard while one circles in a sweeping arc to come alongside, just outside the reach of our oars. Delnorian marines, resplendent in their cream and blue leather armour, gather on the deck with archers behind.

'Stow your oars and prepare to be boarded, or you'll be sunk,' the Delnorian captain yells.

The prince nods to an aide standing nearby. Moments later, our oars are run in, and our ship gradually comes to a serene halt.

The galley manoeuvres expertly alongside, with several marines standing by a boarding plank.

Both Kralgen and Lotane chuckle, sharing a joke, but it only takes me a moment to realise what's provoking their mirth. Our vessel's hull is twice the height of the galley, and as is now apparent to the captain below, his boarding plank won't help.

Lystra strides over.

'Stay serious,' she admonishes. 'We'll do nothing to provoke annoyance or distrust.'

'Captain,' she shouts over the rail. 'Can we assist by lowering our gangplank down to you?'

There's a moment's silence broken only by the ship's creaking timbers and the occasional call of a gull before the captain waves his assent.

Lystra signals to a ssythlan sailor, who dashes off.

'We are supposed to be the crown prince's bodyguard, so from here on, we act as such!'

All mirth ceases, and we make our way up to position ourselves behind the prince, with Lystra standing one step proud of us.

My heart beats quickly with nervous excitement. I shift my weight unconsciously as the ship rolls gently in the soft swell, perfectly balanced. Behind panels on the forecastle are swords, so if a fight ensues, we can take as many of our assailants with us as possible before we fall.

Chains clank as the ship's large gangplank is lowered. As this vessel is so tall, there's a hatch level with the oar ports allowing easy access to a dock. However, in this instance, it will give the Delnorian captain a more convenient way onto the ship than climbing up the sheer side of the hull.

The other Chosen stand firm alongside me. Barely a breeze ruffles our robes as we await, arms folded, hands tucked into the opposite sleeve. We offer no threat, although with Kralgen looming at one end of the line, head and shoulders above everyone else, and Lotane at the other, robe sleeves taut around his arms, we would give anyone pause.

Before long, booted feet crash and shouts rise as the Delnorian marines board the ship and round up the crew. It would be a foolish captain who came straight to the deck without securing behind him first, and this captain is no fool.

Shortly, the ssythlan crew are herded onto the deck and pushed to the stern, where two dozen marines hold them at sword point.

Another dozen swarm up the steps to the forecastle, forming around us in a semi-circle. They raise their shields, locking them together, swords raised threateningly. There's no fear or hesitation in their eyes; these men are veterans.

With no spoken command that I can hear, the line of marines parts and the Delnorian captain strides through.

'Who are you, and what business do you have in our waters?' the captain growls.

His meaty fist is wrapped around the hilt of his sheathed sword, adding further menace to his demeanour. His face twists, the sneer becoming exaggerated, eyes narrowing, exposing his inner distrust.

Lystra takes one step forward.

I remember the last time she befriended a Delnorian captain, and the memory brings a tinge of regret before it's banished by a breeze of righteousness.

'Captain. Welcome on board the Salamander.'

Lystra smiles, bowing deeply from the waist, before standing tall, looking the captain steadily in the eye.

'Please let me introduce my charge, Prince Sylnar of Ssythla.' Lystra sweeps her arm toward the prince and bows again. 'I appreciate your duty requires you to verify who is aboard. Still, now you know, I respectfully suggest your men lower their weapons so this doesn't escalate into a diplomatic incident. The prince is here to discuss an alliance with the High King.'

The captain stares at Prince Sylnar, who gazes back with those unblinking black eyes.

'Captain. Please have your marines assist the crew in piloting my vessel into your harbour,' hisses the prince, causing the captain's eyes to widen in surprise. 'You'd also do me great service by sharing a bottle of wine with me and advising on matters of protocol. It's been a long time since my kind set foot beyond the northern trading posts of my lands.'

The captain turns about and addresses a sergeant.

'As the prince says. Let's get this vessel into harbour.' Turning back, his gaze flicks over me, then Alyssa, before taking in the other Chosen. 'Who are they?'

Prince Sylnar raises his staff to point at us.

'These are my bodyguard. Most were purchased from the Isle of Sin as infants and have been my loyal servants and guards since their coming of age. I believed their human presence by my side would cause less concern than ssythlan warriors. Am I wrong?'

'One's definitely a Tarsian who we're at war with, and the other,' he says, eyeing me, 'is like nothing I've ever seen! They'll be kept under arrest, confined to the ship.'

'No, Captain, they will not!' hisses Prince Sylnar, slamming the staff down onto the decking in annoyance.

I have to admire the ssythlan. He's been gracious till now but has just shown enough of that noble arrogance and authority to make the captain pause. For the first time, there's doubt in the Delnorian's eyes.

'The colour of my bodyguard's skin does not define who they are. They are loyal to me and only to me, not their past heritage. If you feel they pose a threat armed only with daggers in a city containing thousands of warriors, might I suggest you train better warriors!' A long hiss of annoyance slowly fades. 'Let this not sour the wine that awaits.'

Lystra bows, sweeping her arms toward the steps to the deck below.

'If you would kindly follow me, Captain.'

I watch as Lystra, our ssythlan prince, and the Delnorian captain move below. The remaining marines watch over us carefully, smoke puffing forth from their nostrils as if they're bulls ready to charge. Yet we offer no threat, simply moving to stand over the ship's prow as it starts to make way. The oars rattle in their locks, the ship's timbers creak, and my heart beats excitedly as the Delnorian galleys escort our ship toward the harbour mouth.

This time we'll not fail.

***

'It was never going to be easy,' Lotane murmurs alongside me. 'But I certainly thought we'd be closer to our goal than this,' and he gestures with a flick of his fingers.

Lotane and I sit on the harbour wall, our feet dangling over the edge. To our left, Kralgen and Alyssa sit, with Nestor and Fianna a little way beyond them. Keeping a line of sight on each other ensures we can come to each other's aid if required. The Delnorian soldiers and marines here are a bitter, angry bunch. They've experienced too much death to be trusting of foreigners, especially those with skin like Alyssa's. Their faces twist and morph into something hideous whenever their attention falls upon her.

'You're right,' I reply, my shoulders sagging. 'I thought we might even be in the palace by now. We got closer to the king the last time we tried.'

I follow Lotane's gaze as he mulls his next comment. Fishing ships are unloading on a nearby dock, and the smell of their catch is strong on the breeze. Gulls hover, looking for a chance to snatch something to eat, but the hive of workers keeps them at bay. High Delnor is full to the seams with soldiers and civilians, and these fishing vessels bring much-needed sustenance.

Lotane's hand grips my shoulder reassuringly.

'Don't think for a moment this is your fault. It was a good plan, and it wasn't all yours. We might have gotten closer to our target last time, but we almost died too. There was no way they'd not increase security after our last attempt. I can't see how we'd have succeeded if we'd carried on in the same vein. We needed to try something different, and it's still early days.'

Despite our high hopes, our mission isn't starting as we'd hoped. As we'd docked, the city commander, a steely-eyed man named Farsil, had come aboard. He was a no-nonsense man of few words, full of confidence and authority. His arms, minus armour, were covered in a lattice of scars, and one side of his face seemed slightly paralysed. He'd greeted Prince Sylnar with a cold, formal courtesy that didn't bode well, then listened to the prince's wish to meet the High King to discuss an alliance. Yet rather than show deference or interest, his eyes, like the captain before him, had measured the crew, especially Lystra and us Chosen.

He'd offered Prince Sylnar to stay with him while an audience with the king was sought but denied our accompanying the prince despite protestations and threats to return to Ssythla. He must have been good at dice and cards, for he was certainly prepared to call a bluff when he perceived one.

The one concession he'd made was allowing us off the ship while the ssythlan crew were confined to quarters on board. However, except for Lystra, we are under a night-time curfew.

Lystra had headed off an hour ago in the company of the Delnorian captain assigned to find us lodgings. Hopefully, they'd choose somewhere we usually didn't frequent, or the questions that gave rise to would be impossible to answer.

'Sixteen galleys with room for another twenty that must be out on manoeuvres,' Lotane notes.

'I've counted at least five hundred soldiers entering the citadel on the hill,' I reply. 'There's far more activity than when we were here last. Our failed attack likely has something to do with it.'

Hundreds more fill every street everywhere I turn. I'm not sure they have anywhere specific to go, but idle hands are dangerous, so their sergeants have them march from here to there to keep them occupied.

'Those are veterans.' Lotane nods toward a century of heavily armoured men. Their polished shields reflect the sunlight but are also scarred and dented. 'They hold themselves well. Look at the captain leading them, especially his face. He leads men he's proud of.'

'You're right. He reminds me of the Delnorian that Nestor fought, remember?'

Lotane grunts in agreement.

However much we own these streets at night, there are advantages to being out during the day. True, everything is still a thousand shades of greys, blacks, and whites, but most people don't shift with malignancy. Rather, if any change occurs, it's through frustration or anger as opposed to pure evil intent.

However, occasional monsters mingle amongst their fellows, their true selves hidden, except to us Chosen.

'If only these people could see the evil that walks amongst them,' Lotane says softly, nodding to a particularly loathsome-looking creature that, in our eyes, rarely returns to human form. He has a hundred tiny arms with grasping fingers and a dozen blinking eyes on tentacles that wave around his head like some kind of cursed grass in a breeze.

'Maybe we wouldn't be needed,' I add. 'Maybe the High King would be thrown down by his own people rather than us having to do it. I can't imagine what he'll look like to our eyes, but it will be hideous for sure. The amount of evil in that one man must be beyond belief.'

Lystra turning a nearby corner catches my eye.

Her stony face causes several men to move aside as she approaches. There's always a feeling that if you stand in her way, she could walk right through you. Even those who don't know her can perceive the force of her will.

'Come.'

Lystra rarely speaks unnecessarily. Her conversation is direct and to the point, with no room for misunderstanding.

She gathers the others, and we follow her to the furthest end of a pier. Confused, jealous and suspicious looks are cast upon us as we pass workers frantically unloading the latest catch or cargo. We're obviously strangers, walking around without a care in the world. Only the nobility don't have to work, yet here we are on a busy day, taking a stroll, and we certainly aren't nobility.

Lystra finds a quiet spot amongst some coiled ropes and empty crates. The smell of old fish is nauseating, but at least there's utter privacy. We make ourselves as comfortable as possible. Lystra's visage is grim as she looks around.

'We've been assigned an inn nearby, but we're being watched. There's no way we can go hunting at night and go unobserved, so we'll have to harvest souls during the day. No more than three of you can go out at any one time, and you'll have to be extremely careful not to draw attention to yourself.

'The biggest problem is that we won't be allowed to escort the prince further than the citadel gates. However, Sylnar will provide priceless information on what he sees while inside. Perhaps we can use that intelligence to help us gain entrance.

'However, we don't know when or even if he'll be invited to court. Our arrival hasn't been met with enthusiasm. The human dislike and distrust of ssythlans runs deep. It may be that we'll be turned away and have to return to our previous methods to gain entry.

'Whatever happens, we cannot fail to kill the High King.

'The last five years of upheaval, the ongoing war, is all part of the ssythlan preparation to ensure our king succeeds in his ascension. Their gold and gems have helped destabilise the empire across the continent, encouraging kingdoms to seek independence. Now the Delnorian Empire's power is crumbling, and this will be the final blow that will see it vanish forever.'

There's silence as we take all of this in. The ssythlans are behind the current wars! This is something new, and the scope of their planning is breathtaking.

We sit for another hour, discussing how else we might kill the High King if Prince Sylnar doesn't get us access. The High King rarely leaves his citadel, so every scenario involves us getting inside. Poison might work, but whatever food we corrupt is not guaranteed to end up on his table. A further problem is that security is tightened every time we fail, and our chance of success diminishes further.

The sun is starting to drop when Lystra calls a halt.

'We need to head to the inn as we aren't allowed to be out after dark,' she growls, yet she doesn't stand to lead the way. Instead, she reaches out her hand, and we lean forward to clasp one another's wrists.

'What is our mission, Chosen?' she asks quietly, as shadows creep over the land like death's fingers.

'To kill the High King,' we intone as if simply ordering breakfast.

'Then let us rest, and pray that on the morrow, Sylnar is invited to the palace.'

***

CHAPTER XVII

'Four days of virtual inactivity. How many dark souls might we have harvested between us in this time?' Kralgen growls, his fists opening and closing as if he wants to wrap them around someone's throat.

Lystra's glare is enough to stop him from complaining further. There might be no one else in the inn's common room where we're relaxing after breaking fast, but we can't afford someone overhearing such a comment.

However, I share his frustration. For all these years, I've been training or, more recently, hunting souls every single day. To be forced to sit in this world of grey where not even food brings comfort is torture beyond belief.

Prince Sylnar is still ensconced in Commander Farsil's residence, so we're mostly confined to the inn. Every day Lystra visits, only to return with no news. It transpires the idea of ssythlan warriors coming to Delnor's aid to help end the war is not as appealing as we'd hoped.

My reverie is disturbed by sudden movement as Kralgen kicks at a brazen rat running over his foot. He misses the agile creature as it scurries around and barely maintains balance on his chair.

Lotane laughs. 'You're getting slow, Kral. Good thing rats don't carry knives, or I think that one might have got the better of you.'

Kralgen smiles. 'What are you talking about?' he says, nodding at Lotane's weapon at his waist. 'Rats do carry knives.'

Alyssa slaps Kralgen on his broad back, chuckling.

'You win,' she says.

'Damn,' Lotane mutters, not having a suitable comeback, and salutes Kralgen.

'Malina. You, Nestor, and Kralgen can take till early afternoon,' Lystra offers once the laughter dies down.

Nestor and Kralgen leave immediately, going their own way, while I hesitate.

I almost say no. There's nothing to see but grey skies, smoking buildings and people going about their business with evil hidden amongst them. Of course, the other Chosen and I had quietly dispatched a few in the first two days to ensure our Soul Blades were ready to take us home.

Our victims didn't even know what had happened as we walked past, our concealed blades cutting through flesh without leaving a trace, just sucking the souls right from them. My first victim, a cutpurse who'd robbed two elderly women without them realising it, had been at least ten steps behind me before he started screaming. I hadn't thrust the blade into his vitals, so his world would have turned grey just like ours. I wonder if seeing people shifting into something from his nightmares and everything decaying in front of his eyes prepared him for the hell that awaited when he died later that day.

I nod, pulling my hood over my head as I stand. I rest my hand on Lotane's shoulder, but it's more from habit than feeling. Being without a soul leaves no capacity for love, and whilst there's a bond between us, it's of duty and comradeship. Love is but a memory.

There's little joy to be found as I follow the others out the common room door and into the street beyond. Even the young look old in this world of greys. If I could see through normal eyes, would the sky look so angry, full of boiling clouds, or would it be an azure blue? Would that woman's hair be beautiful as opposed to a writhing nest of snakes? I cannot wait for this mission to be over so we can return to the island, our home.

The noise and odour are, at times, overwhelming. It seems that being denied taste, my sense of hearing and smell are heightened, and whilst I need to exercise and escape the confinement of the inn, I soon want to shut myself away.

Market vendors peddle their wares, but I don't even turn my head, not wishing to see the ugliness of greed. Gulls screeching grates at my nerves, and the ever-present smell of fish I loved as a child now turns my stomach.

People push past me as I walk along the street, their eyes lingering if they catch sight of my skin or eyes, but no one says anything. I stroll aimlessly, wondering how we can complete our mission if the ssythlan can't get us access to the palace. Yet whilst my footsteps are as random as my thoughts, I'm constantly aware of the people and surroundings.

A young man resembling a snarling wolf, pushes himself away from a shop front where he was lounging alongside a few evil-looking friends and steps into the flow of people heading toward me.

I catch a glimpse of his empty hands, so he's not out to kill me, which means he believes I'm an easy mark for picking my pockets or stealing my pouch.

Yes. An end to today's boredom. My blood quickens as he closes, stumbles on purpose, and bumps into me, grabbing on. He's an expert; there's no denying it. I'd never have felt him lift my pouch if I wasn't aware of his intentions.

'I'm so sorry, Miss.' He bows in apology and backs away.

'Don't be sorry,' I say sweetly, closing the gap.

He backpedals but bumps into some people behind him, stumbling for real this time. I reach out to grab his flailing wrist, pull hard, and then as he instinctively resists, I step in and elbow him sharply to the bridge of his nose.

It's a cruel blow, and I hear his nose snap above the noise around me. He goes down hard this time, blood flowing in a black torrent as he howls in pain.

'Leave me alone. Help!' he screams fearfully, crawling backwards, tears pouring down his cheeks.

'What's going on?'

'Leave him alone!'

People shout at me but don't dare interfere as I reach down, grab the thief's hand as he tries to keep me away, and twist his thumb so hard that his scream silences everyone in the vicinity.

'My pouch,' I say loudly enough so that everyone can hear, holding out my hand.

'I don't know what ... Owww.'

Sobbing, he reaches inside his tunic, pulls out my pouch and drops it into my palm.

I know I should leave it there; let him go. But I also know he'll steal someone else's hard-earned coins shortly after. But, not with a broken thumb, he won't, at least not today.

With a swift twist, his thumb cracks, and he curls into a ball, mewling piteously while I stride toward the circle of people, most of whom look on in disbelief. The exception are several watching soldiers who clap in appreciation.

As the circle opens before me, the three men the thief had been scouting with move toward me, hands concealed in their tunics, faces evil with intent.

'Come closer, and you'll die!' I say, pushing my hood back, my glare unflinching. Having exposed them, their courage flees, and they back away into the crowd.

With the spectacle over, the noise resumes, reaching a new crescendo as people discuss what they'd witnessed. Even if I'm not hungry, I'll get something to eat and drink, anything to be out of this wailing noise.

Looking around, I notice I'm near the library, and I smile.

If there's going to be one quiet place in this city, then that will be it, and it's been a while since I stopped to read. Maybe I can borrow a book to pass the time.

Yes. The others might tease me as I study, but then, at least everyone will have something to do.

With a spring to my step, I pick up my pace, the steps of the library promising sanctuary ahead.

***

Steeping through the library doors is akin to going back through the Soul Gate. It might still be colourless and decaying, yet there's a sense of something holy. A few librarians and visitors talk in hushed voices, respectful of their surroundings.

There's peace and tranquillity here amongst these tomes, and I find myself somewhat humbled.

All this knowledge. It would take me a thousand years to read it all, by which time there'd be another thousand years of new books written. An eternal quest for knowledge. The thought makes me smile as maybe the books would be about Nogoth and his rule and perhaps even the part the Chosen played in bringing about his golden age.

Instead of heading upstairs toward the section on ancient history, I stay near the entrance. It's a large semi-circular space with grand staircases sweeping up to the left and right. Toward the back of the hall, polished wooden desks are covered in piles of random scrolls, tomes, and books. Moving over, I pick one up to discover a children's story within and smile as pictures of gallant knights leap off the pages.

'Malina, there you are!' Arcan's brittle voice cuts through the near silence like a dropped glass. 'Where have you been? I haven't seen you or that young man sneaking around here recently.'

I turn to watch the old librarian cautiously descend the staircase with two clerks following respectfully behind and smile. Despite the scolding tone of his voice, there's nothing bad about this old man, and his is a lonely job that receives no gratitude of note.

'We went our separate ways, and I've been distracted by other commitments. However, I'll be spending a little more time here from now on.'

'Ssssh,' several people admonish us but don't say more when they recognise Arcan as the author of the conversation.

Nodding, I greet the clerks and receive wan smiles in return as they head toward the back of the chamber, tutting at the amount of returned items, smoke billowing from their nostrils. Overall, it seems that only decent people frequent the library, which is another reason to come here. It's a relief to see peoples' faces and not twisted monstrosities.

'Hmmm. Well, that's good.' Arcan peers at me critically. 'I suppose all those whirls on your robe is your idea of the latest fashion? If your looks don't get you noticed, you'll outrage the other nobility by breaking convention. You should know better, girl!

'Wait here. I'll be right back,' he mumbles, then shuffles off through an archway.

Four young men are sitting at a table with an older man, and I make my way over to discover they're studying books on healing.

'Do you mind?' the old man grumbles as the young men stare in wide-eyed fascination at my look. 'They find it hard enough to focus as it is!'

Moving on, I pick up random tomes, happy to enjoy the silence. Most here are about different plants, and I smile in recognition as names and uses come unbidden to mind. The last one has many that are new to me, but as the shuffling footsteps of Arcan approach, I replace it on a shelf.

'I have something for you,' he says with an embarrassed smile, passing me a small, cloth-wrapped package that's clearly another book. 'Don't get too excited; it's a children's book. I pride myself on knowing most everything about history, but … What's this?'

The puzzlement in his voice and the frown that creases his brow don't bode well.

Quickly tucking his gift through a slit in my robes into a pocket, I turn to look around the edge of a bookcase to see what's caused him concern.

Eight men have entered the library, one of whom has his arm in a crude sling and a hugely swollen nose. Their evil intent is obvious; even if their faces didn't shift from the rough-looking individuals they were into vicious beasts.

Two of the men step forward and start knocking books from their shelves, laughing maliciously as they do so. Murmurs of fear echo softly as the clerks, students and librarians find themselves confronted by these thugs.

'What's the meaning of this!' shouts Arcan, shuffling forward, his staff cracking on the floor, yet he stumbles back as one of the thugs draws a long dirk.

I sigh. It's my fault these scum are here. If I hadn't broken the lad's thumb, then maybe they wouldn't have followed me here and pushed this further.

Stepping from behind the case, I move slowly toward them.

'They're here for me,' I call, drawing their attention.

Arcan's eyes open wide. 'For you? What have you done, girl? I've seen these types. Run! I'll hold them for as long as I can,' he says, gripping his staff tight.

I want to hug him. He's willing to give up his life for me, someone he barely knows. It's for good people like him that I do what I do.

'You shouldna broken me son's thumb, ya stupid bitch. How's he gonna steal proper now?' growls a middle-aged man, eyes bulging with anger one moment, writhing with maggots the next. 'There's another dozen of me lads waiting just outside. Why don't we leave this learned lot alone and 'ave a chat in the fresh air about making fings good.'

I point toward the library door, and *maggot eyes* tilts his head, indicating for me to go first.

'Don't go with them,' pleads Arcan, clutching my arm, his rheumy eyes full of fear. 'They're evil men. The things they'll do to you!'

Gently, to avoid hurting or scaring him, I pull myself free of his grasp. Smiling reassuringly, I step across the polished flagstones toward the entrance with every single eye upon me. The laughter of the thugs rings clearly as they throw more books to the floor.

The library doors are tall and solid, with a simple hinged wooden locking bar that drops into place. Additionally, large metal bolts are at the bottom, which, when released, drop into holes in the flagstones.

'This is a place of knowledge,' I call loudly, having reached the door, 'where wise men come to learn.' I drop the locking bar into place, then bend down, letting the bolts slide home, securing the entrance. 'Your first lesson is that you shouldn't have split your forces and left some of your gang outside.'

I pull my robe over my head, letting it drop to the ground, freeing myself of constraint.

'The second is,' and I smile, 'whilst you might think I'm an easy victim, you really shouldn't judge a book by its cover.'

My magic strains for release, but I bid it silent. I'll definitely use it, but I can't just have the ground swallow these vermin up in front of these people. Even this confrontation will draw unwanted attention, and tales of magic will ensure we never get near the king.

'You fink ya got a clever mouth on ya, but we'll teach ya to keep it shut!' *Maggot eyes* crows.

His men fan out. Each one holds a weapon. Cudgels, dirks, a hatchet and even a mace are gripped in steady hands. Confidence, arrogance, and anticipation ooze from them all.

Pulling my dagger from its sheath, I move to a desk and place it on the wood, spinning it around.

A man with a face looking like a snarling dog runs forward, perhaps wanting to impress his friends, swinging his cudgel fiercely at my head. I duck at the last moment, and as he spins around off balance, his back briefly toward me, I put my hand under his chin and yank backwards and down. Falling, his neck hits the edge of the desk hard, and his legs kick twice before he lies still on the ground, a puddle of urine spreading around him.

Seven left.

Reaching down, I heft his cudgel and pick up my dagger.

With a roar, the other seven charge forward to overwhelm me. Dropping, I roll backwards under the desk, coming to my feet on the other side. Swinging the cudgel, I shatter the shin of the mace-wielding man who'd jumped onto the table, sweeping his legs from under him. As he falls screaming, I plunge my dagger into his neck, grab his fallen mace, then twist and throw in one smooth motion.

It's a heavy weapon, and I know it will take the lad with the broken nose on his forehead as I yank my dagger free and roll under the table again.

Even above the shouts, I hear a sickening crunch as the mace hits.

Coming to my feet, I twist just in time to avoid a thrown dagger that clatters as it skids along the floor as the five remaining men charge back around, their bloodlust and rage something to behold.

Until now, they'd been rash, unthinking, but now they've seen my worth, they slow. There are fewer remaining, but they've become more dangerous. They spread out as I back away, placing my feet carefully.

Shouts and banging on the library door indicate those outside are aware of the fight and are trying to enter. A tall man wielding a dagger almost as long as a short sword sidles toward the entrance, drawn by the hope of reinforcements.

I charge, and as he lashes out, I drop to my knees, sliding along the floor under the sweep of his blade, my dagger slashing his right hamstring as I roll, leaving him howling on the floor, clutching the wound, out of the fight.

As I regain my feet, the remaining four are almost on top of me.

I block a knife thrust with my cudgel, duck under another, but get a powerful kick to my stomach that sends me reeling backwards, winded … yet even as I fall, I'm rolling, creating distance and fling my dagger. It's risky, but I'm rewarded as it takes another in the throat.

The leader, the father of the lad I'd killed with the mace, swings his club, and whilst I deflect it with my cudgel, it's knocked spinning from my hand.

I'm now unarmed, facing three.

I back away between two tables covered in scrolls and tomes. My right arm feels weak, and I'm gasping for breath. With a shout, I sweep both my arms forward, calling upon my magic, and the scrolls swirl upwards, whooshing into the air.

Grabbing a heavy tome, I leap. The closest man armed with a hatchet is distracted, batting away at the papers. I swing the heavy book into his head, sending him tumbling to the ground, then as he rolls over, slam the reinforced spine down, crushing his throat.

The next man thrusts a dagger toward my chest. As I block with the tome, the point becomes stuck in the thick leather binding, so I wrench, twisting the weapon from his grasp. Empty-handed, he lunges forward, looking to overpower me. Aware of sudden movement to my side, I grab his arm and pull him into the arc of a club aimed at my head. With a sickening crunch, he drops to the floor.

Swaying away from the next swing, I sweep up the hatchet, then dance back several steps as the scrolls slowly settle to the floor.

'I'm gonna bloody kill ya, gal,' sobs the leader desperately. His face twists and shifts, but the eyes are wide and betray his fear, whether human or otherwise. 'You shouldna killed me boy. Why you 'ave to go do that? Look at what ya done to me lads too!'

He backs away toward the door as the pounding on it continues. I follow, passing the man with the sliced hamstring. There's a vast pool of blood, and his face is pale as he tries to stem the flow. With a swift swing, the hatchet cleaves through his face. I don't even feel any resistance; the edge is so keen.

Raising the dripping weapon, I point it at the leader.

'A son should live to bury his father, or a father to bury his son, wouldn't you agree? Now, drop your weapon!'

His hand is shaking so much that he might have even if I hadn't told him to do so. Irrespective, the heavy club thumps to the floor.

'Turn around,' I order.

If he's to be believed, there are up to a dozen more scum outside trying to get in. I move behind him, swiftly pulling a dagger from his waistband.

'Kneel!'

Tears run down his stubbled cheeks as he sinks to his knees.

Looking around, I take stock of the other people in the library. It's as though some god has waved her hand and frozen everyone in place, for they're where I last saw them. Even Arcan is standing, rooted in the same spot.

'You, and you!' I say loudly, pointing the hatchet at two of the young medical students. Their eyes lock fearfully with mine. In this world of greys that I see, their faces couldn't be whiter. 'Go to the door. NOW.'

They stand hesitantly, then skirting the bodies and blood, make their way to the library entrance. The thumping has ceased, but voices can still be heard through the wood.

'Unlock, and open them on my command,' I say coldly, leaving no room for disobedience.

Pushing the leader's dagger into my belt, I grab his greasy hair in a fist.

'Open them!'

With shaking hands, the youths pull up the bolts, lift the locking bar, and then heave back on the doors. As daylight floods into the library, eight men and two women are framed in the entrance. Not the dozen I'd been told, but near enough.

As their eyes become accustomed to the gloom, they take in the deathly scene, eyes sweeping left and right before they settle on me, undecided.

I lift the hatchet and, without saying a word, bring it down twice in quick succession. True, swift blows that leave a severed head in my hands and the body collapsing, blood spurting toward the doorway, splashing at the feet of those who stand watching.

'Shall we dance?' I ask, spreading my arms wide, and step toward them, the blood-soaked scrolls flying in a vortex around me.

***

I should feel elated. Eight evil men are dead, and I wonder if the others who fled at the sight me of will mend their wicked ways. Sadly, I doubt it.

Yet what saddens me isn't that they chose to run, but at the looks everyone gave me in the library afterwards. They were more fearful of me than the men who'd come to kill or perhaps even rape me. How is it possible that I was seen as the evil one?

Arcan had said little, but the few words he'd spoken had hurt more than the kick to the stomach that had bruised my ribs. I wasn't to return ever again, for I wouldn't be welcome.

Not that he could stop me, nor could any of them, yet his banishment and words whipped me like steel chains. He hadn't exactly been a friend, but he might have been if I hadn't defiled his holy place. I'd torn a sleeve off a dead body, wiped myself down as much as possible before donning my robes and stepped outside while one of the librarians had gone to fetch the town guard.

My only solace was that Arcan had told me he'd vouch that my killings had been in self-defence, and he didn't know who I was or where I was staying. In truth, he didn't know either, but if the town watch weren't looking out for me, it was one less worry.

Opening the inn door, I step through into the common room. Seeing the other Chosen gathered within, relief pushes away my sadness. Here is my family, who'll not judge me harshly and can appreciate the good deed I've done this day.

Lystra, eyes sharp, tilts her head enquiringly.

'Welcome back, Wolf Slayer. Have you been hunting?'

Kralgen leans forward, eyes lighting up.

'Tell us everything! I've been as bored as hell. I'd rather be dodging arrows than walking about, enjoying the culture of this fine city.'

'To enjoy culture, you need to be cultured, Kralgen,' Lotane laughs deeply, along with Fianna's lighter trill.

Alyssa and Nestor gather around, all intent on hearing the story.

Lotane pats the chair next to him, and I'm the centre of my family's attention.

After I finish my tale, there's a moment's silence before Kralgen laughs loudly, tears running down his face.

'You really killed one with a book?' he wheezes, trying to catch his breath.

'Hush,' Lystra admonishes him. 'You're to be commended in meting out the king's justice, Malina, but this cannot be repeated. We're supposed to keep a low profile and can't afford any unwanted attention. Simple bodyguards don't kill eight men in a library, least of all with their own weapons ... and a book,' she chuckles, smiling.

'You're just jealous,' Lotane teases Lystra.

I'm amazed when she smiles shyly at him.

'It's true. I might just be. Malina gets to have all the fun while we enjoy the culture. Oh, by the way, Kralgen, what exactly does the word culture mean to you?'

Kralgen looks at Alyssa, grabbing her hand, a look of concentration on his face.

'It's not eating with your hands or blowing your nose between your fingers,' he states hopefully.

Alyssa smiles wide, proud as can be.

'That's a good start, Kral,' she says warmly.

Even Nestor, who says next to nothing unless asked a direct question, laughs wholeheartedly along with the rest of us.

'Don't forget that you shouldn't piss in the street either,' he adds.

'Really?'

The look of surprise on Kralgen's face is so genuine that more laughter echoes from the panelled walls. The innkeeper, who we hardly see anything of, puts his head around the kitchen door, sees nothing broken, and closes it behind him.

Gradually the merriment dies down.

'Malina, Nestor, care to do some sparring out back?' Kralgen offers, raising his fists.

I'm tempted to join them, but the thought of getting a punch from Kralgen in my sore ribs leads me to decline.

'Sorry, Kral. Tomorrow.'

Kralgen nods.

'Shame. Still, good thing grumpy Nestor here has a chin as hard as the stone he enjoys playing with.'

Lotane and Fianna snigger but withhold making a ribald comment.

'Lotane, Alyssa, Fianna, it's time to stretch your limbs,' Lystra commands. 'Be back before dark, and don't kill anyone, even if you're tempted to.'

Lotane comes to give me a kiss. I might have gotten used to the greys, the shifting of people from human to monster, yet I can't get used to the absence of love. We go through these motions because the brain says so, but there's no emotion behind it. I can laugh and be happy, but love … that's beyond me and the others when our soul is stripped away by the Soul Gate.

'Be careful and keep your hood well up. We don't want your eyes getting you into a fight,' I say after our lips part. There was no emotion to it, just the touch of skin on skin.

'I'll just wink whenever I see a good-looking woman,' he laughs. 'Shall I give them the blue or the green eye?'

'How about I give you two black eyes if I catch you doing that?' I threaten, punching him on the shoulder.

'Point taken. I'll just keep my hood up and my head down.'

With a final nod to Lystra, he lets himself out.

It's strange how jealousy remains when love has gone. I'd meant what I said.

'I was in love once. He was called Xander.'

I can scarce believe my ears and am tempted to turn around to see if someone else is in the room, but Lystra is looking at me. I don't say a word as her eyes gradually take on a glazed look, losing focus.

'We came from the same town on the Surian coast, although I didn't know him before the orphanage.' Lystra's voice is wistful, soft, and utterly different to her norm. 'There was a plague, I think, and so many adults died. I can't even remember my parents' names, let alone what they looked like.

'What I do remember is hating Xander when we were at the orphanage. He was a bully back then, big for his age and two years older than me. He stole my food nearly every day and would beat me when I tried to fight back. Because of that, I had to take other children's food. I became like him, even though I despised what he did, at least back then.

'Several times, I tried to kill him with a blunt food knife I'd sharpened against the mouldy rock walls, but each time I failed. The beatings the guards gave me after each attempt were worse than his, but the food in the infirmary was better, and Xander couldn't steal it from me either. So, I kept trying to kill him with anything I could get my hands on until they took away my plates, bowls and cutlery and made me eat with my hands.

'Have you ever tried to eat scalding hot soup with your hands?'

It might have been a question, but I know Lystra isn't expecting an answer, for there's barely a pause before she carries on.

'Suntarg was always soup day. They'd boil it good and hot because whatever ingredients they put in were near rotten, and they didn't want everyone puking all night. So they just boiled it for ages. Everyone else got a bowl, but because I'd broken several to get some jagged pottery shards to cut Xander with, I got nothing.

'They made me hold out my hands like this.' Lystra cups her hands together without even looking at me, then carries on. 'Then they'd ladle in the boiling soup. Oh, and if I spilt any, I wouldn't eat for a week. What choice did I have?

'Anyway. The wardens couldn't wait to get rid of me, and I was put on the auction block two years early. Because of that, I got sold at the same time as Xander, and we both ended up at the Mountain of Souls.

'In those first few days, it was all I could do to stay alive, yet, I tell you this. If it hadn't been for him toughening me up at the orphanage, I'd never have survived. I was the youngest there, but I'd been fighting for years, and pain didn't mean anything to me by then.

'Anyway, I swore if he didn't die during training or the purges, I'd kill him when I was strong enough and could get away with it. He knew what I had in mind. I used to sit opposite him every mealtime, knowing how angry he'd be, unable to steal my food cause he'd be killed as punishment.

'So, driven by hatred and with my goal to kill him, I thrived and, over the years, became the best I could be, way better than Xander. Yes, the thought of serving The Once and Future King drove me on too, but back then, nothing shone brighter than the dream of killing Xander. I had it all planned. He was always slow to block a reverse thrust, as he never could read it for whatever reason. Even with a blunted weapon, he'd die if I caught him in the throat. It would take a while with him gasping for every last breath, and I'd hold him closely while I watched the life ebb from his putrid eyes.

'It was just before our first trip through the gate when I knew I could get away with it. No one would believe a grudge could be held for so many years. Yet, when I had the opportunity, I couldn't take it. Don't ask me when it happened or how, but I'd fallen in love with him. I found love with a man I despised and had wanted to kill.

'What's the chance of that?'

I'm mesmerised. All these years, I've never known anything about Lystra other than her name, whereas in the last few minutes, she's bared the soul she no longer carries with her. Yet, even more fascinating is her innocence about how her love developed. She's completely unaware that it was forged by blood magic.

There's silence for a while, and after baring so much, I wonder if she'll share more. I'm truly intrigued. I know the others so well, and whilst I can happily listen to Lotane talk about anything, this is like reading a new book, assimilating knowledge.

'What happened to Xander?' I ask softly. I know there can't be a happy ending, for otherwise, I'd have met him, but the question begs to be asked.

Lystra's sigh is tinged with regret.

'We ruled the night together for two years. Back then, we travelled the world and meted out the king's justice. It was a glorious time, but one day we pushed too far too soon. Blinded by our previous successes, we and the other Chosen attempted to kill the High King. This was before we knew of the final plan and could choose to slay whichever evil souls we wished.

'Despite being equals, the other Chosen wanted me to lead the expedition. The High King didn't lock himself in his citadel all day back then; he hunted the countryside with his knights. Regretfully, the other Chosen and I never received the training you do now, and despite being used to fighting, we knew little of the land. However, that didn't bother us; we were so arrogant, and therein lay our undoing.

'The king's hunters, used to spotting both prey and predator, must have seen us, for we fell into a carefully laid ambush. It was a brutal affair, and the less said about it, the better. Only Xander and I escaped, but he was mortally wounded.

'It was somewhat ironic that he died in my arms after all, and I kept that old promise of mine. I held him close in my arms and watched the life ebb from his eyes. We hadn't returned through the gate, so I didn't feel a thing when he passed. Yet, when I came back, with my soul returned, I'd never experienced anguish like it and wanted to die. After recovering from my physical injuries, I volunteered for every ssythlan experiment as they tried and failed to bind the magical elements to people, yet I alone survived.

'Somehow, the pain and knowing that one day I'd have another chance to kill the High King kept me going. To complete my mission, to reclaim my lost honour and avenge my Xander. All these things sustain me and burn brightly in my mind.

'I envy your love, Malina, and the others. How they fell for each other, I'll never understand. Yet, love is blind, is a saying as old as time.

'Now, sore ribs or not, go and train with Kralgen and Nestor. You're the best group of Chosen I've ever seen, but we need to stay razor-sharp, for whether we live or die, we need to complete our mission, so I can have my revenge.'

***

A distant clanging disturbs my sleep. It's harsh and impossible to ignore.

We leap out of our bunks, and as our habit is to sleep with clothes on, we only need to pull on boots before we open the door to see Lystra striding down the corridor, dagger belted to her hip. I wonder where she's been and if she's somehow responsible for the alarm.

'Get everything, and meet in the common room immediately,' she commands, her demeanour conveying urgency. It's unusual to see Lystra ruffled, but her hair is in disarray and her shirt half unbuttoned.

Another door opens, and a sleepy-eyed patron steps into her path.

'What's all this noise about?' complains the man gruffly, as if she's to blame.

Lystra doesn't even break stride as her fist cracks against his chin, spinning him back into his room. A scream comes from inside as Lystra pulls the door shut and heads for the stairs.

More bells begin to toll as we return to our beds, snatching daggers and looping Soul Blades around our necks. We swiftly descend to the kitchen, which is slowly filling with disgruntled patrons from the ground floor. Pushing through, we enter the common room to find Lystra angrily telling two men to leave.

Not understanding the danger they're in and only seeing an angry woman, albeit a strong one, they stand their ground, saying they've paid for their lodgings and can sit where they like.

Kralgen steps forward, putting a meaty hand around each of their throats and lifts them off the ground in an obscene display of strength.

'If you struggle too much, you might just break your own necks,' Kralgen growls as they kick and gurgle. Either abject fear or Kralgen's grip causes them to quiet. 'Now, you have a choice. I can throw you through the wall and into the kitchen beyond, or you can walk through the door. Which one will it be?'

'Door,' they gasp in unison.

'Where's the fun in that?' Kralgen complains, lowering them to the floor. The look in their eyes as Kralgen looms over them is priceless. They almost tear the kitchen door off its hinges trying to get through.

Alyssa slaps Kralgen on the back, and he beams in satisfaction.

'Wait a moment,' Lystra orders. 'I'll find out what's going on.'

She opens the main door to the street, and we can see soldiers running by as she steps forward. Fast as a snake, she grabs one by the arm and pulls him aside. He angrily tries to free himself, eyes wide with fear as I see Lystra talk to him. She smacks him so hard across the cheek with the palm of her hand that I wince, but he stops struggling and responds before she lets him go.

Stepping back inside, she closes the door.

'A large enemy force has been spotted outside the city,' Lystra breaks the news. 'We'll never be able to complete our mission now as security will be tightened. I'll fetch Prince Sylnar and meet you at the docks. Get the ship ready to leave. We need to get the prince out before it's sealed off.

'Lotane, you're in charge. Now move!'

Lystra steps into the street again, and we follow, pushing out into a maelstrom.

Every soldier in the city is answering the clarion call of alarm and is heading to the walls. High Delnor hugs the southern shore and is defended by a long semi-circular wall that meets and extends into the sea. Large towers and crenelated battlements provide cover from which defenders can fight.

However, we're going the other way, pushing south toward the docks, against the flow of soldiers going the other direction, and our progress is painfully slow. The bells continue to toll, and I think each is being rung with wild panic, for it's hard to hear anything above their sound.

'Kralgen, to me!' Lotane yells, and they lead the way, forging through the crowd as the rest of us follow.

Fortunately, the tide of soldiers thins, and suddenly we're making better time, and it isn't long before we reach the docks.

Dozens of marines are running about, getting their galleys ready to sail. Fortunately, despite the stares sent our way, they're too busy to stop and question our presence.

Lotane raises a clenched fist above his head, and we gather around.

'Look!' he points. 'We'll need to get those smaller boats moved to clear the way for the prince's ship. Kral, you and Nestor cut their ropes and deal with any opposition. Malina, you and Fianna use your magic to move them out of the way.'

'What's that?' Nestor points, drawing our attention.

A flicker of light appears out to sea, and then moments later, fire climbs into the darkness just past the harbour wall. The flames are huge, highlighting five burning galleys being rowed furiously toward the harbour entrance.

More alarm bells begin to clang, adding to the cacophony of those in the city behind us. Flashes of flame arc from the battlements above the harbour. The defensive catapults on the walls throw rocks wrapped in flaming oil-soaked rags. Yet their shots land wide of their targets.

A dozen marines are frantically firing a bolt thrower, shooting volley after volley of the iron-tipped weapons from behind crenulations atop the harbour wall. Yet there's no one visible to hit on the flaming galleys, which continue unchecked.

One is ahead of the others, and it doesn't stop as it passes through the harbour entrance and straight toward the pier, where some Delnorian galleys are moored.

I watch in morbid fascination as it ploughs into the side of a Delnorian ship, flinging the few crew on deck from their feet. Then, as if in slow motion, the flaming galley seems to expand before shattering into a thousand pieces.

One moment I'm standing, and the next, I'm on my back, feeling like I've been kicked in the chest by a horse. Above, the clouds flicker, almost as if on fire. Smoke is everywhere, yet it's so quiet. My heart beats silently five or six times as I regain my senses, and then, like a flood, the noise returns, full of screams.

Instinctively I check on Lotane and the other Chosen. Fortunately, we were far enough from the blast to have only been knocked flat.

I cough, the smoke thick in my lungs, blinking away tears to discover something akin to the fires of hell before me. The remaining fire galleys have stopped in the harbour mouth and are settling in the water. They've been holed by their crew, who are diving from the deck to escape the searing flames. I cast my eyes back to the pier where the first galley struck to find it mostly gone, with little but splintered support piles rising from the water like blackened fingers.

Bodies are strewn everywhere. The blast has either killed or knocked unconscious hundreds of men and women. Some scream piteously as flames blister their skin, and they desperately claw their way toward the water.

Lotane climbs smoothly to his feet, assessing the scene of carnage.

'The prince won't be leaving this way anymore,' he shouts above the roar of flames. 'But we have to stay put as this is where Lystra will find us. However, we'll pull back for now in case the flames spread.'

'No!'

I surprise myself, not only with my resolve but by disagreeing with Lotane.

'We need to help those people.' I gesture to the injured.

'They're not our people,' Kralgen argues. 'In fact, they're more our enemy than friends!'

'Kralgen has it right,' Nestor rumbles, knuckling his eyes.

I'm stunned at their response and look to Fianna and Alyssa, noting their discomfort. Neither wants to disagree with their partners, and I know the tenet that only the strong survive is playing in their minds.

'I know we're tasked with ridding the world of evil, but surely that also means we can save the good where we can,' I shout. 'Most of the injured might not be saints, but we can still help them!

'Fianna, Alyssa, come with me,' I command. 'Let us show true strength to these Delnorians!'

I might have mentioned the Delnorians, but I really mean Lotane, Nestor and Kralgen.

Without another word, I set off at a run with Alyssa and Fianna toward the quay, close to the centre of destruction, where people stumble around in shock.

With every step, the heat rises, and the smoke thickens as the flames spread. My throat is raw, and my eyes are streaming.

We encounter a small group of around twelve marines, unharmed but milling around.

'You men are with me,' I shout, running over to them.

'Who the hell are you?' demands a captain amongst them, eyes wide with fright and panic. 'We need to get away. Look at what's happening. We need to get away. Run. Everybody, RUN!'

I don't hesitate, and my open palm lashes across his face, knocking him to his knees.

'You men are with me,' I shout again, staring at them, pushing my hood back, my hand on the hilt of my dagger. The moment hangs in the balance as they gaze upon me, unsure whether to obey a confident and fierce stranger who obviously isn't one of their own. Yet my stare doesn't brook disagreement, and the penalty for doing so cowers at my feet. Nods encourage me to continue.

'We need to get the wounded back from the flames before they succumb to the heat or their injuries,' I shout. 'Over there,' and I point back to where Lotane, Nestor and Kralgen stand watching, 'is where we'll take any wounded.

'You!' I pick a man who appears calmer than the rest. 'Find bandages, salves, in fact, anything to help with wounds and burns. Commandeer whatever is needed, and don't take no for an answer. Have it ready for the injured. Ask anyone you meet to send for healers. It's an important job. I can rely on you, can't I?'

He nods.

'What's your name?' I demand.

'Caralax.'

'Then go, Caralax. GO!'

'You men,' and I pick three others. 'Take those ropes and go with Alyssa here. Help those struggling in the water. Start as close to the blast as you can where you'll be needed most. The rest of you, come with me!'

I jog toward the piers closest to the explosion's epicentre, leaving the captain on the decking. I've no time for cowards.

Fires are taking hold at different points of the quay where burning debris has fallen. Fortunately, none are yet serious, but it's a threat if they aren't attended to. I pull two marines aside.

'Your job is to douse those flames, or we'll have to pull back if they take hold. Anyone else you come across who is able, send them to me.'

We set off again, the remaining marines following, jumping over wreckage, fallen timbers, pieces of bodies, smouldering rope, and even a heavy mast flung here by the explosion.

Fianna and I assess every injured man we come across. Almost all are bleeding from the ears and nose. Many have limbs torn away, while others have splintered pieces of wood embedded in their flesh. Those who are dead, I turn face down. Everyone alive is carried back to the far side of the quay where I left Nestor, Kralgen and Lotane.

A naked man struggles nearby in water that's full of floating, burning debris. It's such a surreal sight that I stand in shock for a moment, but when he goes under, I tear off my robe and dive in. I find him sinking, kicking feebly in his last throws, and grab him under the chin. So far, I'd resisted using my magic, but now I call upon it, and a sudden current brings me swiftly back to the decking.

Helping hands pull us from the water. His clothes, I realise, must have been stripped away by the blast. One side of his face is scorched, but he's alive. He retches, bringing up water and despite his state, looks gratefully at me.

If I still needed affirmation that this was the right thing to do, he just gave it to me. I take my robe and cover him, allowing him some dignity.

As time goes on, more soldiers report to me for instructions, and the recovery of the wounded picks up pace. However, the flames are spreading along the piers, and everyone is coughing from the smoke. My face and skin, wherever it's bare, feels scorched.

Glancing around, I'm pleased to note the fires behind us on the quay have been extinguished, whereas those consuming several nearby piers are too ferocious. Other vessels that survived the explosion are beginning to smoulder.

'Is there fire oil kept on any of those galleys?' I ask a marine sergeant.

'Of course, they're mostly war galleys.'

His eyes widen as he appreciates the repercussions of his answer.

'Sergeant, take fifty men, split them into two teams. Jump into the water to soak yourselves first, then move those galleys.'

'We can't get near them,' he complains, looking at the flames. 'The heat is too much. We must evacuate because if one blows, the others will too.'

'We'll deal with the flames; just leave it to us. But do your job and move those ships!' I answer instantly, giving no room for debate.

'Fianna. Do what needs to be done. Keep those flames back.'

She knows what I mean. She can use her air magic to push the flames back, allowing the men to board.

'Choose your men, Sergeant,' Fianna commands, and moments later is chivvying them along a pier.

She lets them go slightly ahead, and I briefly see her face contort in pain as she reaches out her arms, and then flames are pushed back by a strong wind.

'The rest of you men,' I shout at those remaining. 'Get axes, saws, or anything that can create a firebreak between the piers and the quay. If we can't put the fire out, we need to let it burn itself out without the whole harbour going up in flames.'

They run off, and for a moment, I'm alone, coughing up black spittle.

A hand takes my arm, and Lotane stands there, a flask in hand. He's doused in blood, and my eyes widen in shock.

He doesn't say anything, just offers the flask with an apologetic look.

'You're a selfish ass!' I croak before taking a gulp of the cool water. It's soothing, and I hadn't realised till now how painful my throat was.

'You are right, and I'm sorry,' Lotane says. 'We might be assassins, but our mission is ultimately to save everyone, including these people. Kralgen and Nestor realise it too. We've been looking after the wounded, although there's not much we can do for most of them.

'Lystra came by with the prince. She was fuming. With the harbour in ruins and an enemy at the gates, we aren't going anywhere. Surprisingly, she didn't say anything about your actions and just told us to meet her at the inn when we're done. Are we done?'

I cast my gaze about. Ships are being pushed, pulled, and rowed frantically away from the flames held back by Fianna's magic. Her strength won't hold out much longer, and I'll need to take her place. There's so much more to do; it will be a long night.

'No. We're not done. Not for a long time. Will you stay with me?' I ask.

Lotane brushes my wet hair back from my face, then tilts his head to one side as if considering something.

Then that smile lights his face, and he pulls me into his bloody arms. I'm also covered in soot and gore, yet I couldn't care less. I might not feel love at this moment, but I know when I relive this memory back at the mountain, I'll feel it then.

'I'll stay with you, Alina,' he whispers. 'Now, and until the end of days.'

***

CHAPTER XVIII

I'm dreaming about Karson, perhaps triggered by Lotane using Karson's pet name for me. He's shouting something at me, a warning perhaps, but I can't make out his words. I struggle to get closer, climbing up the mountain of corpses on which he stands, yet whenever I near the top, hundreds slide down, taking me with them.

'It's her,' says a voice, waking me.

Suddenly I'm being pulled from the bed by rough, strong hands. Arms wrap around me from behind, pulling me tight against someone's breastplate.

With blurry eyes and a head spinning from lack of sleep and inhaling too much smoke, it takes me a moment to react to what's happening. However, a blood rush sweeps that aside, and I bend my head forward, then snap it back hard.

'My nose!'

The grip loosens enough for me to twist free. I turn, and my foot kicks out between my assailant's legs sending him crashing to the ground.

'Restrain that bitch,' he cries.

Damn. Even with blood and tears streaking his face, it's definitely the captain I'd struck the night before. His face shifts with dark intent, nose elongating like a muzzle, ears pointed and furred.

Lotane and the other Chosen are sitting up in their bunks, but two spear points are pressed against their chests, preventing them from interfering as four soldiers move forward.

The first, I spin from his feet with a hard right to his jaw that makes me gasp. It feels like I just hit a brick wall. However, he won't be getting up again soon. As the next man stumbles over his friend's body, I kick him hard in the knee, and he goes down crying.

'If she resists again, spear the rest of them,' crows the captain, looking at me through hate-filled, glowing eyes.

Slowly I raise my hands, palms forward. Quickly, I look at the other Chosen and receive the tiniest of nods in return. They're ready to fight. My magic demands to be released, and with its help, the other Chosen and I might stand a chance, although it will be hard for them to dodge spearpoints sitting in a bed.

As I decide my course of action, there's a commotion outside the room, and Lystra pushes through the doorway.

'What's going on?' she demands. 'We are the personal bodyguard to the ssythlan prince. Unnecessarily arresting one of us could have serious ramifications for you, Captain.'

The captain, who is now on his feet, looks gleeful despite his pain.

'Striking an officer of the Delnorian marines is a crime,' he crows. 'Not only did she assault me last night, but she did so again just now in front of even more witnesses. Foreigner or no, when you're in Delnor, you're subject to our laws. She'll face trial for her crime and will be punished if found guilty, which I can assure you will be the case!'

'What's the punishment for hitting a measly puss sack like you?' Lotane growls, leaning forward, pushing his chest against the spear tips. 'I might find it worth doing myself!'

'Oh, be my guest,' the captain smiles, pleased with himself, yet he doesn't answer Lotane's question. 'Is she your green-skinned bitch?' he goads. 'Probably. Because someone with your disgusting eyes couldn't get anything better!'

Lotane's muscles bunch as a feral grumble rumbles in his throat, and the captain takes a quick step back.

'No, Lotane.' Lystra's voice cracks like a whip. 'Don't interfere. We're subject to Delnorian law, as the captain says. However, that doesn't mean this won't be resolved swiftly. You may not know it, Captain, but our ward, the prince, is staying with Commander Farsil, and I'll be heading there immediately.'

'Even the commander can't override the crown's laws. Now, bring her,' the captain orders.

I'm not worried. I understand Lystra's decision, and she's right; this will just be a minor inconvenience. We could have killed all the guards, perhaps even without serious injury, and returned to the Mountain of

Souls. Yet part of our mission is to protect the prince whom we can't leave behind to answer for over a dozen dead bodies.

A soldier steps cautiously forward, but seeing I won't resist, he roughly turns me around, and cold metal manacles restrain my hands behind my back.

'Slip your boots on,' he growls in my ear and holds my arms tightly as I do as instructed.

'We'll see you shortly,' Lystra murmurs and then I'm being pushed toward the stairs.

Other guests are looking from their doors, but all they see is the town watch arresting a foreigner and a strange-looking one at that. They couldn't care less.

I'm bustled into a cage on a wagon that's waiting outside. The captain mounts his horse, a hideous monster astride his beast, and his squad of men march alongside as I'm driven through the streets.

Despite the early hour, the streets are alive with soldiers and many turn with interest toward me as I'm carried through their midst. In the demeanour of the youngest, I sense fear, not of me, but of potential combat. In complete contrast, I see resignation in the veterans. It's just another battle in just another place, on just another day.

Several shift, but it's fear that drives their transformation more than evil.

The wagon throws me around in the back, the metalled wheels amplifying every irregularity in the road. I have to wedge myself into a corner to stop being knocked senseless.

We arrive at a surprisingly beautiful building built of white stone containing small crystals that catch and reflect the growing morning light. Even soulless, I can appreciate the beauty of this building.

'What is this place?' I ask the driver. I haven't been told not to talk, and he can choose to answer or not.

'The Court of Justice, where your case will be heard and your sentence delivered,' he mutters.

The wagon pulls up outside, and the captain oversees me as I'm taken inside the building to a small cell and thrust inside.

The heavy door clangs shut, and I'm left looking around. A small window protected by bars delivers a feeble ray of light through a window that hasn't been cleaned since it was installed. There's a small bed with a stained straw mattress, but it smells and looks too disgusting to contemplate sitting on.

What am I to do?

I can escape, of that I have no doubt. My magic offers a myriad of solutions. The walls provide shelter, not imprisonment, and I can pass through them with merely a wish, make my way outside, and before anyone knows I'm missing, disappear into the night.

Yet, Lystra said she'd get me released, so I just need to wait.

It's still early, and I'm sure it will be a while before the justices arrive for work. Perhaps with the city under threat, they won't consider my so-called crime worth their effort and release me before Lystra arrives.

Having had my sleep so rudely interrupted after such a long night, it's time to relax.

The floor looks cleaner than the bed, and I'm tired after last night's endeavours.

I sit down with my back to the wall, close my eyes, and almost immediately fall asleep.

***

I'm still so exhausted that I'm finding it hard to focus, even if I could be bothered.

Throughout my training, I'd prided myself on being alert: a requisite to staying alive. Yet here I am, and my mind is full of fog.

Pull yourself together, Malina.

I'm in a cage, still manacled, listening to a bored clerk read out the charges against me.

'The accused struck an honoured officer of the Delnorian marines ...'

The woman goes on and on, using two thousand words when twenty could have sufficed. What a farce and waste of time.

I entertain the thought of killing the guards, the witnesses, the captain, and the judge. None of the guards appears comfortable in armour, and the hilts of their weapons are not worn. It's a sure sign they don't take their practice seriously and would be easy prey despite their numbers.

But I can't. Except for the captain and, surprisingly, the judge, none of them shows as overtly evil. Taking innocent lives to avoid a lashing or a few days in the cell is not justifiable, and I have my order and the mission.

I only half listen as the captain gives a false account of me attacking him in the middle of his rescue efforts and again when he came to arrest me. His words sound nasal, a consequence of his squashed nose. A half dozen marines I'd taken command of also testify to me striking the captain. Following them, two guards who were present at my arrest tell of my further assault.

The lead judge seems almost as bored as I am. He confides with two other assistants next to him.

'You've heard the evidence against you ...' he glances down, shuffling papers.

'Malina,' I offer.

'Well. Thank you, Malina. Now, the evidence appears overwhelming. Do you have anything to say in your defence?'

The man picks his nose and looks at whatever he's managed to excavate, utterly indifferent to my response. He wipes it under the polished table before him to join whatever else is under there.

I just want to get this over with. I'll accept the fine, a few days in the cells, or maybe the lashing I might receive. First, I'll get a little payback on the captain and capture his attention.

'Yes, I do have something to say. The captain is a snivelling coward, and if circumstances were repeated, I'd do the same again. As for my arrest, I had no idea it was him I butted and kicked between the legs. Had I known, I wouldn't have bothered with the kick, as it's apparent he has no balls!'

Some guards chuckle and even the judge's stern features crack momentarily before a serious demeanour returns.

'You show no remorse, not that it matters. The law is the law. You admit to the assault, and let it be noted, would do it again. Even though you're not Delnorian, you are subject to Delnorian law when in these lands. We will now consider our verdict. Return the accused to the cells.'

The cage door is unbolted, and I'm pulled unceremoniously from the courtroom down several cold stone passages. Every ten paces, we pass a cell, and often against the bars, the faces of those awaiting justice press fearfully.

I'm frustrated by how long this is taking. I could be having my lashes by now and shortly be on my way back to join the others.

My cell door is opened, and I'm ushered in. The guard is not rough, nor does he need to be. I'll be compliant and get out of this with minimum fuss.

The flagstone floor isn't comfortable, but I sit and allow my thoughts to wander. I don't regret intervening at the docks, yet I see now the folly of my ways. My actions could have jeopardised the mission despite my motive being good. It won't happen again. The return of The Once and Future King is paramount, and nothing must stand in its way.

Time passes slowly as I wait there, listening to the occasional moan of discomfort from nearby. I'm sure they purposely keep those awaiting justice separated, so we don't communicate, make noise or be a nuisance.

Footsteps echo, coming closer. Two pairs, one loud, one barely audible.

I smile.

The soft tread is that of a Chosen.

With my arms wrapped around my knees, I wait impatiently.

Lystra turns the corner with the guard, who stays back as she approaches the door. I rise and move to stand before her, head bowed.

Embarrassment causes me to flush.

'I am sorry.' I look her straight in the eye. 'I shouldn't have allowed myself to get distracted from what matters the most.'

Lystra's sharp nod, accepting my apology, fills me with relief.

'How long till I'm out? Have the prince and commander talked to the judges?'

Lystra's look surprises me. Do I detect sorrow?

'No. It's apparent the commander is not trusting of the prince and is reluctant to intervene. He spoke with certainty that he must support his own soldiers, not undermine them. The only concession he gave was to hear you speak before sentencing.'

I shrug. 'It would have been good to see that captain humbled. However, that's fine. I'll take however many lashes they see fit to give and not give them the satisfaction of seeing my pain.'

Lystra averts her gaze. In all these years, she's never failed to hold eye contact.

'The mission is everything. Anything that jeopardises it must be avoided at all costs. Do you agree?' Lystra looks at her boots like a child caught misbehaving.

'Yes, of course. What's all this about?'

'The sentence for striking an officer in Delnor during wartime isn't the lash, fines or imprisonment; it's death.'

'Death? For hitting a coward?'

'Yes.'

'Don't worry. I'll just break out,' I whisper. 'These manacles and walls can't hold me. I'll be long gone by the time they realise I've escaped, and they won't even know how.'

'No.'

A cold hand grips my chest at Lystra's unexpected response.

'If you escape, they'll incarcerate the rest of us on suspicion of being complicit until the prince can leave,' she says softly. 'That won't be until the harbour entrance is cleared, which will take weeks. If that happens, they'll confiscate everything but our clothes. Without our Soul Blades and being unable to travel back through the gate, we'll die from being separated from our souls for too long. I can't see another way out of this mess, but if you can discern one, we'll take it!'

My mind whirs.

'Can we leave without the prince?'

Lystra's silence reinforces what I already knew; our disappearance will leave him unprotected and under suspicion. Without the prince, we'd simply use our Soul Blades to escape. Yet, with him in our care, the only escape route is through the city gates, into the unfriendly arms of a hostile force. This would put everyone's life in peril. Ironic that it was my idea for our mission to involve the prince, and now his presence will mean my escape isn't an option.

'I can't see another way that doesn't leave the Chosen or the prince in danger of death or long-term incarceration,' I admit.

Lystra nods forlornly.

'The other Chosen have tried to come up with other plans but failed. I'm genuinely sorry. That being the case, you'll accept the sentence and not escape. That's an order. Do you understand?'

'Yes. I'll do as ordered.'

Lystra nods grimly, then turns away. The guard looks at me and then follows Lystra to escort her from the building.

I sit on the cold stone floor. I'd always been prepared to die during my mission to kill the High King. I'd just never considered it would be at the end of a noose.

***

I stare into Lotane's eyes across the courtroom, recognising the frustration yet also an acceptance of what must be. Not that I'd allowed myself any false hope of being saved because Lystra would have given the other Chosen similar orders to mine, ensuring compliance.

The other Chosen view me with respect, aware I'll be making the ultimate sacrifice, one they'll also make when required of them. In the shadows behind, Prince Sylnar observes.

Resplendent in burnished cuirass shaped to represent a muscular torso, Commander Farsil strikes an imposing figure. At his left-hand stands a veteran officer who has obviously seen recent action. Bandages show between his clothes and armour. Yet, he bears his wounds with stoicism while he studies me intently.

To their right stands my accuser; his swollen nose and blackened eyes give me a small measure of satisfaction. Beside him are the marines who bore testimony to me striking him.

We wait.

It's strange. This place is so silent, almost as if it's removed from the world. Outside its walls, an army gathers, preparing to attack, and here we are, waiting peacefully. I run my fingers over the wooden railing before me, enjoying its smoothness and appreciating the beauty of the patterned grain. The swirls remind me of my body markings and the magic that could help me escape if only I wasn't bound by honour, orders and blood magic.

Behind the judge's dais, two polished wooden doors swing open, and the judge walks in to sit behind his desk, surveying his small empire.

Annoyance flickers across his face as he registers the commander and his aide.

'The military holds no jurisdiction in this court. Your presence, whilst always welcome, will have no effect on this sentence, and ...'

'Nonetheless,' the commander interjects, 'I have been asked to attend. As this affects a man under my command and a foreign noble who has asked for my assistance, I'll have my say. Am I clear?'

The judge frowns. There's malice in his eyes, his face twists, nostrils flaring. He's not used to being spoken to in such a way, and his inner hubris and malignance are plain to see, at least to the other Chosen and me. Nonetheless, he nods grudgingly and waves his hand graciously as if bestowing a favour.

'You have the floor.'

I sense the commander wishes he were elsewhere. He has the defence of the capital to organise, and here he is, listening to a case he has no interest in. If only he knew my reason for being in his city, he'd draw his sword and cleave my head from my shoulders.

For the next ten minutes, the commander questions the captain about the night's events, and all the while, the commander's interest grows. Meanwhile, his aide continues to stare at me, barely blinking. Is he trying to gauge my reaction to the captain's lies or just full of loathing at a foreigner taking up his master's precious time?

I'm listening, but in my head, I picture Lotane's body against mine, the intimate moments we've shared, the jokes he's made. I want my last moment filled with happy memories, not anger at the web of deceit the captain spins to exact her petty revenge.

'Your name is Malina?' the commander asks, pulling me away from the softness of Lotane's caress.

'Yes.'

'Do you agree with the captain's version of events?'

'No.'

'As a point of order, it matters not what she says. We have six witnesses from your military who have testified that she struck the captain,' the judge crows, happy to exert his power back onto the proceedings.

The commander nods. His aide still looks at me, head tilted slightly to one side. He seems familiar, but that could be the uniform.

'Tell us,' the aide raises his voice, 'what happened last night before and after you struck the captain.'

'That is irrelevant!' screeches the judge.

'It is relevant to me!' booms the commander, and the judge flinches and settles back, suddenly finding the filth under his fingernails of apparent interest.

I begin with when the fire ships attacked the harbour, finishing the story with my return to the inn in the early hours.

The commander's eyes bore into mine as I speak. In contrast to his initial indifference, now it's as if he is gauging the veracity of every single syllable.

'Everything you've said is of great interest to me,' he says, eyes narrowing. 'However, what bothers me the most is your accusation of cowardice against your accuser. Who can corroborate your version of events?' the commander asks intently, leaning forward.

'Those beside you. My comrades assisted throughout the night.'

'Irrelevant and also inadmissible!' The outraged judge shouts. 'Testimony from her friends will not be allowed. Of course, they'll lie on her behalf. Also, the assault is not in question; she admitted her guilt. Whatever else happened matters not at all.'

'It matters to me,' hisses the commander. 'This might be your courtroom and the law it administers the king's, but the truth should always matter. Don't you forget it!'

Until now, I'd held no respect for anyone outside the Chosen. Yet, here's a man who cares about right from wrong despite his position of power and influence. He's as hard as the steel at his hip but seems as true as the edge it carries.

'Is there anyone else who can testify, other than your friends here?' the commander presses me.

I look to the marines who'd witnessed my assault, nodding in their direction.

'They all saw me strike the captain, but they also saw everything else I've recounted from beginning to end. They followed my orders the entire night and did themselves and the Delnorian military proud.'

The aide leans forward, whispering in the commander's ear.

'Marines! You're bound by oath and honour to obey my command,' the commander barks. 'Tell me, you!' He points to the first marine. 'Is this woman's version of events true, and if not, what part?'

The marine looks to the captain, who is ashen-faced.

'LOOK AT ME!' booms the commander, and a moment later, the courtroom doors swing open as a guard looks in, ensures all is in order then retreats quickly.

'Tell me the truth, or I'll know.'

The marine corroborates my story, as do the others one by one. The captain looks like he's going to puke. His lies have been exposed for all to see. Even when his face shifts, it remains pathetic and sad, despite its ugliness, not frightening or evil.

Drawing a deep breath, the commander nods at me, something akin to warmth in his eyes, and the aide is smiling too.

'Delnor thanks you for your incredible service. It was you who saved our fleet from destruction with your prompt actions and initiative. Not only that, but your actions saved hundreds of lives. I don't doubt your testimony, and in fact, my aide here believes you personally saved him from drowning. Apparently, he still has your robe.'

I nod back, warmed by his appreciation of my deeds.

Turning to the judge, the commander raises his eyebrow.

The judge squirms, but his face suddenly warps with malicious glee, a wicked smile almost wrapping around his head.

'None of us can override the king's law here; neither me nor you, Commander! It matters not the circumstances before or after the assault. Even if the captain saw fit to conceal his cowardice, she admits to striking him. The king's law states that if a military officer is struck during a time of war, then ...'

'He's no officer. He's a stinking coward,' roars Kralgen, shouting down the judge. 'That turd doesn't deserve to wear a uniform, let alone that of a captain!'

'Silence,' the shrill voice of the judge screams, or you'll find out what sentence I can give you!'

Lystra's hand goes to Kralgen's forearm as she whispers something in his ear, and Kralgen subsides.

The captain is white-faced, yet he glances at me, sure of victory despite his humiliation. If only the commander could see through my eyes. The captain's face twists in unconcealed evil glee, tongue hanging black and long, saliva dripping, eyes snide.

A long silence forms, only to be broken by the judge.

'It seems there's nothing left but to sentence this foreign troublemaker, a sentence which will be carried out immediately unless the commander has any final words of wisdom to share?'

White teeth gleam as a broad smile brightens the aide's face.

'Commander,' he says loudly. 'I believe our islander guest has it right,' and he inclines his head to Kralgen. 'Didn't we demote that coward to private two days ago?' He points at the captain.

The commander's laugh echoes from the vaulted ceiling.

'You have the right of it, my friend. Now you mention it, he *was* demoted to private two days ago. The confusion, it seems, is because he has yet to return his officer's uniform to the quartermaster. That being so, I'm quite sure there's no case for the accused to answer.'

The commander turns to the judge.

'However, the judge here knows the law better than us all. Are there laws protecting a private, or is that just considered a brawl?'

The defeated judge looks from me to the erstwhile captain, then back to the commander.

'No. There's no case to answer,' he growls, resentment clear to everyone. 'Release her!'

'YES,' shouts Lotane, while the other Chosen yell their approval.

The jangle of a guard's keys announces my release.

The commander and the ssythlan leave, heads bowed in conversation, while the bright smiles of the Chosen shine down on me.

As I step from the cage, Lotane and Kralgen lift me high. This should be a moment filled with love, but in its absence, there's a burning relief at being able to continue my mission.

'Only the strong survive!' Lystra shouts.

It's a message of support for me, yet she's looking at the private who is being stripped of his captain's uniform by the other guards.

The aide walks over and sketches a salute.

'The commander requests that you and your,' ... he searches for the appropriate word, 'friends, present yourself to the wall above the central gatehouse within the hour. Don't be late, and ... don't disappear.'

A slap on my back rattles my teeth.

'You owe me one, Wolf Slayer,' Kralgen laughs. 'You see, I'm a lot smarterer than everyone thinks.'

For once, even Lotane doesn't make a joke at the big man's expense.

***

Commander Farsil's back is to us as we're escorted up the rough-hewn steps to the battlements above the gatehouse. His cloak snaps in the wind as he stands firmly planted, feet apart, surveying the enemy forces through a long spyglass under the cold light of day.

His aide, Major Conrol, whom I'd saved, greets us and waves away the guard. Over his arm is my robe, freshly cleaned, and he steps forward to drape it around my shoulders.

'Thank you again for my life,' he says warmly, bowing. 'Now, the commander is waiting for you.'

He gestures us forward. In the distance, spread across a plain, are about four thousand enemy troops in formation. Armour reflects the early morning light while banners dance lightly above. Intermittent forward positions with wicker shields protect the enemy from defenders' arrows.

Lotane's hand rests on my shoulder as we take in the incredible sight. I've trained to fight these last years relentlessly, but never before have I seen a combined force of such numbers.

'Welcome to the best view our fine city has to offer.' Commander Farsil smiles wryly as he sweeps his hand broadly across the landscape.

A thump punctuates his words, and then, moments later, a crash as a top section of wall several hundred paces to the east shatters, flinging debris everywhere. Even from this far, I can hear faint screams. A thick dust cloud begins to form like an evil spirit, and the noise of suffering dies away as if swallowed whole.

'Send another hundred men to that section and barricade the streets for a block on either side in case they try to breach,' Farsil orders, and a messenger runs off.

'Malina,' he begins. 'Whilst all of you helped save our fleet, it was you who led the effort. Such initiative and leadership qualities are exceedingly rare in one so young, and it intrigues me that a simple bodyguard should have such skills. There's far more to you than meets the eye, and that goes for all of you.'

I can sense Lystra's concern at the direction of conservation, and a subtle ripple runs through the Chosen. Kralgen squints a little. Alyssa lightly grips the hilt of her dagger in the same loving way I've seen her hold Kralgen's hand. Fianna appears bright and unconcerned, yet it's a ploy. She'll continue to laugh as she lays open someone's throat. Nestor, well, he hardly shows any emotion at all. As for Lotane, he looks about with that misleading half-smile that never leaves his face, even during moments of extreme violence.

Fortunately, these subtle tells are visible only to someone who has spent years by their side.

'But what matters to me, is why,' Farsil continues. 'Why did you do it?'

Farsil's gaze is intense. This man will see through falsehoods, but I've no reason to tell any.

'I did it to save lives. It didn't matter who was in trouble, they were mostly good people, and I couldn't stand by and let them die, whatever the risk.'

Farsil smiles.

'Hours of tremendous personal risk, acts of heroism, hundreds of lives and dozens of ships saved, and you summarise your reason in two short sentences.'

A loud thump interrupts, and dust rises from another wall section to the west.

'We have catapults, but they don't have the range of their siege engine,' Farsil offers, distracted. 'But it's not their intention to lay siege as they don't have the numbers to take the city, harbour or citadel. They're here causing a nuisance, knowing we'll have to recall troops from sieging Tarsala to drive them away, which will stop Tars from capitulating.

'It's a canny move, and I warned the High King this might happen. We weren't ready to land the finishing blow and pushed too hard too soon. It seems this damned war will go on for longer than we hoped. Too many people are dying needlessly. Soon, they'll be no one left to harvest the crops as they're conscripted into the army, and what then? We'll have even more people dying from hunger and disease. This all needs to stop.'

Lystra clears her throat and bows.

'Our prince has an important mission, and ...'

'Yes, I know,' Farsil interrupts her. 'That was the reason I invited you up here. There's an old saying in Delnor; never trust a diplomat. Yet an even older one is; never trust a ssythlan. Have you heard of that last one?'

Lystra nods.

'The High King relies on my advice when making most decisions,' Farsil continues. 'I hadn't introduced your ssythlan prince to the High King because I was wary of that saying. I wanted to see the type of people he had protecting him, for I judge a man not just by who he is but also by those he surrounds himself with.

'Again, I had my doubts, but Malina here, well, she did something that Delnor will owe her for, for the rest of its days. So, going by her actions and what she has just told me as her reasons, perhaps I was wrong in my initial judgement.

'Bearing that in mind and looking at this rather surprising development before us, it appears the prince's offer couldn't come at a more fortuitous time. Whilst we are still winning despite our enemy's desperate gamble, a fresh ally will decisively tip the balance firmly in our favour.

'I will now make arrangements for the prince to address the High King and his council and recommend we accept the offer of help.'

Lystra's nostrils flare at this positive news. We've suddenly taken a giant step closer to completing our mission.

Yet Farsil isn't finished. He opens his arms wide, encompassing us all.

'Now that brings me on to a final matter. I'd like to present a gift to Malina on the morrow, and I'd like you all to attend. Major Conrol will collect you from your lodgings at dawn, so please be ready.'

He's couched it as a request, but he's a man used to giving orders, and there's no refusing. Yet, for a man as hard as granite, the warmth in his smile is genuine. He steps forward to surprise me with a firm embrace before releasing me.

'A gift for saving lives?' laughs Kralgen. 'Awards should only be given for taking them!'

Alyssa cuffs him. 'Kral's just jealous. You deserve it.'

'I'll be jealous if it's a pretty one,' Fianna laughs, twirling her hair.

Lotane winks at me whilst Nestor shows nothing.

This commander is undoubtedly a good man, even if the Delnorian empire he's part of has kept its boot on the other kingdoms' necks for generations. How he can serve someone as dark as the High King is beyond me, but it must be because he's honour bound.

I feel grubby to be deceiving him.

Taking a flask from his hip, Farsil drinks deeply on its contents before passing it to Lystra, then continues.

'I'd have a brief word with Malina in private. Please wait at the base of the wall,' Farsil states, looking at Lystra.

She hesitates, not appreciating his order, then nods and leads the other Chosen away.

Farsil takes my arm, guiding me to the forward edge of the battlements and the guards move away, giving us space. A gentle breeze blows, and he closes his eyes, smiling as it pulls the hair back from his face. For a moment, he looks younger than his years, but then the weight of command ages him again in a heartbeat. Sighing, he opens his eyes again, gazing out across the landscape.

Despite looking through soulless eyes, I can tell it's a beautiful morning, yet even as we watch, the enemy siege engine flings its deadly cargo, attempting to breach the walls. I wait for him to initiate the conversation, but not for long.

'Where are you originally from?'

'The Islands,' I reply, a niggle of worry in my stomach.

Farsil nods.

'Let me ask it a different way. Where are your parents from?'

'They were from Hastia but died when I was young.'

'Hastia,' Farsil muses. 'Hastia are currently our enemy. Your dark-skinned friend's heritage is Tarsian, and I'd hazard a guess others of your band are Surian, maybe Rolantrian, all enemy lands.

'Don't worry,' he smiles, sensing my concern. 'What you all did proves that whichever country you came from, there's good inside most of us. You've proved yourself a friend and ally. The sad thing is that you shouldn't have to. All those soldiers out there,' and he waves his hand, 'were friends and allies once. Hopefully, one day, peace will return, and the days of killing will end. Once ratified, I hope our new alliance with the ssythlan nation will hasten that day.'

'An end to war is what I truly hope for,' I reply, 'but also poverty, slavery and inequality.'

'If only that were possible,' Farsil smiles encouragingly. 'Such lofty ideals, but let us first settle for a ceasefire and peace!'

'If peace doesn't end oppression and suffering, then surely those things are still worth fighting for!' I reply, certainty in my voice.

Farsil raises an eyebrow, genuinely surprised.

'Sometimes the price you pay doesn't equal what's gained, Malina. We were not all made equal, and people need rulers to guide them just like sheep need a shepherd.'

I shake my head.

'That's a saying made by rulers and shepherds, and it's wrong. So maybe we'll agree to disagree.'

Farsil laughs.

'Yes, let peace remain between us! You know, there's something strange about you, Malina, and it's not just your eyes and skin. That you're a warrior is without question, no one moves with such assurance and balance without constant training. In fact, you and your band have the look of eagles about you; the ssythlan ambassador is in good hands. But amongst your peers, your compassion makes you stand out.

'Hold on to that humanity, Malina, for once lost, it can never be found again. Also, remember that to be wise, you must admit there's a lot you can learn, as only a fool believes they know everything.'

I smile, warmed but also a little embarrassed by his words, while my stomach churns unhappily at our deceit. His eyes hold a genuine desire for peace. He's a man of war who is tired of killing; that much is obvious, just like the captain of the Delnorian galley. I console myself with the thought that despite our mission not being what it pretends to be, it will bring an end to all wars, which is what he wants.

Farsil grips my forearm firmly, then turns away without another word.

As my presence is no longer required, I stride toward the steps and my friends below.

One day this world will know peace, but the price of that will be blood.

***

'I need to sleep,' I say, looking at Karson. 'I'm too tired to argue, to hear how bad I'm becoming, or how much death surrounds me. Please leave me in peace.'

Why does he always have to appear in dreams full of dark promise after a cause for celebration? Clouds boil in the skies, mountains of putrid corpses seem to shift and writhe, the air is fetid and the grass brown.

Karson sits crosslegged, staring back at me. Sometimes he's like the little brother I knew, all smiles and mischief, then at others, like this, serious, full of knowledge beyond his meagre years.

'I care for you from death as you cared for me in life, Alina. Would you rather you never see me again? Don't worry if that's the case. Soon your wish will be granted, for even now, the pull to what lies next is becoming stronger.'

I focus, his words banishing my disinterest.

'Then you're more than a dream, a figment of my imagination?'

Karson scratches his head and then laughs. It's as if the birds are singing; such is the purity of his merriment.

'Does it matter, as long as my words are true? Perhaps I'm nothing but the voice of your conscience or what remains of it.'

My frown stops him from saying more.

'You could be proud of me, Karson. I'm strong and fearless. I saved so many people when the city was attacked, and I've found love. Lotane is such a good man, he's kind and gentle, and you'd have really liked him.'

I blink back tears. I'd have loved them to meet, to know one another.

Karson crawls forward, and then, as his arms wrap around me, I feel his love. Now my tears flow freely, and sobs wrack my body.

'Knowing there's someone to care for you makes me happy, Alina. Just remember, love should be worth dying for, not killing for.'

'You're talking about my mission and allegiance to Nogoth?' I challenge, sensing the underlying meaning of his words. It feels strange to speak The Once and Future King's name aloud, even in a dream.

Karson nods.

A smile crosses my lips as I remember something Farsil said.

'Only a fool believes he knows everything, Karson. Perhaps I'm right, and you're wrong. I don't disbelieve that my future is surrounded by death, but if it's the death of the wicked, then surely, it's a price worth paying.'

Karson's smile matches mine even as he begins to fade from sight.

'Don't forget Malina. Sometimes the price you pay doesn't equal what is gained!'

***

CHAPTER XIX

We've risen early. For years, that's been our routine, and even a red wolf is vulnerable when it sleeps, as Lystra is often heard to say.

I'm facing Nestor, his fists wrapped in strips of cloth, questing.

The sun has yet to rise, but it doesn't matter. We can see in the dark, for we're soulless hunters of the night. We fight in silence. Not because we're sympathetic to those who sleep but because when we reap souls, we want it done without drawing attention to ourselves.

Nestor drops his right shoulder subtly, and I'm ducking forward under his right hook even as he throws it, snapping a swift blow to his stomach as I spin past. I've pulled the punch, but he still hisses through his teeth at the impact. However, his face barely registers the blow. After practising so long with earth magic, I think normal pain doesn't phase him in the least.

'You're telling your punch by dropping that right shoulder early,' I say softly.

A grunt and a nod, then he fires off another without the tell, and this time I have to block, for there's no time to evade. He follows it up with a flurry of punches, and I circle, twisting to the side. After all these years, I don't go backwards unless absolutely necessary, for you never know what's behind and might trip you.

Lotane and Kralgen exchange blows, and whilst they pull their punches on head strikes, their abdomens are so heavily muscled that they don't hold back on body shots. A slap as Kralgen lands a powerful blow makes us all wince, and Lotane steps back gasping, raising his hand, then kneels to catch his breath.

Fianna and Alyssa are exchanging kicks. Blocking and ducking high strikes or jumping over sweeps. They're like dancers.

'Enough.'

Somehow, despite keeping her voice low, Lystra's voice still carries the whip of command, and we instantly disengage.

'Thanks to Malina, we have an event to attend, so let's freshen up.'

Groans meet the premature ending to our morning exercise.

Whilst I'm thankful that Farsil will give me a gift, none of us wants to waste precious time on something so inconsequential. However, thanks to my actions, everyone is excited that the prince will now meet the High King. There will be a good chance of us attending as a ceremonial guard.

We'd talked long into the night about how we could take advantage if we're allowed inside the palace. There are two possible scenarios.

The first was where we'd accompany the prince into the High King's presence. Whilst it was possible, we'd enjoy luck and have an easy kill, more likely, he'd be heavily guarded. Then we'd have little option but for a suicidal attempt, disarming some of the guards and using their weapons in a desperate attempt to kill the High King before we were overwhelmed.

The other option was if we had to wait within the citadel grounds while the prince had the meeting. In this case, Lystra, Nestor and I would use earth magic to conceal ourselves and under cover of darkness, infiltrate the inner palace and hope that we could locate the High King.

Prince Sylnar had joined the discussions but left just after midnight. In a display of great stoicism, he'd told us that if we had a chance to kill the High King, and he died as a consequence, we shouldn't hesitate. His life in exchange was a fair price, as were ours.

Fianna had used her magic to ensure our hushed voices didn't carry, and anyone who'd tried to share the common room with us had been swiftly encouraged to leave by Kralgen's hulking presence. Lystra had also bribed the innkeeper to complacency when he complained about us upsetting the rest of the guests, so we'd been left alone for the most part.

We all head to the inn's washhouse. It's rather novel and reminds me of the waterfall room back home. We take turns scooping buckets of cold water from a trough before pouring it into a long pipe while someone else stands naked under the other end.

Once we're all washed and clothed, we head to our room and don our robes, Soul Blades, and pouches before returning to the common room.

Nestor and Fianna bring us cold food from the kitchen, and we break fast on cheeses, meat, and water. Even after all this time, it still tastes like clay, but we know that even devoid of flavour, it still sustains us.

We're just finishing when Major Conrol opens the common room door and walks in. He's still swaddled in bandages but looks resplendent in full dress uniform. Loops of braid hang from his shoulders while his armour has been burnished to a bright sheen. He exhibits a jovial demeanour that reminds me a little of Lotane. I could imagine them getting on quite well had circumstances allowed.

Seeing our surprise, he appears a little embarrassed.

'I made an effort for the occasion,' he exclaims, full of good humour despite the hour. 'I'm glad to see everyone ready, even if somewhat worn compared to me!'

A tiny frown creases his forehead as he inspects us.

'I must politely ask you to hand over the daggers.' He shrugs apologetically and pulls a small bag from his weapon belt, holding it open expectantly.

There's an awkward pause, but then with a scrape of her chair, Lystra rises, unhooks her scabbarded blade from her waist and drops it in. There's no need for words, so we all follow suit, although Kralgen looks immeasurably unhappy.

Major Conrol chuckles.

'When someone is as large as you, why would you even need a dagger?'

Kralgen smiles, appreciative of the compliment.

The major beckons us toward the door. Stepping out into the grey light of early morning, I'm surprised to see a large carriage awaiting us. It must have arrived whilst we were cleansing, for I hadn't heard its approach.

'After you.' Major Conrol bows theatrically and, with a flourish of his hand, opens the carriage door allowing us to enter.

Kralgen has to squeeze himself in through the narrow opening, and we can't help but laugh as he chooses to sit on the floor with his back to the other door.

'I apologise we didn't bring a separate carriage just for you,' Major Conrol apologises to Kralgen. 'However, we aren't going too far.'

There are no windows in the carriage, which is unusual, and small lanterns hang from the ceiling. Not that we need the light, but it feels like we're in some kind of prison carriage.

The thought jolts me. What if this is all some kind of elaborate plot? We've now been disarmed and could well be blindly on our way to gaol. I glance at Lystra, and I can sense her concern as she considers the same or a similar scenario.

It's quiet in the carriage as it rattles along the cobbled streets. It has sprung suspension, is plushly appointed, and the ride isn't unpleasant, just a little awkward.

'May I see it?' Major Conrol asks, pointing to Nestor's Soul Blade suspended on its chain. He holds out his palm expectantly. We'd kept them visible to allay suspicions of them being a weapon, but they've instead aroused the major's interest.

I tense. If Major Conrol so much as touches the blunt blade, it will pass through his skin, and his soul will be instantly drawn from his body.

Nestor, rarely talkative, surprises us all.

'Major. I must apologise. You may look as closely as you wish, but please don't touch. These are sacred to us and to our religion. It's considered sacrilege if someone other than the wearer or their mate touches it. I struggled through five years of prayer, toil, and sacrifice before being blessed with my Soul Crystal. We believe it helps brings harmony and balance to this world and will ensure we always arrive home safely.'

The best lies are those peppered with truth, and Nestor has explained the Soul Blade's purpose as near as possible.

'Hmmm. So, tell me, why is it shaped like a cross. What does that represent in your religion?'

It's hard to tell if Major Conrol is genuinely interested or is trying to find the lie in Nestor's words. His demeanour is warm, yet we've been slightly on edge since being divested of weapons and confined to this carriage.

Nestor's smile is as wide as the major's. He spreads his arms out. Our places of worship are filled with images of our god. He stands tall and wise with his arms outspread like this and embraces both ssythlans and ...' Nestor shakes his head, a flicker of pain visible for a moment. 'The sacred images show our god embracing ssythlans and ...'

Suddenly Nestor bursts into tears.

'Nestor. Calm down. Everything is fine,' Fianna says, putting her arms around him.

'Nestor gets very emotional talking about our religion,' Lotane offers, breaking the uncomfortable moment as Major Conrol looks on in confusion. 'He's seen holy things that the rest of us haven't, and it's affected his mind.'

Once again, a truth concealing not a lie, but so much more.

Major Conrol shakes his head, a look of sadness replacing his joviality.

'It is said that those who see the true gods are driven mad by their beauty. Perhaps there's more truth to that than I ever realised.' He sits back, satisfied.

'Now, on to other matters. Malina, shortly, we'll arrive at our destination. When we do, you'll come with me whilst your friends are shown to their places.'

'What places are those?' Lystra asks, her eyebrows arching. 'We stay together. Wherever Malina goes, so do we.'

For a moment, Major Conrol allows his friendly mask to slide. Without question, he's done it on purpose, allowing us to see the steel-hardened man behind the smiles.

'Whilst I admire your concern for one of your own, you're not in a position to make any demands whatsoever. However, let me just point out that whilst colourful of skin and somewhat captivating, Malina also looks a bit of a mess. The circumstance requires she's given some clean clothes and her hair attended to, so it doesn't resemble a haystack!'

Lystra doesn't push any further, and the atmosphere in the carriage remains tense.

'I don't suppose I could have my hair done too?' Kralgen muses.

We all burst out laughing, more so because Kralgen isn't joking and looks like a kicked puppy when Major Conrol shakes his head.

'Come on, Major,' Lotane cajoles. 'If you could organise for him to have hair like Fianna's, he'd be far easier on the eye.'

Fianna tosses her head back and forwards, and Kralgen scowls in mock anger at the teasing and this time, when silence falls, it's comfortable.

Occasionally the carriage pauses, and muffled voices can be heard before it rattles off again. It's noticeable we've been heading uphill for some time, and then we're rattling across something wooden.

Major Conrol gets to his feet, although he remains a little stooped in the carriage and braces himself as it comes to a halt.

'I do apologise for keeping you in the dark, but you'll shortly appreciate the need for being somewhat economical with the details of Malina's gift.'

The door is opened from the outside, and Major Conrol steps down before indicating for us to exit.

'And here is the first part,' he laughs.

We're surrounded by over a hundred guards, armed to the teeth.

***

These are not ceremonial guards.

Their scale mail armour and kite shields show signs of battle. Scars are abundant, along with occasional missing fingers or ears. Muscled forearms and chiselled legs show these are not just veterans but an elite fighting force who take their training and fighting as seriously as we do.

Yet not only are we outnumbered by these ferocious men and women but by the sheer number of medals affixed to the chests of those surrounding us and lining a path to the citadel's keep.

However, there's no aggression evident because these guards aren't here to attack us. They're part of the palace guard and are here to honour us.

With a shout and stamp of their feet, they clash their spears against their shields three times, then slam them back into the ground. It's incredible; we aren't just inside the curtain wall of the citadel, which we'd managed before, but inside the main walls of the castle proper.

Catapults and bolt throwers top the walls every fifty paces, and thirty paces back are more defensive engines. Yet before us is manicured grass leading up to a dry moat surrounding the actual keep.

'Welcome to the High King's residence.' Major Conrol smiles, swiftly turning around with his arms raised. He reminds me of Karson at that moment, for he seems to take joy in acting the fool, even though he is anything but.

'Now, Malina, you'll come with me while your friends go with our sergeant-at-arms. Sergeant, would you be so kind as to show our guests to the viewing gallery.'

'SIR!' The man's booming voice echoes from the walls as he stamps forward.

'First, please search our guests, but ensure you respect their religious symbol and place no hands upon it.'

Major Conrol takes my arm and begins to lead me away from the others when Lotane jogs over.

'Excuse me, Major. I've a gift of my own for Malina before you take her away.'

He gives me a gentle kiss, a hug and nestles his face into my neck.

'We'll never get a better chance to complete our mission. Lystra's words,' he whispers.

He steps away, then smiles as if embarrassed before returning to the others.

'Hah, young love,' Major Conrol whispers as if a conspirator, then offers his arm. 'Walk with me.'

Hooking my arm around his, we walk up the shingle path toward the main entrance, where further guards crash to attention before a short bridge. Crossing over, we pass under a raised portcullis and pause before some solid wooden gates studded with iron and darkened by age.

'This citadel has never been taken since records began,' Major Conrol laughs. 'Yet there's the slightest possibility it might see action in the coming days if the city walls are breached. It will be something to witness and sing songs about, that's for sure, but I'd rather a peaceful solution was found to this mess.'

'What happens to the poor folk if the city walls fall? Will they be left for slaughter while you shelter behind the walls with the High King until the enemy are driven off?'

As ever, Major Conrol laughs. It seems to be how he begins most sentences.

'I hope I can lift your lowly opinion of us heartless Delnorians by reassuring you. We've food stores for years, and there are leagues of tunnels under this hill. There's not a single soul in this city who'd be without safe shelter and food. Yet it won't come to that.'

While the main gates remain closed, a small door opens to our left, and the Major leads me into a warren of passages and small chambers. Intermittently, thick, metal-reinforced wooden doors stand open, with holes in the ceilings above.

'Murder holes. Hot oil or sand can be poured through those. Some clever soul made a small maze to entertain anyone who forced entry through the side gate. Not that they've ever been put to use. Sometimes we'll come across people who've been wandering lost for days in these passageways.'

I look around intently, noting how everything looks the same, every chamber, doorway, and passage. All designed to disorientate an intruder.

'People truly get lost here?'

'Hahaha.' Major Conrol clasps his sides. 'I'm sorry. I'm having a joke at your expense. Now, we're almost there!'

Several turns and passageways later, he opens a door and leads me into a large, richly appointed chamber. Tapestries hang on walls, while thick curtains are drawn back from the windows. Mirrors capture and reflect the natural light, while dozens of ornate candle stands add to it.

Along one side of the chamber are rack after rack of ceremonial armours and adornments, whereas on the other, there's fine clothing fit for a noble.

Two beautiful women wait therein. Both are elegant, yet one is as fair as the other is dark. Cinched around their waists with tasselled cord, their finely detailed dresses brush the floor while wreaths of flowers sit upon artfully braided hair.

Yet again, there's no sign of darkness in these people. Everyone connected to the palace seems untainted, from the guards outside who'd obviously fought and killed, to Farsil, Conrol, and now these two women. This must be how the High King hides his darkness by surrounding himself with the light.

'Darna, Sylvis, this is Malina. Ladies, you've fifteen minutes to get ready before my return. Malina. Please, just for the gifting, change from your robes. They'll be here for you afterwards. Can you do this for me, please?' His hands press together as if in prayer.

'As long as I can wear this,' I say, tapping the Soul Blade around my neck.

'Whatever it takes!'

Conrol moves behind a screen, and the distant murmur of voices filter into the room before a door closes.

A small gift. This is nothing like I'd expected and nothing that I wanted. I'm happy with my simple robes and have no need of fineries, yet the Major is a kind soul, and so is the commander, so what harm.

'Stand here, please.'

The dark-haired woman indicates a green mat, and for the next minute, they circle me, gauging my height and build.

'The royal blue, or maybe the naval blue dress, will look amazing,' the fair one says, tilting her head thoughtfully to one side. 'What do you think, Sylvis?'

'Agreed, Darna. They'll accentuate her narrow waist. Please would you remove your religious symbol and robe, Malina. Oh, and the trousers and shirt you're wearing.'

As they turn away, searching amongst the racks of dresses, I do as bid. My Soul Blade, robe, and clothes, I drop onto a chair, the boots I push underneath.

'Oh my. You're naked,' Darna laughs from behind her hands. 'Were you not wearing any undergarments? How scandalous! I've never seen anyone with such a beautiful body, eyes and skin,' she breathes, admiring the swirls. 'Quite mesmerising!'

In my youth, I'd only ever been ridiculed for my corpse-white skin. Now, after years of training, my physique is lean and muscled, with my paleness a thing of the past. Only Lotane has told me how beautiful I am, and I smile my gratitude in return.

'Try this on.'

I'm handed first one dress, then the other, but neither can fit over my shoulders. We try the other way, but my legs are too heavily muscled. This is utterly ridiculous. Lotane's words come to mind. Perhaps I could storm out in a temper and disappear into the citadel. I could use my magic to hide in the walls and pass from room to room, seeking the High King while I had the strength.

The two women start panicking and turn away, picking up and casting aside dress after dress.

Time to act!

I pad quietly to the other side of the room while Sylvis and Darna are distracted, then stop, quietly laughing.

A naked woman trying to assassinate the High King. Perhaps I need to clothe myself first.

Dresses are not me, and I'm secretly relieved they haven't found one that fits. Yet here are fine leather trousers and padded shirts to protect from any armour worn over the top.

Swiftly, I step into some trousers, then pull on a shirt. It seems I'm a far better gauge of size than the two women, for whilst not perfect, they're comfortable. Next, I lift a fine chain mail vest from a stand. It's more ceremonial than practical, for the links are too delicate and would never stop a determined thrust. As I slip it over my head, it jingles as it falls into place, settling down over my hips, almost like a short, silvered dress.

'No, no, no. What are you doing?' both women cry in unison, rushing over to me, horror-struck.

Perhaps I could knock them both unconscious. They've done nothing wrong, so they don't deserve to die. No, I can't harm such lovely souls. I'm here for the king of darkness, not his unwitting retainers.

Suddenly, Sylvis tilts her head to one side.

'You know, we could make this work. We need the dark blue cloak with the fur interior, a tooled leather belt, and some high calf boots, again lined with fur.'

Moments later, the cloak is being fastened around my shoulders, I'm pushing my feet into the softest boots I've ever worn, and a belt is cinching the mail tunic around my narrow waist.

'Not bad,' Darna says. 'But how about we do away with the sleeves and legs. She has such strong limbs. Why not show them off?'

'Agreed!'

Scissors snip, cloth is pulled away, and there I stand, positioned in front of a large mirror like some kind of warrior princess stepped from the pages of Arcan's book of children's tales.

With the book in mind, I move to my robes, pulling it from an inside pocket.

'You can leave that here.'

'No.'

Sighing, a pouch is added to my belt so I can carry it. It's sentimental to me, a good luck charm and a reminder of a friend lost. I also take a moment to recover my Soul Blade.

'Sit here.'

I sit, and a brush is pulled through my hair, trying to straighten the tangled mess. Even though it's short, it's tied back with cord, and a silver circlet is placed on my head to keep my face clear.

'Done, and just in time!'

The sounds of muted laughter and talking rise for a moment, and then Major Conrol is back in the room. He takes one look at me and roars with laughter.

'Oh my. I should have known this is how it would turn out. You look amazing, Malina. Please forgive my laughter.'

'I don't want to sound ungrateful, but fine clothes are not my thing,' I say. 'It's very kind of the commander to gift me this way, but completely unnecessary. I'd be thrilled to have a tour of the keep now I'm here though.'

To be shown around will be a great advantage, and then I can slip away unseen at the right moment.

If Major Conrol's laughter had been loud before, this time, it fills the room. He wipes away the tears that run down his face and catches his breath.

'My dearest, Malina. Never has anyone captivated me with their innocence like you; truly, you're one of a kind. The new clothing isn't your gift; Commander Farsil awaits upstairs with it. There will be a small presentation ceremony at which your friends will be present. However, please be assured it will be over quickly.

'Now, it's time. Thank you, ladies,' he says, bowing to Sylvis and Darna, who curtsy in return.

'Come, Malina. Just follow my lead, and we'll have you back in your fine robe in no time. Although you'll be welcome to keep what you're wearing if you want. I must admit to it being rather eye-catching.'

Leading me across the chamber, we pass behind the curtain, and he opens a door. Before us is a spiral staircase down which the noise echoes, and we turn several times as we ascend to the next level.

We enter a grand hallway to find half a dozen heavily armed and armoured guards standing before two closed doors with banners hanging from poles on either side. They slam to attention when they see us, then one of them turns, slightly opens a door and whispers through the gap before nodding at the major.

The major takes my arm in his.

'This will prepare you for when you get married one of these days,' he laughs as the doors swing open. 'Now, this is your moment, so enjoy it!'

***

'Lady Malina of Ssythla and Major Conrol of Delnor,' the clear voice of a herald announces our entrance.

'A small ceremony. Is this what you call small?' I whisper in disbelief.

'I've attended much larger, so I guess it's relative,' Major Conrol chuckles.

My steps falter as I take in the sight before me. This could well be the keep's throne room, although there's no sign of a throne. Stained windows high up on the walls let in some light whilst dozens of candle stands provide the rest. A gabled ceiling is high above, while viewing galleries line both walls supported by arched pillars. Paintings and tapestries hang everywhere with crossed swords, spears and shields in between.

Several dozen guards stand rigidly to attention on either side of the polished tiled walkway as Conrol escorts me along. Once again, these aren't ceremonial popinjays but battle-scarred veterans, and surprisingly there's no sign of overt evil in them. Their eyes occasionally glow as they look around for threats, but otherwise, they don't shift.

On pews facing a dais, maybe a hundred well-dressed nobles, merchants, and commoners sit. Here and there, occasional dark souls manifest. Faces twist in jealousy, others warp in boredom, some lech and leer in my direction, but overall, these are good folk.

Where are my Chosen?

I look around, feeling somewhat lost and alone.

'Up there!'

The major tilts his head, perceiving the reason for my questing stare.

Sure enough, on a balcony are Lystra, Lotane and the others.

Lystra's nod and taut smile say it all. Despite the occasion, we must use this opportunity to further our goal and take a step closer to completing our mission. The number of people here will make it easier for us to lose ourselves in the crowd. There'll be a search, but they'll never find us if we're careful.

Every balcony is packed, every chair taken. This can't be only for me; something else must be going on.

'This is all for you, Malina.'

The major contradicts my thoughts as if reading my mind.

'Now, there's Commander Farsil. He'll have a few words to say, but just be patient and listen. If you wish to say something afterwards, that's fine, but don't feel obliged. Public speaking isn't everyone's mug of ale.'

The Commander, like Major Conrol, is dressed in his finest. His armour is sculpted to his body, a cloak pinned at both shoulders. Twisted cords denoting his rank hang across his chest plate, where a beautiful pendant is a centrepiece. In this world of greys, it shines, not a little unlike a Soul Blade when it's claimed a soul.

When I'd first seen him, I'd recognised someone tough like Lystra, harder than stone. Yet this man has a soft side that he's also happy to show, and that demonstrates strength. He smiles broadly and opens his arms wide.

'SILENCE!' the herald bellows, and not even a whisper can be heard.

Major Conrol speaks quietly out of the corner of his mouth.

'Wait here until you're asked to step forward.'

He moves away and positions himself behind Commander Farsil's right shoulder.

The Commander looks around. His gaze demands attention even though it looks at no one in particular.

'Someone said to me recently that an award should only be given for taking lives.' Farsil pauses, letting the words sink in.

I smile and wonder if Kralgen recognises his own words as the opening line to Farsil's speech.

'In a time of war like this, when I look around at my fellow soldiers and see the medals adorning their chests, I know those words hold mostly true. When I consider my own awards, including my most treasured, it saddens me to realise that in my own case, it is entirely true. Every medal I wear and hold dear has been bought with enemy lives.

'Those I've killed have been fathers, mothers, sons or daughters, brothers and sisters. For the most part, they've not been bloodthirsty marauders or bandits, but farmers, carpenters, millers and the like. Conscripted against their will, they fought for a cause they probably didn't understand.

'When I look back, I remember those enemies were once allies, friends, and trading partners. We helped them as they helped us. But look at us now. Years of fighting, deaths in the tens, maybe hundreds of thousands ... and we still give medals for taking lives.'

He pauses, giving time for his words to sink in or perhaps to gather his thoughts. I'm entranced. The commander is a great orator and pure of spirit. He's also the polar opposite of what I thought Delnorians were. Each one I've listened to seems to regret this war and wants it to finish. If only Commander Farsil were king, this world would be a far better place. By the gods, the High King must be evil incarnate to be able to manipulate someone like him or even the major.

With a deep breath, Farsil continues.

'Yet it's time to change that tradition. Fifteen years ago, I was awarded the Heart of Delnor, the highest award for service bestowed by this nation. There are just five in existence which can only be voluntarily passed from one bearer to the next should exceptional circumstances dictate. I've carried mine with pride all these years, but now I've found its new owner.

'You've all heard the stories of how a strange woman saved our fleet from destruction, organising our marines when they were leaderless. But that's not the reason she warrants such a coveted award, it's because she acted selflessly to save hundreds, perhaps even thousands of lives. If the fire oil in our galleys had ignited, a firestorm might have swept through our city, leaving our populace decimated. She's not Delnorian, nor were those who helped her. They are from Ssythla, but their heritage harks back to Hastia, Tars, Rolantria, countries that we now see as adversaries. Let us never judge someone by their heritage; let us instead always judge them by their actions!

'My friends, my fellow Delnorians and our esteemed guests from Ssythla, I give you Malina, saviour of High Delnor!'

The roar that explodes around me shakes my very core, exhilarating and frightening all at once. The applause, shouting, cheers, and whistles seem to go on endlessly. My legs tremble at being the focus of this emotional outpouring. I'd never considered my deed so worthy of note. Yet I'm also saddened, for here I am, standing in front of them, a lauded hero, when I'm a fraud.

I'm shocked to realise that I don't want to complete my mission if it means losing the respect and admiration of these people. Both Farsil and the major are glowing with happiness at bestowing this honour upon me. Their act is entirely selfless, and I now know that the Delnorian people are, for the majority, pure of heart.

Major Conrol removes the beautiful crystal pendant from Farsil's neck and beckons me forward.

'Malina. Would you kindly kneel?' Farsil asks, his voice barely penetrating the barrage of noise.

I'm happy to oblige, as my legs are weak. I sink to one knee, lowering my head. The last time I'd knelt like this had been in front of Nogoth, my own king. Remembering him now warms my heart further, but I'm also slightly ashamed, as if I've been unfaithful. So many conflicting and contrasting emotions.

Then a hush descends, from one moment to the next.

Utter silence where before there was noise. The hair on the back of my neck rises, and the magic within me stirs, sensing my disquiet. I fight the urge to look up, for there isn't a feeling of threat but of something else entirely.

'Thank you, Commander,' a soft yet clear voice echoes in the void. 'As ever, your words steer our hearts and minds toward the path of virtue.

'Malina of Ssythla.'

I raise my head to see a kind-looking man. There's no sign of darkness about him, and he appears to be a religious cleric. His robes are simple, shining white in this world of greys. There are no adornments other than a tasselled rope securing them around his waist. Behind him, by several paces, stands his retainer or acolyte, a familiar-looking young man. I look from him to Commander Farsil and back again, smiling, recognising a family resemblance.

The smile is not returned as the lad's gaze remains fixed on me.

'On behalf of Delnor, I thank you.'

The cleric catches my attention as he speaks while taking the shining pendant from Farsil. The crowded room is hushed, hanging respectfully on his every word.

'At Commander Farsil's request, by the power vested in me as High King of Delnor, I bestow this Heart of Delnor upon Malina of Ssythla!'

***

cannot believe it. This is impossible. The High King is darkness personified, the cause of the world's evils. He should have a nest of lava snakes as hair, horns sprouting from his forehead, and fangs dripping with venom as he shifts.

Instead, he remains unchanged, standing before me, eyes full of amusement. Even as he bends down and loops the cord holding the Heart of Delnor over my head, I remain transfixed.

'Malina of Ssythla. The Heart of Delnor is yours to cherish and wear with pride. As a paragon of the virtues we hold most dear, you'll enjoy the King's Favour until such time as you bestow this upon a worthy successor.'

'MALINA. MALINA. MALINA!' The chamber shakes as the crowd roar, and then, silence.

Kill the King. Complete your mission. To obey is to live!

Suddenly these mantras thunder in my head as I gaze upon the High King. All the years of training, the purges, the trials, the souls I've taken. Every moment since I arrived at the Mountain of Souls has prepared me for the moment I have a chance to slay the High King.

Yet, I cannot move.

My shock must be apparent, for along with the High King, both Major Conrol and Commander Farsil laugh kindly at my surprise.

'Uncle,' the young lad says, moving alongside Farsil.

'Hush, lad.' The commander rebukes him with a stern look.

'Don't worry, Malina. It's not unusual to be overwhelmed by such a moment, and I'm glad I still strike awe into someone. Most people don't even blink when they see me. In case you're wondering, the King's Favour is a special gift, which historically has never been called upon. It grants the bearer the right to ask one favour that cannot be refused.'

The room is silent, respectful, and unaware.

Kill the King. Complete your mission. To obey is to live!

'Uncle.' The voice rings loud, even if softly spoken, for nothing else disturbs the moment.

'Nephew, I said to be quiet.'

Tears run unchecked as I fight the years of conditioning, the immediate impulse to strike down this monster, whatever the cost. I've no qualms harvesting evil souls and, in fact, experience pleasure knowing I make the world a better place. But if this man is the High King, he's not evil. He doesn't even wear a crown and dresses no better than a peasant in their finest Suntarg clothes. I don't have to do this, especially now I can use the King's Favour to ask for forgiveness! Salvation is mine!

'Malina. I'm sorry. I can see we shouldn't have sprung this surprise upon you,' the High King says, kneeling down to take my hand, concern in his eyes. 'The times we find ourselves in require great caution ...'

For a moment, his words fade away as my magic brings me a conversation unbidden.

'Uncle, it's her. She's the witch who killed those men who abducted me.'

Now I realise why I recognised him.

'Nephew. That can't be true. She just arrived as part of the ssythlar delegation!'

Yet there's worry in Commander Farsil's voice, and he turns toward the major.

'I thought you were evil,' I whisper softly, clasping the High King's hand. It has never held a weapon, and it's soft and gentle, like my mother's used to be.

'I endeavour to be a good man and a better king, although it isn't always easy.' The High King winks, pulling me to my feet.

The Once and Future King comes to mind, standing in his hall, talking to me, easing my worries, and making me believe in a better world under his rule. The High King is a wise and just man, but Nogoth, despite his protestations, is a god.

'I can see that now. You're a good man and a good king. The thing is … mine … will be better.' My tears stop, my grip tightens, and I feel the purity of righteousness flow through me.

'My king,' Farsil says, stepping forward to the left, his face taking on a hard look as Major Conrol moves to my right while the lad steps backwards, fearful.

But they're too late.

A scorching heat runs through my veins, and the next moment, the High King bursts into flame as I hold onto his hand. His screams tear at my conscience, and then his eyes widen in disbelief before turning to liquid and running down his blackening face.

As the flames have everyone stumbling back in shock, I call upon my magic again, and the floor beneath my feet opens. Then, with screams and shouts of anger, disbelief and outrage rising like a storm, I fall. Air whistles past, but just before I hit the flagstone floor below, I'm slowed and gently land on my feet.

As hoped, I'm in the changing rooms from whence I'd come. Thankfully there's no sign of Darna or Sylvis, and I head toward a mirror, my head spinning. The drain of using my magic so powerfully has left me on the verge of unconsciousness, and I'm only halfway there when I hear a yell, a thump, and a loud crack.

Turning, I see Major Conrol, his clothes smouldering, pick himself up from the floor. He's fallen a long way, and as he steps forward, he braces his sword on the floor. His leg must be broken, but that doesn't stop his advance. His face, which before had shown no sign of darkness, now shifts from one moment to the next. It is full of dark intent, his eyes glowing brightly, smoke pluming from his nostrils and ears.

I've changed him. I made him this, whereas before, he was nothing but a good man.

'You bloody witch. Never before have I wanted to see someone tortured to death, but with you, I'll watch and relish every moment. Have you any idea of how good a man you just killed?'

His eyes suddenly overflow with tears, and he sobs, his anger falling away.

'What have you done, girl? What have you gone and done? We gave you the hand of friendship. We believed in your goodness. Was it all such a lie?'

His strength gives way to grief and overwhelming pain, and he collapses, his broken leg twisted beneath him.

However, through the door at the chamber's end, Commander Farsil charges with dozens of guards behind him. They're a fearsome sight, out for revenge, and I doubt if they caught me, I'd ever see a torturer's chair.

Yet I'm standing by the mirror, and however fast they are, they can't stop me.

I reach out to feel the comforting wetness, and before their widening eyes, step through, the screams of the eternally damned welcoming me as one of their own.

***

CHAPTER XX

It's Suntarg, our day of rest should we choose it to be so. Lotane lies asleep next to me, his breathing even.

I'm envious, for of late, my sleep is troubled, full of grief, and I often awaken to find my pillow damp with tears. Sometimes I consider going back to a dream leaf infusion, but we need to be sharp when we're awake, for the night is frequently our day.

I roll to my side, toying with the idea of waking Lotane. Do I use hands or lips to bring him to life and enjoy his morning vigour, joining our bodies and hearts? I push the thought aside, for he needs to sleep. Beneath the sheets, his ribs are bandaged, and so is my right calf. Sleep is the greatest healer, next to time, and I push aside my selfish needs. However much I need to be distracted, to feel loved, he's my world, and his needs come before mine.

Sitting up, I gently stroke his hair, marvelling at its resistance to ever lie straight. It wraps around my fingers as I run them through his locks. Next, I lightly trace the scar below his eye and the fullness of his lips.

When awake, my heart aches with happiness, but only in the Mountain of Souls do I feel this way. Even though it's early morning, the sun teasing above the horizon beyond the balcony, I marvel at the colours and textures in our room.

Logic has long since told me that this is all part of the conditioning, what keeps us coming back. The island was always beautiful but has since become a paradise now the outside world is a thousand shades of grey. I pick up a sun fruit from a bowl beside the bed, marvelling at its sweetness as I bite into its soft flesh.

But how everything looks, and tastes is just a small part. Here, I feel love, and it's not just given room to grow, but encouraged. The Heart Stone to which we're bound adds to the feeling of completeness, of feeling at home. Then, of course, is knowing that our work makes the world a better place, for we're undertaking the will of The Once and Future King.

Colourful flashing draws my attention to the Heart of Delnor, hanging between the two wolf skulls. No matter how dim, this incredible crystal not only catches the light but also magnifies it.

Yet whilst it's filled with light, it fills my soul with sorrow every time I cast eyes upon it.

Lotane has taken it down several times, knowing the angst it causes me, but each time I replace it. A reminder of friends lost and deeds done.

It's been two months since I killed the High King, and still, my regret lingers. I've killed a good man and am diminished by it.

The others had returned shortly after I, all unscathed, having escaped in the panic that followed the assassination. Strangely, whilst we'd marvelled at accomplishing the deed we'd been trained to do, none of us, Lystra included, had felt like celebrating.

It seems everyone had recognised the goodness in Commander Farsil, Major Conrol, and albeit briefly, the High King and incredibly had questioned whether it had been necessary. However, there was no denying the excitement of the ssythlans upon hearing of our accomplishment. Even the undoubted loss of Prince Sylnar didn't diminish their euphoria. It was, they assured us, the best way to save hundreds of thousands of lives.

The Once and Future King's return would be far smoother now, but more still needed to be done.

So, since then, we'd gone on mission after mission, and with these, I'd felt little to no remorse whatsoever. Each of our targets had exhibited darkness, although perhaps to a lesser degree than we'd been led to expect.

Our first success had been against the King of Rolantria. He'd never gone anywhere without full armour and a host of veteran bodyguards, making any direct approach very dangerous. Yet two days into our surveillance, Nestor had taken a job delivering coal to the castle grounds and, being a hot day, had stripped off his shirt, revealing his muscled physique. Shortly after, the king, with several bodyguards in close attendance, had approached, shifting into drooling, leering caricatures of their usual selves.

The king had given away his weakness.

The next day, having pretended to succumb to the king's sexual advances and thus gaining access to the royal bed-chamber, Nestor killed the king by slitting his throat.

Only a week later, we were in Icelandia.

Following Nestor's success, we'd joked that Kralgen should also seduce the king. Kralgen had apparently thought this through seriously, for the next night, while he was scouting with Lotane, he'd stripped off his shirt and approached the guards outside the Great Hall of the king. Alyssa, Lystra and I had heard his bellowing and ran across the rooftops to find him bare-chested, challenging the king to a duel at the top of his lungs.

He'd been escorted inside, and we thought we'd seen the last of him. However, it transpired he'd drunk ale with the king and his guards throughout the night.

Then, the next day, in an ice arena carved into a massive glacier, Kralgen, watched by us and the entire capital's populace, faced the gigantic king in a duel that lasted the whole morning. It was the most breathtaking display of martial prowess and raw strength I'd ever seen. Then, following his bloody victory, and in Icelandian tradition, Kralgen could have sat upon the Throne of Ice. Instead, we'd left, throwing that nation into a disarray of infighting.

Then only last week, we'd returned from killing the King of Astoria. It had been a messy, brutal, direct affair. A running battle with his personal guard having ambushed him on the way to a country retreat. Lotane had slain the king with a hand axe thrown over fifty paces as he fled on horseback. An impossible throw that Kralgen had tried since to duplicate and failed every time.

It was this latest mission that had seen us all injured to a lesser or greater degree.

Yet our work is far from over and won't finish until Nogoth unifies the broken kingdoms under his one righteous rule. Further rulers and generals must fall before his arrival, ensuring instability remains across the lands.

Slipping from beneath the blankets, I cleanse, then pull on my boots, leaving Lotane sleeping as I head toward the terrace to witness the glorious sunrise. The mountain is a haven of tranquillity at this hour, and my fingertips brush the rough textured passage as if I'm familiarising myself with another's body.

Making my way toward the growing light, I step outside to discover I'm not the first one there. Fianna is enfolded in a light blanket, watching with love as Nestor sculpts the walls with an artisan's eye, face twisted in concentration and pain.

'Have you been here long?' I speak quietly, unwilling to disturb the silence.

'Not long. A few minutes perhaps, ever since it was light enough to see our hands in front of our faces.' Fianna rolls her eyes in mock despair. 'Fortunately, he's as attentive to my body as he is to sculpting, so I can't complain!'

Fianna's laughter seems to wake the entire island. Birds begin to call, and everything comes to life around us as the sun peeks above the horizon.

The north of the island is changing dramatically; thus, Nestor is hard at work amending his masterpiece. As I watch, mesmerised, he adds the new docks the ssythlan engineers have built and the hulls of the ships stationed there.

My attention is drawn to the other end of the terrace, where his earlier work of Nogoth remains. After all this time, he still stays clear of it. It remains a mystery to us all, but questioning Nestor about his reticence to update it only brings him frustration and emotional angst, so I keep my thoughts to myself.

'Help me to stretch if you can take your eyes off Nestor?' I tease.

Fianna laughs, giving me a hug. Since blood magic was used to bind us to our partners, this is the first time she's hugged me.

'As you wish, King Slayer.'

I smile wryly at the new title that's been bestowed upon me. I've protested that Wolf Slayer was my preferred address, but despite Kralgen, Lotane and Nestor all having killed kings, I'm the only one given this moniker.

As Fianna helps stretch my arms behind me, the other Chosen begin to appear. Kralgen yawns mightily as he rolls onto the balcony like a gigantic boulder. He's an utterly fearsome killing machine and now eclipses even Lystra in deadliness. Thankfully as his prowess has grown his ego has diminished, and he's a gentle giant when not fighting. Alyssa shows up moments later, as striking as Kralgen, although in a different way. Her black skin shines as if oiled, and despite numerous white scars, she appears flawless. Lotane appears last, eyes twinkling from under his unruly hair.

'Why didn't you wake me up for some fun?' he laughs with a wink.

'Because she has more fun while you're asleep!' Kralgen intervenes before I can answer.

'Is that why Alyssa always snores when you're on top of her?' Lotane fires back.

Laughter rings across the terrace. The two of them are relentless, and Kralgen's wit is becoming as sharp as his reflexes.

Lystra joins us.

'Let's get some food.'

She no longer snaps orders at us, but we respond as if she did, and it's not long before we're enjoying a quiet breakfast.

'Tonight, we head to Tars,' she says as we eat. 'We'll leave here at midnight, then rendezvous at the Shrine of the Fallen in Tarsala to begin our reconnaissance. Our target will be a general called Landres Sanstom, the overall commander of their forces. He's the power behind the throne, and whilst he might not be nobility, he'll be surrounded by more soldiers than we're used to. So, we tread carefully, ask questions, and leave without incident other than collecting payment for our travel.'

For the next hour, we review possible target locations and rally points before we redress our healing wounds, taking care of each other as we would any weapon or piece of equipment that our life depends on. We stretch, massage out knots, and then go to the training circle to practice with wooden staffs, as they're the only weapon other than the Soul Blade we can travel through with and remain inconspicuous.

I taste the fresh air, savouring its crispness as though every breath is my last while I face off against Fianna. She twirls her staff around her body, a whirring defence that could turn into an attack at any moment.

I hold my own weapon lightly. Too tight, and it can be jarred painfully from my grip if struck with a heavy blow. The best defence is avoidance and deflection, and pitting strength against strength is a waste of energy unless … your name is Kralgen or Lotane.

Alongside us, they favour a more brutal method, laughing as they lock staff against staff. Whilst Kralgen always wins and sends Lotane rolling backwards, they prefer this approach to mine or Fianna's.

Nestor and Alyssa take a style somewhere between the four of us. Lystra steps in and out, changing the dynamic so that, at times, we face two opponents or all gang up on one. That one is usually Kralgen, who embraces the challenge, even if he can't win against such odds.

The day flies by quickly, and it's mid-afternoon when we stop and refresh, cleansing in the waterfall room before taking some lunch.

'It's time for rest, my Chosen,' Lystra smiles. 'We gather by the Soul Gate at midnight, so get some sleep.'

Everyone is full of good cheer as we head to our chambers. We've only known success, and with every evil cancer removed, the world is a better place. The reign of The Once and Future King is further secured by our deeds, and we feel proud.

***

I awake an hour before midnight, rested and full of excitement. The air in the room is somewhat chilly, and with Lotane's body so warm beside me, it should be easy to return to sleep. However, as my mind mulls over the forthcoming mission, sleep eludes me.

Sitting up, I lean over to open my small bedside cabinet. Within are the two books Arcan gifted me, and I consider which to read. Normally the history of kings is my favourite, but maybe some light reading will return me to sleep.

Picking up the ancient children's book of stories and poems, I silently request some light and a softly glowing ball of fire forms on my shoulder. Perhaps it's a rash use of power, yet even having my magic perform the tiniest task gives it a sense of fulfilment.

Opening the book, I'm surprised to see a thin leaf of paper protruding ever so slightly from the uniform pages toward the back. Opening the book, I discover a short, handwritten note in a flowing script.

Dearest Malina.

I believe I might have found what you're looking for.
As I mulled over the king's title you shared with me, it grew vaguely familiar. I had a recollection of my grandfather telling me a bedtime story. So, after sharing your quest with some older colleagues, one of them came up with this. Sadly, it's nothing but an incomplete children's poem.

Even if this brings your search to an end, I so hope you continue to come and keep an old man company in his dotage.

Your friend.
Arcan.

Tears well up, and I blink them back. I doubt he'd call me a friend now. I'd spilt so much blood in his library, and if that wasn't enough, he'd have heard the story of Malina, the assassin who'd killed the High King.

'I am sorry, Arcan,' I breathe softly.

Carefully placing the thin paper in the back of the book cover, I peer at the faded writing on the torn page, my excitement growing.

The golden age of man it was
Of kingdoms low and high
When one night a dark moon bright
Did fill our starlit sky

The dark moon. Yes, this can only be about Nogoth.

Then shortly after, from the west
A wave of wonder came
An army unbeknownst to man
Not seeking land or fame

I can't believe it. Nogoth's previous arrival was immortalised in words. But when I turn the page over, I moan … because the next two sides are faded. Only the final verse is vaguely legible.

I've ruled here   a thousand times
He smiled   led his people away
But be   I'll ret   a thousand years
For I'm Nogoth, King of th …

I finish the last verse, then read it over and over again. If only I could use my magic to bring the other words back onto the page, but my silent request is met by a sense of despondency.

Reluctantly I return the book back to the cabinet. There's no way I can sleep now, and midnight is not far away. Slipping from my warm bed, I go to cleanse, my mind full of purpose. The other Chosen and I will be instrumental in writing the future's history books.

As I look in the mirror, I wonder if a story of a yellow-eyed Chosen will ever make it into a children's poem, and I smile at the thought.

Lotane pads in and wraps his strong arms around my waist. Resting his head on my shoulder, he gazes at our reflections.

'Beautiful, yet so deadly,' he whispers in my ear. 'You slay me with those looks of yours.'

How is it that his eyes remain so bright, or is it only when our gaze falls upon the other that love shines from within? If only we had more time to enjoy this most precious of gifts.

'I hate that what I feel inside for you disappears when we travel through the gate,' I mumble softly, unwilling to say the words too loudly.

Lotane squeezes me gently, making me sigh with pleasure.

'You know I feel the same. But I realised some time ago that if I'm mortally injured or die on a mission, at least you won't do something foolish if you're with me. You'll leave me there, complete the mission, and return home safely without feeling my loss till you arrive.'

I remember Lystra's story and realise that probably something like this will eventually have to occur. We can't keep getting away mostly unscathed.

'You're right.'

'Me? Really?' Lotane laughs. 'You're normally the clever one. I'm just the fool.'

'No,' I say, turning around in his embrace. 'You're my fool, and don't ever forget it. Oh, and if you do forget, and you give your heart to anyone else ... I'll cut it out with a blunt spoon!'

Returning to the bed-chamber, I open a wardrobe and change into the rust-red robes of a Tarsian so that at least our clothing blends in on arrival. Only Alyssa has the dark skin of a native, but as they're allied with so many other nations in their uprising against the Delnor, we won't stand out much.

Lotane dons his own robes next to me.

'You look handsome in red,' I say, smiling, giving him a hug. As I do,
y gaze falls upon the Heart of Delnor, and regret forms like a knot in my
omach.

'Gah.' I shake my head as if that will free me from my disquiet.
nsurprisingly it remains.

'If it still bothers you, we should just put it in a drawer.'

'No.' My voice is firm, but I continue in a more contemplative vein.
1aybe he didn't have to die. Maybe he and Nogoth could have been allies.
ave you ever considered that? The High King was a good soul, even if
s ancestors were evil. He might have seen the error of his ways and
ven up the throne voluntarily. He was already wearing peasant's robes,
) I don't believe he sought riches!'

'This is when being a fool has its advantages,' Lotane laughs softly.
1y mind doesn't ponder on such things, and thus I sleep soundly. That
nd of decision is to be made by kings alone. I'm not saying you're wrong,
mply that the only person with the answer is Nogoth himself.'

Lystra steps into our chamber.

'Good, you're ready. Let's go.'

He's right; I ponder too much, which always causes me disquiet.

The other Chosen are waiting in the passage, so we set off, heading
) to the Soul Gate. There's the usual energy surrounding everyone, the
:nse of excitement that precedes a mission. Fianna is twirling her golden
air under her hood. Nestor runs his fingers along the passageway walls,
) doubt sickened by every imperfection he encounters. Alyssa rolls her
1oulders, loosening her muscles as if she's about to spar with someone.
ralgen and Lotane punch and push each other along like two big
1ildren. At the front, Lystra strides with an unstoppable intensity,
ngle-minded, of clear purpose.

What do the others think when they look at me?

There goes the Wolf Slayer, the King Slayer, the wielder of four
1agical elements. How disappointed they'd be to know I'm full of
)nflicting thoughts again.

What Lotane had said was true. Only Nogoth has the answers. The
st time my thoughts were in such disarray, talking to Nogoth cleared
vay the inner conflicts and helped me see the one true vision. Upon our
:turn, I'll seek his wisdom and know peace.

I hadn't even noticed that we'd reached the terrace, the Soul Gate tall
1d foreboding.

'See you on the other side,' Lystra speaks clearly, her voice confident as if our mission is as good as completed.

She takes a Soul Blade, picks a wooden staff, and closes her eyes, concentrating momentarily. She's holding the image of our destination in her thoughts, and then, with a step, she's gone.

Kralgen gently brushes his fingertips over Alyssa's face before repeating Lystra's actions.

One by one, Fianna, Nestor and Alyssa all follow through the gate.

Lotane sweeps me into his arms. We always hang back, just for this reason. His lips taste sweeter than ever, his heartbeat so strong I can feel it through our clothes. A last desperate embrace and kiss before our souls are stripped away, along with the capacity for love.

Then, like the others, he takes a blade and staff before disappearing through the gate.

It's my turn. I pick my Soul Blade, sheathing it quickly, careful only to touch the handle. Whilst I have my soul, the briefest touch of the blade would be as lethal to me as any one of my victims. How would I ever get it back then? The question nags at me, and I can't believe I haven't considered it before. Would someone else be able to travel through the gate without losing their soul if mine had already paid for the journey?

I must stop getting distracted; now concentrate!

It's important to visualise my entry point, on top of a bakery in the southern district of Tarsaya. On the flat roof, six small chimneys give off the most divine smell. The three to the north are round, whereas the three to the southern side are square. The roof often remains warm, for the ovens are stoked before the bakery closes for the night, ensuring they're ready for the morning. A small but sturdy wooden hatch with five slats gives access to the bakery below. However, I'll go over the north side of the roof, where it drops into an alleyway where stale bread is often left out for the poor and hungry. From there, I'll make my way to the rendezvous, a small shrine adjacent to the city baths.

Opening my eyes, I'm about to step through when above the South Gate, like giant eyes, the blue and white moons smile down from behind a cloud.

The poem comes to mind. How strange that the knowledge of the black moon is only held in a children's tale. I'd never known about it until I'd seen it with my own eyes and then heard it spoken of by the ssythla clerics. Stepping down, I move to the lens and duck underneath it. Sure enough, the black moon is plain to see, and without question, it appears closer to the others than before. Not that it's a surprise, Nogoth's coming is little more than a year away now.

I hate being unsettled, and it's dangerous to be distracted in any way when going on a mission.

When I return, I'll summon Nogoth and tell him how the High King and his generals were good men, that perhaps there's another path to unite the world that doesn't involve killing. Should I mention the poem? Is it even relevant?

I step back to the dais. Thinking of Nogoth eases my angst, and talking with him on my return will be the right thing to do. He told me I was his favoured one and should counsel him, so I'll do as he asked. I'll go to the Heart Stone chamber and gaze through the mirror. Then, once I call for him, I'll see the light of his approach down the dark tunnel. He'll sit on the pure white floor, and we'll talk, and I know he'll listen. I only wish I could sit with him in person, not just see him through a mirror.

Sighing, I step into the Soul Gate.

The screams of the damned and the air whooshing by at insane speeds welcome me. The abject despair and misery scratch at my sanity, threatening to drive me mad. Why doesn't it stop? The journey typically lasts only a moment, yet this feels like an eternity, and I can't take it for much longer.

'Make it stop, make it stop,' I scream.

Then I'm through.

My head is spinning, my eyes are blurred, and I crumple, my legs weaker than a foal.

It's cold, whereas I'd expected the warmth of the baker's roof. The air is stale, absent the aroma of recently cooked dough.

'Open your eyes, Malina,' I growl, pushing myself to my hands and knees, swallowing back the bile that burns my throat. 'You have a rendezvous to get to.'

I groan as nausea threatens to overwhelm me but force my eyes open, seeing as expected a hundred shades of grey.

Yet, there's no sky above me, I'm not on a roof, and I'm definitely not in Tarsala.

Heart in my mouth, I look around, and even as my consciousness fades, I see where I am, and it was exactly as I saw it in my thoughts before I stepped through the gate.

I'm in the hall of The Once and Future King.

***

THE END

Dear fellow fantasy lover.
If you enjoyed this book, then please take a moment to rate or review it on Amazon. It would mean SO much to me.
Thank you
Marcus Lee

THE CHOSEN TRILOGY

If you're ready to find out what happens to Malina and her friends next, then don't wait, and continue the adventure.

Book 2 - THE LAST HOPE

Book 3 - THE RIVER OF TEARS

***

Are you looking for a new magical adventure?

THE GIFTED AND THE CURSED TRILOGY

A dark fantasy trilogy set in a dystopian land, with heroes that are at times more demonic than the evil they face. The bloody battles, quests for revenge and fights for survival are artfully balanced with light romance, tales of redemption, and breath-taking magical gifts.

Book 1 - KINGS AND DAEMONS

Book 2 - TRISTAN'S FOLLY

Book 3 - THE END OF DREAMS

M ❤ M

Printed in Great Britain
by Amazon

39177277R00199